P

Snappy dialogue, a fun story, and a likable character who is deeper than she at first appears— *Sushi for One?* satisfied my appetite for great fiction!

Virginia Smith, author of *Just As I Am*

At last a fun look at Christianity from the eyes of the Asian community. Lex Sakai is a wasabi-hot, fiery heroine that just might find the man of her dreams if she can listen to God, stand up to her controlling grandmother, and learn to trust others along the way.

Anne Dayton and May Vanderbilt, authors of *Emily Ever After*

With katana-sharp wit, Camy immerses readers in the comedy and conflict universal to all families while vibrantly painting the specifics of Asian-American culture. A romance hasn't made me laugh this hard since "My Big Fat Greek Wedding."

Sharon Hinck, author of *Renovating Becky Miller* and *The Restorer*.

SUSHI
for
ONE?

SUSHI
for
ONE?

Camy Tang

■ ZONDERVAN

ZONDERVAN.com/
AUTHORTRACKER
follow your favorite authors

Sushi for One?
Copyright © 2007 by Camy Tang

Requests for information should be addressed to:
Zondervan, *Grand Rapids, Michigan* 49530

Library of Congress Cataloging-in-Publication Data

Tang, Camy, 1972 –
    Sushi for one? / Camy Tang.
      p. cm. – (Sushi series)
    ISBN-10: 0-310-27398-6
    ISBN-13: 978-0-310-27398-1
    1. Dating (Social customs) – Fiction. 2. Man-woman relationships – Fiction. I. Title.
PS3620.A6845S87 2007
813'.6 – dc22

                                         2007006672

Internet addresses (websites, blogs, etc.) and telephone numbers printed in this book are offered as a resource to you. These are not intended in any way to be or imply an endorsement on the part of Zondervan, nor do we vouch for the content of these sites and numbers for the life of this book.

Published in association with the Books & Such Literary Agency, 52 Mission Circle, Suite 122, PMB 170, Santa Rosa, California 95407-5370. www.booksandsuch.biz.

Interior design by Michelle Espinoza

Printed in the United States of America

07 08 09 10 11 12 • 23 22 21 20 19 18 17 16 15 14 13 12 11 10 9 8 7 6 5 4 3 2 1

To Captain Caffeine. I love you.
You're worth a billion of those espresso makers.

ACKNOWLEDGMENTS

Thanks to:

Wendy Lawton, for being the best agent in the entire world.

Sue Brower, for looking past the fact I messed up my pitch and for seeing the potential in my story.

Rachelle Gardner, for your encouragement and enthusiasm in editing my manuscript.

David Robie, for being among the first to believe in me.

Sharon Hinck, gifted writer, awesome friend, generous mentor, encouraging prayer warrior, and feeder of my stamping obsession.

Pamela James, Heather Tipton, and Cheryl Wyatt, for being my friends, sisters, faithful cheerleaders, and prayer team.

Meredith Efken, for staying up way too late talking, for 2 a.m. fire alarms, and for surviving the flying termites with me.

Mary Griffith, for the hilarious stories you tell, the fabulous courses you teach, and for your help along this writing path.

Meredith Efken, Sharon Hinck, Ronie Kendig, and The Critique Boutique, for your fabulous, speedy critiquing.

The San Jose Christian writers group — Shelley Bates, Kristin Billerbeck, Marilyn Hilton, Lisa Kalenda, Dineen Miller, MaryLu Tyndall — for keeping me sane.

Dave Kawaye, for the cheesy *Star Wars* pickup lines. *Muah* to Mirtika Schultz for the Cuban Spanish translation. The ACFW loop, for your horrific bridal shower game stories. Robin Caroll, for your self-defense class expertise. Kayoko Akaogi, for helping me with my Japanese translation.

Stephanie Quilao, for your wealth of experiences, enthusiasm, and fount of fabulous ideas.

My blog readers, for making me feel not so alone in cyberspace.

The Nikkei Volleyball League, without whom Lex and Aiden would have no one to play with.

American Christian Fiction Writers, for being such an amazing group of encouragers, teachers, mentors, helpers, and cheerleaders.

Mom, for encouraging me to read, and Dad, for letting me monopolize the Apple IIe. My family, for being supportive and happy for me.

My husband, for letting me pursue my dream.

Lord Jesus Christ, I would be nothing without You.

Eat and leave. That's all she had to do.

If Grandma didn't kill her first for being late.

Lex Sakai raced through the open doorway to the Chinese restaurant and was immediately immersed in conversation, babies' wails, clashing perfumes, and stale sesame oil. She tripped over the threshold and almost turned her ankle. Stupid pumps. Man, she hated wearing heels.

Her cousin Chester sat behind a small table next to the open doorway.

"Hey Chester."

"Oooh, you're late. Grandma isn't going to be happy. Sign over here." He gestured to the guestbook that was almost drowned in the pink lace glued to the edges.

"What do I do with this?" Lex dropped the Babies R Us box on the table.

Chester grabbed the box and flipped it behind him with the air of a man who'd been doing this for too long and wanted out from behind the frilly welcome table.

Lex understood how he felt. So many of their cousins were having babies, and there were several mixed Chinese-Japanese marriages in the family. Therefore, most cousins opted for these huge—not to mention tiring—traditional Chinese Red Egg and Ginger parties to "present" their newborns, even though the majority of the family was Japanese American.

Lex bent to scrawl her name in the guestbook. Her new sheath dress sliced into her abs, while the fabric strained across her back muscles. Trish had convinced her to buy the dress, and it actually gave her sporty silhouette some curves, but its fitted design prevented movement. She should've worn her old loose-fitting dress instead. She finished signing the book and looked back to Chester. "How's the food?" The only thing worthwhile about these noisy events. Lex would rather be at the beach.

"They haven't even started serving."

"Great. That'll put Grandma in a good mood."

Chester grimaced, then gestured toward the far corner where there was a scarlet-draped wall and a huge gold dragon wall-hanging. "Grandma's over there."

"Thanks." Yeah, Chester knew the drill, same as Lex. She had to go over to say hello as soon as she got to the party—before Grandma saw *her*, anyway—or Grandma would be peeved and stick Lex on her "Ignore List" until after Christmas.

Lex turned, then stopped. Poor Chester. He looked completely forlorn—not to mention too bulky—behind that silly table. Of all her cousins, he always had a smile and a joke for her. "Do you want to go sit down? I can man the table for you for a while. As long as you don't forget to bring me some food." She winked at him.

Chester flashed his toothy grin, and the weary lines around his face expanded into his normal laugh lines. "I appreciate that, but don't worry about me."

"Are you sure?"

"Yeah. My sister's going to bring me something—she's got all the kids at her table, so she'll have plenty for me. But thanks, Lex."

"You'd do the same for me."

Lex wiggled in between the round tables and inadvertently jammed her toe into the protruding metal leg of a chair. To accommodate the hefty size of Lex's extended family, the restaurant had loaded the room with tables and chairs so it resembled a game of Tetris. Once bodies sat in the chairs, a chopstick could barely squeeze through. And while Lex prided herself on her athletic 18-percent body fat, she wasn't a chopstick.

The Chinese waiters picked that exact moment to start serving the food.

Clad in black pants and white button-down shirts, they filed from behind the ornate screen covering the doorway to the kitchen, huge round platters held high above their heads. They slid through the crowded room like salmon — how the heck did they do that? — while it took all the effort Lex had to push her way through the five inches between an aunty and uncle's chairs. Like birds of prey, the waiters descended on her as if they knew she couldn't escape.

Lex dodged one skinny waiter with plates of fatty pork and thumb-sized braised octopus. Another waiter almost gouged her eye out with his platter. She ducked and shoved at chairs, earning scathing glances from various uncles and aunties.

Finally, Lex exploded from the sea of tables into the open area by the dragon wall-hanging. She felt like she'd escaped from quicksand. Grandma stood and swayed in front of the horrifying golden dragon, holding her newest great-granddaughter, the star of the party. The baby's face glowed as red as the fabric covering the wall. Probably scared of the dragon's green buggy eyes only twelve inches away. Strange, Grandma seemed to be favoring her right hip.

"Hi, Grandma."

"Lex! Hi sweetie. You're a little late."

Translation: You'd better have a good excuse.

Lex thought about lying, but aside from the fact that she couldn't lie to save her life, Grandma's eyes were keener than a sniper's. "I'm sorry. I was playing grass volleyball and lost track of time."

The carefully lined red lips curved down. "You play sports too much. How are you going to attract a man when you're always sweating?"

Like she was now? Thank goodness for the fruity body spritz she had marinated herself in before she got out of her car.

"That's a pretty dress, Lex. New, isn't it?"

How did she do that? With as many grandchildren as she had, Grandma never failed to notice clothes, whereas Lex barely registered that she wasn't naked. "Thanks. Trish picked it out."

"It's so much nicer than that ugly floppy thing you wore to your cousin's wedding."

Lex gritted her teeth. *Respect your grandmother. Do not open your mouth about something like showing up in a polka-dotted bikini.*

"Actually, Lex, I'm glad you look so ladylike this time. I have a friend's son I want you to meet—"

Oh, no. Not again. "Does he speak English?"

Grandma drew herself to her full height, which looked a little silly because Lex still towered over her. "Of course he does."

"Employed?"

"Yes. Lex, your attitude—"

"Christian?"

"Now why should that make a difference?"

Lex widened innocent eyes. "Religious differences account for a lot of divorces."

"I'm not asking you to marry him, just to meet him."

Liar. "I appreciate how much you care about me, but I'll find my own dates, thanks." Lex smiled like she held a knife blade in her teeth. When Grandma got pushy like this, Lex had more backbone than the other cousins.

"I wouldn't be so concerned, but you don't date at all—"

Not going there. "Is this Chester's niece?" Lex's voice rose an octave as she tickled the baby's Pillsbury-Doughboy stomach. The baby screamed on. "Hey there, cutie, you're so big, betcha having fun, is Grandma showing you off, well, you just look pretty as a picture, are you enjoying your Red Egg and Ginger party? Okay, Grandma, I have to sit down. Bye."

Before Grandma could say another word, Lex whisked away into the throng of milling relatives. Phase one, accomplished. Grandmother engaged. Retreat commencing before more nagging words like "dating" and "marriage" sullied the air.

Next to find her cousins—and best friends—Trish, Venus, and Jenn, who were saving a seat for her. She headed toward the back where all the other unmarried cousins sat as far away from Grandma as physically possible.

Their table was scrunched into the corner against towering stacks of unused chairs—like the restaurant could even hold more chairs. "Lex!" Trish flapped her raised hand so hard, Lex expected it to fly off at any moment. Next to her, Venus lounged, as gorgeous as always and looking bored, while Jennifer sat quietly on her other side, twirling a lock of her long straight hair. On either side of them ...

"Hey, where's my seat?"

Venus's wide almond eyes sent a sincere apology. "We failed you, babe. We had a seat saved next to Jenn, but then ..." She pointed to where the back of a portly aunty's chair had rammed up against their table. "We had to remove the chair, and by then, the rest were filled."

"Traitors. You should have shoved somebody under the table."

Venus grinned evilly. "You'd fit under there, Lex."

Trish whapped Venus in the arm. "Be nice."

A few of the other cousins looked at them strangely, but they got that a lot. The four of them became close when they shared an apartment during college, but even more so when they all became Christian. No one else understood their flaws, foibles, and faith.

Lex had to find someplace to sit. At the very least, she wanted to snarf some overpriced, high calorie, high cholesterol food at this torturous party.

She scanned the sea of black heads, gray heads, dyed heads, small children's heads with upside-down ricebowl haircuts, and teenager heads with highlighting and funky colors.

There. A table with an empty chair. Her cousin Bobby, his wife, his mother-in-law, and his brood. Six—count 'em, six—little people under the age of five.

Lex didn't object to kids. She liked them. She enjoyed coaching her girls' volleyball club team. But these were Bobby's kids. The 911 operators knew them by name. The local cops drew straws on who would have to go to their house when they got a call.

However, it might not be so bad to sit with Bobby and family. Kids ate less than adults, meaning more food for Lex.

"Hi, Bobby. This seat taken?"

"No, go ahead and sit." Bobby's moon-face nodded toward the empty chair.

Lex smiled at his nervous wife, who wrestled with an infant making intermittent screeching noises. "Is that . . ." *Oh great. Boxed yourself in now. Name a name, any name.* "Uh . . . Kyle?"

The beleaguered mom's smile darted in and out of her grimace as she tried to keep the flailing baby from squirming into a face-plant on the floor. "Yes, this is Kylie. Can you believe she's so big?" One of her sons lifted a fork. "No, sweetheart, put the food down—!"

The deep-fried missile sailed across the table, trailing a tail of vegetables and sticky sauce. Lex had protected her face from volleyballs slammed at eighty miles an hour, but she'd never dodged multi-shots of food. She swatted away a flying net of lemony shredded lettuce, but a bullet of sauce-soaked fried chicken nailed her right in the chest.

Yuck. Well, good thing she could wash—oops, no, she hadn't worn her normal cotton dress. This was the new silk one. The one with the price tag that made her gasp, but also made her look like she actually had a waist instead of a plank for a torso. The dress with the "dry-clean only" tag.

"Oh! I'm sorry, Lex. Bad boy. Look what you did." Bobby's wife leaned across the table with a napkin held out, still clutching her baby whose foot was dragging through the chow mein platter.

The little boy sitting next to Lex shouted in laughter. Which wouldn't have been so bad if he hadn't had a mouth full of chewed bok choy in garlic sauce.

Regurgitated cabbage rained on Lex's chest, dampening the sunny lemon chicken. The child pointed at the pattern on her dress and squealed as if he had created a Vermeer. The other children laughed with him.

"Hey boys! That's not nice." Bobby glared at his sons, but otherwise didn't stop shoveling salt-and-pepper shrimp into his mouth.

Lex scrubbed at the mess, but the slimy sauces refused to transfer from her dress onto the polyester napkin, instead clinging to the blue silk like mucus. Oh man, disgustamundo. Lex's stomach gurgled. Why was every other part of her athlete's body strong except for her stomach?

She needed to clean herself up. Lex wrestled herself out of the chair and bumped an older man sitting behind her. "Sorry." The violent motion made the nausea swell, then recede. *Don't be silly. Stop being a wimp.* But her already sensitive stomach had dropped the call with her head.

Breathe. In. Out. No, not through your nose. Don't look at that boy's drippy nose. Turn away from the drooling baby.

She needed fresh air in her face. She didn't care how rude it was, she was leaving now.

"There you are, Lex."

What in the world was Grandma doing at the far end of the restaurant? This was supposed to be a safe haven. Why would Grandma take a rare venture from the other side where the "more important" family members sat?

"My goodness, Lex! What happened to you?"

"I sat next to Bobby's kids."

Grandma's powdered face scrunched into a grimace. "Here, let me go to the restroom with you." The bright eyes strayed again to the mess on the front of her dress. She gasped.

Oh, no, what else? "What is it?" Lex asked.

"You never wear nice clothes. You always wear that hideous black thing."

"We've already been over this—"

"I never noticed that you have no bosom. No wonder you can't get a guy."

Lex's jaw felt like a loose hinge. The breath stuck in her chest until she forced a painful cough. "*Grandma!*"

Out of the corner of her eye, Lex could see heads swivel. Grandma's voice carried better than a soccer commentator at the World Cup.

Grandma bent closer to peer at Lex's chest. Lex jumped backward, but the chair behind her wouldn't let her move very far.

Grandma straightened with a frighteningly excited look on her face. "I know what I'll do."

God, now would be a good time for a waiter to brain her with a serving platter.

Grandmother gave a gleeful smile and clapped her hands. "Yes, it's perfect. I'll pay for breast implants for you!"

TWO

Grandma did *not* just bellow "breast implants" in the middle of the Red Egg and Ginger party.

Lex's heart stopped for a long, painful moment, then started again at NASCAR speed. Her hands shook and tightened as if they were clenched around a vibrating steering wheel. Except she could never steer Grandma. Pity.

Lex drew a deep breath, fortifying herself for battle. "Grandma, we are going to discuss this somewhere else."

The glow in Grandma's eyes sharpened to sparks. "Why? It's obvious you can't get a boy with salt shakers like those."

Salt shakers?

She had that "Let Grandma fix everything" expression on her face. Her gaze settled lower. "What are you? Double-A? No problem. You know my friend Mrs. Fang? Her second husband …"

Grandma. Outside. Now. Lex toyed with the wonderful daydream of bodily nabbing her and carting her outside so she could strangle her there.

Back to reality—she couldn't manhandle her grandmother, especially since the old woman looked so deceptively delicate.

Lex needed reinforcements. Grandma's yelling should have brought Lex's cousins. Where was the cavalry?

There, several tables away, chatting amongst themselves while Lex was in mortal danger. Trish's body faced Lex's direction, although she cast flirty side-glances at some waiter. Lex lifted her hand and waved.

"Lex, stop flinging your hand around and pay attention," Grandma scolded her. "Now, I think Mrs. Fang brought her husband today."

"But my dress ..." The congealing sauce made a chilly circle over her breastbone.

"He's not going to examine you right here." Grandma's reasonable tone belied the diabolically psychotic mind behind her stubborn, kohl-lined eyes.

Lex cast a desperate glance at Trish and flung both arms high in the air — or at least as far as the tight sheath dress would let her — slapping the chin of a middle-aged relative who had just gotten up from his chair. "Oops, sorry."

At last, Trish saw her.

About time! Lex stretched her eyes wide in a "Need help here!" message, while jerking her head in Grandma's direction.

Trish's expression morphed from curiosity to horror in milliseconds. She nudged Venus and Jennifer, then hurled herself over the crammed chairs in her desperation to reach her cousin. Venus followed with more grace. Jennifer trailed her like a shadow, eyes bigger than *char siu baos*.

"Grandma!" Trish squealed with false cheer.

Grandma scowled at Trish. "What?"

Stumped, Trish's exuberance flash-froze. "Uh ..."

Uh oh. Apparently Grandma still hadn't forgiven Trish for bringing that punk rocker to their cousin's baby shower last month and letting a two-year-old play with his belly button ring.

"Hi, Grandma." Venus inserted herself between Trish and Grandma's annoyed glare. "We need to talk with Lex."

"No, I'm talking to her first. You're so impatient. Come on, Lex, we're going to see Mr. Fang."

"Grandma, I don't *want* breast implants." Lex had a hard time hissing through clenched teeth.

Trish's eyes went from concerned to DEFCON 5. Venus rolled hers. Jennifer's face paled.

Grandma's eyes grew steely like her Chinese cleaver. "That's ridiculous. No man wants a woman as flat as an ironing board."

"Grandma!" Trish's squeak cut through the noise of the people eating.

"Grandma, I need your help." Jennifer's soft voice cooled the tension like a fire blanket. "Mom's trying to pick out new kitchen curtains. Could you look at some color swatches I have in my car?"

Grandma's bulldog expression melted into her sweet Miss Marple facade. "Oh, certainly, dear."

Lex watched in disbelief as Jennifer led Grandma through the crowd toward the door. Grandma limped a little—Lex remembered she'd been favoring her right hip earlier.

"Close your mouth." Venus nudged Lex's shoulder as she turned to follow. "And don't even think of abandoning us to face Grandma in the parking lot."

"Yeah, she hasn't forgotten about you." Trish grabbed Lex's arm in a manacle grip and tugged her after Venus.

Lex felt like Marie Antoinette as she wove between the tables, past the stares of her relatives and family friends. The guillotine had many similarities to Grandma in a completely illogical mood.

She joined the cousins at Jennifer's car.

"Oh, I'm sorry, Grandma." Jenn straightened from rummaging in her car trunk. "I guess I forgot the swatches at work. I had to hurry to get to the party on time."

Oops, wrong thing for Jenn to say. Grandma flicked a sharp look at Lex through narrowed eyes and patted Jennifer's hand. "At least you were on time."

Oh, good gravy. "I'm sorry, Grandma. I already told you I was playing volleyball—"

"You spend too much time playing. Aunty May says you can't find a boyfriend because you've been whacked in the head with a volleyball too many times."

Reminder to self: Get Aunty May a muzzle.

"And your father says you're home every night. Why aren't you dating?"

Greeeat. Grandma even used Lex's dad to spy on her. Lex only needed to save a little more for a down payment on a condo, and then she'd be out of Dad's house, pronto. "I'm not home every night. I have practice with my girls' volleyball team every Monday, Wednesday, and Friday." Grandma didn't need to know that practice ended in the late afternoon and that she played adult leagues three nights a week too.

"That girls' team is taking up too much of your time."

"I just don't like dating. What's so wrong with that?"

"Are you lesbian?"

"*Graaandmaaa!*" Screeched in unison by Trish, Venus, and Jennifer, the word had twelve syllables.

"No, Grandma. I'm Christian." *Have been the last twenty times you complained that I wasn't at Buddhist temple.*

Grandma shrugged. "What's wrong? Half my friends have homosexual children."

Trish bit her lip. "Well, Lex, this *is* the San Francisco Bay Area ..."

"See?" Grandma drew herself up. "You can't blame me for wondering. Now, what's so bad about getting more bosom?"

"The subject of my bra size is closed. Closed, Grandma!"

Grandma pinched her mouth closed and flared her nostrils. Her brown eyes narrowed to slits. "You're missing my point. You never bring anyone with you to family functions."

"Fine. I'll bring a guy to the next family thing."

Grandma's eyes narrowed. "No, that's too easy. You'll just ask one of your volleyball friends."

Lex couldn't win. "Well, then, what do you want?"

As soon as the words came out, she knew they were the wrong thing to say. Grandma smiled a *Maneki* welcoming-cat grin. "I want you to have a boyfriend by Mariko's wedding."

"The end of May? That's only four months away."

Trish leaned in close to hum in Lex's ear. "*You can't hurry love ...*" Lex jabbed an elbow in Trish's squishy side and elicited a soft squeal.

Grandma heard her. "Who's hurrying? You four are already *thirty*—"

"Not all of us." Venus's cheeks burned Hello-Kitty pink.

Grandma shrugged. "You and Jennifer are only a few months behind these two. Close enough."

Lex crossed her arms. "You can't make me get a boyfriend in four months."

Grandma's expression sharpened. "I'll cut funding to your girls' club volleyball team if you don't."

The air sucked out of Lex's lungs like a vacuum cleaner had attached itself to her gaping mouth. She gasped in a sharp breath that stung her throat. "You wouldn't."

"Now you're taking me seriously, aren't you?"

"You agreed to fund them throughout playoffs this summer."

"I didn't sign a contract."

Ruthless. Cruella de Sakai. "Grandma, they're only junior high girls."

"Well then, you'd better make sure they don't lose funding."

"A boyfriend? You'd pull funding just for a boyfriend?" Lex's voice started to take on a screeching edge.

"If that's the only way I can make you listen to me." Grandma turned to walk back into the restaurant, but then she turned on an Italian leather sole to peer at Lex, one eyebrow raised. "And he better be a boyfriend, not a casual friend or a one-time date. None of your chummy volleyball buddies." The back of her silk suit fell arrow-straight as she marched away.

Lex sagged against the car. Trish collapsed next to her. Jennifer stood wringing her hands, while Venus shifted onto one foot and shoved a hand onto her hip.

Suddenly, the door opened from the car next to Jennifer's Toyota. Their cousin Mimi popped her head over the top of the car, eyes wide, swinging her signature calf-length ponytail.

"Whoa! Was she serious?"

THREE

Trish bristled. Lex slammed her arm across Trish's ribcage to keep her in place. Mimi wasn't exactly Lex's favorite person either, but she didn't feel like breaking up another catfight between the two of them.

"You were there the entire time?" Trish's voice came out only a decimal softer than a roar.

Mimi lifted a delicate shoulder in a careless gesture. "It's not as if I had time to announce my presence when you dragged Grandma out here."

"More like you'd rather avoid Grandma entirely." Venus's lip curled in a faint sneer.

"Sure, if she's going to go *loco* and issue ultimatums like that." Mimi fluttered a tiny hand in the direction of the restaurant. She paused, eyes narrowing as she stared at the ornately carved doors. "I better go protect myself."

For some reason, that sounded ominous.

Mimi sashayed away, her teeny four-foot-eight-and-three-quarter-inch body swaying with all the enviable perkiness of a twenty-two-year-old.

Stop it. Lex mentally slapped herself. "Thirty isn't old, no matter what Grandma says."

Venus arched a delicate eyebrow at her. "It doesn't matter. When Mariko gets married, you'll be the next Oldest Single Female Cousin."

The OSFC, unofficial family title. *Rah, rah.* "Why now? I mean, she's always nagged, but never like this."

Trish threw up her hands. "Because Mariko's been OSFC for seven years. Grandma had her to nag until she got engaged."

Venus snorted. "Why do you think the wedding is so fast?"

Lex scratched her head. "I thought she was prego."

Trish and Venus groaned. Jennifer bit her lip, turning her smile into a V-shape.

Venus stared at Lex with a thoughtful gleam in those disgustingly elegant eyes. "Why don't you agree to get implants? Maybe then Grandma will forget about the ultimatum."

"No way! She'll tell *everyone.*"

Jennifer's brow wrinkled. "But ... you've never cared before what people thought about you."

"I've never had them staring at my chest before."

Venus lifted a slim shoulder. "Is it really that bad to add a little padding?"

Lex glared at her. "Get behind thee, 34-C."

She sniffed. "I wasn't always a 34-C."

"Yeah, and your sudden blossoming into gorgeous womanhood didn't make you a more pleasant person."

Jennifer gasped, but Venus and Trish just laughed.

"So then, why don't you listen to me?" Venus's perfect oval face radiated calm reasonability. "I was so fat, I didn't even care about my chest size. That stomach virus was the best thing that happened to me. I found I had womanly curves under all that weight. I didn't have to shop for special-sized bras anymore. And when I could finally fit into a 34-C, I felt better about myself."

That really wasn't helping, considering the fact Lex still hadn't moved out of training bras. "Yeah, well, your losing weight at twenty-five is not the same as my undergoing surgery at thirty." She crossed her arms. "Besides, getting implants would violate our Pact."

Venus also crossed her arms. "No, it wouldn't."

"We vowed that when we fell under the OSFC title, we wouldn't act as desperate as Mariko did. Implants are desperate, don't you think?"

"Wait a minute." Jennifer glanced at each of them. "I thought we vowed to give our dating lives up to God."

Lex thought a second. "Uh ... that too." Wasn't she already doing that? She had no problem waiting around for God to bring the perfect man into her life. The thought of intimacy with any guy still freaked her out a little, even after eight years. She'd get over it eventually, right? And until then, she didn't *have* to date.

Well, until today...

"I thought we wanted to make the point that we're not ashamed to be single." Jennifer took a deep breath and stiffened her spine. "We have a higher priority than marriage and children."

"Well, then ..." Lex frowned. "Grandma's ultimatum violates the Pact. I can't fail my girls' volleyball team—they have a good chance at playoffs. I can't exactly wait around and leave my dating life up to God if I have to be non-single in four months."

Jennifer's brow furrowed and she opened her mouth, but Venus jumped in. "Oh, come on. We all know you. You're not going to just cave into Grandma's demands."

"Well ..." Lex kicked at a rock. "I have been thinking I might be able to find someone else to sponsor the team—"

"See? You'll find some way to work around Grandma's ultimatum."

"And it's not just Lex." Jenn glanced around at all of them. "We should reestablish our Pact, especially now with Grandma being so insistent."

Lex nodded. "We are not Barbie dolls for Grandma to play around with."

Jenn's eyes shone with firm resolve. "We'll give our dating lives up to God."

"And we'll promise not to date desperately just because we come under the OSFC label and Grandma's fire." Venus propped a hand on her slender hip.

Lex could do that—she wouldn't date desperately anyway. She'd have to get up the courage to date *at all*.

"Pact?" Venus stuck out her hand, palm up.

"Pact." Lex slapped her hand down. Jennifer laid hers on top.

"Trish?" Venus lifted an eyebrow.

"Yeah, yeah." Trish joined them.

They broke.

Trish turned away quickly, but Jenn had kilowatts of righteous purity shining from her gentle smile.

Lex flicked her glance away. Jenn always made her feel like such a bad Christian.

"I'm going home. I've got to clean up—oh, no. I forgot my purse inside." She pressed her lips together. She inwardly cringed at the thought of walking back inside the restaurant to face the stares from everyone who'd heard Grandma lambasting her lack of cleavage.

"I left my things too. I'll walk inside with you." Trish's expression radiated sympathy.

"No need. I grabbed them." Jennifer reached down where she'd laid Trish's bulky hobo, Venus's Prada, and Lex's backpack.

"Thanks, Jenn." Thank goodness for Jenn's usual foresight. Lex felt a twinge of guilt for being resentful of Jenn's spiritual maturity earlier.

"See you guys." Jennifer got into her own car, while Venus left to find hers.

Trish walked with Lex toward her aging Honda.

"Bye." Trish gave a little wave.

Lex paused before climbing in. "See you at church?" Trish had been missing church a lot lately.

"Uh ... sure. See ya." Trish nipped into her sporty RAV4 that was parked next to Lex's car.

Lex paused to stare for a moment, then got in her Honda and thrust the key into the ignition.

The engine sputtered, hacked up a loogie, and died.

Lex turned it again. *Click. Click.*

She collapsed back against the headrest. "No way." She jumped out and knocked on Trish's driver's-side window before she drove away. "Got AAA?"

"You're kidding, right?" Trish dragged out her cell phone and her wallet for her card. "You're such a cheapskate. You drive that death mobile *and* you don't have roadside service? You still live with your dad—"

"Yeah, and in a few months, I'll have saved enough to buy my own condo. We'll see who's laughing then."

Trish got out of the car. Lex leaned against the trunk while Trish spoke to AAA on her cell phone.

One of their cousins, her husband, and their two children exited the restaurant. Things must be wrapping up inside.

As the family passed Lex and Trish, their cousin gave Lex a guarded look—the kind young mothers give to the snake exhibit at the zoo as they hustle the kids past. Her husband also gave only an abbreviated wave as they bolted for their car, dragging the kids after them.

Lex straightened. Trish did too. "Did you see—?"

An old aunty and uncle also walked out the restaurant doors. As they hustled past Lex and Trish, Aunty gave Lex a weighty, disapproving look just before she sniffed and stuck her nose in the air.

Trish gasped and thumped her car trunk. "That old bat ..."

Lex looked away. Why did Aunty's look cut her so deeply, when with other people, like at work and volleyball, she really couldn't care less what they thought? A single look from one of the women in her family struck her an almost physical blow, like a mallet pounding sweet rice grains into *mochi*. Lex felt soft and bruised. Was she really that strange to everyone?

Stop that. There's nothing wrong with you. Lex shook off her mood. She was strong and stubborn, and she didn't care who she offended. "I don't want to just give in to Grandma. I don't like being forced."

"Yeah, but how much do your girls mean to you?"

Lex sighed. "The other day, one of the girls' moms came up to me and told me she was so excited the girls could go traveling for playoffs because she hadn't been able to afford it when my mom coached her in high school. How am I going to tell her that the girls won't be able to go if Grandma pulls funding in four months?"

Trish didn't say anything.

"At the same time, how can I meekly walk into Mariko's wedding with a boyfriend on my arm, like a good little granddaughter?"

Trish fingered the filmy chiffon of her dress. "Do you ... do you think you're ready to date?"

Lex tensed at her gentle tone, while at the same time, a restless quivering started in her hands and just under her ribcage. "Yeah, I think so."

"We could tell Grandma about—"

"No. We're not telling anyone about it. It was eight years ago."

Trish blinked at her harsh tone.

Lex immediately deflated. "I'm sorry—"

"No, don't be. I understand."

Of course. More than anyone, Trish understood. She'd stood by Lex through everything—the hospital, the police report, the three years of counseling—when none of the other family even knew it had happened. It relieved Lex to have Trish be with her whenever she needed her. "Actually, it might not be too bad."

Trish looked at her as if she'd said she could fly. "Oookay."

"No, really. I'll ask Kin-Mun on a date."

Trish's eyes bugged out of her head. "No way! Finally."

"See? Desperation does wonderful things to my level of chutzpah."

A thoughtful look settled on her face. "Do you think he'll go out with you? You guys have been friends for decades—"

"Don't you be bashing my age. You're only three months younger."

"Yeah, yeah, yeah. My point—?"

Lex shoved aside the niggling of doubt that had settled south of her stomach. It nagged like Grandma. "I've just never given him the chance to think of me as someone other than his bud."

Trish took a second to absorb that. "Um ... okay."

"And in the meantime, I'll ask some family friends if they'll sponsor the girls' team. Then I won't have to worry about Grandma pulling funding."

"Do you really think you could? You're not a businesswoman like Grandma. She's used to pulling money from rocks—"

"Whenever I put my mind to something, I do it. I can be logical and charming at the same time."

Trish kept her face solidly neutral.

"I *can* be charming." Lex glared at her.

Trish blinked but didn't speak.

"How hard can it be?"

Trish guffawed.

"Oh, shut up."

"Great game, guys." Lex slapped hands with the last member of the team they had just creamed and walked off the volleyball court.

She dodged players from the other court as they sought out their gym bags, and finally snagged some floor space next to hers. She tugged at her shoelaces as she craned her neck, searching for Kin-Mun.

There, his team was still playing on the far court.

The ref briefly removed her whistle. "Last point!" She sent a piercing blast and signaled the serve.

Kin-Mun, in the middle back, passed the difficult floater serve as if it dropped right in his arms. The setter sent the ball arcing to the strong side-hitter, who whaled on it—

Right into the other team's perfectly timed, perfectly setup block. *Bam!* The ball came back faster than the player hit it, landing on the sideline. The line judge signaled it was in. Point and game over.

Dummy! Lex yelled at her distracted self. She should have been taking off her shoes while watching the play. She scrambled to undo her double-knotted laces while keeping an eye on Kin-Mun as he circled with his team for a "Team rah!" and then filed in a line to slap hands with the other team. He beelined for his gym bag and sat on the floor to take off his shoes.

Lex finally undid her laces and tugged her shoes off. She shoved her feet into her street sneakers and leaped to stand up.

Where had he gone? He'd been right there a second ago.

"Lex, great game."

She dashed a passing glance to her teammate as he walked past her with his bag slung over his shoulder. "Yeah, you too." Where was Kin-Mun?

Oh, there, talking to Lex's team captain, Jill. Lex picked up her gym bag.

What would she do, ask him out in front of everybody? She hadn't thought of that. She'd have to wait until they all went outside to their cars, where she and Kin-Mun would have semi-privacy. The plan had seemed so easy two days ago, at Saturday's Red Egg and Ginger party.

Until then, she'd stick to him like gum on his shoe.

"Hey, Kin-Mun. Jill."

"Lex, I was asking Kin-Mun if he'd play with us at the Vegas tournament in a few months. Can you play, too? No one sets him like you do."

Lex shrugged. "Sure, I'll play. Email me."

"Let me check my work schedule first." Kin-Mun's unusually deep voice growled in the noisy gym. Lex had to move in to hear him better.

"No prob. Thanks, guys." Jill drifted away.

"I hope I can play." Kin-Mun sat down to tug off his volleyball shoes. "'Cuz then *Jill* can set me instead of you." He roared with laughter.

"Very funny. I'll tell her you like your sets low and tight to the net so the blocker will stuff it down your face."

"Aw, you're so mean." He rose and picked up his bag.

Excellent. Maybe she could hustle him out of the gym early. "Going out to eat?" Lex started ambling toward the door.

"Yeah ... Where's my ball?" Kin-Mun wove his way toward the folded-up bleachers, examining balls lying on the floor.

Lex went to the other side and helped him search. Anything to get him out to his car faster. She spotted the faded blue Sharpie graphic he'd drawn over the "Tachikara" emblem. "Here it is."

"Thanks." Kin-Mun put the ball into his bag, then dropped back down to the floor to stretch.

Stretch?!

Lex could have a cow or just be patient for once. She dropped to the floor next to him.

They were a little removed from the other players, out of earshot if she spoke low. "Hey, Kin-Mun—"

"Hi guys." Robyn walked up to them. "Will you buy magazine subscriptions for my son's fundraiser?"

Another interruption. She'd never ask him out at this rate. "Sure." Lex fumbled in her bag for her purse. The faster she paid Robyn, the faster she'd leave them.

"Kin-Mun?" Robyn gave him a coaxing grin.

"Uh ... sure." Kin-Mun searched through his bag for his wallet.

Robyn handed Lex the tattered flipcard listing the magazines. Lex barely glanced at them. "*Golf.*"

Kin-Mun gave her an adoringly confused look. "You don't like playing golf."

"I like keeping up with the sport. And I already have *ESPN* and *Sports Illustrated.*" She handed Robyn some cash.

Kin-Mun scanned the magazine listings with agonizing slowness. His methodical nature really annoyed her sometimes. Like now. *Sometime this century ...*

"*Entrepreneur.*"

"You don't invest."

"I'd like to." He handed Robyn the card and his money.

"Thanks, you guys." Robyn finally left.

"So, Kin-Mun—"

"Unca Kin-Mun!"

The screech came only a millisecond before a three-year-old hurtled in between them. Lex caught a flailing hand across her eyes. "Oof!"

A burning sensation crawled across her eyeballs. She squeezed her lids shut, and the pain radiated laterally to the corners. What did that brat—er, child have on his hands?

"Oh, buddy, your hands are all sticky." Kin-Mun's jovial voice spoke through Lex's dark pain.

"Oh-jay." The boy giggled like he'd made a joke worthy of Sesame Street.

Tears finally welled and gushed out. The burning eased. Lex rubbed at her eyes.

"Go back to Mommy." Kin-Mun gave him a pat on his well-diapered bottom as the toddler stumbled away.

"So, Kin-Mun—"

With a fluid motion, he hoisted his lanky frame to his feet. "You going out to eat with everybody?" He turned toward the door.

Kin-Mun didn't even wait for her as he walked out. Lex swallowed her ire as she stood up, grabbed her bag, and followed behind him.

Well, at least he held the door open for her as they exited the gym.

Other players walked beside, in front, and behind them as they all made their way to the parking lot.

"Do you know where we're going to eat tonight?" Kin-Mun dodged a branch that had fallen onto the sidewalk.

Lex shrugged. "Probably the usual."

"I'm getting tired of Michael's Diner."

"Well, then convince some other restaurant to stay open past ten on a Monday night." Didn't they have this conversation every week?

When they reached his car, Lex shifted to stand closer to him as he unlocked his trunk. "So—"

"Hey, Kin-Mun, did you catch the Giants' game the other day?" One of his teammates jogged up, lugging his monstrous bag.

"No, I saw the highlights on SportsCenter. Did you?"

"Yeah, I have it saved on Tivo."

"Hey, can you burn it onto a DVD for me?"

"Sure."

"Thanks."

"See ya." He and his bag lumbered off.

Lex wouldn't be interrupted again. "Kin-Mun, go out on a date with me." Oops, that sounded kinda like a threat.

Bushy eyebrows waggled upward, creasing his tanned forehead, reaching for his hairline. "What?"

"Um ... would you like to go out on a date with me?"

"Date? Like in ..."

"Date."

"Well, we always hang out."

"No, I mean, hang out like more than friends." Man, she hated this kind of DTR stuff. Wait, was this a Define The Relationship discussion? Whoa. This was weird.

"Um ..." Kin-Mun scratched the back of his head and looked down at the ground.

Okay, that was a bad sign, right? No immediate, *Oh, that's some-thing I've never thought of before. Sure, let's try it.*

"Is that it? 'Um'?"

"I like being just friends."

Aaargh. "Nonono. Not acceptable." Oops ... did she say that out loud? Try again. "You've never thought of me as anything else? Not even considered it?"

"You're like ... a brother."

"A brother? One of the guys?"

"Yeah." He started to smile.

"What am I, genderless?" It came out just short of a screech. Grandma was *not* correct, she didn't need bigger breasts to catch a man.

His smile flitted away. "No. You're like ... a sister. Yeah, a sister."

Was she really not attractive — *No, stop that thinking right there. Don't be ridiculous.* "But I'm not your sister."

"Uh ... no, I guess not."

"So why would you think of me as a sister?"

"I dunno."

Lex needed to hit the restart button on this entire conversation. "So why not give it a try?"

"What?"

"Dating."

"Why?"

"Why not?"

As Kin-Mun stood there, Lex could almost see his left-brain logic gears whirling. "Uh ..."

"Give me a good reason."

"Well ..." He scratched his head again. "I guess."

"Great!"

Kin-Mun jumped at her exuberance. His smile seemed a little pained. Maybe she had shouted too loud.

Now to make plans so he couldn't change his mind. "I'll email you. We can go out this Saturday night. You're free, right?"

"Uh ..." Gears whirling some more. "Yeah — "

"Great! You can take me to FJL."

Kin-Mun's face brightened at the mention of his favorite Italian restaurant. "Okay."

"I'll make reservations. Pick me up at seven."

"Okay."

Lex walked away. That hadn't been too bad. He had just needed a little prodding.

FOUR

Yes, I'll hold." Lex loosened her grip on the phone handset. "Will you stop pacing? You're making me nervous."

Trish plopped on the orange-and-brown striped couch. "So, Kin-Mun's reluctance doesn't bother you even a little bit?"

Trish's knowing look put Lex's back up, even as a small part of her whispered, *He wasn't that reluctant, was he?* "Can we talk about this later? I'm on the phone." Lex leaned back in the ancient La-Z-Boy and rested her elbow against the scarred oak side table.

"You're not talking to anyone right now."

"I'm not going to be distracted by you."

"I don't distract you."

"You make me emotional, and I need to be pleasant and calm with Mr. Tomoyoshi."

Trish rolled her eyes but shut up.

"Hello, Lex?"

Lex turned her attention to the phone. "Hi, Mr. Tomoyoshi."

"Haven't seen you in the restaurant in a while. How are you doing?" The kind, jovial voice matched Mr. Tomoyoshi's wide girth and generous nature.

"I'm doing well."

"Still playing volleyball?"

"Yup. In fact, I'm coaching—"

"I still remember when your grandma brought you into the res-taurant and you wouldn't leave your volleyball in the car, and you

37

ended up hitting it into your ramen noodles and splashing yourself." He laughed.

"Heh. Heh. Yeah." Was that the only memory Mr. Tomoyoshi had of her? He mentioned it every time she spoke to him. What about her graduation party in his Japanese restaurant? Or her dad's *yakudoshi* birthday party? Or the numerous other times she went in there to eat and didn't have a horribly embarassing mishap? "So, Mr. Tomoyoshi—"

"How often do you see your grandma?"

"I just saw her at my cousin's Red Egg and Ginger party."

"Oh, Chester's niece? That must have been nice."

For the other guests there, maybe. "Yeah. Good food." Not that she'd had any of it.

He chuckled. "You tell your grandma to have it in my restaurant instead next time."

Hmm. Traditional Chinese party in a Japanese restaurant. She wasn't quite seeing it. "Sure. You've got the best food."

"Aw, thanks. You're such a sweet girl."

Lex grimaced at the "girl" remark. "I'm still coaching a junior high girls' volleyball club team."

"Oh, good for you. Way to give back to the Asian community."

Lex wouldn't mention that most of her girls were from downtown San Jose. Well, a few of them were Asian. "I'm happy to do it. They're the daughters of the women that my mom coached."

"Ah, I miss your mom."

Lex swallowed convulsively. "Yeah. So anyway—"

"How's your dad doing these days?"

"He's good. He's bowling a lot."

"I see him every so often. He's walking a little slower these days, you know?"

"Uh ..." Actually, it didn't seem that way, but Lex wasn't about to argue with one of her elders, let alone a potential sponsor. "Sure."

"Well, you should cut back on some of your volleyball so that you can take care of him. We're all getting older."

Lex was fully aware of the cultural and moral obligation to care for her parent in his old age, even if said parent insisted he didn't want to be cared for. But why did people always think she needed to be reminded and that she needed to give up everything in her life to do it? She'd seen friends and relatives who gave up dreams to care for their family, and it was just sad, frustrating, and tiring for them.

Lex chose to ignore his comment. "Speaking of volleyball, my girls' team will be traveling for playoffs over the summer, and I wondered if you'd be willing to sponsor us or donate to the traveling costs."

"Oh..."

"In Mom's memory, maybe?" Yeah, she'd get his sentimental side.

"I'm sure I could do something. Let me get back to you, is that okay?"

"Oh, yes! Thanks, Mr. Tomoyoshi." In her mind's eye, Grandma's dragon claws receded into the milky mist ...

"Should I plan to make the check out to your dad for you?"

"Uh ... no, why?"

"Oh, well, so you don't have to take care of the more complicated money stuff."

That was the problem with growing up in the Japanese American community, where everyone knew Grandma and Lex's family. The older people still tended to think of Lex as, say, eight years old. "I take care of all the team's finances, Mr. Tomoyoshi. You can make the check out to the volleyball club."

"Okay. I'll call you in a few days about it."

"Thank you so much, Mr. Tomoyoshi." Lex dropped the handset into the cradle. "Take that, Grandma!"

Trish yawned. "Yeah, yeah. So what about Kin-Mun?"

Lex held her hand out to her. "Pass the remote."

Trish grabbed it and clasped it to her chest like the Holy Grail. "No way. I want to actually have a conversation with you."

"I can talk and watch TV at the same time." Lex reached over and scrabbled at her clenched fingers.

Trish turned away. "Answer my question first."

"What question?"

Trish gave her a *Tell me you're not that stupid* look. "Kin-Mun?"

"Oh." Lex folded her arms. "What about him?"

"It sounds like you bullied him into going out with you. You never consider other people's feelings."

"Do too. I just know what's best for them."

"So Kin-Mun reluctantly going on a date with you is what's best for him? Or for you?"

"Both. Now gimme the remote."

Trish jerked it out of Lex's reach and sat on it. "You're not even a little concerned?"

Well, it wasn't very flattering to learn he thought of her like a broth — sister, but she wasn't about to admit that to Trish. "He's just never thought of me that way. Besides, I have a plan."

"Another one?"

Lex playfully smacked Trish upside the head. "This is a good one. You're going to take me shopping."

Mention of her favorite — and only — sport made Trish sit up straighter. The TV blinked on, then off.

"Gimme the remote. You're going to break it."

"Tell me why you're actually volunteering to go shopping."

"I need you to help me wow Kin-Mun."

"Do you mean a *makeover*?" Trish's mouth dropped to her lap.

"You're drooling."

"Am not." Trish swiped at the corner of her mouth. "You must be desperate to agree to a makeover."

"I'm not desperate. I'm being practical. He's never seen me in anything other than casual clothes. He needs to see me as sexy and attractive." Non-sister-like.

"Is it really going to work?" Trish's face oozed skepticism.

"Gee, thanks for letting me know I'm such a hopeless case."

"If he isn't already attracted by your personality, how is a new skin going to do it?"

"You of all people know how visual guys are. I mean, what did my brother look at while we watched SportsCenter? The Axe commercials with all those half-naked girls shaking bootay."

Trish's mouth formed a giant *O*. "You're not going to go half-naked—?"

"What? No. It's not like I'd have anything to shake." Lex smacked her nonexistent butt. Her athletic but sadly flat body in a bikini would send Kin-Mun screaming for the funny farm.

"So ..." Trish scrutinized Lex's body with that "fix-it" look she usually wore when working on a new biology experiment at work. Yup, Lex had her hooked.

"Can you do it?"

"If I can't, no one can."

Trish with a license to shop was a frightening sight.

Trish with a license to shop for someone else was like Godzilla ripping apart Tokyo.

Lex drank in the smell of roasted coffee as they entered Tran's Nuclear Coffee Shop, but it failed to stimulate her tired muscles. The shop was empty for a Tuesday early evening. She sank into a cold metal chair and propped her elbows on the glass tabletop. "Get me a soy latte. Double shot."

Trish dug in her purse for her wallet. "Going hard-core today, eh?"

"I'm going to need a week to recover."

"You don't have a week, you have three days. But that's okay, because you'll floor him in that dress even if you look like Franken-stein's bride."

"You're just a fount of encouragement."

"I try." Trish tossed a cheeky grin over her shoulder as she flounced to the counter to order their drinks.

Lex rubbed her side and lower back where the pins had stuck her earlier. She'd never before tried on clothes that had pins in them.

Shouldn't duds with that many numbers on the price tag have the pins already removed? And even her finely tuned balance couldn't teeter on those stiletto heels for more than a millisecond. Hundreds of dollars for the privilege of twisting her ankle.

This better be worth it. She had created a monster. The only thing Trish would love more would be if she could spend someone else's money on *herself.*

"Here you go, Lex—"

"Eeeek!"

She'd know that squeal anywhere.

Paper cups don't make much noise when they splatter double-shot soy latte all over the tile floor. But Mimi's piercing voice made up for the lack of shattering glass.

"Did you have to spill *my* coffee?" Lex eyed the brown soy lake with sorrow.

Trish wasn't paying attention. Her basilisk glare tried to turn Mimi into stone. "What are you doing here?"

"Getting coffee. Duh." Mimi swung her long ponytail in a sulky arc.

"You bumped into me on purpose."

"As if. You ran into me when you turned."

"Lying little pipsqueak."

"That the best you got? Bring it on, sister." Mimi did a head-wagging thing, making her ponytail tick like a rapid metronome.

Time to intercede. "Can you *not* have women's mud wrestling in the middle of Tran's?"

Trish opened her mouth, but Lex thrust a palm in her face. "You. Quiet. You." She shoved a finger between Mimi's eyes. "Buy me another latte."

Mimi's eyes sparked black fire.

"Or I can loose Trish on you. You've got a disadvantage with that ponytail."

Mimi's pink cupid-bow mouth disappeared, but she whirled and stomped toward the counter. Lex followed.

"Double-shot soy latte." Lex leaned against the counter and looked around while Mimi ordered her own drink. A coffee shop employee came out front to clean up the mess.

By the window, an Indian couple chatted away, and in the corner, a guy ducked under his table. He must have dropped something. Back at their table, Trish looked hot enough to steam milk with her finger.

Standing next to Mimi, even leaning against the counter, Lex felt gargantuan at five-foot-seven.

Mimi fingered the Tiffany heart pendant at her throat—a gift from one of her numerous boyfriends, probably—and slid it back and forth on the chain. "Been working out, Lex?"

She asked the question with a little too much innocence. Despite her honeyed voice, the question had peeved undertones. Most likely at forking out four dollars for Lex's latte, straining Mimi's college-student budget. "No."

"Oh. Well, you just seemed *larger* than usual."

Two could play at that game. "Still shopping in the children's section?"

The old dig got the same old response. Mimi's button nose scrunched up and she puffed out her cheeks. "Better than shopping in the boys' section."

"I'm not as sensitive about my washboard figure as you are about your vertically challenged state."

"At least I'm not—"

"This has been such a refreshing conversation, Mimi—" Lex nabbed her latte as the barista slid it onto the pick-up shelf. "But we do have that mutual avoidance clause in our relationship. We'd better abide by it." Lex lumbered away.

No, she didn't *lumber*, she walked with *athletic grace*. And her height usually did her a bit of good on her Asian coed volleyball team. She wouldn't let Mimi bring out that childish insecurity again.

Back at the table, Trish didn't even turn her laser-beam gaze from Mimi, who still waited on her mocha freeze—which wouldn't add an inch to her little curvy body . . .

Stop it, stop it, stop it. "Trish, why are you and Mimi like Sugar Ray Leonard and Roberto Duran?"

"Huh?"

She'd descended into SportsCenter cant again. "Never mind. Oil and water. You and Mimi are like oil and water." Not that Lex got along any better with Mimi, but Lex didn't have the burning desire to tackle her every time she came into sight.

"She's a cat." Trish hissed like one.

"She's beneath you. You're being juvenile."

"I'm being bitter. There's a difference."

"So she dated one of your numerous boyfriends. Get over it."

"Not just one of my boyfriends. It's become her personal mission to steal every boyfriend away from me. Every time I bring a guy to family events, she's all over him."

"Oh, come on. Not every guy."

"I can list at least six who dumped me as soon as they met her, and then dated her within two weeks of our breakup." Trish pinned Lex with a challenging glare.

Lex couldn't really argue against stats. "Well, you forget one small detail. They all dump Mimi too. She still bothers you, why?"

"It's the principle."

"It's your inflated ego. Go lead on yet another boy, revel in your seductive muse power, and move on, sister."

"Your powers of empathy astound me."

"Heads up. The brat's coming back for more." Why was Mimi approaching them again? Idiot. This time, Lex wouldn't break up the catfight. Her money was on Trish.

Mimi sauntered close to the glass table and leaned in between the two of them. "So Lex, why does that guy keep staring at you?"

"What?"

Mimi nodded her head toward the other end of the shop.

"The guy with the newspaper?" Trish didn't bother to keep her voice down. "That's silly."

"His newspaper is upside down." Mimi shifted onto one hip and buffed her glittering extensions against her sparkly top.

Lex squinted. "Are you sure?"

Trish squinted too. "You can see better."

Mimi exhaled a frustrated sigh. "Trust me, it's upside down."

"Well, I can't see his face." Lex leaned left and right but couldn't see around the newspaper.

"If we stare at him long enough, maybe he'll drop the paper."

The three of them bored holes into the paper for a whole minute. They probably looked like idiots. Or actors trying out for Cyclops in the new X-Men Broadway play.

"This is stupid." Lex blinked her burning eyes.

"I agree." Trish swiveled away. "Mimi, don't you have somewhere to be? Like Timbuktu?"

Mimi's tinkling laughter rang out. "Oh, you're so original, Trish. By the way, I saw your mom putting flowers on Grandpa's grave yesterday. She came all by herself, poor Aunty." To belie the dig about Trish's lack of filial duty, Mimi's mouth pulled down into a puckering frown.

Trish bristled. "I was working. Not all of us are still in school. Some of us graduated in four years."

Mimi tossed that annoying ponytail. "Oh, well. That's good. I mean, after all, unlike you guys, I have plenty of time."

Trish's face turned into a persimmon.

An electronic trill broke through the tension. Lex dove for her cell phone like a lifeline. She glanced at the caller ID. "Hi, Kin-Mun!" Lex noticed Trish's face cooled down a bit as she listened. Except stupid Mimi didn't move away.

"Lex, I have to cancel for Saturday night. Something else came up."

Lex could have sworn she smelled something like day-old sushi. "What something?"

"Work stuff."

"Oh." Her heartbeat slowed down from frantic to disappointed. "Maybe next week—?"

"Sure. I gotta go."

"Okay. See y—"

"Oh, wait, can I talk to Kin-Mun?" Mimi snatched the phone out of Lex's slack grip.

"Hey!" Lex clawed at her phone.

Mimi danced out of the way. "Just a sec."

"You don't even know Kin-Mun."

"Sure I do. We met a couple weeks ago." Mimi spoke into the phone. "Hi, Kin-Mun?"

Lex took an angry sip of latte. If she didn't keep her hand occupied, she might slap her cousin.

"Yeah, it's Mimi. Are we still on for Saturday night?"

FIVE

Aiden Young peeked over the edge of the newspaper just in time to see the thin girl spew coffee all over Trish.

"Aaack!" Trish leaped up and flapped her hands. "This is new! That was coffee! Leeex!"

Aiden hid behind the paper again. Trish, the drama queen.

"Trish, you're such a drama queen." The tall, slender girl—Lex?—had a deeper voice than Trish, but he heard an uncertain quaver in it that hadn't been there before. He peeked over the newspaper.

Lex thrust out her hand at the junior high girl. "Phone."

"But I'm—"

"Now."

The young girl jumped at Lex's bark, but then rolled her eyes as she finished her conversation on the phone. "Sorry, Kin-Mun—"

Lex snatched the phone away and snapped it shut. Her face was as gray as a thundercloud. With the other hand, she propelled Trish toward the restroom at the far end of the coffee shop.

Now was his chance. Aiden flapped the paper shut, picked up his coffee, and hustled out the door.

From the parking lot, Spenser waved as he activated his car alarm. "Sorry I'm late."

Talk about rotten luck. Aiden intercepted him in the middle of a parking stall. "Let's go to Peet's Coffee instead."

"No, I did an extra hard workout today just so I could have a caramel mocha freeze." Spenser flashed his toothy, little-boy grin as he walked past Aiden and yanked open the glass door.

Maybe Trish would stay in the bathroom with that girl while Spenser ordered.

The junior high girl with the long ponytail passed him as he headed back into the shop, her eyes smoky beneath half-closed lids. Up close, he realized she wasn't as young as he first thought — she looked about college-age. Her mature gaze seemed appraising, and she looked like she might stop and speak to him. He brushed past her and followed Spenser to the counter.

"Caramel mocha freeze with extra whipped cream." Spenser rolled the syllables with relish.

Aiden lounged against the drink pickup counter with his back to the restrooms. Hopefully they wouldn't come out soon, and if they did, he hoped Trish wouldn't recognize him.

Spenser approached the pickup counter, stuffing bills into his wallet. "So, how ya been?"

"I'm good." He was still too flustered to spill the news — that he'd seen that spoiled flirt Trish, months after they'd finished physical therapy for her shoulder, and that he'd been instantly floored by the gorgeous girl with her.

He could still see her in his mind's eye — Trish's sister? Cousin? With her smooth, athletic grace, that beautiful face. But would she be another hypocritical Christian like Trish?

Spenser gave him a sharp look. "You sure you're okay?"

"Yeah. How's your son?"

Spenser sighed. "At his mom's house this weekend." He tapped a quick rhythm on the pickup counter. "So did you read that article I emailed to you?"

"Yeah."

"Interesting, huh?"

"Sure." Aiden glanced back at the women's restroom door. Still no sign of them. Could the barista go any slower?

Spenser looked away. "We don't have to talk about it if you don't want to."

"No, I do." But right this moment, he didn't feel up to another discussion about God. Not that their conversations weren't interesting—the Christian and the agnostic—but he'd been distracted.

The restroom door opened. Aiden's entire body stiffened, but he didn't turn around.

The Indian man walked past him back to his girlfriend sitting near the window.

"You're a little tense." Spenser gave a sidelong look.

How to explain the predicament without looking more like an idiot? His gut reaction had been to avoid Trish. After all, she hadn't taken it very well when she made that blatant pass at him, forcing him to firmly shut her down and transfer her to another physical therapist.

But then one glance at her cousin made him forget his initial desire to leave the shop, and he'd sat there staring at Lex. Too stupid to leave before Trish had come back to the table with their drinks.

He should just come clean. Of anyone, Spenser wouldn't judge him—although he might poke a little fun. "Actually—"

"I said I was sorry." Lex's voice coincided with the *whoosh* of the restroom door opening.

Where was Spenser's mocha freeze?

"Oh, look, you missed a spot." Trish's sulky voice faded as the door closed again. No footsteps. They must have gone back into the restroom.

"Caramel mocha freeze, extra whip." The barista slid the drink across the counter so hard it almost toppled to the floor before Spenser caught it.

Aiden took a deep breath. "Let's go somewhere else."

"Sure." Spenser slurped through the straw as he headed out the door.

He'd managed to avoid Trish and Lex. Strange how Lex had frightened him more than Trish. Well, it didn't matter now. He'd never see her again.

"You know, Mimi had a point," Trish said, back in the bathroom to scrub at the remaining liquid.

Lex dabbed at Trish's shirt. "I don't care if she had an intelligent thought for once."

"Hey, a little more gently, please. Do you know how much I paid for this?"

"Do I look like I care?"

"You could have aimed at her instead of me."

"I'm sorry. Next time I'm lied to, dumped, and shocked in the space of three seconds, I'll remember to spit my coffee in a more convenient direction."

"You can't blame her, though."

Lex looked up to make sure Trish hadn't blown a mental gasket. "What are you talking about? I can't believe you're saying something nice about Mimi."

"It's not something nice about Mimi, it's an insult to you."

"Oh, well that's so much better."

"Think about it. You and Kin-Mun have been friends for so long. If you guys had anything between you two, don't you think it would have happened already?"

"I told you, he just never saw me—"

"Oh, dream on. Mimi had every right to ask Kin-Mun on a date. How could she have known you'd suddenly go vampy on him?"

"That's rich, coming from you, when you just complained about Mimi stealing *your* boyfriends."

"No, there's a difference. Mimi knew they were attached to me—er, belonged ... she knew they were mine."

"She knew Kin-Mun was mine. And she knew about Grandma's ultimatum. She knew I'd be looking for someone."

"Unlike you, Mimi can't be 'friends' with a guy. She either loves them or dumps them. Since you and Kin-Mun weren't lovers, she figured you never would be."

Lex shot the crumpled paper towel into the trash. "Why are you defending her? I'm the injured party here."

"You're stupid is what you are. You wouldn't listen to me about Kin-Mun. He isn't right for you."

"How could I know he wouldn't be thrilled to date me? There's nothing wrong with me, Trish. I'm fine the way I am. I don't have to change for anybody."

"No, you don't."

"I don't need to look different."

"Not at all."

"I'm fine the way I am."

"Well, you need to aim better."

Lex eyed the mocha stain on Trish's sunflower silk top. "I'll pay for dry-cleaning."

"No, it won't come out. I want that pink top you bought today. You won't need it now."

"Just thwack my heart open with a Chinese cleaver, why don't you?"

"Puh-lease. I know you too well. In about an hour, you'll get over this 'Oh poor me' phase. And then, guess what?"

"What?" Lex sighed.

"You are going to be kamikaze mad at Kin-Mun."

"Kamikaze mad? What—I'm going to ram my car into the side of his house?"

"No. You'll be so mad that you wouldn't waste that pink blouse on a date with him if he groveled." Trish smiled, as persuasive as a geisha. "I'll get that nasty pink thing off your hands and out of your sight."

"I'll think about it."

"Don't think too long. I have a date tomorrow night."

SIX

I should go look for a condo." Lex took a bite of Chunky Monkey ice cream and stretched her legs onto the battered oak coffee table.

Trish looked up from the edge of her Cherries Garcia. "What? Why?"

"It's part of plan B." She rubbed at a drop of ice cream on the dull orange and muddy brown of the living room couch.

"Kin-Mun was your plan A? Not much of a plan A, if you ask me."

Lex had expected to feel upset for longer. Could she really get over someone so fast? "I guess I fell for an illusion. Or an ideal."

Trish stuck her nose back in her ice cream. "Why a condo? I know you were saving money for a down payment, but now it looks like you'll need that money to pay for the girls' playoffs travel."

"I don't have enough for the entire team's travel expenses. Besides, I'm sure I can get someone to sponsor the team instead. If they'd ever call me back." Lex glared at the silent phone.

"It's a lot of money." Trish fished out a cherry.

"So, I also need to keep searching for a boyfriend."

"You don't need a boyfriend. Just somebody to bring to Mariko's wedding."

"Grandma's expecting a boyfriend, not just a date. She's going to be looking for some lover-like behavior." Lex shifted her seat in the sagging couch springs.

"You realize that whoever you bring, Grandma's just going to complain about something he's not."

"What do you mean? She'll be ecstatic I'm dating. She'll love him."

"Wanna bet? It'll be the same thing she did to Mariko. 'He's too short, he's too tall, he's too skinny, he's too fat, he's not Japanese, he's not Chinese' ... Mariko could never win."

"Well, Mariko dated some pretty pathetic losers."

"I think Mariko's only marrying what's-his-name because Grandma couldn't find anything wrong with him."

"Why should I care what Grandma thinks of my dates, anyway? She's not the one kissing them good-night." Suddenly Lex's throat tightened. She couldn't swallow her ice cream.

Trish gave a quick, wary look. "Are you going to be okay—?"

"I'm fine." Lex scraped at her ice cream with her mouth still full.

They ate in silence for a moment, then Lex gave the coffee table a frustrated kick. "Why do we care so much what Grandma thinks? We're pathetic."

Trish kept eating. "It's ingrained fear."

"Yeah. Even when I know I'm right, it's hard to disagree. Why are we so intimidated?" Lex took another bite. "She's only ninety pounds. We could take her."

Trish ignored Lex's tongue-in-cheek. "She's bigger than ninety pounds."

"What do you mean? She's only—"

"No, I mean she's *larger* than ninety pounds."

"Oh. Yeah." Lex set down her ice cream and stared at the phone, willing it to ring. "Well, I have four months. I'm sure I can find some nice guy."

"You know, even if you dump him after the wedding, by that time you'll have found another sponsor for the girls' team, right?" Trish waggled her spoon at Lex. "Why are you stressing? Just pick up somebody from volleyball or something."

"I dunno." Lex crossed her arms and curled up in the sofa. "I hate being forced to do this."

Trish paused mid-bite. "Are you not ready yet?"

"Of course I'm ready. I just don't like being prodded like a cow. If I'm going to do this, I'm going to do it my way."

"What's the difference? Grandma still gets what she wants."

"I have control of my life, not her. I'm not going to date every Tomeo, Daiki, and Haruto like Mariko did. I'm ready to date, but I'm not stupid. If I'm going to be out with a guy, he has to pass certain criteria."

"Criteria? What are you going to do, ask to look at his teeth like a racehorse? Or under his hood like a car? 'Flip up your shirt, please. No back hair? Okay, you've passed inspection.'"

"*Baka.*" Lex swung a pillow at Trish. "No, I've been studying Ephesians in my women's Bible study. It's got all the traits of a godly man. I've been making a list."

Trish chortled. "A list? An Ephesians List? I'll bet it's a mile long."

"No, it's only six points."

"Just six? Let me guess. Heartbeat? Check. Can read? Check. Worships the ground I walk on—"

"Shut up. It's a good list." She ticked them off on her fingers. "One, he has to play volleyball very, very well."

"Oh, that just widens the field. That's in Ephesians?"

"Well, I have to 'submit' to him—you know, 'wives, submit to your husbands'—and I'm not submitting to anybody who can't beat me in volleyball. Two, he has to be physically attractive. It's the whole 'oneness' thing. I have to actually want to 'be one' with him."

Trish snorted with laughter.

"That's gross! You're getting ice cream everywhere."

"Sorry." Trish covered her mouth.

"Three, he's got to be Christian."

"That's third? Not high on your priorities, hmm?" Trish poked her in the ribs.

"Er . . . it's in no specific order. Four, he has to have a good, stable job."

"Where did Paul say he has to be rich?"

"Not rich. But Ephesians tells men to love their wives just as they feed and care for their bodies. So that means my boyfriend—or future spouse—needs to have enough money to feed and care for me, right? Five, he'll be faithful. No sexual immorality, impurity, all that stuff."

"That's in Ephesians too? I have to read my Bible more."

"Six, he won't lie to me. 'Put off falsehood and speak truthfully to his neighbor.'"

"How are you going to know if he's lying?"

"Um . . ." Lex dropped her legs from the coffee table. "Well, hopefully he won't. He shouldn't manipulate me or deceive me in any way. So, what do you think?"

Trish shrugged. "I guess that's doable."

"I just want to be careful, you know?"

"Yeah, I know." Trish set down her empty carton. "So what's up with buying a condo?"

"Think about it. A house declares independence. What's more, to the family, it's not a form of independence that's outright defying Grandma. It's an acceptable form of independence because it's considered an investment."

"Oh, I get it."

"I need to make a statement. Even if I show up at Mariko's wedding with a boyfriend, I want to show Grandma that I'm not completely under her thumb."

"Grandma's not a monster."

"Easy for you to say, she hasn't threatened anything important to you."

"She was actually pretty nice to me the other night."

"Huh? Why?"

"I introduced her to my new boyfriend."

"So who's the flavor of the week?"

"Shut up." Trish stuck out her tongue, then launched into her giggly mood when talking about a new guy. "I met him when I went out to lunch last week at Sako Sushi. He's a waiter. He gave me fresh chopsticks." Trish dimpled. "And he spoke Japanese to Grandma."

"Score!" She gave Trish a high-five. "No wonder Grandma liked him."

"I'm telling you, being on Grandma's good side is better than where you are now. Find a boyfriend."

"Well, I'll start at work tomorrow. Maybe my coworkers have some leads."

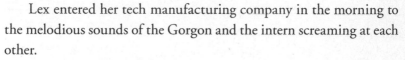

Lex entered her tech manufacturing company in the morning to the melodious sounds of the Gorgon and the intern screaming at each other.

"If you make the mess, you clean it up!" The administrative assistant's bellow resonated from the entrance foyer down the hallways to the managers' offices.

"I had a family function to go to!" Cari, the newly hired intern, had plenty of the head-wagging thing going on.

Lex's entrance through the glass doors didn't even pause the argument.

The middle-aged woman gave the hip intern a look that lowered the air-conditioned area to below freezing. "You spilled the entire bottle of soda. At least you could have gotten paper towels!"

"Somebody pushed me! It wasn't my fault!"

"It doesn't matter! Grow up and take responsibility or don't come to the afternoon office parties."

Cari's blue and purple glitter eye makeup glinted in the fluorescent overhead lights. "Even you can't keep me from going to the office parties, you old hag."

Good going, girlfriend, insult the Gorgon. Make her difficult to work with all day for everybody else.

Lex kept to the periphery of the foyer and managed to nip back to her cubicle. She guessed she wouldn't be asking Cari about her favorite singles' hangouts this morning. Maybe this afternoon. She wouldn't be able to hold a civil convo with the admin all day—she'd have to ask someone else about real estate agent recommendations.

She passed two of her coworkers—privately she called them the Gossip Twins, GT1 and GT2—huddled as usual in a cubicle furthest from the managers' offices.

"Did you hear that she got called in yesterday?" GT1 always thought her voice didn't carry, but Lex could hear her two cubicles away.

"I heard she got reprimanded for rubber-stamping the documentation." Smug and superior, GT2's softer-pitched voice still rang audibly.

"Was she too lazy to check it?"

"She got distracted when her boyfriend called."

Both Gossip Twins were young and sociable. For a flickering moment, Lex considered asking them about a good place to meet guys, but ... She walked past their giggling session.

Lex arrived at her cubicle and found a large note scrawled on her yellow sticky pad: *See me.—Everett.*

What now? Lex had finished her CAD work yesterday—ahead of schedule, thank you very much—so what could Everett complain about now?

"What do you need a new chair for?" Everett dispensed with any greeting as soon as Lex appeared at his office door.

"My back is giving me problems, so I need an ergonomic one." *Like, duh.*

"Your chair is fine. It's not broken, is it?" His bald pate had begun to glisten and blush. Great. Temper tantrum ahead.

"Well, the back adjustment screw is stripped—"

"Then get maintenance to fix it. You don't need a whole new chair." Everett tossed the purchase order onto his haphazard desk, where it disappeared in the sea of other white papers.

"Mark looked at it, and he says—"

"Who the heck is Mark?" Everett's violent head-rearing dislodged a few combed-over wisps.

"Mark is our head of maintenance."

"Oh." Everett harrumphed. "So, what'd he say?"

"He said to get a new chair."

"Why can't he drive down to Office Depot and pick up a chair?"

"We went last week, but none of them fit. My desk is too high and my legs are too short."

"So you need this $250 chair?"

"It was the cheapest ergonomic we could find."

"You don't need a special erko — ergic — nomic chair."

"My old chair is causing my lower back to hurt."

"Nonsense! It's all that volleyball you do."

That did it. An *ume*-red haze dropped over Lex's eyes. "I played for years before coming to work for this company and never had back problems until I got that computer chair at my desk."

"Delayed reaction injury. The answer's no." Everett somehow found the purchase order from his desk — or maybe he didn't, but he thought he picked up the right paper — and crumpled it up.

Lex considered screaming "Avalanche!" and flinging the layer of papers over the edge of his desk. Or maybe she could dump him out of his posh leather chair like a dump truck and run off with it to her cubicle. Or maybe she could yank out his computer cables and hold them ransom until he gave in.

Lex's teeth ground against each other. She whirled and exited the Chamber of Torture.

She almost collided with someone rushing past. "Oops, sorry, Anna ... What's wrong?"

Anna dashed at her eyes, and her blotchy face scrunched up even more. Her nose turned neon.

"Oh, no. Is it your manager again?"

"Yesterday we were working together so well ... laughing and joking. This morning, she yelled and threw her flowerpot at me. She said I did shoddy work."

Lex rolled her eyes as she walked down the hall with Anna back to the cubicles. The more distance from her manager's office, the better.

Lex walked close to a sniffling Anna but balked at putting an arm around her shoulders. She wasn't as uncomfortable touching women as men, but she still didn't like the physical contact.

The tears gushed from Anna's swollen eyes. "I just don't get her. She's so moody whenever I talk with her, I never know if she's going to smile or bite."

"If you want me to help you—"

"No, it's not the work. It's the mental anguish of working with her." Anna broke down into wrenching sobs.

Lex's desk didn't have tissues, so she reached into the cube next door to snatch some from her box. Anna crumpled them in her hand and dabbed her face.

Lex stayed with her until she calmed down. Anna blew her nose—loudly—and looked around for a trash can.

Lex followed her gaze. What had happened to her trash can?

"Uh ..." Lex peeked into the cubes on either side of her. Both missing trash cans. What was going on?

Anna's hand flapped around, still searching for a landing spot for her tissue.

Lex swallowed a sudden upsurge of bile, but held out her hand. "Here, give it to me. I'll find a trash can." Poor girl. Lex couldn't make Anna feel worse by letting her anti-bodily-fluids phobia show on her face, although her cheeks felt clammy.

Anna shuffled away, and Lex zigzagged through the cubicles, searching for a trash can. Who had pilfered all the trash cans?

"Aaaieeeeee!" Cari's shriek pierced through the cubicle walls like a spray of bullets.

Despite Cari's obvious distress, Lex would have avoided yet more drama, but just her luck, she stood a few cubes down from Cari's. The girl bolted out of her desk, hands chicken-flapping, mouth wide open and emitting more screams, legs pumping up and down like on a stairmaster.

Jerry followed behind her, weaving slightly, face pale. "I'm sorry, Cari ..."

Cari ignored him, instead wailing and flicking her purple manicure at the beige and mauve design on her skin-tight T-shirt.

No, not a design. The streak that splashed from one shoulder across her chest was vomit.

From Jerry.

"I was sitting! At my computer! He was standing! Behind me! And he just *bleaugh*!" Cari erupted into fresh hysterics.

Lex clapped one hand—not the one holding the dirty tissue, which seemed rather insignificant now—to her mouth. Her stomach roiled. *Don't breathe. Don't look.* Right now, that morning cereal didn't want to stay in her tummy. *No, don't think about the cereal!* Lex needed to get to the women's restroom.

Jerry sagged against a cubicle wall, which tilted precariously. "I'm sorry, Cari." He heaved a long, slow sigh. "I only had a few beers last night ..."

Suddenly his eyes grew large. His face dulled to Elmer's glue. He pressed his large, loose lips together.

And unleashed all over the carpet.

A collective chorus of "Ewww!"s rose from the other people who had gathered to Cari's frantic call.

Lex couldn't speak. Could barely breathe. Her vision started to cloud ...

Jerry coughed and spit.

Lex dashed to the bathroom.

SEVEN

L ex sat outside on a curb in the parking lot. The feeble sun warmed her head and made her straight hair feel like a helmet. She took another deep breath, and smelled blessed *nothing*. Nothing strong, that is. A whiff of mowed grass, a tingle of mulchy earth, a tease of something flowery, but mostly just fresh, unscented air. Nothing to cause her volcanic stomach to erupt again.

She stared at the ants weaving circles around her shoe soles. She wasn't a very good ant worker at this startup company. She wondered if ant queens were anything like unreasonable Everett or Anna's moody manager.

Maybe she ought to qu—

No, that was bad. Shouldn't she be content? *I have learned the secret of being content in each and every circumstance ...*

Lex wondered if Paul ever had to endure an illogical argument with Peter like Lex had with Everett. Peter must have been a more reasonable guy, right?

No, she needed patient endurance. She had to run the race. She had to love her enemies.

She needed a stronger stomach.

She should just qu—

Don't say it!

Chirping. Chirping. *Strange-sounding bird ... Oh! Her cell phone.* "Hello?"

"Lex, it's Chester."

Her cousin rarely ever called her. "What's up?"

"I'm going to make you smile today, coz. There's a job opening here."

"Shut up! No way. For what position?"

"Uh ..."

Oh great. "Don't try to lie to me, Chester."

"Receptionist."

Lex groaned. "How much pay?"

"Minimum wage."

What a pay cut. But still—a rare opening at SPZ! Even if SPZ wasn't one of the hottest new dot coms in Silicon Valley, Lex had only ever dreamed of working at the sports website mecca of North America. Sports, all day, every day. High school, college, and pro. Stats galore. It made Lex's head spin.

Could she be a receptionist? Just the thought made her cringe a little. Wearing makeup and nice suits and being polite to stupid people? Like Lex didn't already have to be nice to stu—er, difficult people. "It's a foot in the door, right, Chester?"

"Sure. Except for some internal shuffling, SPZ hasn't hired anyone since last July. And Lex, you're going to owe me big time—I know the hiring manager personally."

"I'll email you my résumé tonight."

"Turn that thing down!" Lex leaned back in her chair to holler through the kitchen door into the living room. The TV volume didn't move.

She sounded off. "Dad! Richard!"

"Okay, okay." Her older brother Richard slid off the couch and grabbed the remote from the coffee table. The sound of the basketball game lowered a miniscule decibel.

Lex stared at her archaic laptop. She pushed her chair back so she could lean her forearms on the kitchen table, and the metal feet shuddered against the cracked linoleum.

"Education: San Jose State University ..."

The commentator's voice cut through her concentration. "Whoa! What a shot by Kobe Bryant. The Lakers are up by three ..."

"Major: Electrical engineering ..."

"Can you *feel* the heat? Suns tie ..."

"Work experience ... City Beach Volleyball Club: Receptionist ..." She didn't have to put down that they fired her after two days, right?

"Four seconds left, and oh! That foul must've hurt ..."

"Manufacturing Engineer at Pear Technology for two years ..."

"And he missed the second free throw! The Suns have a chance for the playoffs!"

"Ooh, ooh—" Lex jumped up from her chair and darted into the living room. She had to see this. She caught Steve Nash sending a beautiful shot sailing through the air, the flicker of camera flashes ...

"He did it! Suns win!"

Lex and Dad roared and pumped victory fists while Richard moaned and sank lower into the sagging couch.

Lex stepped on something soft as she turned back to the kitchen. Richard's dirty socks, which he'd pulled off when he arrived at the house earlier tonight. "Richard, you've got three other pairs in the corner." Lex nodded to a stack of gray socks by the end of the couch. She kicked the ones under her feet in his direction too.

"Oh, good. I'm running out."

"And you can't do laundry here, the washer's being a pain. Do it at your apartment."

"The laundry room charges two bucks!"

"Not my problem." Lex walked back into the kitchen.

Her gaze fell on the stack of plates and cups in the sink. She turned around to shout back into the living room. "And wash your dishes before you leave tonight!"

"Yeah, yeah."

"I mean it!"

"Dad dirtied dishes too."

"And Dad's usually the one who washes yours! Wash your own dishes tonight!"

"Is it that time of the month?"

"I don't have to cook for you on Sunday, you know."

Richard's groan meant he'd do the dishes. Pizza and Chinese takeout got old fast for a bachelor living by himself.

Lex sat at the table again and touched the trackpad.

Nothing. The mouse arrow didn't move.

"No! No no no no no!"

"Whatcha doing?" Richard sauntered into the kitchen and sat in the chair next to her. His arm brushed hers, and she twitched away.

"Résumé. At least, I was until the computer froze." She tried a few keystrokes.

"You finally quit from Pear?"

"Not yet." Lex glowered at the unchanging screen.

"Which company is this for?"

Lex pounded a key over and over. "SPZ."

"Whoa! Doing what? I'm the programmer—I should be the one applying."

Lex shot him a wicked look. "Oh, you'd be perfect for the position." She did a hard restart of the laptop.

He knew her too well. His excited expression shifted to guarded and wary. "What position? Lemme guess. Janitor?"

"No, this is more in your line, since you're so chaaahming." Lex fluttered nonexistent lashes like his most recent psycho ex-girlfriend had done.

Richard closed his eyes and exhaled low in his throat. "Give it up already. She went back to China. What's the position for?"

"Receptionist."

Richard coughed. "You? Receptionist? Miss I-don't-want-to-hear-your-problems?"

"Hey, it's at SPZ, baby! And I can't stay at Pear anymore."

"You're finally admitting it? You've been keeping your good-Christian-girl stiff upper lip for two years."

"Can you not knock my faith for just one second?"

"Okay, okay. So what's making you think of quitting?"

"The Gorgon admin. Cari the Princess. The Gossip Twins. Everett the Super Swine. Jerry the Drunk."

"You do nothing but *monku-monku-monku* about those people. The difference today was ...?"

Lex didn't want to relive the horror. "I realized I'd never want to meet anyone those people knew."

"Meet? What?" Richard's slashing brows met above his stern nose.

Uh, oh. Her big mouth. Much as she loved Richard, no way could she tell him about Grandma's ultimatum. "I was going to ask for the names of real-estate agents they've used, but they were so impossible that I realized I didn't want their recommendations. Then Chester called, and I thought, 'I should just quit and work someplace I'd actually want to be.'"

"It's a pay cut, right?"

"But think about it. It's SPZ. The single largest sports presence on the net. It's like the iPod of the sports world. How much better can you get?"

"Something besides a receptionist position that pays less than nothing."

"You're thinking too negatively. I'll be surrounded by sports all day. I'll be in Nirvana."

"While answering phones and talking to stupid people?"

Richard knew her too well. "Maybe I can get promoted or transferred. Never in my wildest dreams did I think I could work there. They hardly ever hire new blood, and I don't have the skill set, but here's my chance."

Richard glanced at the rebooted computer. "You wanted a real-estate agent? You can't move out if you're working for minimum wage. Not in the Bay Area, anyway."

True ... "But I have some saved up. If I live a few more months with Dad, I'll have enough for a down payment. And I'll rent out a room—lots of people do."

"I know a real-estate agent."

"Oh?"

Richard flashed that famous grin, the one that made women flock to him like cats to an *ahi* steak. "He's your type too."

"No th—" The disgusted refusal came automatically, but then Lex remembered what had changed in her crazy life. Namely, Grandma's claws. "Well ... okay."

Richard's eyebrows disappeared under his four-hundred-dollar sculpted haircut. "Really?"

Hastily, "Well, I don't have any other recommendations."

His eyes narrowed, and a smirk made his dimples flash. "For a real-estate agent, or a date?"

"Shut up."

Richard smiled.

George had a face like an Asian Backstreet Boy—clean-cut, good-looking, with that indefinable sparkle-charm. A hint of sexy.

"Nice to meet you." Lex dropped his hand like a hot cup of tea, opening and closing her fingers. She still couldn't get used to even professional touches by strange men.

He didn't get the hint. His other hand landed on her shoulder—meant to be a reassuring gesture, but she became as skittish as a racehorse. *Get your hand off me.*

"I've got some great condos that you'll fall in love with." George finally dropped his arm when Lex took a giant step back.

"Let's go see them."

"I'll drive." He gestured with pride to his gleaming Lexus SUV.

"I'll follow you in my car."

As she looked at condos, Lex felt like Goldilocks, except without little Junior Bear to lend her his chair and porridge and bed.

The first condo was too far away—not from her current workplace, but if she got the job at SPZ, it would be more than an hour's drive.

The second place had an astronomical price tag—not too bad on her current salary, but it would take 130 percent of a minimum-wage paycheck. And Lex would have a hard time hiding her potential job switcheroo plans, at least until the loan application came through.

The third house was a dump labeled as a "fixer-upper"—affordable on a receptionist's salary, but she'd be eating ramen noodles every day for a couple years. Plus, it had that ratty air of a place that would start to fall apart as soon as she breathed her first sigh as the legitimate owner.

"Well, that's all I have for today." George walked her out to her rusted bucket, looking forlorn next to his hulking Lexus.

"Thanks, George. I appreciate you taking me to these places." *Even though I can't afford most of these houses if I quit, but if I tell you I'm going to quit, you and the loan officer are going to abandon me faster than a smoking Pinto.*

"Are you going home now?" George leaned against her car frame. Her Honda gave a sighing creak.

Weird question for an agent. "Uh … yeah."

"I wondered if you'd like to go out to dinner with me tonight."

Whoa, momma! Did he just ask for a real date? He didn't go the safer, less committed "Give me your email address" route that most engineers in Silicon Valley took. Not even the Starbucks coffee-hour option. Full-blown dinner. *You landed yourself a winner, toots.*

She should have hurled herself in his arms. Instead, she hesitated. Dark memories wove on the edges of her mind. Her gut clenched for only a moment, then released.

No, you're bigger than that. You can do this. The volleyball girls needed her. Grandma wouldn't win.

"I'd love dinner, George. Where?"

EIGHT

Thank goodness for the casual California dress code. Lex entered Crustaceans Restaurant in Santana Row and knew her simple cotton skirt wouldn't look out of place. Some diners were dressed up, but others wore jeans.

She actually felt kind of special being seated with such a good-looking guy. Except that George also noticed the appreciative feminine glances he collected.

"Do you know those girls?" Lex nodded at the scantily-clad gigglers who were batting their eyelashes from a couple tables away.

George whipped his attention back to Lex. "Uh ... no." He flashed that bright, warm smile. Lex would have felt enveloped by it if she hadn't seen the girls over his shoulder still ogling him. *Look all you want, girlies. He's with me.*

He seemed to welcome the attraction, which didn't bode well for item number five on her Ephesians List — the whole faithfulness issue. Well, she had all dinner to weigh him against the List.

Lex skimmed the menu, but she knew what she wanted to eat. Same thing she always got.

George glanced up at her. "Want to split a crab wonton appetizer?"

"Sure. Good choice." To add to the List: *Must enjoy good food as much as me.*

The waitress appeared at the table like a genie, and dressed like one too, in a gauzy jewel-toned Vietnamese dress. "Do you know what you'd like to order?" Her bell-like voice tinkled.

George's eyes didn't immediately raise from his menu to the waitress's face—he took a rather slow journey over her slender curves. Lex's jaw flexed. That was strike two on the faithfulness point of the List. This might be a short date.

"We'll share the crab wontons. I'll have a Caesar salad and the garlic-roasted crab with garlic noodles."

At least he had good taste in food. "I'll have the same." Lex handed the oversized menu to the waitress.

George leaned forward. "You work at Pear Technologies?"

She winced. *So* not her favorite topic. "Yeah."

"How do you like working there?"

"Um ..." Her boss was Captain Hook, her coworkers were nuttier than the seven dwarves, and she was worked harder than the Israelite slaves in Egypt. Not the most P.C. answer. "It's okay."

An awkward silence fell between them. Actually, it felt more like the embarrassed quiet that hushed a restaurant when someone dropped a platter full of dishes onto the floor.

"So, Lex, have you read the bestseller by that Asian author who goes by the pseudonym Mr. Roboto?"

Lex blinked. He was kidding, right? "Uh ... I don't think Mr. Roboto is Asian."

"What do you mean? Of course he must be Asian. That famous song was Chinese or something."

She stared at him so hard, her eyes crossed. He was a complete idiot. "'*Domo arigato*' is Japanese, and that song was by Styx."

George gave her a *Well, duh* look. "And they did that '*Sukiyaki*' song too."

"What?" Wasn't '*Sukiyaki*' by Taste of Honey or something like that?

He sat back, his eyes heavy-lidded. "You didn't know that? I thought you would, being Asian and all." He smiled. All that was missing was a condescending pat on her head.

Her gaze narrowed. Was it really possible for him to be such a blockhead?

Here in the Bay Area, hardly anyone brought up her Asian-ness—it would be like living in Dallas and commenting on someone's Texas drawl. A part of her was in shock at how he'd been both insulting and idiotic, while her hand itched to smack that condescending smirk off his face.

Control yourself, babe. You're in Crustaceans and you're about to have a fabulous free meal. Remember the free part. She managed a strained smile. "You're so multicultural." *Oh, gag me.* "What's your ethnic background?"

"Oh, I'm an American citizen. I grew up in San Jose ..."

To add to the List: *No ignorant ethnic remarks.* Wasn't that already in Ephesians somewhere?

While he spouted off on his childhood, her mind wandered. Maybe she should have politely shut him down instead of appeasing him. This date had already started downhill. Why waste her whole evening?

The burning question: *Is the garlic crab that important to you?* She hadn't had it in three months. Ninety-seven days, to be exact. And George was paying. Decisions, decisions ...

"You know, you remind me of someone." He squinted at her. Problem was, he squinted quite a bit below her chin.

Lex sensed another goober remark up ahead.

George snapped his fingers. "I know. You remind me of my ex-girlfriend."

Hadn't anyone told him that mentioning ex-girlfriends while on a date was like begging to have his car keyed?

"Yeah, you look exactly like her ... except she was cuter—er, younger."

Younger? She was only thirty!

"And she had a different body." He sketched an impossible hourglass in midair—something like a 42–12–42. "And she had a larger caboose."

The room darkened. A blood-red haze blurred his face in her vision. "That's a little too personal."

He waved a hand. "Oh, I don't mind talking about it."

"Well, I do." *You cretin.* She could barely spit the words past her gritted teeth.

Oblivious to the gathering storm, George leaned forward. "But today's technology is so great."

She spoke as slow and measured as a speech therapist. "And-what-is-that-supposed-to-mean?"

"Well, you know … plastic surgery. It can help … *people* … look so much better."

She couldn't speak. Her vocal cords weren't responding.

The moron kept talking. "You can get surgery for cheap. If you go to Mexico, you can get it for half the price as the U.S." He beamed at her in friendliness mingled with pity.

She wondered how she could dispose of his body.

George was begging to get decked. With a two-by-four. Or maybe the aluminum baseball bat Lex kept in her car trunk. She'd forgotten to include on the List: *Must never mention body parts, or else risk decapitation.* They hadn't even gotten their appetizers yet. He'd ruined her entire evening and she wouldn't get dinner.

She was starving. She wanted crab.

No, she would walk out on him, breathe fresh air, clear her head, shake the dust from her shoes.

Or she could endure the evening and stick him with the bill. This place didn't exactly have McDonalds' prices.

Escape or revenge?

Freedom or suffering?

Peanut butter sandwiches or garlic roasted crab?

A steaming plate appeared in front of Lex—the crab wontons, nestled in a lettuce leaf. Blond deep-fried dumplings.

Maybe she'd walk out without braining George …

Another waiter swept past their table holding two platters of Crustaceans' signature entrée. Rich, briny crab. Nutty brown butter. Lex's stomach growled. "Let's just finish dinner." Granted, it came out sounding a bit strangled.

George smiled and tucked his napkin into his shirt collar.

Lex paused as she settled her napkin in her lap.

Her look must have clued him in, because he stiffened his shoulders. "This shirt cost me three hundred dollars and the tie is Ermenegildo Zegna. I'm not getting it dirty. Do you know how much good dry-cleaning costs?"

Why was she surprised by anything that came out of his mouth by now? *Just eat and leave.*

As Lex pierced a wonton with her fork, its bubbled surface flaked pastry onto the stainless steel tines. She brought it to her mouth. The outer shell crunched against her teeth while the satiny, cheesy filling melted on her tongue. A ribbon of sweetness from the fresh crab lingered in her mouth.

Aaaaaahhhhhh ...

George bit into a wonton with relish. "I had a girlfriend who could make these."

Lex bit her tongue. The pain made her start and drop her fork with a clatter against the porcelain plate.

Her next wonton didn't taste so divine.

He looked like he would expound on his master-chef ex girlfriend as soon as he finished chewing. She needed a tangent. "Do you cook?"

"I make a jambalaya that women swoon over ..."

Could the man ever say something that didn't involve other females? Lex listened with half an ear to his masterful feats of culinary genius. At least getting their food meant that he didn't talk as much.

The Caesar salad arrived, aromatic with garlic, studded with caramel-colored anchovies. The crisp lettuce popped in her mouth with freshness. The perfect balance for the wontons, and a way to ready her palate for the crab to come. The dressing sizzled with hot pepper, tangy vinegar, creamy mayo, and bright lemons.

George cut into an anchovy. "Salads are a great way to lose weight."

That was random. "Um-hm." *Just keep chewing, Georgy-boy, so I don't have to listen to you.*

"But you need exercise too. Increase muscle mass, increase metabolism."

Where was he going with this? Lex cleared her throat. "How often do you work out?"

"Three times a week minimum, but I try to make it more often."

Lex did a discreet appraisal. Not a powerhouse, but not flabby. He probably only made it to the gym twice a week on average. She sighed. She and George didn't even have athleticism in common, because she worked out much more than he did. "Do you play sports?"

George swallowed a bite. "I'm taking kickboxing right now. You should try it, it's fun."

On the volleyball court, she didn't mind getting bruises and floor burns on her body, but blows to the head wigged her out. Kickboxing? No, thank you. "Mm-hm."

"It's great exercise. You'd tone your body a bit."

Uneasiness and suspicion caused a prickling at the back of her eyeballs and a humming along her jaw. "What do you mean?"

His handsome smile could charm the knife away from a serial killer. "You'd fit your clothes better and feel great about yourself."

What?

Sure, she didn't have curves, but she never thought she looked out of shape. She glanced down. Her tucked-in blouse ballooned out from her skirt waistband. She thought the loose top would hide her flat chest while the pleated skirt would give her hips, but maybe it gave another illusion entirely. Did he actually think she looked *fat*?

Lex didn't say anything for a long time. A weird emotionless feeling had descended on her. She blinked, wondering what her reaction should be.

Gee, I ran five miles yesterday, and the day before that, I did lateral movement drills on a sand volleyball court. Not enough toning?

You know, I didn't care much for sparring sports, but you're making me rethink that.

My life has been completely changed by your sensitive insight into my weight and self-esteem.

The waitress saved him. Maybe she had a premonition of George's imminent demise and swept in to rescue him. She removed the salad plates and presented the garlic roasted crab with a flourish.

Hot, pungent aromas steamed Lex's face as she leaned over the plate for a long, ecstatic breath. An exotic mix of spices melded with the warm richness of browned butter. Only a whiff of brine. The shells had a warm, healthy sunset color. Her mouth watered.

She lifted the top shell and inhaled a sweet tang of the sea. She picked out a forkful of feathery meat and took a bite.

She magnanimously forgave George for everything. Because of him, she sat here in pure bliss.

George nattered on about fat cells, he checked out the miniskirt of the woman sitting at the next table, and she thought he called her Alicia once. He could call her Big Bird for all she cared. She had reached Shangri-la.

"Hiya, Lex!"

She plummeted straight into hell.

Mimi posed beside their table. Her sleek black dress revealed her curvy hips, while her perky C-cups squished under the low, tight neckline. She flashed white teeth framed by lipstick that screamed "Red Light District."

"How nice to see you here, Lex." Mimi tossed her shimmering, calf-length ponytail. She then ignored Lex and sidled up to George. "Hi, I'm Mimi, Lex's cousin."

He seemed dazed by the jiggling mounds waving in his face. "George."

Her mesmerizing, half-lidded eyes drew close to him. "You seem familiar. Have we met before?"

Wait a cotton-pickin' minute. What was Mimi doing? She already had Kin-Mun, and if the two-hundred-pound hunk of steroid-built muscle glaring at them from across the room indicated anything, Mimi had men by the dozen. Why go after Lex's measly lamb? Well, granted, George was more like good-looking slime, but still. Lex sat forgotten on the other end of the table, a lump on the couch watching a bad soap opera.

George lived up to her abysmal expectations with a delighted reply. "I promise, I wouldn't have forgotten you if we had."

"Are you sure? I could have sworn I saw you at a naked coed Ultimate Frisbee game."

His answering look smoldered with wicked glee. "Oh, darling, I would only flaunt this body for a private audience."

Lex tried not to gag. George wasn't the sharpest knife in the drawer, but she expected a little consideration while she remained within reasonable distance. Like *three feet away* across the dinner table.

Mimi gave her a sly sidelong look. *Can't keep your date's attention, Lex?*

Heat rushed into Lex's face like her head had been stuck in an oven. Her chest tightened in pain, and her lungs felt punctured. She gasped for a breath that burned down her throat. She hunched her shoulders, trying to shrink within her clothes, make herself smaller, more delicate, more feminine.

"Oh!" Mimi's graceful hand touched her shell-shaped ear. "Where's my earring?" She bent to search the floor, affording a generous view down her dress.

George paused a moment to stare down at her like a predatory wolf. Then he scooted his chair back and bent to peer at the patterned carpet.

When his head fell at level with hers, Mimi lifted her chin at him. He also tilted toward her. She smiled a slow, sensual bedroom smile, as if daring him to move the scant inches between them and press his lips to hers.

George gave an inane smile.

A spasm squeezed through Lex's chest. Ignored and spotlighted at the same time. Shut out by the two lovebirds exchanging heated glances. Laughed at by everyone else in the restaurant who witnessed the poor plain Jane losing her handsome escort in front of her eyes.

Mimi rose languidly to her feet. A business card appeared between two fingers. Where had that come from? Her bosom? As she tilted it toward George, he plucked it from her without breaking eye contact.

She dragged a seemingly innocent finger down her neck in an unselfconscious gesture. "Nice meeting you, George."

"The pleasure was all mine."

Mimi's eyes flickered to Lex. "How do you two know each other?"

"Me and Lex? Oh, her brother set us up."

Wait a minute. No, he didn't. Richard just asked George to show her some condos. Why did George say that? It took a second for Lex to pick up what he didn't say.

Had Richard asked him to ask Lex out to dinner?!

No way. Richard wouldn't be that stupid. Or suicidal—because he'd know his sister would hunt him down if she found out.

But drowning her anger, a sludge-filled sea of utter mortification pulled at her with a slow undertow. She'd needed her brother to get a date.

And Mimi would tell everyone.

Lex would never live this down. She closed her eyes to block out the sight of Mimi's sparkling gaze and surprised, mocking expression. In Lex's world of warm darkness, Mimi's high, trilling voice cut through.

"Oh reeeally?" A giggle. "Well, next time I'll be sure to take advantage of Richard's dating service."

Lex's eyes flew open. She needed to salvage her pride behind some white-hot anger. "Stow it, Skipper."

Mimi's smile hardened. She looked like she did when she had ripped the head off of Trish's Barbie doll when they were younger. A warm, vindictive rush pooled in Lex's heart at the thought that no amount of push-up bras and scanty clothing could make Mimi look taller than an elementary school student.

Lex tilted her head toward the far table. "Now be a good girl and go home to Papa."

Mimi turned to George and leaned her face in close. "I hope I see you sometime?"

He gave a confident movie-star impression. "You just might."

She sashayed away.

Lex regarded George with a neutral face and burning eyes. His smile faltered.

Over his shoulder, she spotted the waitress approaching. She snapped up a hand. "I need a box." Lex glanced at George's untouched crab. He'd been too busy spewing out pheromones. "He will too."

The waitress nodded and hurried away.

George blinked in astonishment. "You didn't like the crab?"

"I'm not hungry."

He seemed deaf to her clipped tone. "That's good. Lower calorie intake will definitely — "

She couldn't believe him. "Do yourself a favor and stop talking."

He halted mid-sentence, his mouth open, but recovered quickly. "Ah ... Lex, your brother and I are good friends."

Another lowering suspicion shot tension down her spine. "And?"

"You see him pretty often, right?"

She pressed her mouth together and regarded him with a narrowed gaze.

"Can you ask him to pay you back for my half of tonight's dinner? I, uh ... I'm out of cash."

NINE

Richard was so dead. He was deader than dead.

Lex jammed her key into the lock and pushed her way into the house. She'd like to indulge in a good slamming, banging, crashing fit, but Dad was sleep—

"Hey, Lex."

"Dad? Why are you still up?" Lex closed the door and dropped her bag on the couch.

He struggled to sit up in the recliner. "How'd your date go?"

Lex glowered at the Styrofoam boxes. "I got leftovers." And she didn't have anything better she could say about it.

He sighed. "I hoped he might be a nice guy."

Lex froze on her way to the kitchen. Dad hadn't even paid attention to her love life when she'd been fantasizing over 'N Sync. "Why?"

He shrugged, a floppy up-and-down motion with his shoulders, letting his arms hang down.

It usually meant he was hiding something.

"Why the sudden interest, Dad?" Lex thrust every ounce of steel into her voice so he wouldn't avoid her question.

He peeked sidelong at her. Lex crossed her arms.

"Well, I'm going to bed." He hoisted himself up from the recliner.

Lex slid into the doorway to the hall and blocked it with her body. She set her mouth in a firm line and glared.

It didn't always work, but it did tonight. He seemed to sag as he stood there. "Grandma called."

Lex closed her eyes and resisted the urge to bang her head against the doorframe. "About?"

"Complaining you weren't dating enough. Not making enough of an effort." He wouldn't look at her.

"What else?"

He didn't answer for a long moment. Lex wondered what else Grandma had put into his ear that he wasn't telling her. Finally he sighed. "Do you think you could try to find a nice boy to date? Just to make Grandma happy."

The words struck like a blow from a sword into her gut. A spasm tightened her stomach, then disappeared. She inhaled a shallow breath.

Dad never asked anything of her. Never. He let her find her own way, do her own thing. He made her stand her ground against Richard, he let her choose whatever interested her in college.

This was like the warrior on his knees.

"Yeah, Dad. I'll find somebody." The words sounded strong and sure despite working around the tightness in her throat. "I'll make sure he's a Suns fan."

Dad smiled like his old self. Lex moved aside so he could shuffle off to bed.

"Oh, Lex." His voice echoed down the small hallway. "Mr. Tomoyoshi called. He said to tell you he's sorry, but he can't sponsor the girls' team."

What?! Lex turned to stare at her father. Did she hear the wrong thing? "He said no?"

Dad nodded. "Why'd you ask him? Isn't Grandma sponsoring your team?"

"Ah …" Lex's mind scrambled. "She might not after Mariko's wedding. So, I'm asking people just in case." Oh no! What if Grandma found out? "But don't say anything, okay, Dad? Grandma didn't say for sure she wouldn't do it, and she'd be hurt I was looking."

Her father nodded and headed back down the hallway with a yawn.

Well, Lex would have to be satisfied with that. She didn't even want to consider what would happen if Grandma found out.

She'd have already talked to Robyn if she hadn't been late ... Yeah, yeah. Story of her life.

Her grass doubles match now over, Lex gulped water from her Nalgene bottle and looked around for Robyn. She'd just seen her ...

"Good game, Lex." Kin-Mun, her doubles partner, toasted her with his own water bottle and swiped at the sweat pouring down his face.

"You too." They'd committed to this tournament weeks ago, and Lex had worried that there would be awkwardness because of their almost-date. She had discovered that her initial feelings of complete devastation—okay, maybe it hadn't been that dramatic—had dissipated as quickly and completely as water on a hot hibachi grill, but she wasn't sure how Kin-Mun would feel.

She shouldn't have even wasted the neurons. She didn't understand how, but Kin-Mun chose to pretend nothing had happened, and they'd played together as fluidly as usual. They'd returned to their competitive, easy-going, *platonic* relationship with unbelievable ease. Lex supposed that was a good thing. Kin-Mun was the best doubles partner she'd played with yet.

"You were on fire." Kin-Mun grinned.

Yeah, she felt on fire right now despite the cool temperature. She fished her towel out of her bag and tried to stop Niagara Falls from pouring down her forehead. "Have you seen Robyn?"

"I saw her at registration earlier."

"I arrived at the tournament late, so I couldn't talk to her before we started. Where is she now?"

Kin-Mun used his extra inches of height to scan the grass tournament grounds. "Far side, near court three, talking to Jill."

Lex hoofed it over to court three. Robyn knew practically everyone who played volleyball—she would know whom Lex could approach about sponsoring the girls' team. Lex hoped she could broach the touchy topic of money with Robyn alone and with tact, for a change.

Robyn smiled and waved hello at Lex but didn't pause her conversation with Jill. Sounded like something to do with the Nikkei Volleyball League that put on this grass tournament. Lex shifted to one foot, ready to wait.

"Lex!"

Her least-favorite person at the moment approached, sticking out from the T-shirt-clad crowd in his stylish jeans and some designer shirt that made him look muscular. Lex felt mad enough and powerful enough to take Richard down, right there in the middle of the park. She opened her mouth to lash into him when she saw he'd brought a human shield—an okay-looking guy, Richard's age and probably single. Had Richard talked to Dad? Did he know he was in the doghouse?

Lex gave him a feral smile. "Richard. My most favorite, chaaahming brother."

He froze, hand still lifted in a welcoming wave. "What have I done now?"

"*George*, you doofus."

Richard had the grace to wince. "I told him not to do anything stupid."

"Oh, you mean like open his mouth?"

Richard's smile became pained. "Uh ... Lex, I came up because I wanted to introduce you to my friend, Aiden." He gestured to the non-descript guy hanging back behind him.

Aiden held out his hand, light eyes intense on Lex's face. "Hi."

She returned his brief, firm handshake, and a quiver raced up her arm and down to her toes. Must be nerves. "Hi."

She wasn't in the right frame of mind to be civil to another of Richard's friends. She peeked over at Robyn—still deep in conversation with Jill.

"Richard!" A coy feminine voice made him turn and flash that famous *Come hither* smile.

"Hi, darling." He walked away.

No, no, no! Don't leave me alone with—!

Lex attempted a feeble smile at Aiden. He looked so calm and bland. Nice-looking, but not striking enough to make her heart pound—he already had a point against him from her Ephesians List. Although he did meet her eyes directly, which was something Richard and her father never did. "So, Aiden, what do you do?"

"I'm a physical therapist. I work at Golden Creek Physical Therapy in south San Jose."

"Oh." Lex suppressed a shudder. Why did anything having to do with injuries give her the willies? Another thing to add to the List: *Must have an occupation I can say without wigging out.*

Silence.

Lex glanced at Robyn and tried to will her to finish with Jill so she could talk to her. From their serious expressions, it looked like something important.

Her gaze bounced back to Aiden. "I'm a manufacturing engineer at Pear Technologies."

Aiden nodded. "Richard told me."

"How do you know Richard?" Always a good question. Richard collected friends like he used to collect baseball cards.

"He's friends with one of my patients. I met him last week."

"Oh." He wasn't even one of Richard's close friends, but Richard threw them together. Well, may as well go down the List. "Do you play sports?"

"I run. I'm training for a marathon right now." Even when talking about something he obviously enjoyed, Aiden didn't change his calm expression except to give a half-smile.

Man, he was boring.

She sighed. Robyn still talked to Jill, and Lex didn't feel like being polite anymore. "I hate running. I only do it because I need to, for training."

Aiden blinked. "Oh."

Lex plunged ahead. "Do you play volleyball?"

"No, but I'm thinking of picking it up."

Scratch Aiden as date material. No way she could respect—much less date—someone who didn't play volleyball at a higher level. "Take classes. That way you'll learn proper form and technique."

"Uh ... okay." He looked at her as if she were a crazy cousin he had to humor.

Lex didn't care. This topic was her pet peeve. "I hate playing with people who have sloppy form."

"Oh ... Okay."

"It's dangerous on the court. I can't tell you the number of times I've seen near-miss accidents ..." She should shut up, she was ranting. "Um ... It was nice meeting you." Lex would go and stand next to Robyn's elbow to let her know she needed to talk to her.

"You look so much like Trish—" He ended his sentence oddly, as if he hadn't intended to say that.

Lex paused in the act of escaping. "She's my cousin."

"Yeah, Richard told me."

"How do you know her?"

"From ... the gym." His eyes drifted left.

"You really think we look alike?" Lex almost didn't want to hear his answer. Trish had a bubbly personality. Trish had a decent cup size and curvy hips. Trish attracted men like Fight Night in Vegas.

"You look exactly like her."

She realized he was studying her face. How weird. "Naw, she's prettier."

He shook his head—smart man. "Do you ... go to the same church?"

The way he said the word made Lex uncomfortable. "Yeah. Santa Clara Valley Asian Church." Although come to think of it, she hadn't seen Trish on Sunday last week.

Aiden blinked, and a glass shutter dropped over his eyes. He still had that bland, polite smile, but suddenly he seemed farther away from her, even though he hadn't moved an inch. "Oh, that's nice."

"Do you go to chur—" From the corner of her eye, Lex saw Robyn finally break with Jill and move toward the registration table. "I'm sorry, Aiden, but I need to grab Robyn about something. It was nice meeting you." She dashed off after Robyn's figure weaving between the crowd of volleyball players.

"Lex!" Richard stepped in front of her.

Lex tried to sidestep, but he moved with her. She stabbed an accusing finger between his eyes. "What's the big deal, bucko?"

He jumped back before she poked his eye out. "Uh ... You didn't like Aiden?"

"We had nothing in common. What's with you playing Love Connection?"

Richard winced. "Consider it an attempt to make up for George. I feel bad about that."

Lex searched for Robyn. She thought she saw her bright yellow T-shirt in the crowd. She whipped back to Richard with her best menacing glare. "You stay out of my love life."

"Did Aiden tell you he knows Trish?"

"Yeah, so?"

"Remember when she had to have physical therapy for her shoulder?"

"You mean that injury from work? Aiden was her therapist?"

"At first. Then she got transferred to another therapist at his facility."

"And this is important to me, why?"

Richard's expression baited Lex. "Trish made a move on Aiden, but he wasn't interested, and he got her transferred to another therapist. She was so peeved that when she found out Aiden's agnostic, she made a big deal about not dating him because he isn't Christian."

Oh good one, Trish. Way to make Christian girls look stupid. Lex rounded on her atheist brother. "So you introduced him to me to see if I'd diss him too? You dork." She *had* dissed him, but it was because she had to talk to Robyn, not because he wasn't Christian. "We didn't even talk about religion, so it doesn't matter." She stuck her finger at his face again. "In case you missed it the first time—Stay out of my love life. I don't want to date any of your friends, because they're all just like you."

Richard spread out his arms. "What's wrong with me? I'm chaaahming." He laughed.

Lex growled and bopped him on the shoulder with her fist. "I'll deal with you later." She dashed after Robyn.

"Let's go." Aiden hustled past Spenser, who was flirting with a cute volleyball player in a sports bra.

With a hasty goody-bye to the underdressed girl, Spenser followed him to the parking lot. "Already? I thought we were going to stay to watch the whole tournament."

"I didn't think athletic girls were your type." Aiden hit the button to deactivate his SUV's car alarm.

"They're not." Spenser grinned. "She came up to me, buddy."

His gregarious friend attracted girls like stray dogs to a sausage truck. "Well, I've seen enough volleyball today."

Spenser opened the passenger side door. "So are you going to listen to me and learn to play volleyball?"

Aiden hesitated.

"What's the problem?" Spenser climbed in and buckled his seat belt. "You get so many clients with volleyball injuries, it'll only add to your reputation to play it and understand the sport, the kinds of injuries."

Aiden glanced out his window back toward the park, picked her out as she talked to a shorter Asian woman with a yellow shirt. Lex stood slimmer than Trish, more graceful. Deeper voice, more outspoken.

"I saw you talking to her." Spenser's voice had that ribbing tone.

"I'm a masochist."

"What do you mean?"

He didn't answer. He should have left it alone. Shouldn't have reacted when Richard carelessly pointed out his sister on the grass volleyball court.

"Who is she?"

"You remember that girl, Trish?"

"The one who came on to you?"

"That's her cousin."

Spenser peered at Lex again, brows knit. "Is she anything like Trish?"

"She's Christian." That sealed it for him. Yup, his interest in her had officially ended.

Spenser sighed but didn't bring up the religion argument again.

Belatedly, Aiden realized the indirect insult. "No offense."

Spenser cocked an eyebrow at him. "None taken."

He started the engine. Maybe it was a good thing he'd met Lex. She looked just like Trish, except way more attractive. He should run in the other direction.

But she'd been beautiful playing on that volleyball court ...

She'd also been blunt and borderline rude. His attraction had taken a nosedive when he realized she didn't feel the same physical pull that he did.

He started to pull out of the parking space when a horn blared. He hit the brakes. A hefty Explorer roared past.

Great. Just thinking about the girl would get him killed.

TEN

Lex's heart thudded from her chest down to her stomach as soon as she walked in the glass doors Tuesday morning. Directly ahead of her, the conference room was jam-packed with her coworkers.

She checked her watch. 9:15 a.m. She had stayed until almost eleven last night—Everett had checked in on her before he left at seven—so she *knew* she hadn't gotten an email or a phone call about an all-hands meeting.

She tried to discreetly edge into the room, but Everett threw her a nasty look from his seat on the far side. She remained standing by the open door, next to Jerry, who swayed visibly. He bumped into her arm. She took a side step away.

The admin's whining voice carried over everyone's nodding heads. "And so, because of all the extra work I've been getting, from now on you have to submit a copy of this form—" She waved a white sheet— "in triplicate, a week before you need it done. No more last-minute things."

"Even for a customer?" Anna's incredulous voice burst out.

The Gorgon admin's cheeks colored a dusky orange. "Well, if it's for a customer—"

"Everything is for customers. We don't ask you to pick up our dry cleaning."

Lex almost burst a sinus trying to stifle her sniggering. The admin did exactly that for Everett because she had a crush on him.

The Gorgon babbled, trying to regain control of the situation.

Lex's mind wandered. She had a lot to do today, and sitting—or in her case, standing—in a useless meeting meant she'd need to stay late again.

When the meeting finally broke, Lex hurried to her desk.

Yup, she had an email. Sent this morning at 8:30 a.m., calling for "an important mandatory meeting" at nine.

"Lex, I want to talk to you." Everett appeared at her elbow, blowing steam. "In my office."

A hissing, fizzing pressure started to build in her gut. No way. He knew Lex had stayed late last night, so her being fifteen minutes late this morning shouldn't be a problem.

Shouldn't. This was Everett, after all.

He slammed his office door behind her. "How dare you miss an all-hands meeting?"

"You didn't send the email until 8:30 a.m. today." Lex's gut bubbled.

"You're supposed to be into work by 9 o'clock."

"I stayed here working until eleven last night." She spoke low to try to keep her voice calm. *I have learned the secret of being content . . .*

"How do I know you're telling the truth?"

Lex had to take a slow breath through flared nostrils before she answered. "You checked in on me before you left last night at seven."

"You could have left right after I did."

"I sent you an email at eleven, just before I went home."

Everett's thunderous brow knit, then he circled the desk to check his computer. His face grew redder. "Ah . . . You could have altered your computer time stamp."

"What?" *I have* learned *the* secret *of being* content . . . *content . . . content . . .*

He straightened to face her. He seemed to feel stronger with the desk in between them. "The bottom line is you should have arrived earlier, no matter how late you stayed. It's an embarrassment to me when you sneak into a mandatory meeting late."

Lex felt like an overworked racing engine about to bust a gasket. "It wasn't that important a meeting."

"Every meeting is important. You're on probation as of now."

The edges of her vision clouded in, but not because she was going to faint. No, she was going to slap that silly, superior smile off his face. "You can't put me on probation."

"And why not?" From Everett's loose fish lips, sarcasm sounded stupid and silly.

"Because I quit."

Oh my goodness, did she really say that?

Everett's eyes and mouth became the size of three baseballs.

Lex's brain boiled. She could feel it. And it felt good. "I quit. I could work at Starbucks and get more respect than I do here, and with the hours I put in, it's the same hourly rate."

Lex turned and yanked open the office door. She paused at the threshold to turn and face him. "Everett, you are a complete schmuck!" Wow, that felt good.

She stomped to her desk and grabbed the plastic bag holding her lunch. She collected only her personal items—well, she did steal her favorite pen— shouldered her purse, and marched out the door.

The sunlight hit her full in the face as she exited. Illuminating the realities she'd ignored while packing up her desk.

What. Had. She. Done?

Go right back inside and fix it. Forgive your enemies.

No way, Jose. Not speaking to Everett ever again.

Patient endurance, remember? Go talk to the Gorgon admin. She handles all the HR stuff.

Like she'd listen to me.

Nope, this was right. Sure, it would be tough—okay, maybe a little less than impossible—for an engineer to get another job in Silicon Valley. But she had stared into the horrific face of incompetence in Everett, and she wasn't going to take it anymore. Even a receptionist job—even someplace other than SPZ—would be better than that.

She marched to her car. She'd fax, mail, and email a copy of her resignation letter from home. Clean, indisputable cut. She was free. Unfettered. Flying high.

And financially unsound.

Well, not dead broke. She had enough to survive on for years since she lived at home, but no loan officer would touch her now. Goodbye, condo.

Her cell rang. "Hello?"

"Alexis Sakai?"

"Yes." She straightened.

"This is Wendy Tran from SPZ Human Resources. We received your résumé, and we'd like to bring you in for an interview. Are you free tomorrow?"

Aaack! She was late!

Lex leaped into her klunk-mobile and peeled out of the driveway. She navigated Highway 85 like a pro, zipping in and out as she drove north to Sunnyvale. Other drivers bore down on their horns with relish.

She got onto De Anza Boulevard. SPZ's massive square office building lay just ahead. She darted into the right lane—

Squeeeeeal! Bam!

The jolting impact to her right front slammed her car to a halt. Ripping pain across her chest. Then eerie silence.

Bright sunlight. No sounds.

She gasped in a heaving breath. Then another. Her ears started working again, and she heard the honking from the cars stuck behind her.

Her chest hurt. Was she having a heart attack? No, the seatbelt had cut through the thin fabric of her interview blouse. A red swatch burned across her breastbone.

This wasn't happening. This wasn't happening. This wasn't happening.

The other driver, an older man who looked frighteningly like Everett, had a mouth worse than a sailor. Lex remembered her dad's admonitions to always keep her trap shut, especially if it just might be entirely, horrifically, and irrefutably her fault. She traded insurance information.

The car didn't look *that* bad. Her bumper was only hanging off a little—nothing duct tape wouldn't fix, right? And while the frame had dented inward and scraped against her right front tire, couldn't a mechanic just pound it back into shape?

Lucky for her, the accident happened only a few feet from the entrance to a strip mall parking lot. She had more than enough strength to push her tiny car the few feet into a stall.

Except her interview started thirty minutes ago and she smelled like rubber tires.

Lex jogged—well, teetered as fast as she could in pumps—to the SPZ building a block down. She burst through the glass doors into cool air conditioning and collapsed at the receptionist's desk. "Lex Sakai, and I'm late for my interview."

Instead of a receptionist, a security guard sat at the desk and gave her a bored look. He punched in a few keys, a mini-printer buzzed out with her information on a card, and he handed her the ID tag. "Go down the hall, turn left, and wait in Conference Room C12."

Lex clipped down the hallway, peeking briefly into a few open doors. A couple large empty offices, a couple conference rooms. She curbed left around the corner.

"Hey!"

Something warm—no, make that something *hot* splashed on her blouse. Lex bent over too late—some of it trickled down her shirt into her underwear.

Coffee. Extra-strong, from the smell. All over her white blouse and staining a narrow vertical strip down her pencil skirt.

A heavily made-up woman glared at her. "Serves you right for not watching where you're going."

The nerve! "You could use a few less calories anyway, toots."

The woman opened her fuchsia lips in a soundless gasp. Then with a high-pitched grunt, she huffed off. Lex felt hot enough to steam the coffee out of her clothes as she watched the woman waddle into an office and slam the door.

Lex hadn't passed any restrooms, so she moved on until she saw a breakroom—probably where the coffee came from. She nabbed some paper towels and hustled back to conference room C12.

She dabbed at the stain while she waited. Ten minutes. Twenty minutes.

What gives?

She made her way back to the receptionist's desk. A different security guard sat behind the counter.

"I came in twenty minutes ago and the other guy told me to go to conference room C12, but no one's come to meet me yet."

"Name?"

Lex stabbed a finger at her name tag.

The guard typed her name into his computer. "Oh. Miss Sakai, you were supposed to be in conference room D22. They've been waiting for you."

Lex swallowed a hysterical scream. "Where is it?"

"Up the stairs, to the right, second door on the left."

Her stupid pencil skirt wouldn't let her take the stairs two at a time. She entered the conference room hot and panting. Three pairs of eyes glared at her.

One older gentleman with a ring of silver hair set down the phone. "The security guard told us you'd been sent to another conference room." From his tone, he didn't seem to believe her or the guard.

"I'm sorry." *Pant, pant.* "The first—" *Pant, pant*—"security guard—" *Pant, pant, wheeeze.*

"Never mind." A middle-aged man with a long, thin face waved her to a seat and introduced the silver-haired man and a young, antsy man. "We didn't get copies of your résumé. Do you have extra ones?"

"Yes, sir—" Lex opened her leather folio and grabbed—

One sheet. Where were her other copies?

In the printer. At home. Forgotten as she rushed out of the house. "Uh ... I only have one copy."

The antsy man rolled his eyes.

Lex sat down on the chair, resting her hand on the smooth plastic armrest—

Eeewww.

Something sticky-slippery, like a cross between glue and butter. All over the armrest, and now coating her palm.

This was going to be either a very short or a very long interview.

ELEVEN

The interview ended up being pathetically short. After a few questions that made her sound like a complete moron for applying for a receptionist position with no corporate receptionist experience, they pushed her out the door, which barely missed hitting her backside on the way out.

Her only saving grace had been that they didn't even bother to rise to shake her hand good-bye, so she didn't have to try a left-handed shake when her right hand looked fully functional. She entered the lobby and immediately saw the women's restroom on the other end. With a yellow *Cuidado: Piso Mojado* sign in front of the propped open door.

She peeked in and saw the janitor, a surly-looking Hispanic man. "Can I just come in to wash my hand?"

"*No entre. Es peligroso.*"

"I just need to wash my hand."

"*No, esta resbaloso.*"

"Please?"

"*Por dios! Lea el cartel!*"

Guess that was a no. She headed toward the men's restroom just as someone exited and caught a glimpse of other men inside. Nope, she couldn't sneak in to use the sink.

A couple of oversized couch-chairs sat against the wall across from the restrooms. She walked over and flopped down—

"Stop!" A man's voice came out of nowhere.

Squish.

Comfy overstuffed chairs — especially those upholstered in modern zippy colors — weren't supposed to squish. Something colder than her skin seeped through her skirt.

Lex slammed her hands down on the chair arms to hoist herself up. She was reminded of the stickiness on her palm, but not in time. Upholstery fuzz clung to the gummy residue on her skin. With a heave, she shot to her feet.

Her skirt stuck to her bottom with a disgusting, wet feeling.

A forty-something man in a polo shirt and slacks approached. "You okay? I saw the janitor clean a stain off the seat cushion a few minutes ago."

Lex then noticed that the scent of industrial cleaner hung heavier in the air here than near the bathroom. She glanced back at the seat cushion and the psychedelic colors slammed her with an instant headache. "The fabric must hide the water mark." She almost didn't want to look at her behind, but she twisted around for a peek.

"It's not too bad." Then he looked away, face glowing. She guessed he belatedly realized he probably shouldn't be staring at her tush. Not that she had that much tush in the first place.

His ringed left hand — *darn, married* — carried a worn leather briefbag like the ones she'd seen on Levenger.com, except his had a faded Indian badge attached to the flap. Stanford's old mascot. "Wow. How did you get that?"

He shifted his bag in front. "Isn't it great? I got it from a retired football coach. All my coworkers are jealous."

"I am too. I wasn't born yet when Stanford retired that mascot."

His eyes seemed to glitter with curiosity. "Did you go to Stanford?"

"No — not smart enough. I went to San Jose State, and my cousins have all gone to Berkley."

He tilted his head and his forehead wrinkled slightly. "You know a lot about Stanford for a Cal fan."

She shrugged to hide her embarrassment. His tone reminded her of when her male cousins teased her about her sports fanaticism.

Then she remembered where she was. SPZ. Sports Mecca of Silicon Valley. Largest sports presence on the net. She was a sports nut just like any one of them. *Oh, yeah*! "Where did you go to school?"

"Sac State."

"Oh, did you see the game last night? I thought Lloyd would hit fifty points."

"That foul on him was so wrong."

"Thornton should have taken Stuart out. He hasn't been shooting well since he came back from that ankle injury."

"Jamieson was smart to keep Costello on him."

"Yeah, that was brilliant. Stuart didn't have a chance."

His direct, intense gaze reminded her of Aiden, except this man's eyes were harder, more shrewd. "What do you think of UC Davis baseball this year?"

"Disappointing. All their key players graduated last year, and the new coach is failing his fresh blood. But their wrestling team is doing really well. I think they're going to go to nationals."

"You follow a lot of different college sports." His mild tone contrasted his shrewd eyes, which seemed to search her face for her answer, not just listening to what she said.

"I love sports. I grew up with just my brother and my dad."

"Not to be rude, but it's kind of surprising."

Lex gave a rueful snort. "Yeah, you kind of expect an Asian to be a doctor, lawyer, or engineer, right?" Like most of her cousins, who were pushed to excel in school, which just fed the stereotype.

"You're here for an interview?"

Lex grimaced as she glanced down at her stained blouse and felt a fresh breeze spin a cold finger up her skirt. "For uh ... receptionist. I'm actually a manufacturing engineer, but I've always wanted to work at SPZ and thought I'd get my foot in the door."

"Oh." He smiled, the lines deepening around his wide mouth. "Russell Davis." He held out his hand.

"Lex Sakai. Trust me, you don't want to shake my hand."

"Got a business card, Lex?"

She flipped open her folio—her brother had given her one of his extras, so who cared if she got her hand gunk on it? She passed him a card.

"Thanks. It was nice talking to you."

"You too." She watched him walk away. Professional despite her appearance and her smell. She sniffed her shoulder. Yup, she still smelled like rubber and car grease.

What a nice guy. Too bad he hadn't been the one hiring.

Well, Lex would need to look for another engineering job in the morning. Maybe she'd find something with a nice pay raise so she could buy a condo. She didn't dislike living with Dad, but she had turned thirty and thought she really ought to be on her own.

Lex weighed her options while waiting for the tow truck to haul her klunker-mobile to the nearest body shop, who said it would be ready in a couple days. She paid an exhorbitant price for a full-size rental car—all they had last-minute—and reveled in the fact that the engine actually turned over the first time she tried.

Thing is, now that all her potential sponsors had said no—which was really strange, come to think of it—she'd either have to get a boyfriend or use the money saved for a down payment for the girls' playoffs costs. Too bad it wasn't enough. If she really had to, maybe she could borrow the rest of what she'd need from Dad and Richard.

Maybe she'd do that. Things weren't really so bad. Good thing she still lived at home.

"Dad, I'm home." She slammed the front door and juggled her keys with her sticky folio and the old T-shirts from her trunk. She had sat on them to protect the rental car seat from the chemicals peeling the skin off her butt.

"Dad?" She kicked off her shoes and went to open the garage door. She tossed the T-shirts to the ground in front of the washer.

"Where are you?" She moved into the hallway toward her room.

He rounded the corner and jolted as he saw her. "Lex! You're home early."

"Not really." She eyed the cordless phone clutched in his hand. "Who called?"

"Nobody. What happened to your clothes?"

Lex pressed a hand to her temple. "I separated a lady and her coffee. I better go change." Her skirt felt cold, wrinkled, and tight against her legs.

"Uh ... Lex." He scratched the top of his head.

Her sixth sense snapped to attention. "What, Dad?"

"I, uh ... got laid off today."

"*What?* Oh, I'm so sorry."

"It's more like early retirement." He played with the edge of his button-down shirt.

Both of them were now unemployed. "Are we going to be okay? Lay it all out right now. No pussy-footing."

"No, we'll be okay. I'll be able to do some consulting with other air-conditioning companies in the area. And you'll get another job soon, right?"

"Yeah." Maybe that jibe to Everett about Starbucks wasn't so far off. She'd go to Jennifer's house — Lex wasn't the only one still living at home — and use her parents' high-speed Internet to check for jobs.

"How did the interview go?"

"Great." Lex walked into her bedroom. "I made a great impression."

On Friday night, Aiden walked into the gym and was engulfed by the echoing booms of volleyballs slamming against the wooden floor as players warmed up. He found Jill, the woman he'd talked to about joining the recreational volleyball club.

"Hey, Aiden. Ready to play?" Her bright smile reassured him.

He glanced at some of the players on a hitting line. Their grace and rhythm as they leaped and hit the arcing balls was leagues above the people from his community college volleyball class. "Does my team know I only started learning?"

"Oh, yeah—I'm your team captain. You're replacing a fourth round guy. Don't worry about it." Jill gestured toward the middle court. "Let's head over there."

Aiden adjusted his gym bag across his chest and approached the court, where four other Asian players peppered the ball back and forth to warm up.

Jill pointed to the folded bleachers on the back wall. "Get your shoes on and I'll introduce you to the team."

He dropped his bag on the floor near the bleachers and sat down to change into his volleyball shoes. He stretched a bit and looked around at the other players.

Most were more experienced than he was—some significantly so—but he noticed a few players, both girls and guys, who were about his level. His shoulders relaxed. Each team seemed to have at least a couple strong players and a couple weak ones.

A familiar feminine voice. "Hey Jill, warm up with me." A slim figure darted onto the middle court.

No way. Maybe God wanted to punish him for not believing in Him or something. Maybe for talking about church to Lex with such derision in his thoughts. Because there she was, on his team.

Her excellent form marked her as one of the best players on the court. She not only set with fluid movements, strong and precise like a dancer, but she also glowed with inner confidence, evident in the calm expression on her face, the way she focused on the next ball thrown at her to set.

He knew she'd be on his team even before Jill beckoned him over. "Lex, this is Aiden. He's replacing Neal. Why don't you warm up with him?"

The dampening look in her dark eyes could have extinguished grass fires.

He bristled, although he kept his face cool and impassive. However, he wasn't a doormat, and this snobby player wasn't going to intimidate him. "Gee, contain your excitement." He tossed the ball to her.

She gave him a startled look as she bumped it back to him with amazing precision. His return wasn't bad—just not as good as hers.

"You're not bad." It came grudgingly out of her mouth.

"I'm taking classes at the community college because someone told me to learn proper form."

Her face flushed as pink as a lollipop, starting from her neck and creeping up to her hairline, but she didn't respond.

After they bumped a few minutes, he took a few hits on the hitting line. He tossed the ball to a short Asian girl—he thought her name was Carol—and then took his first approach. He sailed through the air, opened up his chest, then swung at the ball that seemed to float in front of him.

Wham! It sailed so far out of the court that it hit the base of the folded bleachers on the far wall. Well, at least he'd hit the ball squarely and hadn't flubbed it.

A piercing whistle cut through the hitting practice. "Let's get started!" The ref—a player from the third team playing on the middle court that night—swung his whistle from the cord around his neck and leaned against one of the net poles.

Lex walked up to the net and called to a tall Asian guy on the other team. "Hey Kin-Mun, sure you're not too sore from last week?"

His smile exuded testosterone. "Nope. I must be a bus driver 'cuz I'm ready to take you to school!"

Lex laughed. "You're easy. I can pick up anything you hit at me."

"Wanna bet a pizza on it?"

She held out a fist, and they bumped knuckles. "You're on. Loser buys."

In the team circle, Jill introduced the other players. Carol leaned close to whisper to him. "Watch out. Lex is going to be intense this game 'cuz she's playing against Kin-Mun."

"Is he her boyfriend?" Aiden had heard bad tales about significant others playing against each other. Not that he cared if Kin-Mun was Lex's boyfriend. Nope, he didn't care at all.

"Naw, they've been friends forever. If they haven't dated by now, they never will."

"Aiden, you know coed rotation, right?" Jill asked.

Everyone stared at him. It seemed like people were holding their breath. "Uh ... sort of."

"Define 'sort of.'" Lex looked at him hard.

"My class instructor explained it to us, but I've never played it."

Lex groaned and looked at the ceiling. The other players were more restrained.

Jill laughed. "Well, we'll try it. We'll tell you where to go."

They set up with Aiden in middle back — the easiest position for a guy in coed rotation — so he could watch how the other guys moved in the complex pattern. Except it stuck him in the prime passing zone.

He shanked the first serve. However, Lex — the front-row setter — raced down his high, wide pass and made a brilliant set to their strong side hitter, who slammed a line drive past Kin-Mun's three-story-tall block.

"Haa!" Lex heckled Kin-Mun under the net. He made a face at her.

The game continued with the two scores neck and neck. Lex dove and rolled. She screamed possession as she ran down shanked passes or blocked hits. She became a blazing fireball on the court.

Stop watching her. And stop liking it.

Just observing her made him step up his game. He dove for balls. He became more territorial when passing. His passes marginally improved.

"Game point!" The ref signaled the serve.

Lex served. Kin-Mun, in the front row, passed the ball and then set up for a hit. Aiden leaped to block ...

He actually got a touch on it. The ball sailed high.

"Got it!"

"Mine!"

He and Lex shouted at the same time. He was closer to it. He ran—

"Oomph!" He and Lex went down in a tangle of limbs. He slapped his hands on the floor to keep his face from planting nose-first. Lex toppled next to him.

Another body tripped over his arm and dropped on him. *Ow!* An elbow hit his ribcage.

"Umph!" Lex groaned next to him as yet another player flipped over someone's legs and came down on Lex's head.

Somewhere, Jill was laughing.

Lex's face lay six inches away from him. She lifted her head and glowered at him.

Aiden already knew he should say his last prayers now. Lex was going to kill him. Slowly.

She was going to kill him. Slowly.

Lex sat on the sidelines watching the last game of the night. She hated sitting out, but she had to take her turn.

"You can't be too mad at the guy." Robyn, whose team referee'd on the far court, watched Aiden dive for a shanked ball. His assertive play made up for a girl's timid defense in the back row.

"We lost that first game. Kin-Mun is never going to let me forget this."

"Oh, come on. It's only pizza."

"I had such high hopes for this season when I saw the team Jill had picked. Even Neal wasn't a bad fourth round guy. But then Neal had knee surgery and we got Aiden."

"I think Aiden's better than Neal."

Lex turned her head to stare at her. "How?"

"Aiden gives 110 percent on the court. He's more aggressive than Neal, and he stays in position."

Lex couldn't argue with Robyn, but she still didn't like having him on her team, where she had to see him every week. "He's awkward."

"He's not that graceful right now, but hopefully he'll get better."

Lex pursed her lips.

Robyn motioned to him. "He's also a pretty cool player. He doesn't get upset."

Aiden always had that calm, composed look on his face. "He's so bland."

"He doesn't cuss at himself or anybody else. He never gets emotional. Unlike somebody I know." Robyn nudged her.

"I'm not emotional."

"Suuure. You *never* yell at anyone on the court."

Kin-Mun's team reff'd the game. He saw her glowering, and he did his dorky "laugh and point."

"Ooooh, I'm never going to live this down."

"It's your fault. You heckled Kin-Mun first."

Lex huffed. She couldn't keep her massive mouth shut.

She had more important things to worry about, anyway. Like employment. And a volleyball sponsor. "Do you know anyone else who might be able to sponsor my girls' team?"

Robyn's mouth opened to the size of a *musubi* rice ball. "You mean Jim said no?"

"Yeah."

"Why? What did he say?"

Lex frowned, remembering. "He seemed kind of evasive. I figured he didn't like hurting my feelings by saying no."

"I don't understand. He can totally afford it." Robyn peered at where Jim reff'd a game on the third court. "I'm going to talk to him."

"Don't. I'll find another sponsor."

"I can't think of anybody else who has the money to do it."

Lex sighed. "I'll keep looking."

"I don't understand why Jim said no. It must be something serious that happened, or someone scary who threatened him not to do it."

Lex laughed. "Who in the world would scare him? King Kong?"

TWELVE

L ex's head whirled. Not just from circling the biology labs where Trish was supposed to be, but also from the chorus of chemicals smelling up each lab. If she hadn't run into Trish's boss, Lex would still be wandering through the labs trying to find her.

She walked down the sunny path to the other biotech research building, but she couldn't enjoy the warm day. Trish hadn't been to church again. Come to think of it, she hadn't talked to her cousin for a couple of weeks, and they usually gabbed pretty often. Was she okay?

Lex entered the glass doors to the lobby of S-building and stopped in her tracks. "What are you doing here?"

Aiden turned and backed away like she had the bird flu virus. "Hello to you, too."

Lex peered over the counter of the receptionist's desk at the empty chair. "Did you ring the buzzer?"

"Five minutes ago." He hit the buzzer again. "Happy?"

"Satisfied."

"What are you doing here?" Aiden looked genuinely curious.

"Looking for Trish."

Alarm flickered across Aiden's face, but then he assumed that bland-as-rice expression. "She works here?"

He had so much control over his expression. Lex wondered what it would be like to rile him. "She doesn't work in this building. Anxious to see her again?" Lex smirked.

His eyebrow twitched—a crack in his calm mask. "Can't get away from you two."

"What?" Lex feigned shock. "You're the one who's stalking me, buddy."

"You came through those doors after I did. Looks like you're the one who can't leave me alone."

He was teasing her. Lex smiled. Maybe he wasn't as colorless as she first thought.

The receptionist clicked through the magnetically locked doors from the labs into the lobby area. "Who are you seeing?"

"Trish Sakai."

"Spenser Wong."

The receptionist called Trish and Spenser to snap at them about their guests at the front.

Spenser came first—a tall, broad Asian guy with the Hollywood look of Chow Yun-Fat and Russell Wong rolled into one. He didn't even glance at Lex. "Hey, Aiden. Ready to go to lunch? It's gotta be fast today. I have an assay running." They left out the front glass door.

Trish came through the magnetically locked door a few minutes later. "Hi, Lex. What are you doing here?"

"Want to go out for lunch?"

"Sure. Come in, let me finish up my experiment."

Lex trailed Trish to yet another smelly lab. Trish donned a lab coat and pointed to a chair a few feet away. "Stay there while I finish pipetting these." She seated herself in front of a big inset hood with air whooshing up through a pipe in the ceiling.

"Why did you come all the way here?" Trish had to shout above the noise as she manipulated some delicate instruments and canisters of liquid inside the hood.

"I can't find you anywhere else. Why haven't you been answering your phone?"

Trish had her back to Lex so she couldn't see her expression, but Trish's silence said it all.

"What gives? You haven't been to church lately, either."

"I've, uh ... been with Kazuo."

"The Japanese waiter?"

"Yeah."

"Even on Sunday mornings?"

"We, uh ... go out for breakfast."

A dark suspicion nagged on the edges of Lex's mind, but she didn't voice it. Maybe if she ignored it, it wouldn't be true. "Oh."

"I saw Grandma once a couple weeks ago. We were having breakfast at Hobee's."

"How did dear Grandma look?"

Trish gave her a sidelong look. "Leeex. She's not a monster. She was having breakfast with Mr. and Mrs. Tomoyoshi."

Oh, no. Lex's heart suddenly put on twenty pounds and thudded to the bottom of her stomach. She buried her head in her hands. "What were they talking about?"

"How should I know? I just went over to say hi. I mentioned you. How you were trying so hard to find a sponsor—"

"Trish!" Lex jumped off her chair. "You didn't!"

"Didn't what?"

"Tell Grandma I was looking for a sponsor."

Trish pouted and knit her brows. "Oh, did I say sponsor? I must have said boyfriend. Yes, I'm sure I said boyfriend." But the quaver in Trish's voice and the whiteness of her face said otherwise.

Lex remembered Mr. Tomoyoshi's abrupt about-face. Jim's evasive no. The other business owners who politely turned her down.

Grandma's influence rooted deep into the Japanese American community because Grandpa's bank's loan services had been so reliable for everyone. Lex knew without a doubt that Grandma had been talking to business owners—warning, bribing, or calling in favors so that they wouldn't agree to Lex's petition of sponsorship.

"Trish, how could you?"

"I made an innocent mistake." Trish chewed at her bottom lip. "What are you going to do?"

Lex took a few deep breaths, but it didn't calm the simmering in her gut. "I'm going to talk to Grandma."

Lex didn't hate children, but right now, she just wanted them all to be quiet.

"Grandma!" Lex's yell could barely be heard over the cacophony of children's voices inside Lotus Preschool. Grandma stood at the far end of the playroom, listening while Lex's cousin's son Eric prattled about his day. If only Grandma would listen to her grandchildren that way.

"Hi there, Eric. Grandma, I need to talk to you."

"Eric, say hi to your cousin Lex."

"Hi your caw-zin Leksss."

"Grandma ..."

"We'll talk after I drive Eric home to his mommy. Don't you want to see your mommy?"

Eric smiled up at his great-grandma and placed a sticky hand on the immaculate cream skirt.

"No, we'll talk now. It took me long enough to track you down," Lex insisted.

"I always pick up Eric on Wednesdays." Grandma watched Eric take out plastic dinosaurs from the toy box. Such an attentive, loving great-grandma. Ha!

"Grandma, stop influencing all the business owners."

"I don't know what you're talking about." She aimed her sing-songy tone at Eric instead of Lex.

"You know exactly what I'm talking about." Lex suddenly felt rather stupid demanding her Grandma do anything. She couldn't even prove that she'd influenced Mr. Tomoyoshi or Jim. "If I want another sponsor, it's none of your business, because you're the one who decided to drop the girls' team."

"I haven't dropped them yet." Grandma's sugary sweet voice had a definite sharp edge. "Didn't we have an agreement?"

"You can't force me to just find someone to love. Tons of my friends are actively looking for a significant other and not finding anybody."

"Your problem is that you weren't looking at all."

"Dad doesn't care!" Lex flung out her arms — luckily, there weren't any bodies over two feet tall in her vicinity. "Why does it matter so much to you?"

Grandma blinked, and for a fraction of a moment, she looked old and tired. She absently rubbed her right hip, the one she'd been favoring the day of the Red Egg and Ginger party. Then in the next moment, the look melted away.

Had Lex imagined it? Grandma never seemed *old*. She always had the perfect clothes, perfect poise, perfect health. Or maybe that's what she wanted people to think. Was Grandma feeling her age just like the rest of the human race? Was that what was behind her campaign for more great-grandchildren?

Grandma's fierce eyes stabbed into Lex with renewed force. "It's for your own good, you know."

Lex rolled her eyes. *Save me from bossy, control-freak grandmas with good intentions.*

Grandma's eyes narrowed to black toothpicks. "See? You're not taking me seriously. Well, you'll take me seriously if you can't find another sponsor."

"Why are you punishing those junior high girls? This has nothing to do with them."

"They matter to you." Shrewdness glittered in her hard gaze, the same smarts that made her such a good partner for Grandpa's business. "I am not playing games, Lex. If you don't start looking for a boyfriend, I can talk to other people who matter to you too."

A sliver of ice dropped down her shirt. "What do you mean? You wouldn't."

"You've seen how much influence I have. What if Richard were evicted from his apartment? What if your father's car were repossessed?"

Would she really do that to her own son? Her grandson? Just for one granddaughter?

Lex had challenged her, put her back up. Like a Tasmanian devil, Grandma didn't take growls from the enemy as warnings — they were acts of aggression. And she responded in kind.

Grandma bent and picked up Eric. "Time to go home, sweetie."

Her direct gaze made Lex back up a step. "I had better see more effort, Lex." Grandma walked out of the daycare.

Lex refused to play dead just because Grandma snarled. But she wouldn't be stupid either. She dashed in late to the Singles Group meeting on Thursday night with twofold purpose — date trolling, but also sponsor seeking, in the one place she knew Grandma couldn't penetrate.

Church.

Grandma didn't understand Lex's and her three cousins' faith, but even Grandma wouldn't go up against God.

Lex had tried talking to the older members of the church last Sunday. They were all distantly friendly to her, a little aloof. They tended to prefer to hang out with their friends, who were their own age and spoke to them in Japanese or Chinese or Korean. The language barrier itself made their relationship with Lex a bit wide. She felt uncomfortable asking them for sponsorship — almost as if it would be rude.

She also realized she didn't talk much with the married-with-kids crowd. It seemed kind of rude to ask them for sponsorship when most of them barely remembered her name. She didn't have a clue who else she could approach.

So she stuck with the church family she knew — the singles.

Except Lex had lost precious pre-Singles Group mix and mingle time. Trish had said she'd pick Lex up, but after twenty minutes and no Trish — not that Lex had been ready by 6:30, but she'd been ready by 6:40 at least — Lex had jumped into her Honda and limped to church.

The worship leaders tuned their guitars — Lex had about five minutes. She regretted now how plainly she'd informed all the guys about her non-interest in anything more than friendship. She suspected they were all a little afraid of her.

But maybe she could lean on their sense of Christian charity. "Hey, Alvin."

"Hi, Lex." He had the wary look of a trapped animal.

Lex mentally went down her Ephesians List. Alvin was a Christian (faithful attendee) and had a good job (engineer), but there was no physical attraction (bug eyes and wide mouth made him look like a toad), he didn't play an interesting sport (fishing, which Lex didn't have the patience for), and he had really bad dandruff (enough said).

"Alvin, would you consider donating to a junior high school volleyball team?"

His eyes lit up, which made him look really freaky, like a frog with electric eyes. "Oooh, a junior high school ministry? How great."

"Uh ... not exactly a ministry."

The lights went out. "No?"

She did ministry-like stuff, didn't she? "Well, sometimes the girls confide in me about boys and stuff, and I try to talk to them about God."

"Is it evangelical?"

"Uh ..."

"Do you open their eyes and their hearts to the depth of their sin, leading to death, and their need for a personal savior?"

Lex blinked and stared at him.

Alvin took that to mean encouragement. "Do you lead them in a prayer of confession and surrender to Christ, inviting Jesus to dwell in their hearts?"

"Not ... exactly. I coach them to play volleyball."

"Do you have outreach where you invite non-believers to come and experience the love of God's children?"

"Um ... well, anyone can join. It's a club team."

"Do you have prayer and worship before and after each game?"

"That would be a no."

"What do you do with them?"

"I tell them God loves them and cares about their problems. I tell them I'll pray for their girlfriends to forgive them, and for boys to notice them, and—"

In shock, Alvin eased away from her. "That's not a ministry. That's just recreation."

"What's wrong with recreation?"

His mouth pursed so small it almost disappeared into his chin. "I'm afraid I can't donate God's money to something that won't give Him all honor and glory."

Lex glared at him. "Fine."

Next victim.

She had to choose with care. Didn't want another Alvin—

"Okay, everybody, take your seats." The worship leader strummed a full chord on his 12-string acoustic guitar.

Rats. Too much time wasted with Alvin.

She took her seat and then drew into herself when they started with the song "Indescribable." She sang the words, trying to ignore how uncomfortable they made her feel. Why couldn't God be describable? He needed to work on expanding the English language. She didn't like the whole limitless aspect of deity.

Then they moved to "How Great is Our God," and Lex could hang with that. God is great. She sang and felt that same pull of greatness that made her first believe—the power that had overwhelmed her so that she had no choice but to believe.

The associate pastor—who took care of the singles and youth groups—talked about trusting God. Pretty appropriate, since she was trusting God to make sure she succeeded in finding a sponsor, finding a boyfriend, or even both. Hey, she had resources, right? She could do it.

As soon as the pastor prayed to close the meeting, Lex had found her next target. She bolted out of her seat and plopped down next to Randy.

"Hey, Randy, what do you say to contributing to a junior high girls' volleyball team? Great opportunity to—"

"Sorry, Lex. I only support overseas missions."

Lex blinked a few times. "Why?"

"Jesus called us to make disciples of all nations."

"America is a nation."

Randy waved a hand. "We have ample access to churches, whereas people in other nations have no chance to hear the gospel."

Her neck itched, which meant a flush rose up from her chest, which meant she wasn't controlling her temper very well. "People die from poverty in America as well as in India."

"But the people in India haven't heard about Christ, so they're more important to reach."

Her cheeks felt like she had a lemon in her mouth. "I want my family to become Christian. Most of them are Buddhist. And they live in America."

Randy shrugged.

Breathe in through your nose, out through your nose. Well, she didn't bother to go down the List with Randy. Another thing to add to the List: *Make sure his theology doesn't exclude basically any American who doesn't know Christ.*

Lex glanced around at the sparse crowd of people for Singles Group tonight. She was oh-fer-two, but maybe —

Her cell phone chirped. "Hello?"

"Leeex?"

"Trish? What's wrong?"

"Leeex." Belch. "Can you come pick me up?"

"Are you drunk?"

Lex met Randy's horrified stare. Oops, she had said that rather loudly. A few other people tried not to look like they were listening.

"I'm jus' a leedle tipsy," Trish answered her.

She got up and headed toward the door, slinging her purse over her shoulder. "Where are you?"

"Um ... Club Yellow Fever."

She'd have to MapQuest it. "Stay where you are, okay? Are you inside the club?"

"I'm at my car ... I can't open the door." *Giggle.* "I think I lost the handle."

THIRTEEN

Lex had gotten her pepper spray and stuck it in her pocket. She considered sneaking her brass knuckles into her purse but thought the bouncer might object.

She shouldn't have worried. After parking next to Trish's car but not seeing her, Lex entered the club doors, where no one stood guard.

Pulsing dance music drummed against her liver while darkness winking with wild lights made her feel like she was looking at a Christmas tree through sunglasses.

How was she going to find Trish?

She phoned Trish's cell, but no answer—not surprising if she didn't have it on vibrate. Which she never did. Lex hated to admit it, but the bar was a logical place to look.

What had made Trish get sloshed like she did at that one frat party in college? Looked like lots of these people were roaring drunk too. A laughing blonde smashed into her. "Oops, sorry."

Ugh. Sour martini breath.

Lex tried to avoid touching anyone, slowing her progress. She wove in and out, ducked and darted, side stepped and backtracked.

A half hour later, she'd circled the entire dance floor twice, searched the bar three separate times, gotten a stiletto in her instep, and had beer spilled on her pants. Trish would have fifteen "missed call" messages on her cell phone if she ever thought to check it.

Lex headed toward the bar. One last pass, and then she'd blow this joint. She inched around a large group of people near the entrance to the dance floor, trying to avoid being touched or splashed by swinging arms still attached to glasses of drinks.

A hand landed heavy on her shoulder.

She snapped rigid as steel. Her self-defense classes flashed through her mind. "Haaaiyaah!" She nipped backward and grabbed the offending hand, turning around and twisting the hand palm-up at the same time.

"Owowowowowow — Lex! It's me!"

"Richard! Dummy, you know better."

"Leggoleggo — aaah." Richard flapped his wrist. "I called your name but you didn't hear me."

"Oh." She had the grace to feel sheepish.

"Hey, lemme introduce you to someone you'll like. He's into sports too."

She perked up at that. "Really?" She then deflated and glared at Richard. "What's the catch?"

"Huh?"

"Is he married? Gay? Living with his mother? And what is he doing in this bar?"

He thumped her forehead with his finger before she could slap him away. "He's a nice guy. Trust me."

"Ha! That guarantees he's a dweeb." But she followed him. She had to admit she was intrigued if Richard's friend really was into sports. Maybe, like her, he didn't normally come to places like this. She could look for Trish while she moved through the crowd, right?

Lex appreciated Richard's extra height and heftier bulk as he cut a smooth path through the people chatting and drinking. Lex huddled in his wake and twisted her body to avoid being brushed by the people around them. They passed a few small bistro tables, all with a dozen people around them. Finally, they reached a booth — boy, the guy snagged a booth! — in the corner, where the noise level muted slightly.

Three guys lounged against the padded seat, each nursing the latest of several drinks, if the empty glasses indicated anything. Oh, great. Conversing with drunks. Her favorite crossword puzzle.

"Lex, this is Tigh Anders."

A broad but not fat man with a toothy smile stood to shake her hand. His paw engulfed hers like being swallowed by a whale.

His touch lingered too long. Lex snatched her hand back. *Strike one.*

"Richard tells me you know a little about sports." Tigh's tone wasn't condescending, although his words bordered on the edge. *Ball one.*

Lex smiled tightly. "Some."

Tigh gestured to the other two nameless men. "We were just talking about Hosh's return to the Niners this season."

"Unlikely."

Tigh's brows rose, then he grinned. "That's what I was saying. Smart girl."

Ball two. Lex didn't falter. "He's not being aggressive enough with his rehab. He can't even run the mile at 80 percent his normal."

Tigh looked thoughtful.

Ball three.

He scratched his chin. "I thought it might be a publicity ploy."

That was a new idea. "Oh?"

"The reporters were already comparing his slower recovery with Bennett's super fast recovery last season, when he protested a little too loudly about being steroid-free."

Tigh had an interesting theory. *Base hit.*

He gestured toward the dance floor. "Dance?"

Well, he'd earned a single.

The nervous juggling started in her stomach as she followed him to the dance floor. *Stop wigging out, it's a fast song, you're too hung up on being touched by guys anyway, stop being a freakazoid.*

She had loved dancing once. She could again with the right partner. Sure.

Lex tried to groove to the beat. Tried not to jerk when someone's limb tapped her from behind. Tried to smile at Tigh. Then he moved closer.

She froze so tight that her shoulder blade muscles shook. His big hands circled her waist lightly, but enough to make her jolt and twitch away.

He must have thought they were dance moves, because he grabbed her waist fully and tried to sway her hips to his rhythm.

Lex's stomach cramped. She shoved his hands away and pulled back.

He followed, face fuzzy and confused but still amiable. This time his hands roved higher, cupping her ribcage.

"Leave off!" Lex twisted away.

Tigh's face darkened. He shouted a few names at her.

She shouted a few back.

Lex tromped off the dance floor. Stupid! She knew he'd been drinking. She headed toward the exit door while she called Trish's cell phone one last time.

"Hello?" Hiccough.

"Trish! Where are you?"

Giggle. "By the bar. This nice guy—"

Lex snapped her phone closed and shoved her way to the bar. Her encounter with Tigh had made her so tense that the extra contact didn't unnerve her as it did before.

There. Trish lounged against the bar with a middle-aged man who tried to look down the V-neck on her blouse. Lex grabbed her. "Did you come alone?"

"No." Trish dissolved into abject depression with a speed only alcohol could accomplish. "My boyfriend ... the slime ... had a fight." Sob. "He left me, the dork ..." Trish burst into tears.

Lex got her out into the parking lot, where the fresh air seemed to have the opposite effect as normal. Lex leaned against the car trunk while Trish emptied her stomach.

"Lex, right?"

She looked up and noticed the antsy guy who had interviewed her at SPZ. He actually sounded jovial. "Hello."

"Yeah, I thought I saw you in there."

When she danced with Mr. Hands or when she dragged Miss Apple Martini away from the bar? "I didn't see you."

"Yeah, I see you met Tigh Anders."

A weird, unpleasant tingling raced over her shoulders like a hairbrush drawn across her skin. "You know him?"

"Oh, yeah. He works at SPZ."

The tingling rose up the back of her neck and buzzed in the base of her skull. "What's his department?"

"Oh, he's my manager."

Only a few times in her life had Lex indulged in stress-eating. This was one.

Lex inched into the drive-thru line and fumbled with her purse. She had cash, right?

"Are we at In-N-Out?" Trish shoved her nose against Lex's not-so-clean window. "It's yelllow."

"WelcometoInnunOut. Whaddayawant?" The order speaker blasted static at Lex.

"A 3 x 3, Animal style, with fries and a strawberry shake."

"Fffvertwinntwo."

What? Lex drove forward while digging in the bottom of her purse. Didn't she have a stray bill? She counted the money in her fist. Three bucks.

"You dint get me anything." Trish pouted. "I wanted a double ... triple ..." She started counting fingers.

"You may as well be good for something." Lex slapped Trish's knee to the right so she could snatch Trish's purse.

"Thazmine!"

By the time Lex made it to the window, she had a ten-dollar-bill to hand to the girl in her white and red uniform.

The aroma of grease made her mouth almost feel the crispiness of the fries, the juiciness of the burger, the softness of the bun. Lex pulled back into the In-N-Out parking lot and found an empty stall.

Her first bite unknotted the ball in her gut.

The second bite loosened her wooden-hanger shoulders.

The fries made her headache ease.

The shake brought it right back with brainfreeze.

Well, if she could say anything about Tigh, he had reunited her with In-N-Out Burger, her first unhealthy meal since the fiasco with George. Words like "stupid Lex" and "doofus" and "guano-head" really didn't convey the emotion of the moment—the crashing and burning of her dream of working at SPZ.

She wouldn't have wanted to work for such a handsy guy anyway.

Yeah, the ecstasy of talking nothing but sports all day at work wouldn't be worth it. Not at all.

Lex started sobbing into her shake.

"Are you crying?" Trish shoved her face two inches away from Lex's nose. "Aw, poor Lexie. Trishy will make it all bett—better."

Trish's foul breath seriously cramped Lex's enjoyment of her burger. Lex pushed her away, and Trish tipped over to lean against the door, already starting to breathe deeply.

Lex finished her fries. She didn't really feel much better. Well, no. She could never be unmoved by fresh french fries. But she still felt like a teetering Jenga tower.

What was it Scarlett said? "Tomorrow is another day."

Whoop-de-doo. Cheeriness for the unemployed.

TUMS, TUMS TUMS TUMS, TUMS …

So, maybe the shake had been a bit overboard.

Lex's stomach rolled as she stumbled into the living room. She would look for more job listings in the morning, send out a few more résumés. She should be fine for several months because she and Dad were sharing expenses. Problem was, could she find anything?

She locked the front door behind her. Dad had left the light on—

No, he hadn't left his chair. He looked up at her. "You're late tonight."

"I had a sort of emergency."

Bushy eyebrows waggled up. "Emergency?"

"A Trish emergency. Relax."

He did. "Oh."

That prickling had started again across her shoulders. "Why are you still up, Dad?"

He started that floppy shrug again, but Lex gusted out a sigh. "Oh, just tell me."

Stopped mid-shrug, Dad looked like the Hunchback of Notre Dame. He lowered his shoulders.

"You'll have to move out, Lexie. I decided to sell the house."

FOURTEEN

G et your rear ends lower!" Lex clapped her hands to make the junior high girls pick up the pace of their drill.

She needed to hop to it and find an apartment. Something cheap.

"Lower!" She pointed at an eighth-grader who only crouched halfheartedly. The girl bent her knees and waist into a deeper crouch before exploding into a sprint to the next cone.

Lex needed to move fast. Dad's house would sell quickly. But with the dismal housing market, could she find an apartment she could afford in only a few weeks?

"Move over for the girls behind you." Lex signaled to a girl who stood panting at the end of the set of cones she'd just completed. She shifted out of the way as the next girl darted to the cone in a sprinting crouch, then straightened, also breathing heavily.

Now that she'd booted herself from the SPZ job, she needed to put more effort into another engineering position. The job listings on craigslist this morning hadn't been encouraging.

"Bend your knees when you jump!" Lex slipped into the drill lineup and demonstrated with a deep squat before exploding up in a mock block. She then dropped to a defensive crouch and sprinted to the next cone. "You're being slowpokes!" Lex straightened and clapped her hands again.

She had quit her job, and she'd soon be homeless. How could she even have time to think about getting a sponsor for this team — much less a boyfriend?

"You're pushing them kinda hard today, aren't you?" Vince, her assistant coach, leaned close and murmured low so the girls wouldn't hear.

Lex moved away from his close proximity but absorbed his words. She sighed. Yeah, maybe she projected her frustrations on the team. She'd ease up—

She saw it happening and felt the pulse through her muscles as she tried to move in to prevent it. Her top hitter, Kathy, leaped into a blocking motion just as another girl sprinted toward her cone. As Kathy landed, her foot rolled off the other girl's sneaker. A sickening *crunch-pop* echoed through the small gym.

At the sound, a blow of nausea hammered through Lex's gut. It slowed her steps as she rushed to Kathy's side. She didn't want to look. What if the ankle lay twisted at a sickening angle? What if there was blood . . . ?

Lex took a deep, harsh breath, tightening her jaw, her neck, her shoulders. She dropped beside Kathy and swatted away the girls crowding her.

Kathy heaved with sobs. The ankle hadn't swollen yet, but it would look like a grapefruit in a few minutes. The shoe needed to come off before the swelling welded it to her foot.

"This is going to hurt, Kathy." Lex untied her shoe, grabbed her heel to stabilize her foot, and tried to ease the sneaker off.

"Owowow! Stopstopstop!"

Lex slowed her movements but didn't stop. Kathy wailed. Finally the shoe dropped to the ground.

Lex tried to hide her concern. Kathy didn't usually complain about pain—she'd taken hard dives to the floor without a word. This was bad.

"Let's get her to urgent care. I'll drive." Maybe she had only sprained her ankle: If the team lost another player of Kathy's caliber, they'd get tromped in playoffs this summer.

"I'll carry her." Vince stepped in and squatted beside her. "Both arms around my neck . . . good. Ummph!"

Lex ran to get her purse and gear. Her cell phone rang. "Hello?" She shouldered her gym bag with a grunt.

"Alexis Sakai?" A vaguely familiar woman's voice.

"Yes." Lex followed at Vince's heels.

"This is Wendy Tran from SPZ Human Resources."

They were calling her to turn her down? Well, it was nicer than an email.

"Lex, what about practice?" One of the girls tugged at her shirt.

"Vince isn't going, just me. Finish the drill."

The girl groaned but went back to report to the other players.

"Miss Sakai?"

"Sorry ..." What had been the woman's name? "You were saying?" Lex fumbled for her car keys and hustled to beat Vince and Kathy to her car.

"It is my pleasure to offer you a position in the SPZ college division."

"*What?*"

At that moment, Vince stumbled over the curb and Kathy let go of his neck. She bounced on the ground while he staggered onto one knee.

"Oh my gosh!" Lex rushed to Kathy.

"I'm so glad you're pleased." The SPZ HR woman sounded pleased herself.

"OW! OW OW OW OW OW!" Kathy clutched her ankle and rocked back and forth.

"Just hold it up." Lex put a hand under Kathy's thigh to keep the foot off the ground.

"Excuse me?" the HR woman asked.

"You said college division?—Kathy, honey, don't squeeze your ankle—I never applied to the college division."

"You didn't? I have your application here and the offer letter from the director."

"Sorry." Vince knelt beside Kathy. "Let's try this again."

"No way!" Kathy tried to back up, but her heel bumped the ground, and she winced. "I don't want to get dropped again."

What was the woman's name? Lex's stupid memory. "Who gave you my application? Kathy, he won't drop you again."

"He will too!"

"I got it straight from the head of the department, Russell Davis."

"Okay, Kathy, one, two, three, heave!" Lex clapped the phone closer to her ear. "Russell? Russell with the Stanford Indian on his briefbag?"

"Yes, that's him."

Whoa. Even with her skirt soaked with Pine-Sol and coffee decorating her shirt and who-knew-what on her hand? "What exactly is the position? Another receptionist? Put her right there, Vince."

"You don't know? It's for Alumni Association Liason."

"Oh." Lex didn't want to sound more ignorant, so she made her tone reflective and intelligent. She hoped.

"You'll receive the offer letter tomorrow. Can you start work on Monday?"

"Yes!" That answer she knew. She climbed into the driver's seat.

"Great. We'll expect you at eight o'clock at the front desk, and we'll take care of you from there."

She was going to whoop Kin-Mun's fanny this time.

Lex served the ball directly at the weakest passer, a tall front-row banger who would probably shank the ball. He did. It made for a frantic set, and the banger couldn't get an effective hit.

Her team picked up the ball, and the setter ran a four that caught Kin-Mun's defense by surprise.

Point.

She couldn't resist doing a "laugh and point" at Kin-Mun on the other side of the net. They each had teams for this weekend tournament—it was Kin-Mun versus Lex. That was all that mattered—bragging rights.

Two tall Caucasian men stood a few feet away. Both seemed to be staring intently at Lex.

What gives? She shrugged off an uncomfortable shiver as she served the next ball.

However, her serve went long, and the right wing passed the ball perfectly to the setter, who sent a perfect set to Kin-Mun, who made a perfect line shot. Side-out and point for his team.

Lex dropped to ready position. What would Kin-Mun's serve be? Probably a short floater.

Wait a minute, did that Caucasian guy just take a picture of her?

Lex shanked Kin-Mun's deep, hard serve. Point, his team.

She ground her teeth together. She pounded a fist into her thigh, hoping the pain would make her focus.

Point. "Come on, guys, call your balls!"

Point. "Let's pass! Come on!"

Point. "Double-block!"

Point. "Timeout!" Lex shifted onto one hip as she stood in the back row and waited for her team to gather around her. "What gives?"

One of her hitters eyed her. "You're yelling a lot."

"Am not! Er ... Am not." The two Caucasian guys were talking to each other, but peeking looks at her from time to time. They didn't look at any other player. Lex was totally creeped out. "Let's go, guys. Let's beat Kin-Mun—I mean, Kin-Mun's team."

Lex's setter rolled her eyes.

They lost by five points.

Lex went to slap hands under the net with the other team, then dropped to the floor next to her bag. She sagged against the far wall as she sucked down her Gatorade.

When she closed her eyes, she saw all the dropped balls, the blocked hits, the shanked passes. Half of those had been hers. She couldn't believe how badly she'd played. Those two guys and their creepy staring had rattled her game so much. Where were they?

Gone. Figures. She'd probably have walked up and slugged one of them. Yeah, the taller one. He'd go down harder.

"Lex, what happened? You disappointed me." Kin-Mun dropped next to her.

She moaned into her hand. "Let me wallow in peace."

Kin-Mun nudged her. "I have some news that will perk you up."

Lex shifted away. "Nothing you can say would make me feel better."

"Sure about that?"

His mischievous voice piqued her interest despite herself. "What?"

"There's an opening in Wassamattayu."

Lex jolted. "No way! Are you sure?" The wait list for the prestigious sports club was years long. Lex had been on it for at least five.

Kin-Mun shrugged, but his smile said it all.

"Their volleyball team never has openings."

"A woman dropped. The menisci in her knees are almost gone, so she can't play anymore."

Lex's mind whirled. For a recreational player like herself, Wassamattayu was the pinnacle of her volleyball career. The club belonged to a national organization of other elite clubs, all with stringent athletic requirements for their various sports teams, so that tournaments between clubs were highly competitive. "I need to find out where I am on the waiting list."

"Sorry, can't help you there."

"And I need to train for tryouts. How many women are they going to invite for tryouts?"

"Usually ten." Kin-Mun glanced over at the court.

"I have to get picked."

"My team's reffing. Catch you later." He hurried to get onto the court.

Not only had she always dreamed of getting into Wassamattayu sports club, it might solve all her problems. Membership wasn't cheap, so all the members were not only stellar athletes, but the majority of them were quite solvent.

She'd be able to meet tons of wealthy, young players who might be open to sponsoring a girls' volleyball team. Or she'd find her handsome, sensitive, Christian soulmate who would match her sports ability.

If she got invited to tryouts. If she was picked. And if she got the money for the membership deposit, due before tryouts and reimbursed if she wasn't chosen.

It hadn't been something she worried about when she'd been a moderately well-paid engineer at Pear. Lex had received her offer letter from SPZ, but it hadn't shed any more light on the requirements of her position. While not paying minimum wage, it didn't come close to her previous pay range.

Too many ifs.

The thought of Grandma's ultimatum made her head ache. Lex couldn't ask most of her Asian volleyball friends to sponsor her team—Grandma had gotten to them. But maybe she could try for the primary purpose of the ultimatum—a date.

Her gaze roved around the gym. Who could she ask to pose as a boyfriend?

No, she couldn't do that. It had to be long-term or Grandma could pull funding if she and her date suddenly "broke up" after Mariko's wedding.

Okay, who could Lex go on a date with? Her eyes went down the line of players lounging against the wall. Married, dating, married, married, dating, just broke up, just divorced, married, dating.

Who was single?

Jim, Steve, and Neal.

Jim still had that weird girl stalking him.

Steve was a little obsessed with his *Star Wars* figurine collection.

Neal complained too much about his volleyball injuries.

The volleyball community was too small. Lex knew pretty much everyone. She needed new blood.

SPZ would be new blood. And Wassamattayu, if she got in. Until then ...

There were a few guys she didn't know very well. As she went down the line, she realized they were all Caucasian.

Really?

She scanned the crowd again. Yup. The ones she didn't know were mostly Caucasian or Hispanic men.

Am I racist? How awful. Is it because—?

He had been Caucasian.

She shuddered. She shoved the dark memory aside. These guys were probably all really nice. She should get to know them.

Sweat trickled down her neck. She discreetly sniffed.

Maybe later, when she smelled better.

FIFTEEN

First day on the job. *Don't mess it up.*

Lex entered the SPZ lobby on Monday, and this time a perky twentysomething sat behind the receptionist's desk. "Alexis Sakai."

The girl typed in the name. "S-a-k-a-i?"

Lex blinked. "Yes."

The girl exchanged a conspiratorial smile. "I'm a quarter Japanese." She studied the screen, then picked up the phone. "Mr. Davis, Miss Sakai is here in the lobby." She listened, then hung up. "He's off to a meeting, but he'll talk to you later. Grey Meyers will be meeting you here." She printed out a name tag for Lex. "This is just temporary until you get your security badge."

"How much are you getting paid?" *Aiyaaaah.* Lex and her big mouth. "I'm sorry — "

The girl's face had gone politely blank, but then she twinkled with impishness. "I'm in the high end for corporate receptionists. I demanded as much as some of these engineers."

Lex gave a weak smile, but her knees started to shake. What had Russell seen in her? How could she be qualified to be a liaison "anything"? She gripped the edge of the receptionist's desk and dug her fingers into the unyielding surface, welcoming the pain from her nails.

"Alexis?" A tall, thin young man rounded the corner of the receptionist's desk. His pale eyes surveyed her impassively, as if he were shopping for toilet bowl cleaner.

"Call me Lex." *Eeewww*, his handshake was like squeezing a wad of wet tissue paper.

"I'm Grey. We're in the same group."

Great. Her first coworker already gave her *Run away! Run away!* vibes.

He gave her a sly look from beneath half-lowered lids. "So, what's your previous experience as an Alumni Association Liaison?"

What is this, another interview? She clamped her jaw shut before the thought shot out of her mouth. Lex glanced at the receptionist, who discreetly rolled her eyes. It gave her courage. "Russell thought the superior aspects of my background would help me do a good job." There, she'd been nice and tactful.

Grey led the way to the stairway behind the desk. "I was just curious."

Curious, my foot.

They ascended the stairs together. "The last AAL was Judy Baloney. She quit after her maternity leave ran out."

"You must have been sad to lose her."

Grey shrugged. "Not really."

Lex stumbled on the steps. He gave her a sardonic look.

"You didn't like her?" Lex wondered if God would consider this gossip. But she needed to know Judy's mistakes so she wouldn't repeat them.

Grey shrugged again. "She was eye candy."

"*Say what?*" Lex's tact crumbled, since Grey obviously had none.

"She didn't know much about sports, and the alumni associations didn't respect her all that much." A fierce expression zapped onto his face, then disappeared. He turned a carefully insipid look on her. "Several men within the company jostled for a transfer to her spot."

Aaaaahh. Lex was beginning to understand. Except she wasn't another Judy Baloney. "Then Russell certainly picked the right person when he hired me."

Grey's eyes hardened. "Tigh Anders was surprised Russell hired you."

Tigh? Mr. Hands from the club? "How strange. I never interviewed with Tigh or gave him my résumé. Does he hire by how well someone dances or something?" She bared her teeth at him. She almost growled and barked.

Surprise widened his eyes for a second, then those lazy half-lids concealed his thoughts again. He shrugged.

Lex frowned. If she wanted to be summarily dismissed, she'd have stayed at Pear.

They entered a large area crammed with cubicles. Lots of male voices. It reminded her of those movies about Wall Street traders, except apparently not all of them were on the phone.

"Lex, this is Dan and Jordan." A Caucasian and an African American man cut off their conversation when they saw her. Speculative gazes pinned her to the floor.

An iron rod slammed down Lex's spine. She returned a gimlet stare.

"Welcome to the team." Dan's voice had a menacing thread.

"Lot of work." Jordan's hard eyes flickered over her masculine work suit. A thin hand scratched the scruff on his narrow chin.

Lex crossed her arms. "I'm used to hard work." *Watch out, bucko, I'll arm-wrestle you under the table too.*

He flexed a scrawny bicep.

She cracked her knuckles.

Grey interrupted the testosterone-estrogen duel. "This way's your office."

I get an office? Luckily, Lex's teeth still ground together from her circling with Jordan, so she didn't blurt it out and advertise her ignorance. These boys reminded her of her male cousins. She had rolled with enough punches and knew how to hit their soft spots.

Lex followed Grey down the row of cublicles.

"Here's your office." Gee, Grey's voice could have been a tad more resentful.

Office? More like closet, and not the walk-in kind. It looked like Judy left in a whirlwind — papers scattered on the floor, dirt and purple petals dusting the carpet around a circle where a flowerpot had rested, the occasional waft of nail polish remover. Some sparkly flower stickers, painted butterflies, and cut-out hearts decorated the front of the metal file cabinet. An emery board and a half-open, mostly-used eyeshadow compact lay next to the desk leg.

And on top of the desk, a stack of pink "While you were out" slips. Lex caught the dates on some of the top ones—today.

Were they all—? She flipped through the stack. They were all from today. And a couple from Sunday too.

Grey had an almost amiable smile as he watched her sift the pieces of paper. Did her dismay blare out from her face? "There are also messages from last week in the desk drawer. Enjoy."

He closed the door when he left, which doubled the floor space in her "office." She squeezed around the edge of her desk to get behind it and collapsed into the squishy chair.

The little pink message slips giggled at her.

She planted her elbows on the desk and buried her face in her hands. She didn't even know what to do. Looked like Judy had been cute and feminine—how could Lex fit those stilettos?

A firm knock at the door. More roosters come to strut? "Come in."

Russell Davis entered with the first friendly smile she'd seen since that nice receptionist. "Sorry about that, I had a meeting."

"That's fine." Lex climbed to her feet.

"No, no, there isn't enough room to stand." Russell had to walk all the way inside in order to close the door. He perched on her desk— taking up half the surface area—while she sat back down. Somehow his proximity didn't crowd her.

Might as well begin as she meant to go on. "So, Russell, why did you hire me?"

He laughed. "Did it surprise you?"

She thought of the HR woman's call. And the magnificent timing of it. "That's one way to put it."

He peered out the window into the back parking lot. "Well, when we talked, you demonstrated all the traits of who I wanted for this position."

"That's another thing. What exactly is this position?"

His eyes crinkled in laughter. "That's right, you don't know yet. The Alumni Association Liaison is like a receptionist specifically for college alumni associations. You're the intermediary between them and SPZ. Information, scheduling, promotion, news. You answer questions or find the answers, forward requests, implement suggestions. Alumni associations deal solely with you as the representative of SPZ."

"How in the world am I going to be able to do all that? I'm a manufacturing engineer, for crying out loud."

"Our last liaison—"

"Yeah, I heard about her already."

He studied the dirt pattern on the carpet with a brittle expression. "The AAs didn't warm up to her, and she didn't relate to any of their representatives. You will."

"How do you know that?"

He smiled, and the lines deepened on his face. "You know a lot about college sports, and not just the major ones."

She flipped her memory back to their conversation. "For all you know, I could only be familiar with wrestling, basketball, and baseball."

"True, but I could also tell you're the sort who wouldn't mind learning other sports if you had to."

Lex tilted her head. "Well, that's true." She nodded at the closed door, then met his gaze directly. "There are a lot of guys out there who wanted this job."

He grinned. "You can take 'em."

"I'm serious, Russell."

"They don't understand that the AAs, by and large, prefer dealing with a female liaison." He shrugged.

It probably wasn't right, but Lex wasn't about to complain.

Russell continued, "But I also didn't want another woman like the previous liaison."

Lex glanced at the sickening stickers, butterflies, and hearts on the filing cabinet. "Well, I can assure you I'm nothing like her."

"I knew you weren't. You're right for the job. And I think you'll enjoy it." He got off her desk, backed up a step, and yanked open the door.

Three men bolted to their feet from a crouching position.

Russell glared.

They froze.

"Don't you have work?" His tone could have made a volcano ice over.

They scattered.

He turned back to her and nodded at the pile of pink slips. "For today, return those phone calls. Introduce yourself so the AAs know there's been a changing of the guard."

"Okay."

"If you have questions —"

"I'll bully one of the guys."

He grinned and walked out of her office.

Lex booted up her computer. The IT department had already sent someone to reset the user. "ASakai" had been preprogrammed into the login window. Password? She typed in "ASakai" again.

Voila.

Aaaah. She could always tell a good company by their IT department.

She already had email. Wendy Tran — that's what that HR chick's name had been! — had arranged for her orientation at 2:00 p.m. in the HR department. That meant she had to answer these calls this morning.

Lex picked up the first slip. Arizona State. Mark Burns.

Deep breath. What did Russell say? People hadn't related to Judy. But what had Judy done? Said? How could Lex know she wouldn't do the same thing and alienate this Mark guy? She'd mess up on her first day at work. She'd be a total failure.

Deep breath again. She needed to think for a second here. Russell had implied that Judy hadn't known much about sports. Well, Lex didn't know about every college sports program in every college in the U.S. What if she congratulated Arizona State on their terrific golfing team when the University of Arizona had just whooped their butts in the last tournament? She'd ruin SPZ's reputation and the company would fold.

Deep breath one more time. Pull a Nike. Just do it. *You're only introducing yourself. And if you mess up and they fire you, you won't be any worse off than you were last Friday.*

She dialed.

"Arizona State Alumni Association. This is Mark."

"Hi, Mark. I'm Lex Sakai from SPZ."

"Who?"

"Lex Sakai. I'm the new Alumni Association Liaison."

"They got rid of Judy?"

"No, she left because she got pregnant." Ooops, that didn't come out right. "I mean, she left for personal reasons."

Mark muttered something that sounded suspiciously like "Good riddance."

Lex cleared her throat. "Anyway, I was calling to let you know—"

"Did you get my message—I left it for Judy—about the web advertising for the new PAC–10 volleyball tournament we're hosting?"

"Cool! You're hosting a volleyball tournament?" That came out only a little lower than a squeal. "I mean, how exciting." What a lucky break—she could hang with college volleyball.

"This year, we've invited Arizona, Washington, and Cal."

"Oh, the game between ASU and Washington should be really good. Their new coach is building a strong team."

"Yeah, but we've just got a freshman who was originally red-shirted. Outside hitter, six-foot-six."

"Who?"

"Lorianne Lee."

"Chinese?"

"Half. Mother is Swiss."

"I'm looking forward to watching her, then."

"Yup." The pause seemed thoughtful rather than awkward. "You follow baseball?"

Lex racked her brain. She remembered watching a little ASU baseball. "You guys doing okay this year?"

"Shaky."

"Well, your captain graduated. He was great last year."

"Yeah, he held the team together like Elmer's. The new captain's Dave Garrett."

"Oh, I remember him. He's not bad. I think if they give him a few months, he'll get the hang of it."

"Yeah, I think so too. Well, it was nice talking to you, Lex. If you're ever in Phoenix, give me a call. I'll get you tickets to anything playing that weekend. Even football."

Whoa! "Thanks, Mark. I appreciate that. Anyway, can you email to me the info on the advertising you wanted for the volleyball tournament? I'll get right on that." She had no clue what she needed to do, but she felt good enough to take on all those jealous chumps out there in the cubicles. "A-S-A-K-A-I at SPZ.com."

"Sure, I'll do that. Thanks, Lex." *Click.*

"Yes!" Lex punched the air with a triumphant fist.

Blip. Oh, she got an email. A sitewide bulletin. "SPZ sponsorship program." Huh? She clicked on it.

Suddenly, a head popped into her open doorway. Grey, peeking in at her. Except his eyes had expanded to the size and color of softballs. "Whoa."

"What?"

"You know sports."

"Duuuh. That's why Russell hired me." Her gaze flickered to the email. *Starting in the fall quarter, SPZ will offer—*

"No, I mean you really know sports."

Lex dragged her gaze away from her computer screen. "What—you think someone needs a *Y* chromosome to know sports? Think again, buddy." She turned back to the message—*SPZ will offer full sponsorship to three local youth club teams—*

"No, I just—"

"Will you let me read my email?!"

Grey disappeared like smoke. Great, now she probably had a reputation for being snappy and emotional.

She returned to the email bulletin. This would be almost perfect. If SPZ picked her girls' team to sponsor, they'd start funding in September.

After playoffs.

But supposedly Grandma would sponsor them until Mariko's wedding in May. If Lex could fool Grandma into funding them through playoffs, she wouldn't need to keep a boyfriend after August. SPZ would take over funding.

Could things get any better? She rocked at her new job. She had a new possibility for sponsorship. And she now worked for a 90-percent male workplace—there had to be at least one guy here who was Christian, who didn't want her job, and who fit the items on her Ephesians List (which wasn't really that long).

The sponsorship program just firmed her resolve. Lex needed to find a guy to date until August. She needed someone who would wow Grandma enough to keep her as sponsor through the summer. She needed to take advantage of the large population of testosterone-charged sports nuts and meet more of them (one of whom she'd just scared away—brilliant).

Oh, and she needed to fill out the application for this sponsorship. She searched her desk.

Judy had taken all the pens.

SIXTEEN

Aiden ached all over, but somehow he also felt really good. He peppered the ball back and forth with Jill. His movements felt strong, his form good. He bumped, set, and hit with more confidence tonight. He felt more anticipation to play than in previous weeks, because of the Stanford Volleyball Camp he'd been taking on Saturdays.

"Where's Lex?" This was late, even for her.

Jill caught the ball instead of bumping it. "She called and said she's working late. She's not coming tonight."

His arms didn't feel as strong as a second ago. He jogged in place a little, but the energy didn't come back.

She's only one person. Stop caring so much about—

He didn't. He didn't care at all. He barely knew her. She was just a cute girl, on and off the court. That was it. He was noticing a cute girl.

Wonder if she'll come by later tonight?

He did great on the hitting line. More accurate hits, better contact between his hand and the ball, better control over his upward momentum. No one else noticed.

Lex would have.

Yeah, but Lex noticed every flubbed hit too.

Stop thinking about her. Don't even think her name.

The game started. Aiden shanked the first pass, but he remained impassive—he didn't cuss or react like most players. Rather, he felt his face had been chipped out of marble, made up of stiff and hard edges.

He could do this.

"Oh, look, there's Lex." Carol pointed at a figure still in work clothes and heels clicking across the back of the court.

"Hey guys!" She waved and sat down on the bleachers.

"You aren't playing?" Jill ignored the ref's glare and turned to her.

"No." Her mouth screwed up in a disappointed grimace. "I forgot my clothes and shoes at home, and it'll take too long for me to go all the way there and come back."

"Come on, guys!" The impatient ref blew her whistle.

Yeah, come on, guys. Aiden moved away from Carol and got back into position. Since when had he become so competitive? Lex must be rubbing off on him.

Then he saw them — two Caucasian guys, strangers to the league. They stood by themselves, not watching the play.

Watching Lex.

The whistle blew. Aiden tried to focus back on the game, but he almost missed the shanked pass sailing his direction.

"Aiden, get it!" his teammates yelled.

He set the hitter too tight to the net, and the other team's blocker pounded the ball back over.

One of the two Caucasian guys gestured at Lex. The other answered.

Lex had noticed them. She had that angry but wary look darkening her face, as if she were torn between going over and throwing a punch, or calling the psych ward to come with straitjackets.

Strange, the two men didn't look like stalkers. They had the build of athletes. If not for their business casual dress, they'd have fit right into the crowd of volleyball players.

"Aiden, that's you!" his team yelled again.

Get your head back in the game! He thrust his arms out to pass the serve, but it sailed too close to the net and Jill had to leap and try to punch it up. It caught in the net and dropped.

The two guys walked toward the exit doors. Aiden hadn't realized the tension across his shoulders until the muscles loosened.

The whistle blew. Ball served. The back row sent a sweet pass. Jill set it curving toward him. Aiden leaped . . .

He knew the guy on the other team who would be blocking. Tall, with long arms. He couldn't hope to slam the ball through him.

Aiden swung, but then cocked his wrist and rolled the ball over the blocker's fingers. The spinning momentum sent the ball dropping fast into the center of the court. The two girls on wing dove from both directions to try and get it.

Point, side-out.

"Good shot." The blocker slapped hands with him under the net.

"Thanks."

They served. The other team set the same player. Aiden couldn't hope to stuff him, but he posted his block the way they'd taught him at camp. *Just protect your section of the court.*

Bam! The ball glanced off his hands in a high arc, easy to pass. Jill set to him again. Out of the corner of his eye, he saw the other team's second front-row player sprint in a little late to the double block. Aiden cut the ball at a sharp angle and hit the sideline.

The down-ref stood by the pole. "Nice cut."

"Thanks."

He heard Lex hooting. He turned, and she clapped and beamed at him.

Beamed at him.

His legs twitched with energy. He could jump higher than the rafters. He was in the zone, his groove was on, and he was on fire.

On the next serve, the other team shanked the ball and they had to bump it back over. Carol set him, high and arcing.

Aiden saw a window—the blocker had left the line shot open. He cranked.

Blammo! On the other team, a girl dropped to the ground.

His heart stopped. Dread spiraled across his chest. He gagged and sucked in a heaving breath. *What have I done?*

He ducked under the net and raced to her side. "I'm so sorry."

She stared dazedly at the ceiling, but she didn't seem too injured.

Well, except for the "Tachikara" emblazoned across her nose and over her left eye.

"How can I not worry about it?" Aiden banged the back of his head against the folded up bleachers.

Lex adjusted her seat and stretched her legs. She hated wearing heels to work—even the short ones made her calves and hamstrings tighten. "Everyone who plays understands these things."

"I should have left the game." His gesturing arm glanced off her. She shifted sideways on the wooden bleacher seat.

"No, if you left, that would be the coward's way out. You finished out the game. You shouldn't have let it hurt your play like it did."

"That girl I hit left the game—"

"Camy? She's a ball magnet. She gets brained just walking across the back of the courts during warm-ups."

"I hit it right at her—"

"You hit it exactly where you should have, the only place you could—on line, which the blocker gave you. She should have been back further to dig it."

Aiden stared morosely at the second game being played. "I should sit out the other two games too."

"Oh, shut up."

Her abrasive tone seemed to amuse him. Well, anything to snap him out of this funk. Lex clapped when their hitter gave a great deep corner shot that had the other team's middle back diving at the ball. "You know, you've been playing better lately."

His expressionless face warmed a bit. She could almost swear a glimmer of a smile appeared. "You think?"

"Yeah."

"I've been taking the Stanford Volleyball Camp the past few weeks."

"Oh, hey! That's a great clinic. It's showing—"

"Hey, Lex."

Kin-Mun had appeared in front of her. She hadn't even noticed. "Hi."

He gave that familiar smile, the one that turned her stomach into a toasty mug of chocolate. "I heard you got a new job."

She nodded. "Alumni Association Liaison at SPZ."

"Awesome. Do you like it?"

"It's terrific. I get paid to research about schools' sports teams and then talk shop with their alumni association reps."

Kin-Mun laughed. "You must be in heaven. One of my cousins used to be an alumni association rep. They made a lot of money off of sports."

His words had a weird catch, an odd hesitation. She shrugged it off. "Yeah, they like using SPZ's web presence to promote their school sports."

"Ever talk to UW?"

"Yeah, I have to call them next week. Why?"

"Oh, no reason." Kin-Mun glanced at the game being played. "I'll be in Seattle next weekend. I'd love to catch the football game but don't know if I'll be able to get tickets."

Lex wondered if she could. Other AAs had offered her free tickets when she talked to them, but not all. And next week would be the first time she spoke to the University of Washington Alumni Association.

"Ah, well." Kin-Mun smiled down at her, and her cup of chocolate reheated. "I'm glad your job is going so well. Going out to eat with everyone tonight?"

"Yeah. We're going to Chili's."

"Great. Save me a seat."

"Sure."

Kin-Mun sauntered away.

"He's a good friend?"

Lex had completely forgotten about Aiden sitting beside her. "Yeah, he and I go way back."

Except Kin-Mun had seemed almost interested in her tonight. Weird. No, exciting. Well, weird and exciting.

Lex needed to get those tickets.

SEVENTEEN

Sorry, Lex, but tickets have been sold out for a few weeks." Her heart dipped, but only for a moment. "Roger, I know most alumni associations have their own block of seats. You couldn't spare me a couple?"

"Well, now." Roger's voice had started to drawl. "I might be able to."

She knew it. "I could offer some discounted advertising rates."

"Naw, we don't really need more advertising."

Shucks. "Not even a premium story on our home page? What would you like to highlight about UW?"

"Our baseball team is doing really well, but it seems we can't fill up seats."

"A home page story would do that for you." She reeled him in.

"A few scouts at the next game might be nice too."

Aha! That's what he was fishing for. "SPZ has connections to many scouts." She had ten of them to call back today about new high school team stats that had just gone up on the website.

"Well, Lex, let me talk to a few people and get back to you on those seats."

"I'd appreciate it, Roger." She hung up. She now understood the rush when magnates closed a deal, or when stockbrokers scored on Wall Street.

Lex reached for her water bottle. Empty.

She glanced at the silent phone. She had time to refill it before Roger called back. She hooked the loop in the Nalgene bottle's cap and headed down the walkway toward the water cooler.

She sidestepped Grey's long legs sticking out into the hallway as he sat in his cube, having some serious phone conversation involving San Jose State baseball. Jordan's voice drifted from his cubicle—probably also on the phone—but too late, she saw his foot shoot out into the walkway in front of her.

Her arms flailed as she tripped. *Thwack!* Her water bottle connected with something solid.

"Ooomph!"

She thrust out her hands, but the flimsy wall toppled instead into Dan's cubicle. *Konk!* Sounded like the partition collided with Dan's head.

"Ow!"

Lex and the partition went down. She flipped over as Dan's body slowed the wall's crash. Her hand, which had still hooked the loop in her water bottle, swung wildly and suddenly let go.

Two things happened at once.

The cubicle partition slammed Dan into the ground. Her water bottle, free and flying out sideways, crashed into the top-heavy water cooler.

Down went the partitions.

Down went the cooler.

Water soaked through the thin office carpet and rushed at her like an ocean wave. It saturated her pants.

"Lex! Are you all right?" Grey appeared. He grabbed one arm, and Jordan, the other. They carefully hoisted her up. While grateful for their help, she disentangled herself from their hands as soon as she could balance.

Dan ran to upend the water cooler bottle and stop the office flood. "Are you okay?"

"I'm fine."

"Are you sure you're good?" Grey asked. "Nothing broken?"

Dan had a huge red spot on his temple, but he focused all his attention on her. "Yeah, are you sure?"

"For the last time, I'm fine. Dan, are you okay? Jordan?"

Jordan froze in the act of rubbing the swollen part of his jaw. Oops, that must have been what her water bottle had first collided with. He flashed a Prince Charming smile. "I'm great."

Okay, she'd walked into the Twilight Zone. "What is wrong with you people?"

Dan blinked. "What do you mean?"

"When did you all suddenly become nice?"

Grey lifted a hand over his chest. "Lex, we're hurt. We respect you deeply as a coworker."

"Since when?"

"We've heard you on the phone." He passed her water bottle to her. "The AAs like talking to you. You're doing a great job."

His eyes seemed sincere. Lex warmed to his praise.

Grey pointed to some papers on his desk. "Their advertising orders are up by ten to twenty this week alone."

She hadn't thought they'd noticed. She shouldn't have assumed they were all still having hissy fits about her getting the AAL position.

"Dan, get her a few more towels. Here, I'll go to the next office and fill your bottle from their cooler." Grey took her bottle from her.

"Thanks."

"Jordan, you help her back to her office."

"No, I'm fine." She started back down the walkway.

"Here are some towels." Dan looked so earnest, Lex feared he'd mop up the water from her derriere if she didn't stop him, so she took the towels from his hand. "I'm good, thanks."

"If you need anything, just ask." Dan smiled.

"Thanks." She turned into her office and closed the door.

Ugh, her butt was soaked. She sopped up her pants and dropped the towels onto her chair before sinking down.

They were actually pretty nice guys. She'd misjudged them. And really, they weren't bad-looking. Plus, they knew as much about sports as she did. When she asked any of them about the Chico stats or the latest Pistons scouting report, they were quick to get her the info and even chat intelligently about it.

Maybe she'd find a boyfriend right here. Even outside of her group, there were tons of men who lived and breathed sports. She wouldn't need to get into Wassamattayu to find a date she could talk to.

Not that she still wouldn't be willing to give up her firstborn child to get into Wassamattayu.

The phone trilled. She almost snatched it up mid-ring, then slapped her hand. *Don't be too eager.* She let it ring one more time. "Lex Sakai, SPZ Alumni Association Liaison."

"Lex, it's Roger. We're all go for the tickets."

"Great! Thanks, Roger. I'll talk to my scouts. I can get several to a few games in the coming weeks." Yeah, she knew a few whose arms she could twist.

"That'd be fine. Thanks." He clicked off.

Lex called a few scouts and left messages for them to call her back.

She had other things to do while she waited, but her mind kept going back to her favorite topic of the month, the Wassamattayu tryouts. She tossed a tennis ball in the air. "Am I high enough on the waiting list?"

The tennis ball dropped to earth.

"Who can I call to find out?"

The tennis ball remained silent.

"Who would know someone who works at Wassamattayu?"

"Wassamattayu?" Grey poked his head into the doorway and held out her Nalgene bottle. "Here's your water."

"Thanks. Yeah, they have an opening for women's volleyball."

"Oh. My cousin got asked to try out for men's soccer."

What luck! "Did he get in?"

"Naw."

"Oh." Rats.

"When did they open tryouts?"

Lex shrugged. "I heard about it a week ago."

"They're probably scouting the waiting list now."

"They scout the waiting list?"

"That's what my cousin said. They don't invite anyone they haven't seen play."

Lex's throat tightened. Her heart did a rapid thump-thump. The two Caucasian guys. At the tournament, at the Nikkei gym. Good thing she never went over to punch their lights out. The thought made her clutch the edge of her desk in horror.

"Thanks for the info."

"Not a problem. Had a good weekend?"

"Yeah, watched lots of ESPN." She'd done some weight lifting in front of the TV. If she didn't get asked for tryouts, it would be for nothing. "How about you?"

He shrugged. "Nothing. Decorated the couch. But next weekend I'm visiting my cousin up in Berkeley."

"You're close?"

"He's like my other brother." Grey's gaze wandered to her tiny window. "You haven't, by any chance, talked with the AA for Cal recently?"

Lex knew she usually didn't pick up on social cues, but the disinterested mask on his face, the twitchy way he drew patterns on the surface of her desk, made her narrow her gaze. "I talked with them last week."

His eyes gleamed like gold fire. "Think you could score me some tickets to the basketball game this weekend?"

Lex felt ... plastic. Not real. Like a thing. Grey didn't move, but suddenly a gulf cracked open between them that made him seem not real either. And she realized she didn't like being used. Imagine that.

"You can leave now." She leaned back in her chair and stared him down.

"What's wrong—"

"You have three seconds before I throw this water bottle at your head, you slime."

He scurried out.

The phone rang, her outside line. She really didn't want to talk to anyone. Maybe she could let it go to the main operator. No ... talking sports with someone might cheer her up. "SPZ Alumni—"

"Lex, it's Jennifer."

Lex straightened in her chair. "What's up?"

"I'm in your area—I had to drop Mom off at a friend's house for Mahjong. Have time for an early lunch?"

What timing. "I'll meet you at Union."

"I'll have the House Special Hong-Kong-style noodles."

"I'll have the same."

The waitress bustled off, hollering in Cantonese through the doorway to the kitchen.

Jenn sipped her jasmine tea. "Are you doing okay?"

"Yeah, why?" Lex blew to cool her tea.

"Well ..." Jenn twirled a lock of her long hair. "You don't usually volunteer to go to Union for lunch."

"What do you mean? I love Chinese food." Lex rubbed at the clear glass covering the tabletop.

"Not when you're training."

"How'd you know I was training?"

Jenn's eyes popped up, alarmed. "Was I not supposed to know? I'm sorry. Richard told me—"

"Relax, Jenn, it's not a secret or anything."

"Oh." Jenn's shoulders sank back to their normal hunched position.

Lex didn't feel like nagging her again about her posture. She started playing with the spoon that went with the little condiment canister of spicy peppers in oil.

"So ... is work going okay?" Jenn bit her lip. "Nothing ... bad?"

Poor Jenn. She had an excess of tact while Lex had none. "Why? Do I look extra stressed?"

"No ... just that ... when you're training extra hard, you eat better than Denise Austin."

Lex laughed, and her mood lightened. "So Denise Austin wouldn't eat Hong-Kong-style noodles?"

Jenn's sweet smile peeked out. "Are you really trying to tell me they aren't unhealthy?"

"It's just salty and saucy over deep-fried chow mein noodles." Just saying it made her feel like fat was congealing in her veins and depositing on her hips.

Who cared—she was out and didn't have to deal with Grey or any of those dorks. "The day was a little bad, but it got better when you called. We haven't been out to lunch in a while."

Lex unloaded. She kept talking even while they chowed down on their salty, saucy, and deep-fried lunch.

"I mean, Jenn, I knocked the partition on his head. Not even a grimace from him."

"And that poor guy you nailed in the chin." Jenn bit into a piece of broccoli.

"Exactly. They were all, 'Are you all right?' Not even yowls of pain." Lex chomped on a crispy noodle. "It was all for the tickets."

Jenn didn't answer.

Lex glanced at her.

Jenn screwed up her face. "Well ..."

Lex sighed. "That's encouraging."

Jenn shrugged and kept eating.

"I thought I'd look for a boyfriend at work. You know, for Grandma's ultimatum. I only have three more months. But now I can't tell the cools from the creeps."

"Yeah, that's tough."

"I just don't like being forced to date someone. What is it with Grandma and great-grandchildren?"

Jenn paused with a piece of char siu pork in her chopsticks. Her extra-large brown eyes leveled with Lex's. "You don't know?"

"What do you mean?"

"Lex, for our parents and grandparents, children are their immortality."

Lex was suddenly dipped into a bucket of ice water. Grandma favoring her right hip, that vulnerable moment when she'd looked so old and tired. Was Grandma feeling her age and working to increase her legacy? An extension of her own life?

"I also think ... I hope this isn't gossip ..."

Lex waited. Jenn would spill eventually.

"I heard Grandma telling Mom that she stopped seeing her friend Mrs. Matsumoto."

Mrs. Matsumoto had babysat each of the cousins. She was also Christian, and very vocal about it too. "Grandma and Mrs. Matsumoto clash all the time. They're too much alike—both outspoken."

"No, this time I think it's serious. I don't know what Mrs. Matsumoto told Grandma, but she won't talk to her at all." Jenn feverishly jabbed her chopsticks at her bed of crispy noodles. "I think that's why Grandma's after us. After you."

"Huh? Speak up." Jenn had a tendency to not only lower her husky voice, but to also talk to her chest.

Jenn looked up with a troubled gaze. "I don't know this for sure, but ... maybe she's being hard on you because you're always so adamant about dating a Christian."

Lex blinked. Mainly, that had been a tactic Lex used to keep Grandma from throwing the sons of her Buddhist friends at her. "That doesn't make sense. Grandma's never liked the fact we four are Christian, but she's never been outright hostile about it ..." Until now.

Jenn went back to stabbing her noodles. "I'm wondering if Mrs. Matsumoto said something that really made Grandma uncomfortable."

"And so she's cutting off Mrs. Matsumoto and poking at us. At me."

Jenn nodded.

Lex sighed. That meant this whole thing could be so much more complicated. She hated complication.

"You know ..." Jenn bit her lip again.

"What is it?"

"You're not going to like hearing this."

"I'm not going to bite your head off."

"Well ... those tickets are probably influencing men outside of work." Jenn's eyes radiated sympathy—not a pitying kind, but the kind that wished she could take away Lex's pain.

"What do you mean?"

"Kin-Mun."

She started as if a blast of air hit her in the face. "But he didn't ask for the tickets. I'm the one—"

"How did he bring up the subject?"

Lex thought back. *Hi, Kin-Mun. Oh, new job. Yeah, going to Seattle. Wish I could go to the game ...*

Her lungs collapsed. Or maybe her heart caved in. Regardless, she felt a huge echoing emptiness in her chest.

"Well, now I'm just depressed." Lex sat back in her chair. To add to the List: *Must either not know about the perks of my job or not care about college sports events.*

"I'm sorry. I shouldn't have brought it up." Jenn pushed her plate away.

"No, don't feel bad. I needed to get my head out of the sand." Lex stared at the steaming noodles and sighed. "I need a new strategy. I can't really trust anyone who knows enough about my job."

"That rules out your workplace, but not all volleyball guys."

"And not Wassamattayu. I had planned to find another sponsor, but Grandma's got her claws in practically the entire Japanese American community."

"Oh, Lex. Grandma really does love us. She thinks this will make us happy."

"Who are you kidding? Grandma just wants to make herself happy."

Jenn's eyes dropped. "It's easier for you. She's always at my parents' place. Sometimes it's just better to give in, don't you think?"

"No, I don't. That's not how I am." Lex signaled for the waitress. "I'm not going down without a fight. Grandma can't get at everyone—I just need to be more unconventional."

Lex liked the beach but hated sand. It got everywhere, like it did now—into her shoes and socks, working into the waistband of her shorts and under her sports bra.

And like an idiot, she kept doing volleyball drills.

No, she wasn't an idiot. She was dedicated. She needed to focus on the prize—getting into Wassamattayu, assuming she'd be invited to tryouts. She had to get into even better shape.

The Hong-Kong-style noodles for lunch yesterday hadn't helped her any.

She finished her side-to-side shuffles and folded in half, panting. The breeze from the nearby business park cooled her and made the outdoor volleyball net ripple. The sun had warmed the sand, and it radiated heat like a toaster oven.

She set up for blocking drills at the net. Old and left out in the weather, it had been provided by the accounting firm from the business park, and it sagged toward her. Well, it hung between the two poles. Good enough for her. She squatted, then leaped.

The net slapped her elbow. *Ow!* She paused as the pain tingled and subsided down her arm. She wished she'd been more careful in self-defense class an hour ago. As long as the bruise didn't affect her passing, she'd be fine.

Voices made her hesitate. Her back muscles stiffened.

In the large parking lot, a group of men all in their thirties, a mix of Asian, Indian, and Caucasian, headed toward the sand volleyball court. No, toward the basketball court nearby.

Most dressed in shorts and sneakers, but a few still had on business casual slacks and polo shirts. An evening pickup game, probably coworkers from one of the businesses. Nothing to worry about.

A few glanced at her. Were they really neutral glances?

Stop it.

There were a lot of them. What about mob mentality? Didn't she read about that in *Newsweek* once?

You're being paranoid.

She was by herself.

Now you're just illogical.

Maybe she should get into her car and leave.

You need the training. They're harmless guys.

Lex took a deep breath and stared at the gray, tattered net. She was such a basket case.

She squatted deep and leaped in a rapid series of three blocking motions. She sprinted a step to the side, then leaped into another three blocks. She continued all the way down the net.

She stood sucking in air by the pole, the net flapping against the metal in a soft, hollow ringing sound. The group of men had reached the basketball court and started stretching, practicing free throws. Very little chatter. Some good-natured ribbing and heckling.

It relaxed her. They looked and sounded like her brother or her male cousins and their friends. The pickup games in Campbell Park, her whining to be included and holding her own against them.

A movement in the parking lot caught her eye.

A tall, wild-haired Caucasian man, dressed in a cotton button-down shirt and slacks—both creased from a long work day. Staring intently at her.

She hardened her eyes to hide the violent shiver that shot from her neck to her lower back.

He wasn't someone she knew. With his narrow face and scraggly beard, he reminded her of recording artist David Crowder, but since he probably worked for one of the tech companies in the business park, Lex wouldn't be surprised if he had the IQ of Einstein and a couple PhDs under his belt. If only he'd stop staring at her.

Lex considered marching over there and getting in his face. He couldn't stare at women and get away with it. She pursed her lips and stepped off the sand court.

A car horn. An SUV zipped into view and parked near the sand court. Her heart ramped up for a second, then Aiden got out. Funny, her heart rate didn't slow back down.

Okay, so maybe she wouldn't start a fight with Mr. Santa Cruz. "What are you doing here?" She shaded the sun from her eyes with her hand.

"I should have figured you'd be here. The people at the volleyball clinic suggested doing sand drills, and some players from Nikkei told me about this court."

"Yeah, there aren't many free sand courts in this area."

"So do you mind if I join you?"

Why not? Maybe she'd push herself into an even longer, more intense workout. That would be great. She'd be in terrific shape for tryouts. "Warm up and get moving."

They spent an hour doing sprinting, blocking, hitting, and diving drills in the sand. Aiden knew a few new drills he'd picked up at the Stanford Volleyball Clinic, which challenged Lex even more. She felt exhausted but great after they finished.

They sat on the grass bordering the sand court, sucking down water and toweling off the rivers of sweat pouring down their faces. Lex had a new respect for Aiden's terrific lung capacity—at points, she'd been the one breathing harder. It must be from his running.

"How's your new job going?" Aiden dusted sand off his bare feet.

A knot tightened at the base of her neck. Aiden had heard about her job when she'd been talking with Kin-Mun. "It's okay." It would come any minute now—*Can you get me tickets for ...?*

"Different from engineering, I'll bet."

"Yeah."

Aiden looked her directly in the eyes. "You and I are a few of the lucky ones. Doing exactly what we love doing. Being good at it."

In the warm, understanding light from his gaze, Lex felt energized and relaxed at the same time. The knot in her neck melted away. "You love physical therapy that much?"

He nodded. "It's a rush, seeing a knee surgery patient jogging on the treadmill, seeing a carpal tunnel patient up their weight on the gym machines."

Lex had always thought about the injuries associated with PT, not the healing. "That's neat."

"And you get to talk sports all day. It's as if the job was made for you."

It was, wasn't it? For the first time, Lex caught a glimmer of the hand of God in all the crazy turns her life had taken lately. She hadn't been talking to God much, but He'd still been orchestrating things. It gave her a weird feeling—both comforted at being taken care of, but also antsy that she hadn't been as independent and in control as she thought she was.

Before she knew it, they'd been talking for over half an hour. Lex left reluctantly to go home and start packing for her move. She had a lot of stuff, so she might as well start early.

It was only as she waved at Aiden and drove away that she realized he'd never mentioned game tickets even once.

Her cell phone chirped. Home phone number. "Hey, Dad."

"I'm glad I got a hold of you, Lex. I just got off the phone with our real-estate agent."

"She sold the house already?"

"Even better. We got a huge bid."

"That's great, Dad." She tried to muster more enthusiasm.

"But one thing the buyer stipulated is fast escrow."

"What do you mean? How fast?"

"I'm sorry, Lexie. We have only three weeks to move out."

EIGHTEEN

And now for her favorite pastime—dealing with her bridezilla cousin. Lex had left it off as long as possible, but now it was late afternoon on Friday. She closed the door to her office, then sat and dialed Mariko's number.

"Hello?"

Lex paused. The voice sounded sweet and silky—very un-Mariko. "Mariko, it's Lex."

"What do you want?" Mariko barked in her normal voice.

"I can't make it to the bridal shower tomorrow."

"Yes. You. Can." Each word stabbed like a knife.

Lex sighed. Mariko had gone hormonal. "Look, you and I both know I'm only a bridesmaid because Grandma dictated the bridal party to you. You don't want me there messing up your fun with your friends."

The pregnant pause cheered her. She could almost see Mariko waffling: *Grandma ... fun with friends ... Grandma ... fun with friends ...* "No deal."

"Aw, why not?"

"Grandma will kill me, that's why." Mariko's voice had a pinched tone.

"She won't be there. How would Grandma ever find out if I didn't show? Who would tell her?"

"Uh ... Grandma will call and ask me how it went."

That was a lame excuse, even for Mariko. Lex trusted her like she trusted Uncle Howard not to tell bad jokes. "What's going on?"

"Nothing." But her snap lacked genuine annoyance.

Why did Mariko adamantly want Lex to be there? "Did Grandma put you up to something? Did you invite some guy to introduce me to?"

"N-no! Like I'd go through the effort for you."

"You wouldn't. But you would for Grandma."

"You're so full of yourself. You will show up, and you won't ruin anything. You're always ruining things."

Lex's throat tightened. She swallowed painfully. "I do not." She cleared her throat. "I do not." There, she'd said that a little stronger.

Luckily, Mariko wasn't listening to her. "Why'd *you* have to be the next OSFC? Then you wouldn't be in my bridal party at all. Why couldn't Venus have been next OSFC—she'd at least look good in the pictures. Or Jennifer—she's always so easygoing. You are *not* leaving me to explain to Grandma why you couldn't come."

Lex tightened her grip on the phone. "Why are you doing this? What did I ever do to you?"

"You were born thirteen months after me, that's what."

Lex exhaled a hot breath. "Take it up with my dad."

"You don't realize how hard I had it all those years, being OSFC."

"Wah, wah, wah. It's all about *you*." Lex wanted something to smash. "I am *not* going to your stupid shower just so that you can shove some guy at me."

"It's not a stupid shower—"

"Do you know what kind of a week I've had?" Lex started ticking things off on her fingers. "I have to move out in three weeks, I had to divvy up all my stuff so Dad can have a garage sale this weekend, Dad's moving in with Uncle Howard and they don't have room for me! How would you like to be homeless and possessionless, all in three days?"

Mariko's low, menacing voice carried clearly over the phone. "You *will* be there tomorrow or I'll call Grandma personally and tell her you didn't want to meet Burt."

"Ha! You *are* shoving some guy at me."

"You're so juvenile. Be there at nine." *Click.*

Lex collapsed in her chair. Life was so not fair. A bridal shower with Mariko and all her girly-girly friends, laughing and having a good time, excluding tomboy Lex. Laughing at Lex while some totally uninterested guy tried to pretend he was. Then Grandma on the phone as soon as she leaves: "Well? How did he like her?"

This couldn't come at a worse week. Forget about finding a boyfriend—Lex had to find housing. She felt doubly abandoned because it seemed like Dad couldn't wait to get rid of her.

No, she shouldn't think that way. Dad had been distracted lately. He loved her. He and Uncle Howard would enjoy their bachelor apartment. She shouldn't resent him for that. She was such a lousy daughter. What—did she expect Dad to take care of her for her entire life?

May as well look for a few apartments online, since she wouldn't have Internet access in ten days. She toggled her mouse to take her computer out of sleep mode.

Oh, she had mail. From Russell.

Lex, Congratulations! The SPZ Sponsorship fund has selected your junior high school girls' club team for funding beginning in September ...

What? She had to read it again.

Selected. Not rejected.

She had funding! Lex unleashed a whoop into her silent office.

She read the rest of the email. *The SPZ Sponsorship fund committee is enthusiastic about the opportunity to encourage more girls to join next year, to build community, to create opportunities for girls, and to influence other children in the area.*

Funding is pending your team's finishing record in the summer playoffs. This is not to demand perfection from your team, but to evaluate your own coaching skills.

Well, she supposed they wouldn't want to back a hopelessly losing team. But oh, man. She'd look so bad if the girls' team got killed during playoffs.

A press release has been sent to the newspaper—

Press release? So, if the girls' team did badly, she'd not only look like a doofus, she'd make her *company* look bad to the entire community.

Lovely. No pressure.

Now Lex really needed Grandma's money for playoffs. SPZ funding didn't start until September. Mariko's wedding was in May.

She needed a chump — er, boyfriend, until September. They also needed to actually look like a couple at the wedding.

Lex chewed on her lip. A niggling burrowed around in her gut. She needed to find someone she wouldn't mind looking lovey-dovey with. Well, that's what she had the Ephesians List for, right?

She wouldn't look like an idiot at the wedding, would she? A picture of Mariko and her posse of Asian Barbie dolls flashed in front of her. So glamorous, so with-it, so charming. Lex wasn't ugly, but she wasn't glamorous, she was never with-it, and she'd really rather not be charming to anyone.

No, there was nothing wrong with her. She'd show those girls, her aunties, Grandma. She had appeal. She wouldn't be pitied, and certainly not by them. She could top those ninnies and their ninny boyfriends —

Ding! The lightbulb went off.

She'd wow them with a superstar date. A boyfriend so dazzling they'd bow to her superior man-appeal.

She had called the A's new pitcher just yesterday about an event with his old alma mater. They'd hit it off. She wondered if he'd agree to be a date for a wedding with guaranteed good Chinese food?

Or the new Giants' shortstop. His best friend, UCLA's alumni association's representative, *adored* Lex for all the scouts she'd sent to the ball game last weekend.

Lex leaned back in her chair and beamed at the ceiling. This was going to be great.

They were after her.

Lex didn't know how Grandma had found out about the free college game tickets. Maybe she'd bugged Lex's phone. She wouldn't put it past her.

But it didn't matter how, anymore. The news was out. All of Grandma's friends' sons knew about it.

And they were all after Lex.

Her cell phone started ringing as she shut off her computer for the night. "Hello?" Oops, she only had fifteen minutes to get to Nikkei.

"Rreksoo Sakai?" The male voice speaking with a heavy Japanese accent made her pause as she grabbed her purse from her desk drawer.

"Speaking."

"*Hajimemashte. Boku wa Akaoki Toya. Anata no obaasan—*"

"I don't speak Japanese." But she knew a few words, and Toya had definitely mentioned Lex's grandmother. A dark suspicion made her grit her teeth as she made her way outside.

"Oh ... you no speak?"

"Fourth generation, bud."

"Ah, no. No 'Bud.' Toya—"

"Toya, what did you need?"

"Ah. You grandmother, she friends with my mother."

"Oh, no."

"She say you pretty girl. You like sports. You get tickets for college games, yes?"

"What?" Lex dropped her car keys. "Where did you hear that?"

"*Okaasan—*"

His mother. "No, not interested. Good-bye."

"But—"

She closed her phone and slid into her car. The phone rang. "Hello?"

"Rrek Sakkai?"

Chinese accent this time. Oh, no. Maybe she could throw him a curveball. "*Moshi-moshiiii! Otearai e itte mo iidesuka?*"

"Uh ..."

"Ichi, ni, san, shi, go! Hitotsu, futatsu, mitsu, yotsu!"

"Er ... *Ni hao ma?*"

Come on, hang up. Lex didn't know many more Japanese phrases. She supposed she could repeat the "going to the bathroom" phrase. *"Otearai—"*

Click.

Lex stared at the offending phone in her palm. She could turn it off. But what if Wassamattayu called?

It rang. *Nononononono.* She let it ring again. Unknown San Jose number. With a painful grimace, she flipped it open. "H-hello?"

"Lex Sakai?" American accent.

"Yes?"

"Hi, my aunt is friends with your grandmother ..."

Lex fielded two more calls on her way to volleyball. She skidded into the parking lot and rammed into a stall. Collecting her gear, she hustled toward the high school gym doors.

"Lex Sakai?" One of three Asian guys stood near the open doorway.

She stiffened, then peered through the door at the volleyball players just inside. What was she thinking—that some strangers would attack her five feet away from her friends?

She turned to the one who had spoken, a tall, thin boy who looked like he had just graduated college. "Listen, guys, I'm late for volleyball. I'll talk to you all later." If they stayed around until later. She rather hoped they didn't.

A second boy moved forward to block her way with his broad chest. "Okay, so you know your grandmother told our moms about the tickets." He grinned and spread his hands wide. "We've all been nagged. We understand. We're easy."

The first guy moved closer. "We don't have to go out on a date. If you have tickets to the Cal game this weekend, and you're not going, just give them to one of us. We'll tell our mothers we had a terrific dinner and a movie."

Lex's jaw ached from dropping it so far down. How was this better than being actually courted for those tickets? "You've got to be kidding me."

"What—you're going to the game?"

With a growl of frustration, she pushed through. Dummies! Idiots! They had put her in the perfect mood to slam some balls—

"Lex Sakai?"

"*What?*" She twisted around, following her bark with a feral glare.

Right at the two Caucasian guys who had been watching her for the past week. The ones who might be Wassamattayu scouts. *Just shoot me now.* "Ah … Sorry, guys. I thought you were someone else." She simpered.

Their expressionless faces reminded her of FBI agents on TV. Or Aiden when he got frustrated on the court. The shorter one handed her an envelope.

Her gym bag plopped to the ground. She ripped it open. *You are cordially invited to participate in tryouts for Wassamattayu …* "Oh my gosh! Thank you!"

"You're welcome." Grim-faced, the taller one nodded.

"We were very impressed. You play with power and precision." The shorter man's tone reminded Lex of a business report.

Lex beamed. "I could almost kiss you!"

He cleared his throat. "I'd rather you didn't."

Lex needed money.

How ironic that something so important to her might be over before it began.

She knew Wassamattayu charged several thousand dollars per year for membership—but that hadn't worried her when she worked for Pear Technologies. She would have been fine taking the money out of her savings and then living cheaply at home until she made the money back at her higher-paying engineering job.

Now she had to cough up five thousand dollars as a deposit before tryouts. It would be refunded if she didn't get chosen.

She re-read that line. She *would* be chosen. She'd train extra hard.

But the money worried her. Now she had to rent an apartment instead of living free with Dad, and her SPZ job didn't pay as much as Pear. And she had thought she'd use her savings as a backup plan — even though it wasn't enough — for the girls' playoffs expenses.

Aiden dropped down next to her to take off his shoes. Both their cell phones rang at the same time.

Lex barely glanced at the number before ending the call and tossing it down on the floor. She'd missed six calls during the night. How many friends with eligible sons did Grandma have? She sighed and glanced up.

Oh, no. Talk about persistent.

The tall, thin guy had stayed. The other two had left. Lex groaned and dropped her head. A pulsing headache started right behind her eyeballs.

"So, Lex." Mr. Persistent bent at the waist, hovering over her. "Let's talk tickets."

"Let's not." He hadn't even introduced himself, the pushy creep.

Her foul mood only made him smile. "Come on. It's an easy answer for both our problems — my mother, your grandmother."

An idea dawned. Lex shoved aside the immediate guilt that followed. "What do you do?"

Mr. Persistent blinked. "Uh … I'm an optometrist." He dug out his wallet and handed her a business card.

He was solvent. And she needed money. He probably wouldn't be willing to cough up five thousand dollars for the weekend Cal game, but he'd know friends who'd be willing to pay for other tickets …

Nonono. She couldn't believe she was even considering it. Aside from being, oh, slightly *illegal*, she couldn't betray the alumni associations who gave her the tickets in good faith.

Mr. Persistent smiled with that same slick confidence her brother Richard had.

"No." She thrust the card back at him. "No."

His smile widened. "Lex—"

"No."

"Aw, come on—"

"She said no." Aiden's sharp voice cut through them. Lex had forgotten he sat beside her. He'd apparently ended his cell call and overheard Mr. Persistent.

He tossed Aiden a dark look before gazing at Lex with chagrin that almost looked real. "Keep the card. If you change—"

"I won't." She turned away from him and started tugging off her shoes. She didn't look at anyone. Certainly not Aiden.

She waited until she got the second shoe off. "Is he gone?"

"Yeah." Aiden dug in his bag for his street shoes.

She stared at her feet, wiggled her toes in their socks. Finally she raised her eyes to him. "Thanks."

His look rested on her, gentle but not probing. "Anytime."

A warmth settled over her ribs. She liked having him ... not say anything. Especially since practically every guy wanted tickets from her.

Except him.

Lex glanced at her discarded cell phone.

It rang.

NINETEEN

Mariko had given her notorious sweet tooth full rein. Lex stared at the table of food and could already feel the sugar eating cavities into her enamel. Banana nut bread, sesame-crusted Chinese doughnuts, almond cookies, fruit cocktail and almond custard, steamed egg cake, even honey walnut prawns. On the non-Asian side was rum cake, blueberry pecan muffins, strawberry almond rolls, and croissants. The radioactive coffee Lex had bought that morning from Tran's Nuclear Coffee Shop burbled in her stomach.

"Not hungry?" Lex's cousin Tiki fluttered impossibly long lashes as she bit into a chocolate croissant.

Okay, one, what Asian had eyelashes that long and curly? They had to be fake. And two, how did this size-zero chick get away with eating a chocolate croissant with gusto? Tiki even had a *son*.

"So, Lex, I heard Mariko has a surprise for you."

Lex peered down her nose at Tiki. "She's wasting her time."

Her cat-eyes glittered with mirth. "Oh? And why is that?"

"I don't need a man when I've got Byron Harvey." Only the points leader on the Sacramento Kings's roster.

Tiki blinked. Her face had a vacant look that matched her brain capacity. "That's ... nice."

Lex pursed her lips. "Uh ... I'm trying decide between Byron and Geoff German."

Tiki's plucked brows wrinkled. "Who?"

"German. The new pitcher for the Oakland A's?"

Her brow cleared. "Oh. Baseball." She said it the way she'd say *toilet.*

Lex's diaphragm dropped like a trapdoor. These dodos didn't know any of her sports heroes. A professional athlete as a date to Mariko's wedding would be like a Pulitzer Prize winner at an Illiteracy Dinner.

"Tavi's crying." Tiki flounced away to soothe her shrieking baby.

Lex's shoulders sagged. Well, at least she didn't have to suck up to the UCLA alumni association rep in order to get Byron's number. She probably couldn't have convinced Grandma it was true love anyway.

"Okay, everybody, let's start the games." Mariko stood in the middle of the living room as perky as a cheerleader.

Tiki sidled up to Mariko, bouncing her crying one-year-old. "Where's Burt? He's supposed to be here to babysit."

Mariko shushed her with a hiss.

The door opened.

Mr. Babysitter had the coloring, build, and look of Russell Crowe as he entered the Colosseum to fight the gladiators. Shoulders back, chin up, firm jaw, eyes stern and ready for warfare.

"There you are!" Tiki mobbed him, shoving baby Tavi into his arms. "See, Tavi-wavvie? Here's Uncle Burt." She danced back to Mariko's side. "Okay, we can start now."

"Burt, sit *there.*" Mariko stabbed a lacquered nail at one of two chairs sitting side by side. "Lex, you sit—"

"Yeah, yeah." Lex plopped down next to him.

He jiggled baby Tavi like a jackhammer, brushing her arm with his elbow.

She hopped her chair a few inches further away.

"Okay, everybody, take five clothespins." Tiki passed them out. "Stick them somewhere on you."

Lex stuck them out from her blouse sleeves like a porcupine.

"Okay, if someone catches you saying the word 'wedding,' they can take a clothespin. Whoever has the most pins at the end wins!"

Tiki clapped her hands and bounced on her toes as if this were the most clever game ever invented.

Lex unclipped herself and handed all five clothespins to Mr. Babysitter. "Here. Wedding."

"Lex!" Tiki's face matched her pinky lipstick. "Can't you even try to get into the spirit of things?"

"Nope." Lex said the word with relish.

Mr. Babysitter shifted the now-hiccoughing Tavi to one arm and grabbed Lex's pins. "Thanks. I'm not saying another word all afternoon."

"Okay, everyone, now take some toilet paper. However much you like." Mariko giggled as she passed around the toilet paper rolls. Several of the other women also started giggling and pulling off wads and wads of paper. Lex tore off one sheet.

"We're separating you into two teams. You guys are team one—" Mariko pointed to three Barbies (Lex didn't remember their names), Lex, Mr. Babysitter, and baby Tavi. "The rest are team two. Now, pick a model and make her a bridal gown from the toilet paper!"

You have got to be kidding me. Why did Mariko cheer? It would be hard to find an older or dumber bridal shower game in history.

"Lex, you're our model." Tall girl with fried blonde hair.

"Because we know how to make a good dress." Asian girl with green contact lenses, making her look rather alien-like.

"No. Way." Lex crossed her arms.

"Oh, come on." Buxom girl with short hair held out her length of TP. "The less you fight, the faster this will be over."

She had a point. It wasn't as if Lex was going to help them make the dress, and Mr. Babysitter had his hands full. "Fine." She flung out her arms and clipped Green Contacts's nose.

Mariko should have set a time limit. The Three Stooges dithered over where to put every single length of TP.

"Over her shoulder?"

"No, then it won't drape for a nice train."

"How about dipping down in front?"

"No, that'll upset the lines."

Lines? It was a TP dress, for crying out loud. And did they need to touch her so much? "Just put it on!" Lex swiveled so she could give all three her hottest glare. Mr. Babysitter sat apart from them, holding baby Tavi a little like a football.

The doorbell rang. Since Lex's group was the only one in line of sight with the door, Buxom Girl darted to open it.

Lex twisted around. "No!" She looked ridiculous. She didn't want anyone to see—

Too late. The door swung open. "Got a package. I need a signature." A UPS deliveryman stood there in his brown uniform. He did a double-take at seeing Lex mummified, with Fried Blonde wrapping her head in more TP for a veil.

Lex's glare lanced right through him. "What are you looking at?"

He jumped. "Nothing, ma'am." He grabbed the electronic pad from Buxom Girl before she could scrawl more than an initial and raced away.

They finally finished, and Lex stood glowering while the girls laughed at her—no way would she believe they were laughing at the dress instead—until Mariko nodded, and she could tear it off her body.

"Oh! Be careful!" Green Contacts tried to save their creation.

Lex stuck her face close enough to see her pupils shrink. *"It's toilet paper."*

"Okay, next game is Guess That Lingerie!" Tiki trilled a sadistic laugh. "We asked everybody to bring some sexy lingerie for Mariko— they're all laid out here—so now each of you will guess who brought which outfit!"

Was Tiki dropped on her head as a child? What kind of inane game was this?

Baby Tavi let out a particularly shrieking wail—man, that kid had cried nonstop so far—and Mariko glanced in Lex's direction. "Lex, you go first."

"No way." Lex thrust out her jaw.

Mariko's eyes spit daggers at her.

Lex burned holes in her Shiseido face with her laser-beam vision.

Mariko took a step toward her.

Rrrrring!

Saved by the cell phone. Lex would even welcome a call from one of Grandma's friends' sons right now.

Maybe it was ... the number looked familiar, but she couldn't place it. "Hello?"

"Lex, it's Aiden."

Lex flashed a brilliant smile at Mariko. "Sorry, I have to take this." She escaped into the kitchen.

"Hey, Aiden, what's up?" She peeked into the refrigerator. Maybe Mariko had some carrot sticks ...

"You have my cell phone."

Lex straightened, clipping her forehead on the edge of a shelf. "What do you mean? You're talking to me." She rubbed her raw skin.

"From your cell phone."

Lex peered at the phone. Oh. "When did this happen?"

"Last night at volleyball. Remember? We both answered our phones."

"Oh, yeah." She'd tossed hers down without answering. She hadn't even noticed it when she put her phone away.

"Where are you now?" Aiden asked.

"Cupertino."

"I'm in the area. Want me to come by so we can switch phones?"

"Yes!" *Whoa, easy there, Rover.* "I mean, that would be fine."

"Give me your address."

Lex recited Mariko's address with the gusto of the kids in Sunday school. "Need directions?"

"No, I'll MapQuest it. I'll call if I get lost."

She hung out in the kitchen, munching on an apple until the mortifying lingerie game had finished. She took her seat next to Mr. Babysitter, who was trying to juggle a squirming Tavi and a cup of syrupy punch someone had given to him.

180 / Camy Tang

He held out his cup to her. "Can you hold this for a sec?"

"Sure." She grabbed it.

Mr. Babysitter changed to a weird stiff-armed bouncing thing with the squalling baby. Tavi had crescendoed to a piercing howl.

Mr. Babysitter's eyes held pure panic as he turned to her. "Know anything about babies?"

"No." He couldn't pay Lex enough to lay a finger on Tiki's spoiled brat.

Baby Tavi paused his wide-mouthed crying to burp. A drop of cloudy drool trickled down his chin.

Ew. Lex flipped her eyes away faster than Dad with the remote control. Mariko bustled past her, wafting some sickly sweet scent her way. Lex's abused stomach rumbled, then stilled.

Baby Tavi had quieted to sniffles, snorts, and hiccoughs, all of which started to sound very wet and slurpy and gross. He now had a large spot of ochre-colored drool on his bib. *Don't think about the color!* Lex tried to shut one eye so she couldn't see him.

She breathed a shallow breath in through her nose, but then caught a whiff of something distinctly urp-smelling. She gagged.

"Mariko, I'm not feeling well."

Mariko tilted her head down as she glared at Lex. She propped a hand on her hip, making her bangles jingle like chains. "You stay right where you are."

"I'm serious, Mariko."

A pink glitter extension aimed at her. "Stay put."

Lex's stomach heaved again. Maybe if she didn't move, it would settle down.

A gushing liquidy sound. Warmth dripping on her hand, soaking through her slacks.

Don't look, don't look, don't—

The smell of regurgitated carrots assailed her. Her eyes flew open in shock.

Orange-yellow splattered on her hand, her forearm, all over her leg. Lucky her. Tavi had the projectile thing going.

Her stomach rose to boiling. She clapped her hand over her mouth and nose, trying to think cool, calming thoughts while her gut roiled.

Unfortunately, she forgot about the cup of syrupy juice in her hand. It spilled all over the source of her misery.

Well, she got most of it on Tavi's bib. And his head. And Mr. Babysitter's pants. And Mariko's floor.

"*Aaaaiiiiieeeee!*" Mariko's piercing shriek sent a jolt through Lex's body.

Lex couldn't move. She stared at Tavi's red-orange grinning face and pressed a shaking hand to her midsection.

Tiki rushed to Tavi's side, but then stood there flapping her arms canary-style when Mr. Babysitter shoved the newly anointed baby at her. "Ew ... ugh ... er ..."

"Lex, how could you?" Green Contacts circled them, but she also kept out of reach of Tavi's flinging arms. "He's just a baby."

"He started it." Lex tried to wipe the baby urp from her hand onto Mr. Babysitter's pants.

"Hey!" He shifted away from her.

"Your pants are already dirty."

"So are yours."

Hmm. Good point. Oh, no. Lex's stomach started boiling again. "I'm going to be sick."

The circle around them expanded faster than a balloon. Mr. Babysitter's dismayed gaze passed over each of the women. "Somebody take the kid!"

Lex gagged in Mr. Babysitter's direction.

"Aim at your own pants!"

The doorbell rang.

Green Contacts waggled a finger at Lex. "Put your head between your legs."

Lex tried to glare at her through the tears gathering in her eyes. Rats. Being sick always made her cry. Not now, not in front of *these* people ...

"Is Lex Sakai—?"

Aiden.

He stood in the open doorway, the sunlight bright behind him. Her knight in shining armor.

"Save me," she croaked.

He felt like a knight in shining armor.

Lex looked paler than mochi rice-dumplings. Tears streaked down her face, and she held her orange-colored hand out from her, as if in denial that it belonged to her.

Aiden strode to the refreshment table and grabbed the entire stack of cocktail napkins. He had to use half the napkins on her hand, the other half on her pants. "What's wrong? Dizzy?"

She shook her head. She kept her eyes screwed shut, her mouth pinched closed.

"Nauseated?"

She nodded.

The women chattered around him, as intelligible as a flock of pigeons. He ignored all advice, questions, innuendoes, and flirting.

A girl who looked a little like Lex sank her talons into his upper arm so she could hiss in his ear. "Get her out of here."

Lex rose on shaky legs. Aiden held her elbow as he guided her to the door. One of the women slung Lex's purse over her shoulder.

Mr. Babysitter had sat there while the women cleaned up the baby with wipes, then mopped up his pants. As Lex headed toward the door, he rose to his feet and faced her, looking like a bulldog. "These were Giovannis. I should make you buy me new ones."

Aiden expected a blazing hot answer from her, but Lex just peered at him, her eyes dazed.

The guy slanted his beady eyes at her. "I might be more forgiving if you can get me Giants' tickets."

Lex inhaled a raspy breath and swallowed hard before answering. "It's only college games, you doofus." She turned toward the door.

Aiden put a steadying hand on her waist, but a jolt of tension tightened her entire abdomen at his touch. He immediately removed his hand.

She didn't seem to mind his grasp of her elbow. Her weight sagged against his hand. He shuffled her out the door, and someone slammed it behind them.

When he opened the door to his SUV, she flinched away from his leather seats. "My pants."

Where had he put those extra T-shirts? Trunk? No, backseat. He spread them over the leather and let her climb in gingerly.

He got behind the wheel. "Home?"

"Blossom Hill and 85." She sat with eyes closed.

The tears spilled down her face. She wouldn't open her eyes. He wondered if she wanted to shut out the world.

Somehow he knew it wasn't sickness. Her entire body had seemed to shrivel where she sat. How many people had ever seen her weak and vulnerable? Her hand clutched the door handle, knuckles white.

Some knight you are. Catching her at her worst. I'm sure she's thrilled about that. He caught the tremble in her lower lip before she drew them tight.

"It's okay. I'll take back roads and drive slow."

A small smile appeared on her face. His heart expanded.

He punched it down immediately. Dummy. She was Trish's cousin and a Christian. Wasn't Trish's hypocrisy enough?

"Drmmmnn."

"What?"

She reached down for her backpack purse at her feet. "Drm-mmnn." She fumbled inside, then pulled out a foil packet of tablets.

Lex looked at him, finally, as she held out the packet. Her bleary gaze captured his eyes, pleading, but somehow calm. Trusting.

He pulled over and took the medicine from her. "Dramamine?" He popped out an orange tablet.

"For the nausea." She bit down on the tablet, then pulled a bottle of water out of her purse.

Aiden drove on, listening to her directions. Her voice started to slur, her eyes drooping with sleepiness. "It's the medicine. Makes me tired." She yawned. "Follow Santa Teresa all the way down. A few miles." She sighed. Then sighed again. "I'm so sorry, Aiden."

Knight in Shining Armor. "It's okay."

"I'm so glad you came."

"Well, I needed my phone."

"Forgot about that. You're so nice to come pick it up." She yawned with a little sound at the back of her throat. "You don't make me feel bad. Not like those girls."

"They made you feel bad?" He shouldn't be encouraging her to talk, not with her disoriented like this.

She snuggled back into the leather seat, eyes closed. "They snipe. You don't. You don't fuss either."

She fell into a restless doze. She roused with a slurred, "Wedding cake."

"Dreaming about a wedding?"

She smiled but didn't open her eyes. "Mm-hm. You're not a bad guy."

"I'm glad you think that."

"Really. I could like you." She turned her head toward the window and sank deeper into the seat.

"Huh?"

She gave an enormous yawn and mumbled something that sounded like, "Will you marry me and save me from Grandma?"

He jerked the wheel back before he crashed the truck.

TWENTY

For the first time in weeks, Trish had come to church. Lex had come alone, not expecting her cousin to show up, but then Trish had slipped into a seat at the back about twenty minutes late.

Lex fidgeted in her pew, craning her neck to make sure Trish didn't slip out before the worship leader finished the closing prayer.

"Amen."

Lex shot out of her seat and scurried toward the back of the church. Trish had already slipped out the door.

If Trish had been at Mariko's shower, Lex wouldn't have said whatever she said to Aiden to make him unceremoniously dump her at her front door and sprint away. She had been so sleepy from the Dramamine, she couldn't remember. At least she'd remembered to go with Dad and get her car back from Mariko's house.

"Lex."

She skidded to a halt and turned around. "Venus. You didn't go to your church today?" Venus had switched from Lex's church after one too many of the single guys had been too persistent in their attention.

"No, I came here. I wanted to see you."

"Why?" Lex saw Trish duck into the women's room. Good. She had time to talk to Venus.

"I heard about the bridal shower."

A low moan rumbled out of her throat. "Let's not go there."

"How about a detox mud wrap?"

"Huh?" Lex frowned. "My stomach is still sensitive, Venus."

"No, dummy, a detoxifying skin treatment. It's at Belview Spa."

"I don't think my skin's that important."

"It's to *relax*, idiot."

"Oooh. Wow, that's nice of you, Venus." She saw Trish exit the women's restroom. "Hang on, I need to talk to Trish. Trish!"

Her cousin didn't turn around. She raced out of the building as if Mrs. Cathcart was chasing after her, asking her to teach Sunday school. Lex detoured around a few clusters of people chatting, then followed Trish out the door.

She stumbled out into the parking lot in time to see Trish nip into a cherry-red Mazda convertible with a slick Asian man at the wheel. They peeled out of the church lot.

Left behind. A hollowness ached in her stomach. Trish had never run away from Lex before. Why would she not want to be with her?

"Was that her boyfriend?" Venus's heels clunked against the blacktop.

"I guess." Lex couldn't hide the soft snuffle as she cleared her nose. "She didn't want to talk to me."

"Her loss. Stop feeling sorry for yourself. Come on." Venus walked toward her car, a silver convertible. "I'm driving."

"Pfffaugh. I can't look, I'm going to puke ..."

Venus gave an exasperated snort. "You don't have to look at it. Close your eyes."

"When I do, all I see is brown goo. Ugh ..." Lex's stomach shifted, as if uncertain whether to be nauseated or not.

She squeezed her eyes shut and sank deeper into the tub of mud. Actually, the heat felt amazingly good. Her old lower back injury—from the chair at work—had felt like a rock shoved at the base of her spine, but as she stretched out in the mud, the pressure slowly receded.

She heard the mud slurp as Venus shifted in her own tub. "Feels good, doesn't it?"

One thing about this sticky soak, it gave her mind license to wander into places she'd rather not go. Like why Trish had run away. The hurt at being left standing in the parking lot.

No, let's not go there. Think happy thoughts. Her brain didn't oblige, instead moving back to Mariko's shower. The mud looked a little like—

"Relax." Venus practically barked it at her.

"Your tone isn't very relaxing."

"Your face is all screwed up, so I know you're worrying about something."

She glanced over at Venus. "Did you hear Dad sold the house?"

"No, when?"

"Wednesday. But I have to move out in two and a half weeks."

"Where to?"

"Uh ... I'm looking." Lex needed to get going and look harder for a place to stay. Maybe she could rent a room from a house instead of a whole apartment. "Did I tell you I got into Wassamattayu tryouts?"

"That's great! When are they?"

"Next weekend. Problem is the high deposit fee."

"They charge for tryouts?"

"They refund it if you don't get picked. They want to be sure you can afford the league fees to play."

Venus sank deeper in her mud. "I'll pay for it for you."

"No!"

Venus gave her a lazy sidelong glance. "It's not a problem."

She knew Venus had a high position at her game development company, a few levels down from the corporate stratosphere, but Lex wouldn't be indebted to her. Not like that. "No, I have money saved."

"I thought that was for a down payment on a condo. Isn't that why you suffered through all those years living with your dad?"

"It's not enough for a 5 percent down payment. It's not enough for the girls' playoffs this summer either." Lex fidgeted, and the mud slapped against the sides of her porcelain tub. "That's why I was thinking I'd use it for Wassamattayu."

"Wouldn't it be better to use it for playoffs and then try to raise only a little more?" Venus shot her a sharp look.

Wassamattayu was the pinnacle of her volleyball career, but posh gym-member Venus could never understand that. "Wassamattayu membership isn't just for me. The club is filled with wealthy, sports-oriented yuppies. It's the perfect place to look for a sponsor for the team. For any of them, the cost for the girls' playoffs would be hardly a blip in their checking account, and they could get a tax write-off."

"Assuming you can convince one of them. Kind of a gamble, isn't it?"

Venus's dry voice sent a fizzle up Lex's spine. "They're athletes. We speak the same language. They'd understand my dilemma and be happy to sponsor the team."

"If you say so."

Her skepticism decided it for Lex. "I think it's a good idea. I think I'll use the money for Wassamattayu."

Aiden was beginning to think God liked playing practical jokes.

He drove all the way out here to south San Jose to run some hills, and whom did he see? The one person he'd be most embarrassed to talk to. Did she even remember her proposal of marriage?

Lex didn't even live in this area. What was the deal?

She hadn't seen him yet — she struggled up the hill, limping a bit. It looked like her ankle was bothering her.

He should avoid her. She represented everything his alarm system warned against: friends with a pushy girl he'd had to reject pretty hard, *related* to same girl, fanatically Christian enough to go to church regularly versus just talking about it. Common sense should tell him to stay away.

Except she was also attractive enough to make him lose his good sense. And then there was the small fact that she happened to be on his volleyball team, stole his phone, proposed marriage, and then way-laid his marathon training course.

He picked up his feet to catch up to her.

She veered left down a side street and out of sight.

His stomach bottomed out and left a little hollow spot down there. He needed to continue on his training course or he'd never be in shape for the race. He lost a little of his kick as he climbed the hill.

The first hill stretched his lungs as he sprinted to the top. On the way down, he cut through an empty grocery store parking lot and turned right around the corner of a trash shed.

"Ooomph!"

He hit someone soft, light. He staggered. She went down.

Lex. He'd collided with Lex. *No way. God, you have a strange sense of humor.*

He could have sworn he heard laughter.

"Are you okay? Your ankle—" He offered a hand to help her up.

She waved it away. "I'm fine." She hoisted herself up and took a few steps. "See?"

"You're limping."

"Am not." Her bottom lip shot out.

His eyebrow shot up a fraction before he got his face under control. "Okay. You're not."

She glared at him. "Are you making fun of me?"

"Not at all."

"Hmph." She looked back up the hill, and her face sagged.

"Are you training?"

"How did you know?"

"You told me you never run except for training."

"Oh." Her pale cheeks flushed rosy in the morning sun. "I'm, uh ... sorry I was so rude that time."

His neck relaxed. "It's okay." A simple apology and he caved. He was pathetic.

"So, are you training?" Lex asked him back.

"Yeah." He glanced at the hill. "I have a marathon in a few weeks."

"Oh. Well, I'll let you get to it." She turned into the parking lot and pulled her car key from her pocket.

"But I thought you were running."

She grimaced. "I feel kind of lazy today. I've ... had a lot of stuff happen. Besides the bridal shower."

"No, don't do that. Come on." He started jogging up the hill. "Come on."

She stared at him with a confused, annoyed look.

He gestured her to come. "Don't be a pansy."

He knew it would spur her. Yup, she broke into a run after him.

"I'm not a pansy." Her eyes on him were fierce.

"Of course not." He turned his blandest face at her.

She frowned.

He grinned.

Lex had rarely seen Aiden smile. He was usually so reserved, so controlled. Gosh, it made him look like Orlando Bloom. Her heart did a little jump-skip before settling back into a steady rhythm.

He ran a *lot* faster than she did. She shouldn't be so surprised. She'd never jogged with a true runner before. She usually set the pace with her volleyball friends, but here she struggled to keep up.

"Come on, you can do it. Just a few more feet at this pace."

"Rah—" *Pant, pant*—"rah."

"I'm a physical therapist and a trainer."

"So you're—" *Pant, pant*—"a professional bully."

He laughed. "I thought you wanted to be in shape."

"In shape." *Pant, wheeze.* "Not dead."

"Okay, now lift up your knees."

Her legs burned hotter than the Arizona sun. Her lungs would burst any minute now.

"What are you training for?" Aiden asked her. He wasn't even winded, the slime.

She gulped in air. "Wassamattayu."

"Wow. Congratulations. Volleyball?"

"Yeah."

"Pick up your knees more. When are tryouts?"

"Saturday."

"Oh, just a week. Come on, don't be lazy, pick up your knees. You want to do well, don't you?"

Determination prodded her like a lance to her fanny all the way up the hill, down the other side, and up another one. Perversely, it pleased her when Aiden started to sweat.

They made it back to the grocery store parking lot none too soon. Lex's entire body ached, even her skull.

"I'm sorry. You didn't get a very hard run because of me." If it had been her, she'd be mad and frustrated, but Aiden just shrugged.

"I had a harder training yesterday. I'll do a little more after you leave."

No way.

He cocked his head as he studied her. "You might want to close your mouth. There are a few bees around."

She scrunched her face at him.

He smiled, transforming his face from nondescript to dreamy.

Why hadn't she seen that before?

TWENTY-ONE

Rats, rats, rats! Of all times to be late! If not for that accident on the freeway, she would have been early instead of seven minutes late.

Lex screeched into the expansive parking lot for Wassamattayu's complex just off Central Expressway. She grabbed her heavy gym bag and ran/waddled into the lobby.

"Lex Sakai, volleyball tryouts."

The receptionist pointed her to the back of the sports club.

She entered the massive gym and tried not to pass out in awe. She always evaluated a new gym, and this one blew them all in the dust. Lofty ceilings, perfectly aligned lights so they weren't glaring, set at the right brightness to more than adequately light up the courts. The soles of her sneakers crackled against the freshly waxed floor. New aluminum bleachers with wooden seats, folded up for now, lined all four walls, but even if they were pulled out, there would be ample space around the court. The highest grade nets available stretched tautly across the two courts—no sagging or bouncing from those puppies.

Nine other women stretched or warmed up on the sidelines. There were no other Asians, and they all towered over her by four inches or more. Not a good sign.

The women seemed to eye each other—no band of sisters here. Lex recognized several from volleyball tournaments. They were all strong players.

Don't psyche yourself out. She pulled on her shoes and started stretching. The last women stretching started warming up, throwing the ball to flex their shoulder muscles, then moving into bumping, setting, and finally peppering back and forth.

Lex stretched as fast as she could. Why had she been late again? She could have sworn she had been watching the clock. Regret and guilt pulled her shoulder muscles together, made her heartbeat quicken.

No, stop that. You can't tighten up now.

She finally approached a threesome warming up — apparently three women who knew each other well. "Anyone want to warm up with me?"

The girls stopped laughing at each other. "We're done." A stick-straight blonde with ice-blue eyes grabbed the ball and motioned for her entourage to follow her off the court.

Lex's hands started shaking as her chest cavity became a furnace. Forget Nebuchadnezzar — she'd have fried Shadrach, Meshach, and Abednego if she got any hotter. The other women warming up in pairs avoided looking at her.

Her vision expanded as it did whenever she got ready-to-slam-a-ball-in-somebody's-face livid. The lights became brighter, the gym larger. She caught every movement — the miniscule swaying of the net, the dangling of the cords at each end, the tiniest shifting of weight from one woman as she prepared to pass.

Lex marched to the wall and threw the ball to warm up her shoulder. She had ceased to feel — all her energy focused on that ball. She was a raging fire, a nuclear star.

She moved to her most technically challenging bumping exercises, then shifted to setting. Lex hadn't warmed up solo in a long time — usually she peppered with a teammate, having fun, loosening up. Now, her muscles flowed like water, each movement precise with the higher level of challenge. She ought to do this more often.

A group of men and women entered the gym, one of them blowing a whistle to get everyone's attention. Lex joined the circle of women around them.

"I'm Darren, coach for both the coed and women's teams here at Wassamattayu. You all are trying out for a single position that will play on both teams." He paused to glance at his clipboard. "Wassamattayu is part of a larger network of elite sports clubs. You should have received a schedule of tournaments for both the coed and women's teams."

He gestured to the others with them, rattling off names. "These are members of the coed and women's team, and Krista here is my assistant coach."

Krista stepped forward. "Okay, let's start with some drills."

The drills were easy compared to the stuff Lex put her junior high school girls through. She also learned a few new ball control exercises she could add. The drills tired her but didn't wipe her out. She stood mopping her sweaty face while several of the other women bent double, gasping for air.

Hehehe.

She knew most of them would be better at blocking—their height alone made them more effective at the net. Lex got touches during the blocking drills, but no stuffs like some of the women. However, she performed well on the setting drills.

Lex was among the last group on the hitting line, after watching her six-foot-tall nemeses pound the balls inside the ten-foot line. She'd learned to hit smarter.

Lex sent a few good hits into the center of the court for her first two. Before she started her third hit, Darren stepped up to the other side of the net to block her. He nodded to her.

He hadn't blocked any of the other women during their drills.

She grinned. For him, she'd need a high set. "Five, please."

The setter sent a beautiful arcing ball that seemed to float in mid-air. Lex started her approach, planted, and lifted off.

Darren set up a good block, taking away the easy shot in the middle of the court. Last-minute, she torqued and sent the ball down the line. It landed squarely on the strip of white. Excellent.

Darren continued blocking for the other two girls in her hitting group. One got stuffed, the other hit it high and out.

Lex's turn again. This time he inched in to make the line shot harder. Lex cut the shot, a sweet short angle, right under his left armpit.

He grinned at her as they both landed.

Energy zoomed through her veins like liquid caffeine. Her lungs felt twice as large, her muscles twice as fast.

For the defensive drills, they paired her with two other girls at the back of the court. Lex subtly adjusted position, further from the brunette—who was a ball hog—but closer to the blonde—who was slow. She picked up a few hard, short shots near the net and got under the other balls so she made perfect, soft passes to the setter.

And then it ended. Lex felt like she'd hardly broken a sweat. She'd had more tiring sand workouts with Kin-Mun than the four hours from today.

The other women had left by the time Lex finished changing her shoes. Darren stood near the door, waiting for her.

As she passed, he gave her a high five. Looking around quickly, he leaned in toward her. "You nailed it."

Her insides glowed—she felt as if she were made of light. "Thanks."

"I talked briefly with Krista. It's pretty clear who we're going to pick." He lowered his voice even more, but his smile was like ethanol, making her burn brighter. "Lex, I'm looking forward to playing with you."

Where else to celebrate besides Hot Pot Town Restaurant with her three cousins?

Unless one of them brought a guy who wasn't a brother, a cousin, or even a close acquaintance.

Venus nudged Lex as Jennifer approached the restaurant from the parking lot with Mr. Gecko in tow — pale, buggy eyes, constantly licking his lips. "Who's that?"

"Her boyfriend?"

"Jennifer looks like even she can't stand him." Trish stared hard at the two of them. "Look, she keeps moving away from him whenever he gets close." Her phone rang. "Oh, it's Kazuo. Hey, babe ..." She wandered a few feet away.

Venus leaned close to Lex. "Did Trish explain why she ran away from you at church?"

"She said she never heard me call her."

Venus eyed her with a *How stupid do you think I am?* look.

"Yeah, I don't know if I believe her either." Lex shook her head.

"That boyfriend is bad news."

"Well then, you try talking to her. She avoids being alone with me."

"Fine." Venus was raring to go.

"Oh, I forgot to tell you. I found housing. I called one of the ladies from church. I heard her niece wanted to rent the extra room in her town house. Bedroom on the second floor, carport in the back. I'll go look at it tomorrow."

"That's great."

"Things are totally looking up for me."

Jennifer joined them. "H-hey, guys."

Gecko had sidled up to Venus, trying to give her a discreet look down. Venus backed up a step and unleashed her famous organ-shrinking glare. His eyes popped open, and he scurried closer to Jennifer like a Chihuahua.

"Who's your friend, Jenn?" Lex didn't want to call him Gecko all night, although Venus probably wouldn't mind.

"Um ... this is Hector."

"Perfect." Venus sneered at him.

"How'd you guys meet?" Lex planted a cool smile on her face.

"Oh ... Actually, we just met tonight."

Lex raised her eyebrows at Jenn.

"Well Lex, when you called, Grandma was at our house."

Oh, no.

"And she asked me to invite Hector along." Jenn cast a desperate glance at the restaurant doors. "Should we go in?"

Lex hooked her talons into Jennifer's arm to hold her back as Hector followed Venus to the restaurant, trying to ogle her backside. *Creep.* "Jenn, what's the deal? Why didn't you just tell Grandma no?"

"*You* try telling Grandma no."

"Why'd you tell her you were going out with me? You know what she's been up to."

"Grandma's been over at our house a lot lately. It's *wearing* on me." Jenn snatched her arm away and marched into the restaurant.

Lex stood a moment, too surprised to move. Jenn never snapped at people.

She gestured to Trish, who went inside without her.

"Lex! Wait up!" She heard another voice.

Lex turned and saw her brother. "Richard, what are you doing here?" With yet another male friend?

He hustled up to her, while a dark-skinned guy followed at a slower pace. "Grandma told me you'd be here."

Lex fought the urge to scream.

He ignored her, instead motioning to his friend. "This is Oliver."

"Hi. Nice to meet you." No way was Oliver one of Richard's friends. They all tended to have the same slick charm, but Oliver seemed rather mild-mannered, like a tanned, Asian Clark Kent. "Bye, Richard."

"Wait a minute, where are you going?"

"We're having dinner."

"I know. We'll join you."

Lex lowered her voice to a hiss. "I don't remember asking you."

Richard chucked her under the chin as he breezed past her toward the restaurant doors. "I'm your brother. I don't need to be asked."

Lex stormed after them.

Hot Pot Town looked more like a warehouse than a restaurant. A mish-mash of tables packed every open space, and they managed to find a cafeteria-style table near the food buffets. The waiter started their tabletop burner topped by a steel kettle of chicken broth — the "hot pot" — and took their drink orders.

Lex wandered to the refrigerated raw meats and selected chicken and beef, sliced so thin she could almost see her white plate through them. Each of them would cook their own selections in the broth at the table. She had moved to the marinated seafood when she realized Gecko followed her.

"So, you're Lex?"

"Yeah."

He didn't get the message from her clipped tone. "I'm Hector."

"I know." *And I don't need to know anything more about you.* Hmm, the marinated scallops or shrimp? She got a scoop of each.

Gecko hovered near her shoulder. She jerked away from his invasion of her personal space.

"So, Lex, what do you do?" Joviality so heartily false it sounded like a Barney movie.

She slammed him with a hard, direct glare. "Don't even. I know Grandma told your mother — "

"Aunt, actually."

Lex shrugged and went back to the black bean sauce chicken.

"Well, then, since all the cards are on the table ..." Gecko's voice grew more forceful, less pleasant. "Let's be honest here. I'd just like some game tickets." Gecko smiled as if he'd said something intelligent.

"No." Ohh, they had Chinese broccoli and bok choy.

"Aw, come on." Slime coated his voice. "I'll make it worth your while."

"Since we're being honest, Geck — Hector, I have to tell you that you'd be a pretty boring date." Lex spooned some corn onto her plate.

"Who's talking date? I can make it worth your while *the other way.*"

His attempt at being subtle, she guessed. He'd make a lousy *Yakuza.* "You mean money?" She pitched her voice rather loud.

He sucked in his cheeks and flapped his hands at her. "Keep it down."

"You mean money?" She said it even louder, if possible.

"Yes, yes, just shut up."

She rescued a piece of fish before it rolled off the edge of her plate. She had finished getting food for the hot pot. "The answer's no."

"I can pay as much as you want—"

Lex turned toward their table, but Gecko stood in the way and laid a hand on her arm. She jolted away. "Listen, buddy, jailbait isn't my first career choice."

"Who's to know?"

"What about the word 'no' do you not understand?"

"Oh, come on—"

"Hey, Lex."

She'd never been so glad to see Aiden. Yet again. "What are you doing here?"

Aiden lifted an eyebrow. " 'Why, hello, Aiden. How are you?' "

She smiled. "Hello, Aiden. How are you?"

"I'm fine. I'm here with my friend Spenser and his girlfriend."

"I'm here to celebrate Wassamattayu tryouts."

"Great! How'd they—"

"Excuse me, *Aiden,* we're having a conversation." Gecko thrust his face in between them.

Aiden's face became stone. "Sounded to me like you'd already finished."

"Not by a long shot."

"Excuse me?" Lex turned to Gecko and eyed his prominent Adam's apple. A good hard blow right there would shut him up.

"Your grandma promised me those tickets."

"Well, that's just too bad."

"I was counting on them."

"Gee, you can count?"

Gecko's bloodshot eyes looked like they were going to pop out of his skull. "Look, you—"

Aiden's whipcord figure slipped between them. "The lady said no."

Lex backed away from them. Other people had started to notice their argument.

Gecko's face twitched like a rabid rabbit. "I wasn't talking to you."

"Well, I'm talking to you." The edge to Aiden's voice had the ring of a sword being drawn. "She said no. Just leave it."

"Get out of my way."

"Let's discuss this outside."

"I'm not going anywhere with you." Gecko suddenly thrust at Aiden's shoulders, making him stumble backward.

Lex turned to get out of the way.

Aiden's arm reached out to break his fall. His shoulder hit Lex right at the knee joint.

She felt and heard a sickening *pop.*

Pain like a vice grip exploded around her kneecap, in the soft area under the knee, along the inside edge of her leg. She fell to the ground, raw meat and vegetables landing on her stomach, her legs, her hair. She grabbed her right knee.

No. Oh, God, no.

Swelling rushed into the joint like a scalding river. Sharp stabbing in her joint, in cacophony with the hard pulsing of the pain, trying to break out of her skin.

No, please, no.

She lifted her leg, and her shin dangled at a slightly odd angle from her thigh.

No, not now. No.

"Shhh, Lex, it'll be okay." Venus's face appeared in front of her.

Lex hadn't realized she'd been screaming.

TWENTY-TWO

Aiden held open the front door as Lex hopped inside, one arm hooked over Venus's neck. Poor Venus bent over like an old woman to make up for the height difference.

Lex didn't say anything. She collapsed on the sagging couch, breathing hard, trying not to grimace too much from the pain. Jennifer rushed into the living room with a couple pillows she'd snagged from Lex's bedroom, easing them under Lex's knee.

She stared at her knee, ballooned out to twice its normal size. She started crying again.

Venus shielded her, while Jennifer whispered something to Aiden. Venus turned to wave at him as he left. "Thanks, Aiden."

Lex still hadn't said anything. She couldn't open her mouth. Her brain ordered her to say something—at least thank him for driving her home—but her throat had closed shut with Crazy-Glue. He had checked her knee at the restaurant, but his grim look and firm command to see a doctor ASAP had crushed her hopes.

Venus's face had a sad, calm cast to it, like a pale *Noh* mask. Jennifer's eyes glistened with tears as she sat at the other end of the couch. Venus sank down onto the sturdy coffee table. "When does your dad get back?"

"Tnnm." Lex cleared her throat. "Ten." Saying the word exhausted her.

They sat in silence, listening to the familiar ticking of the old cuckoo clock. Fog filled Lex's head. But the mist cleared a little, and she realized who was missing.

"Where's Trish?" Her voice had a soft, plaintive tone she didn't recognize as her own.

Venus glanced at Jenn, who bit her lip. Venus touched Lex's shoulder. She jumped.

"Trish . . . had to go."

Lex didn't remember seeing Trish at all — inside or outside — after the — She swallowed. "When? Where did she have to go?"

Venus's eyes darted away. Jenn fiddled with a loose thread from the couch.

"One of you has to tell me." Her sentence ended on a sob.

Venus sighed. It sounded frustrated. "Trish — " Venus bit her name out — "decided to meet up with her boyfriend."

The news struck Lex like a slap to her face. She exhaled sharply but couldn't breathe back in. She pressed her lips together to stop them from trembling.

"It's not you, Lex. It's her." Venus's eyes had narrowed into black *goma* seeds, dead and dangerous in her face. Her fingers curled as if around Trish's neck.

It didn't make the emptiness right below Lex's rib cage somehow fill up again.

"Do you . . . uh . . . want to watch SportsCenter?" Jennifer reached for the remote control.

"No!" Lex's hand snapped out to grab at her. A knife chopped into her knee. She winced and gingerly touched her kneecap.

She couldn't watch people doing athletic things. Not now. Not when her own body had failed her like this.

She'd seen several people tear their ACL — the ligament connecting the tibia bone to the femur. She'd watched them on crutches both before and after the surgery, the long recovery. Some of them never played volleyball again . . .

No, don't think that way! Lots of people came back just as strong from ACL surgery.

However, lots of people didn't tear their ACL right after nailing Wassamattayu tryouts. Right after finding a room on the second floor of a town house.

Lex crumpled her face, trying not to cry again. She sniffled. Jenn handed her the box of Kleenex from the end table.

Venus took a tissue too. "One good thing has come out of this."

"What?" Lex blew her nose.

"Mariko is going to be fuming."

Lex wasn't supposed to do this alone. Trish had let her down again, right after her apologies and protests that she wanted to help her injured cousin.

Lex took a shaky breath at the entrance to the MRI center. *You can do this, even alone.* She had to do a sideways hop to both pull open the glass door and manage her crutches, but in the past week, she'd gotten pretty savvy on her crutches from navigating the cubicles at work. Behind her, the taxi sped away to a duet of honks from the two cars it cut off.

She hobbled up to the receptionist's counter. "Lex Sakai. I have an MRI scheduled for two."

The sour-faced woman checked her computer. "You're late."

"I'm sorry. My ride never showed up—"

"You're lucky. We don't have anyone after you, so we can still work you in."

"Gee, thank you." Her voice didn't quite have a meek, grateful tone. The woman glanced up at her. Lex gave a weak smile.

"Have a seat until the tech calls you."

As if it weren't bad enough her heart pounded in her chest, she had to deal with snippy people. Lex hobbled around the arrangement of chairs in the waiting area. She finally managed to get into position to sink into one when a door opened at the far end of the room.

"Lex Sakai?"

Anakin Skywalker stood in the doorway. After he turned bad, and sans cape. Glorious golden curls contrasted with his bloodshot eyes and fanatical "world domination" expression. His head looked like it floated in midair until he gestured with his black-clad arm. Then she saw that his all-black ensemble had blended into the background.

"You're late." His voice rumbled deep and menacing.

"I'm sorry, I—"

"Just follow me." He turned down the hallway behind the door.

Gee, that's not creepy at all. She had a surreal sensation of following Luke into the cave.

She maneuvered back around the chairs, but just before she reached the doorway, it closed in her face. Brilliant technician hadn't even stayed to hold it open for her.

She turned the knob. Locked.

Frustration overtook the nervous twitching in her limbs. She pounded on the door and almost lost her balance on the crutches. As she righted herself, the door swung open to Mr. Dark Side's dour face.

He gave her a set of scrubs and showed her a closet-sized changing room. The room didn't even have a chair for her to sit on. She had to balance on one leg while she unstrapped herself from the Velcro-and-metal brace her sports doctor had given to her at her appointment a few days ago. It made her feel like a cyborg. The brace crashed to the ground.

She shed her warm-up pants and hopped into the flimsy paper shorts Anakin had given to her. The cotton top followed.

She left her brace and her clothes on the floor. Getting out of the changing room reminded her of her office at work. She backed up, pulled open the door, and then stepped out. Anakin sat in a hallway chair waiting for her, foot jiggling. Another frown when she appeared.

He led her into a small, sterile room crammed with the biggest toilet paper roll she'd ever seen. Except it was made of hard plastic instead of toilet paper. A table was attached to the roll, and he stabbed a black-painted fingernail at it. "Hop up."

The cold temperature and complex machinery made her shiver. Too much like a hospital. She took small steps to turn around— quite difficult with two extra "legs"—and sat down. "What about my shoes?"

He loosed a frustrated grunt as he turned around and exited. He returned with a plastic bag. "Dump your stuff in here."

She shed her shoes. "I left my clothes back in the changing room."

He looked like she'd asked him to give her his firstborn child. "Fine, I'll get them." He pointed at her leg. "Put that in the holster."

Like a gun about to go off? Sounded like her temper. She lifted her knee gently to drop it into the plastic thingy that looked like a big stalk of celery.

Anakin came around the other side and grabbed her leg.

"Ow! What are you doing?"

"Just positioning it correctly."

He pulled and pushed. Lex gritted her teeth, wincing with each rough movement. Her knee started to feel warm again, like a fever in the joint. "Watch it! You're going to injure it more."

He gave a last tug. "Okay, lie back."

He left the room—thankfully—but then the table started to move her toward the toilet paper roll.

"CAN YOU HEAR ME?" His voice shot out over the ceiling speaker as loud as a rock concert.

"Turn it down. Are you trying to give me hearing problems too?"

"How's this."

It was a statement, not a question, but she answered anyway. "It's fi—"

"Okay, now keep perfectly still or else the MRI won't work."

Bam! Bam! Bam! At first Lex thought they were gunshots. Then she realized the sound came from the machine.

Wait a minute. How long was this going to take? She didn't know how long she could stand the firecrackers from the toilet paper roll . . .

It seemed like forever. Luckily, the machine didn't snap, crackle, and pop the entire time. Finally, his voice blasted over the loudspeaker, making it vibrate. "Okay, you're done."

Praise God.

She got her clothes back on, although pulling up the warm-up pants was like threading a wet noodle into a keyhole.

As she left, the tech handed her the MRI photos.

"Th—" Thanks for what? The second worst day of her life?

He didn't notice her hesitation. He just shook his head.

"What is it?"

"You'll need to verify with your doctor, but it looks like you tore your ACL. You'll need surgery."

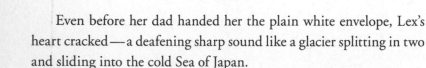

Even before her dad handed her the plain white envelope, Lex's heart cracked—a deafening sharp sound like a glacier splitting in two and sliding into the cold Sea of Japan.

You have been accepted into the Wassamattayu sports club for the coed and women's volleyball teams . . .

She folded the letter up precisely, sharpening the folds, sliding it back into the envelope. She laid it on the coffee table next to the couch where she lay with her knee propped up.

Darren had called earlier that day to tell her of her acceptance.

"Darren . . . I tore my ACL last week." Her voice cracked. Her nails dug into the phone, making her cuticles ache.

"Are you sure?"

"I had an MRI and saw my doctor today. I have surgery scheduled for a couple weeks from now."

"Lex . . ." A heavy *whoosh* over the phone as he sighed. "We have an Injured Reserve list, but it's usually as long a wait as the wait list."

Tears stung her eyes. She snapped her jaw shut and bit her tongue.

"I'm sorry, Lex. I'll put you on the IR list. Maybe in a few years."

Click.

The severing of all her hopes.

She swallowed as she stared at the envelope. Insult to injury. Insult to ACL injury.

She picked up the envelope and tore it neatly in two. Then again. And again. Tiny pieces rained into her lap like white tears.

"I can't do it again, Lex." Trish's bloodshot eyes darted toward Lex, then out the living room window. Her shaking hand picked at the fuzz on her sweatshirt.

"Do what again, Trish? I've never torn my ACL before." Lex had hoped Trish's arrival at her house meant she'd drive Lex back to work, but no way would she get into a car with Trish in her condition. "Did you call in sick to work? I've never seen you this hungover since college."

"I'm not hungover." Trish answered too quickly, too emphatically. She scrubbed at her cheeks, which only turned them from pale bags to pink bags.

"No, you were just too *tired* to pick me up for my MRI. Which was at 11:00 a.m."

"I already said I was sorry." Trish didn't sound like it.

"You know what? You can make it up to me if you'll help me the few days after my surgery."

"That's just it, Lex. I can't do it again. This is just like the last time."

"What last time? My sprained ankles?"

"No ... you know ... after the rape."

Arctic winter flash-froze her heart. Lex had never spoken the word. Trish hadn't either, until now. The ugly sound settled in the room like dirty snow on a roadway. "I don't understand."

"You were so depressed afterward."

Lex didn't clearly remember the days, even weeks after the attack. She remembered feeling like weights were on her legs, her arms. She opened her mouth, but she couldn't speak about it.

Trish kept talking. "I understand the trauma for you and all that, but being with you drained me emotionally."

Lex remembered Trish with her in those days — Trish as her constant, the only bright star in her blustery night. Trish's smile, Trish's touch on her arm, her shoulder, her head — the only touch Lex could tolerate at the time. Outside of her dad and brother, only Trish knew what had happened to her. She hadn't even told Venus or Jenn, much less Grandma.

Lex swallowed. "I was counting on you to help me through the surgery."

Trish shook her head, her eyes on the walls, the ceiling, out the window. "Kazuo says I'm giving too much of my time, that you're being too clingy and demanding."

"What?"

"I can't do it again, Lex."

Lex sat there, breathing hard and fast. And really, what could she say? *Oh, okay. I promise not to be a basket case now that I've lost my knee and Wassamattayu in the same day.*

Trish sighed into the silence, then turned and walked out the front door. She shut it firmly behind her.

Lex stared at it. She realized she hoped it would open again, and she looked away.

Her gaze fell on her bulky leg, braced in a black web of Velcro and metal. The physical pain didn't come close to the aching in her heart every time she saw it. Her first major surgery.

She'd never thought it could happen to her. A few sprained ankles, a few torn muscles here and there. Nothing serious.

This . . . This sucked the life out of her soul. She felt hollow and fragile.

She never felt hollow and fragile. She was always strong and healthy.

Maybe she'd never be strong or healthy again.

Lex squeezed her eyes shut as a tear spilled out. She bit her tongue, hard. The pain helped her focus, kept her from exploding into a billion little fragments.

Who would take care of her? She and her dad moved out this weekend. She could no longer handle the stairs for the room in the condo she'd found, so she had called and taken a ground-floor studio in south San Jose, the only thing she could afford, sight unseen because she couldn't get a hold of Trish to check it out for her. Maybe she had been relying on Trish too much lately.

Had Lex been smothering her? When she usually only saw Trish once or twice a week at church or Bible study? But she tended to call Trish when she needed her for something. Maybe that was smothering.

Lex sighed, but it came out like a sob. Just call her a wet, smothering blanket.

Who would take care of her? Dad? No—Dad had never been comfortable with helping her with personal stuff. He'd always stayed away from it, leaving one of her aunts to help her when she was growing up.

Jennifer? She'd be sympathetic and mothering, but she had to work. Venus? Lex had never been as close to prickly Venus as Trish.

She had no one . . .

The phone rang. Lex measured the distance between the couch and the cordless, then hauled herself to her feet to pick it up on the fourth ring. "Hello?"

"Lex, it's Venus. This is going to weird you out, but I suddenly felt like I should call. Maybe it was God trying to talk to me."

Lex burst into tears.

Venus sighed. "I guess God was right."

Say good-bye.

Lex memorized the shape of the funny door knocker on the old oak door, the crooked front window, the sagging roofline. Besides that rental house in college with her three cousins, and that very brief time she'd had her own apartment—dark memories there—she'd only known this house. Mom had died here. It felt like leaving her all over again.

Behind her, Venus slammed her trunk. "Is this all?"

"Yeah. Dad bought me a storage unit and dropped off the rest of the boxes yesterday." Separated from all her things.

Venus got behind the wheel and strapped her seatbelt on while Lex got into the passenger side of the beat-up Honda. "Are you sure we should take my car?"

"With mine, we'd take two trips because the trunk isn't big enough."

"I'm just not sure this thing will make it with all the extra weight."

"It had better." Venus fired up the engine. It roared to life, then died.

"See?" Lex thrust her hands out, as if saying a mantra to the goddess of old cars.

Venus gave her a mean sidelong look. "Grow up, will you?" She banged her hand against the dashboard, then turned the key.

The Honda came to life.

"How did you do that?"

"Cars respond to bullying more than praying."

The car whined and complained on the freeway, especially at the speed Venus made it maintain. Once on streets, it rebelled, belching smoke and jerking every time it started up from a red light. They limped into the driveway to her new apartment building, the Honda moaning and sputtering.

Venus slammed her door and stabbed a finger at Lex over the oxidized hood. "How do you stand driving this thing?"

Lex flung her arms wide. "Do you see me with enough money to buy a new one?" She moved on her crutches to the manager's apartment.

A cheerful Hispanic woman answered the door, patting her gray bun in place and reeking of garlic.

"Hi, I'm Lex Sakai. I'm renting a ground-floor apartment."

"Oh, yeah, yeah. I've been waiting for you. Oh, injured your knee? No wonder you need a ground-floor unit. You'll like this one. The last owner who had pets moved out seven years ago, so the smell's gone away by now. Here's your key—oh, I guess you can't carry it and walk with crutches, can you? I'll carry it and show you to your apartment. Watch the hanging pots—oops, that one nailed you, huh? Be careful about Mrs. Delarosa's pansies, over there. Sometimes I think if people just breathe on them they die, but she gets so upset. Aw, don't worry about Mr. Parks's dog, he can't get past the security door, and he's more bark than bite. Mr. Parks walks him twice a day without fail. Here we are. I'll open the door for you. There. Welcome home!" The woman flung open the door and waggled a few ringed fingers like Vanna White.

Musty smell—it had been unused for a long time. Just enough floor space for her bed and her boxes, although it would be a squeeze to get to the bathroom. The short carpet was stained but clean. Same with the walls. A mini kitchenette took up an entire wall.

"It's ... fine." Lex managed a polite smile.

"Oh, there's your friend with your boxes. I'll let you unpack. Here's your key, I'll leave it on the counter. If you need anything, just ask me." She bustled away.

Man, that woman could talk. But friendly. Probably nosy too.

Venus crossed the threshold and stopped. Stared. Tried not to grimace. "Are you sure about this, Lex?"

"Do I have a choice? I couldn't afford anything else."

"This place is a dump."

"Venus, what happened to 'speaking the truth in love'?"

"That is love. You're lucky I don't dump this box and leave you stranded."

Lex knew she was kidding, but the dingy surroundings seemed to almost weigh her down.

Venus dropped the box she held into a corner. "I'll bring in the pieces of your bed." Lex was glad they were light enough for her to handle by herself.

After she left, a head popped into the open doorway. "Ha-roh?"

"Hi." Lex smiled in greeting at the wizened round face, the round body, even the gray hair caught up in a bun as round as the ones in the Chinese bakeries.

The eyes disappeared as she smiled, her mouth in the shape of a plump pot sticker. "I Mrs. Chang. Next door."

She'd picked up at least a few phrases from Venus and Jenn's Chinese dads. "*Ni hao ma?*"

Mrs. Chang exploded into cackles. "You accent terrible."

Lex laughed.

"Japanee?"

Lex nodded.

"You eat *chou dofu*?"

What was that? Lex shrugged and shook her head.

"I get you some." Mrs. Chang disappeared.

Venus appeared with one side of her aluminum bed frame. "Neighbor?"

"I think so. She's Chinese."

"Does she speak Cantonese or Mandarin?"

"Dunno. I can't tell the difference."

Venus sat a hand on her hip. "Why not? Trish can, and she's as 100 percent Japanese as you."

"This coming from a 50 percent Japanese."

"At least my dad taught me Mandarin, thank you very much."

"Trish can tell because she sings — she's got a musical ear. The only note I can tell is if a volleyball is bounced and it makes a flat squish."

Venus snorted in amusement in spite of herself. "When's your dad coming by with the box spring and mattress?"

"He said he had something to do until three. So he'll swing by the house, pick it up, and bring it here around four."

"Something to do? Like what?"

Lex shrugged. "I never asked. He didn't want to talk about it."

Venus propped her hands on her hips. "Your family's lack of communication is something else. How do you guys get anything done?"

"Hey, hey, hey. I grew up with one brother and a single dad. I'm lucky when they tell me good morning."

"Ha-roh?" Mrs. Chang peeked her head in again. "I bring you—"

Venus snapped as straight as a Japanese bow. "Lex—"

"Thanks, Mrs. Chang." Lex took the plastic food container filled with brown-beige cubes. Oh, it looked like fried tofu.

Eww, what was that smell?

Venus's mouth had frozen in a plastic smile. She murmured to Lex, "Don't open it. Just say thank you to Mrs. Chang."

"What are you talking about?" Lex tugged at the container. She loved Chinese food. She ate anything Jenn's dad served her, even when he didn't know the English name for it.

"I'mgettingtherestofyourbed." Venus disappeared like a ninja.

Mrs. Chang motioned to the food and beamed. "You like? Good."

Lex cracked the cover open.

Ugghhh.

She didn't think anything could smell so rotten in her life. She cranked the lid back down. Her eyes watered, but she slapped a toothy smile onto her face. "Th-thanks, Mrs. Chang."

"You want more, you ask me." She turned and strolled away.

Venus reappeared with another part of her bed, then gagged as she entered the studio. "You dummy. I told you not to open it."

Lex wiped at the tears gushing from her stinging eyes. "What the heck is that?"

"Stinky tofu. From what I've been told, it's an acquired taste."

"You can actually eat that?"

"My parents' cat won't even eat it."

"Ugh." Lex tossed the container onto the counter. "I heartily apologize for not listening to you."

"You? Apologizing? That's a first." Venus drew her eyes wide.

"Oh, bite me."

Venus chuckled and started putting the bed frame together. "This is kind of a long commute to work for you, isn't it?"

"It's only temporary."

"Is your boss okay with your leaving?"

"Yeah, Russell okayed my leave, no problems." Lex tugged at one of the Velcro straps on her brace. "Besides, the doctor said I could go back to work six weeks after surgery. But I'll still be in rehab, so I'll need to take off time to go to physical therapy sessions each week."

"I guess I'll have to take you to PT until they say you can drive."

Lex winced. "Yeah. Thanks a lot, Venus." She coughed at the dust in the air. "After the surgery, when my knee can handle stairs again, I'll look for a room in a town house."

Venus snapped the aluminum frame into place. Something seemed to catch her eye. She squinted toward the far corner. Lex glanced over. A small spot on the carpet.

The spot moved.

"Aaaiiieee!" Venus climbed to her knees on top of a box of books. Lex sat on another box and drew her legs up.

The mouse scurried away.

TWENTY-THREE

She couldn't pray.

Lex huddled in the middle of her bed and stared at the clock. She should try to get some sleep for surgery tomorrow. It would also keep her from thinking about the bottled water in her fridge that she'd like to chug in defiance of the "no water after midnight" rule the surgery nurse had given her.

Even after a week in her apartment, Lex still kept her ears strained for rodent-like sounds. The mouse hadn't made a repeat appearance, but she still surrounded her bed with traps.

The blessedly silent studio seemed like a cage with walls too thick to let her prayers through. Would God even hear her if she did pray?

I'm pretty mad at You, You know. Yeah, You probably already know.

Maybe she should read her Bible. Except ... it still lay packed somewhere in her boxes. Besides, she had no idea where to read. Knowing her luck, she'd open it up to a list of genealogy. Or worse, some bloody, violent war.

She felt abandoned, just like when Mom had died. The chemo that made her sick, and then the futility of it all. Dying at home, with Lex's hand holding hers. Mom had even dressed up for the occasion.

Lex shivered. It probably wasn't the wisest thing to think about Mom and dying the night before knee surgery.

She needed to be strong. She should think about what she did have. She had Venus taking care of her after surgery. She had a ground-floor apartment, found last-minute, and the mouse hadn't returned. She had a terrific surgeon—the doctor for the Oakland Raiders, no less.

So go to sleep and let him do his thing tomorrow.

Lex lay down. Listened to the quiet apartment.

Couldn't sleep. Obsessed about water.

"You're not going to need anesthesia." Venus nudged her again. "You'll fall dead asleep on the table."

"Can you not use the word 'dead'?"

Lex shifted in the uncomfortable chair in the surgery center's waiting room. Actually, it wasn't that uncomfortable, she just didn't like sitting in it. Especially when she wanted to drink a lake and eat a horse.

The door at the other end of the room opened, and a nurse clad in colorful cartoon scrubs smiled at her. "Lex Sakai?"

She trudged through the door into the main area of the surgery center. The nurse directed her to a bathroom, where she set a gown, socks with rubber treads, a bonnet, a bag for her clothes, and a urine cup on a chair.

Lex picked up the cup. "I haven't drunk any water since yesterday." She sounded kind of whiny.

The nurse had a venti-size order of patience. "That's okay if you can't go, but please try. Now change into everything, but you can keep your underwear on." She closed the door behind her.

At least this bathroom had a chair. Lex unstrapped her leg brace and undressed, shivering in the chilled tile room. The bootie socks were warm, but the gown gaped in front (at least it didn't gape in *back*). She also managed a trickle into the cup and left it on a shelf with a huge sign "Urine cups."

Oh man, she was thirsty. She wanted a tall glass of ice water, chilled beads of condensation dripping down the sides, pooling at the base.

She whimpered.

Lex exited the bathroom, and the nurse who'd been leaning against the wall waiting for her, gave her a pat on the back. Lex twitched away, even though the nurse had meant her touch to be reassuring.

She led Lex to a small room with two recliners separated by a curtain, each in front of a TV set. Venus stood inside, talking to a dark-skinned Asian man who seemed to be demonstrating a strange contraption. He saw her and introduced himself as Alan.

"This is your CPM machine—Continuous Passive Motion machine. After surgery, you'll put this on your bed and strap your leg into the cradle—" he pointed to a metal cradle lined with soft faux lambskin—"and turn the machine on. It will bend and straighten your leg very slowly, and for only a few degrees at first. You'll increase the degree during the next two weeks."

"Alan told me how to set it up when I get you home." Venus was far from flirty or chummy with Alan, but it had been years since Lex had seen her so relaxed around a male. He must be one of the few who had the courtesy not to ogle her gorgeous face and lust-inspiring figure.

The nurse sat her in the recliner and then covered her with warmed blankets. *Warmed.* A perfect temperature. The gown didn't seem so skimpy anymore.

"Take this marker and write 'yes' on your surgery leg and 'no' on your good leg."

Okay, now that was just scary. "You mean sometimes they open up the wrong leg?" Her voice had a screech at the end.

The nurse winced at the sound. "No, don't panic. They don't open you up. This will be arthroscopic, so he'll only cut three small holes into your knee."

"He can repair it with only three small holes?" Her voice still had that screechy thing going on.

"Oh, yes, it's the best kind of surgery. Don't worry." She set a hand on Lex's shoulder. Lex jumped.

Another nurse joined her. They started an IV on her and scrubbed down her bad leg with some neon orange soap that looked like it zapped every last germ.

The nurses left, and Venus sat in a chair next to her.

Suddenly, the magnitude of what Lex was about to go through smacked her across the head with the force of a two-by-four plank. She'd be unconscious. And she might not wake up.

Her stomach started to ripple. Her hands trembled where they lay against the warm blankets. She licked her dry lips, swallowed against the ball of fuzz lodged in the base of her throat.

She had to go to the bathroom. The warm blankets added to her incontinence problem.

"Venus, flag down a nurse."

"Why?" Venus tore her eyes from the TV.

"I need to know if it's okay to go to the bathroom."

"Sure," the nurse chirped once Venus had explained everything. "Just take your IV bag. There's a hook next to the toilet."

Venus had to carry the bag while Lex grabbed her crutches and hopped to the bathroom. Once she sat down, the IV line also got in her way.

Back in her recliner, she felt a little better, although her stomach still jiggled.

A nurse peeked in on the older woman sitting in the other recliner. "You'll be going into surgery in a few minutes, Mrs. Tyler."

Lex couldn't see her around the curtain, but she heard Mrs. Tyler's quavering voice speaking to her husband. "Charles, look at me."

"Mm-hm."

"Turn off that TV. Look at me. This might be the last time I talk to you."

"Now, don't be scared, honey—"

"Don't be scared? How can you say that to me now?"

"It's a simple procedure—"

"I might never wake up."

Lex's chest squeezed tight.

"Charles, promise me you'll give me a nice funeral."

"Honey—"

"And don't invite your cousin. I can't stand her. And promise me you'll marry again. You need someone to take care of you." Her voice ended on a sob.

"Honey, you'll be fine."

"I'll miss you so much, Charles." *Sniff, sniff.*

"I'll miss you too—I mean, what are you talking about? You'll be okay."

"And don't forget to water the gardenia plant."

The nurse bustled in. "Mrs. Tyler, they're ready for you."

"Oh! Good-bye, Charles. Don't ever forget me."

A nurse wheeled the weeping woman out the door. As she passed Lex, she clutched her bad shoulder—marked with a "yes"—and her distraught husband trailed behind.

Lex and Venus stared at each other with wide eyes after she had left. Venus bit her lip. "You, um ... want me to pray for you?"

"Yeah ... yeah, I guess."

"Dear God ... Thanks for Lex. Thanks for her *really skilled* surgeon. And *really good* nurses. And *really excellent* surgery center. Please help her feel calm. And, uh ... help her wake up afterward. Amen."

"Gee, Venus, you pray so eloquently."

"Hey, it's a prayer."

"True."

A new patient strolled into the room, this time a college-aged, athletic redhead. "Hi." She smiled at Lex and Venus.

Lex searched her joints for any swelling. "Are you sure you need surgery?" she asked the girl.

"Oh, sure." She sat in the recliner and automatically held out her arm for the IV. She peeked at Lex around the curtain. "I re-tore my ACL a month ago, so the swelling's gone down."

"Oh."

"Yeah, this is my third ACL surgery."

"*Third?*"

"Uh huh. I keep snapping them like rubber bands. But Daddy's an ex-football player, and he has great insurance. He coaches a college team now, but he's loaded."

Lex suddenly had visions of years of surgeries draining her pocketbook. "Venus, I need to go to the bathroom again."

"What's your problem?" Venus grabbed the IV bag.

"I have to go when I get scared."

"Oh, great."

Lex relieved herself—wow, she had a lot this time—and sat back down just in time for her anesthesiologist to arrive.

Dr. Frank looked like he'd sucked a lemon. He adjusted his glasses and glared at her over the rims. "Any allergies?"

"Not that I know of."

"Any family history of heart disease, yadda, yadda, yadda?"

Did he just say, "Yadda, yadda, yadda"?

"Uh ... no."

He sighed and pursed his lips. "How'd you tear it?"

"Accident."

He grunted. "Well, obviously. How?"

"Someone fell into me."

"Hmph." He scribbled in his chart. "Okay, that's it. Oh, and I have to disclose that there's a slight chance of complications, nothing is 100 percent guaranteed, yadda, yadda, yadda. Understand?"

He liked that "yadda" word. "I guess."

"No questions?"

"Uh ..."

"No." Venus pinned him with a hard gaze. "Just make sure she wakes up again."

"Yeah, yeah, yeah." He left.

Lex's legs quivered. Her mouth had become Death Valley. "Venus, I need to go again."

Venus rolled her eyes but reached for the IV bag. She paused as she studied it. "Hey."

"What?"

"It's almost empty. It's dripping awfully fast."

Lex studied the drip-drip-drip. "Yeah, I guess so."

Venus flagged down a nurse and pointed it out.

"Oh! Sorry about that. We forgot to slow it down after we got the antibiotics in you." She changed the bag and slowed the drip.

"I didn't flush all the antibiotics out of me, did I?"

"No, don't worry, dear." The nurse bustled away.

After another trip to the bathroom, Lex sat with Venus, not saying anything, just watching a rerun of *Oprah* on TV. Finally, the nurse peeked in. "We're almost ready for you. A few minutes."

Lex's fingers fidgeted on her lap until Venus slapped her hand down on them. "Stop that. You're driving me nuts."

"You're nuts? Think about me."

"You are so egocentric, you know that?"

"I'm about to go into surgery. I think I'm entitled."

"You're going to wake up, perfectly fine and as crabby as ever. So stop making my day worse than it already is."

"Okay, Lex, they're ready for you now." The nurse walked over to Lex with a wheelchair.

Lex stood and moved into the chair, surprised her legs didn't collapse under her. She grabbed Venus's arm. "Take my mom's diamond earrings. I want you to have them."

"Oh, stop."

"And that picture frame we fought over as kids? It's in my closet. You should have gotten it."

"Will you shut up?"

"But make sure I get cremated with my ratty bunny. He's on my bed."

Venus shoved her face in close. "I'm going to deck you so you don't need anesthesia."

Lex swallowed. "I need to go again."

Lex opened her eyes. Hey, she was in a different room. She could have sworn she'd been wide awake when she counted down to eight in the surgery room. Now she felt fuzzy and she couldn't move her leg.

Oh, no! She was paralyzed!

She would panic *after* she threw up.

"How are you?" A smiling nurse who was *way* too cheerful nudged her bed and did something with her IV. She started raising Lex into a sitting position.

"I'm going to puke." Her mouth had weeds growing in it.

"Not quite yet." The nurse tugged at her IV and injected something.

Another ten minutes, and Lex realized her mouth had suddenly dried up. She tried to speak but couldn't move her tongue. "Wa ... wa ..."

"Juice?" The nurse shoved a straw into her mouth.

"Nnn ..."

"Drink up."

Lex shook her head. The room spun.

"Rise and shine." The nurse bounded over with Lex's crutches. *Where's the fire, lady?* Lex's leg started to ache with fierce, bone-deep pain.

"Let's get you to a chair."

"Wha—?" She could barely sit up.

"The anesthesia is still in your system. Move around and it'll clear. Otherwise, you could sleep here all day." She giggled. "And we're not a hotel."

Lex stumbled with her crutches as the room tilted around her. She could feel the fiery energy of the nurse as she practically carried her the few feet to a recliner, her IV bag trailing on a wheeled stand. A weird Igloo cooler was attached to her leg by a thick tube, making her leg freezing cold. The nurse carried that with Lex to the recliner.

She collapsed on the chair and just wanted to sleep some more.

"You're almost ready to go home."

Home? She couldn't even form coherent sentences yet. Where was Venus? Who was this Pollyanna-on-steroids nurse? How could she even walk to the car with her leg bigger than a slab of mutton and frozen solid?

"Hey, Lex." Venus appeared.

Little Miss Sunshine hovered over her shoulder, driving a wheel-chair like a race car. She unhooked the tube attached to the Igloo cooler. "Time to go."

Lex eased herself into the wheelchair. She'd barely sat down before Miss Earnhardt took off, zooming down the hallway, out a side door. She skidded the chair down a ramp and nicked the curb as she turned toward Venus's car.

It wasn't a hard knock, but Lex's bones jarred like she'd been sideswiped. "Ow!" She grabbed her knee but only felt thick layers of bandages.

The NASCAR nurse screeched to a halt beside Venus's car. Lex paused to breathe.

"Come on. If you move, the fuzzies will go bye-bye." The nurse jiggled the wheelchair.

Was this woman for real? Lex shot to her feet and swayed as the darkening sky rotated around her like a carousel. She grabbed at the passenger door.

It took some painful hopping to turn herself around and sit in the seat. It took even more angling to get her straightened leg into Venus's little car.

"Slide the seat back."

"It's already back all the way."

Her leg hung over the edge of the bucket seat, but her heel didn't quite touch the floor, making her knee throb. The nurse wheeled away.

Lex didn't remember much about the long drive home from the surgery center, except for the pain that flashed through her leg every time the little sports car hit a bump in the road.

"Can't you drive any smoother?"

"Pardon me, Your Highness."

Venus finally eased into the carport at her apartment. Lex couldn't open the door all the way because of the car next to her. As she angled herself out, she banged her foot against the door. "Oooh."

Venus appeared with her crutches. Lex moved backward out of the carport, but then she discovered her mistake.

The ground sloped down from the carport, and Lex hadn't braced herself for the change in grade. She started tipping backward.

"Venus!"

Splat. Lex landed hard on her backside. The impact sent a jolt through her leg. "Oh, my knee, my knee."

Venus knelt at her side. "At least you landed on your butt. Lots of padding."

"Speak for yourself, bubblebutt. My tailbone is throbbing."

"Your Insult-o-meter spikes when you're in pain, doesn't it?"

"Wouldn't yours?"

Venus hooked her arm around her waist. "Okay, one, two, three-eee. Oomph."

Lex's butt barely cleared the ground before it bounced right back down. "Yow!"

"Sorry." Venus studied her. "I don't know if I'm strong enough to raise you up."

"Hand me my crutches."

Even with Venus's arm around her, even with the upper body weight training Lex had been doing for Wassamattayu tryouts, she heaved and strained to get upright again.

It was going to be a long night.

TWENTY-FOUR

She needed to go to the bathroom.

Lex stared at the ceiling, wide awake after sleeping for who knows how many hours on the surgery table. Venus's soft snores from where she sprawled in a sleeping bag matched the rhythmic whirring of the CPM machine as it bent and straightened her leg.

Poor Venus. She had collapsed, exhausted after setting everything up for Lex, not even thinking to ask about the mouse (which still hadn't reappeared). Lex couldn't wake her now.

The machine bent her leg, and she bumped her head against the wall. Her stupid bed. She couldn't have known it would be too short for her to lay full out with the machine, even diagonally. She couldn't move the bed away from the wall because there wasn't room, what with the box Venus had dragged to the foot of the bed. They'd needed to anchor the CPM machine so it wouldn't slide off and take Lex's leg with it. She waited for the machine to straighten her leg and then turned it off.

Lex unhooked the ice machine — one of the reasons Venus was so tired. After discovering Lex's tiny fridge didn't have an ice maker, she'd gone to the grocery store for a bag of ice, which now melted slowly in the large cooler Lex used for volleyball. Venus would need to get more ice tomorrow too.

Lex had to hop sideways to squeeze out from her bed — no mean feat while clutching her crutches. She almost tripped over the extension cord — the new one Venus had gone out (again) to buy because the only other one had been two feet too short.

The bathroom seemed an ocean away. And she had to go really badly.

She bumped and hobbled to the tiny bathroom, dropping onto the toilet. At least the Novocain hadn't worn off yet, and her knee had only a dull ache.

She'd been so mean and crabby to Venus all day. She would be better tomorrow.

At least the worst was behind her.

"Novocain's wearing off." With a vengeance. The dull ache from last night had turned into a thousand needles in her joint.

Venus looked up from her *Star* magazine. "Ready for your Vicodin?"

Another bone-deep stab. "Yeah."

Venus rummaged in her purse for the prescription she'd picked up for Lex. "Ever taken Vicodin before?"

"No."

"It might give you constipation."

"Is that all? Okay."

"Venus, I'm going to be sick." Lex twisted over the edge of the bed and stared at the floor.

"Wait!" Venus rushed — well, inched, past the boxes to her side with a plastic bag.

"Sorry." Lex grabbed the side of the bed to try to make the room stop whirling and dipping.

"Here." Venus thrust the bag into her hands, just in time for another wave of nausea.

Lex started crying. "I feel so sick."

"Shut up and concentrate on not throwing up."

"I can't."

"And why not?" Venus thrust a paper towel into Lex's plastic bag.

"Because I have to go."

Venus's eyes crackled with sparks. *"Again?"*

Lex's sobs renewed. "I'm sorry."

"Stop crying."

"I can't. Nausea makes me weepy." She burst into fresh tears.

Venus's sighing breath tangled in Lex's hair. "Come on." She unhooked the ice machine, turned off the CPM, and stuck her arm under Lex's ribs.

Upright was way worse than lying prone. Lex kept the plastic bag close to her face as her stomach clenched tight. Venus helped her stagger through the boxes and onto the toilet.

She couldn't even sit up. Hot tears ran down her face as she sagged over, clamping her mouth shut to the tidal waves of nausea ebbing and flowing in her stomach. Venus leaned against the wall, sweating and panting from carrying her.

Back in bed, Lex turned her face to the wall while Venus re-hooked her ice machine. "I just want to die."

"There is no way you're going to die after putting me through all that." Venus's razor-sharp tone would have stopped Mel Gibson from dying in *Braveheart*.

"Why am I feeling so sick?"

"Have you ever taken any narcotic before? Codeine?"

"No."

"How about your family?"

"Oh. Dad reacted badly to codeine when he got a bad cough, and the doctor prescribed him this strong syrup."

Venus squeezed her forehead hard with her hand. "You're kidding."

"What?"

"Vicodin is related to codeine. If your dad reacts badly to codeine, you'll most likely react the same way to Vicodin."

Lex closed her eyes. "Oh." She wished she'd known this sooner. "I just want to diiiiiie."

"I'm calling your surgeon."

"It's Saturday."

Venus grabbed her cell phone. "He has a pager."

Lex listened carefully, but Venus remained polite while on the phone. She snapped it shut. "There's nothing else you can take that won't make you sick."

"Nothing?"

"There's other stuff not related to codeine, but if you're super-sensitive like this, the other medications might also make you dizzy. The doctor said you can take Tylenol."

"*That's it?*"

"Well, you're already taking ibuprofen. It'll work in tandem. He said it might be enough. Or you can continue to take the Vicodin."

Rock and a hard place. Wonderful. "I'd rather be in pain than puking."

Venus shrugged. "Your call."

Lex stared at the wall clock for the next few hours while Venus read her bits from *People* magazine. After a while, she started to notice what felt like fiery-hot pins across the surface of her knee.

"Venus, something's wrong."

"In a lot of pain?"

"Not the same kind. It feels like … sunburn. With jeans on."

Venus winced. So did Lex.

She felt it when she got up to use the restroom again. The room had stopped spinning, but as soon as she swung her leg off the CPM machine, fire ants crawled up her shin and bit her kneecap with relish.

"Ow ow ow!" Lex pressed a hand against the thick bandage.

"Do you want the Vicodin?"

"*No.*" Lex waited for the burning to subside. "It's weird. It feels like really bad sunburn."

"Well, your doctor's appointment is Monday. You'll have to last until then."

Monday couldn't come soon enough.

The bone-deep ache returned after the Vicodin wore off completely. It hadn't been a good weekend.

Monday morning, Venus drove her to the doctor's office. Lex eased down into the waiting room seat.

The woman sitting next to her had a horrified look as she stared at Lex's face. After two days of biting her sheets and sweating into her pillow while her knee throbbed with each motion of the CPM machine, Lex knew she looked like death warmed up in the microwave.

"Lex Sakai? Come on in."

She hobbled into an exam room. Another patient passed her — the young redhead who had been on her third knee surgery. She walked without bandages or crutches, just her leg brace. Her surgery knee looked a little pink, but swelled only slightly more than her good side, with three small round Band-Aids. She smiled and waved at Lex.

Lex felt too weak to do more than growl at her.

She got up onto the exam table with Venus's help. The doctor came in and shook hands with both of them. "How does it feel?"

"It's burning, like a sunburn. I had to stop using the CPM machine."

"Hmm, not good. You need to keep using the CPM machine so your knee doesn't freeze up. Let's take the bandages off and see how it looks."

He took off the outer Ace bandage to reveal the flat, water-filled plastic pad that had attached to the ice machine. Oh, so that's what it looked like. Lex had only felt the coldness.

Then he took off the gauze and pads underneath.

Whoa, momma. Blisters covered her entire kneecap. The swelling hadn't gone down at all, unlike the redheaded girl's knee.

"Your body didn't shunt the fluid away, so it formed subdermal blisters."

Whatever that meant.

"I'm going to drain the fluid."

Lex didn't quite get what he intended to do until he whipped out several humongous needles, and then drew up some clear liquid with another one. "I'll numb the area a little." He injected the fluid a little above her knee. It pinched but didn't seem to reduce sensation.

Then the doctor grabbed the big needle.

Suddenly, all she could feel was white-hot pain pain pain pain pain ... She grabbed the table, but her fingers scraped over the paper covering and the smooth vinyl. *Whoa, Momma!*

The doctor moved the tip of the needle to another blister. Lex's teeth scraped against each other. The cuss words started flaming through her head sharp and fast.

Let no unwholesome words come from your mouth—

Oh, shut up. God has it in for me or something.

God didn't answer, not with comfort or a lightning bolt. Lex felt completely alone.

TWENTY-FIVE

L et's ask Mimi for help."

"What?" Lying in her bed, Lex paused as she adjusted the pillows behind her aching back. "You're kidding me, right?"

Venus pulled out her cell phone. "She doesn't have any scars from that auto accident a few years ago, and it burned her pretty badly. She might know how to help your blistering."

Lex had last seen her cousin when she stole her slimeball date George at Crustaceans Restaurant. "But Mimi? She's not your favorite person either."

"Do you have any other ideas?"

Lex started up the CPM machine again and winced at the rippling pain from the blisters that gradually dulled. "I guess not."

Venus made the call, which, after some initial snarling, went well. "Mimi said she'll be right over."

"She's probably coming to gloat over how terrible I look. I'm not holding out hope, Venus."

"Let me warm up some soup for you. You haven't eaten in three days."

Lex shifted her back against the pillows. The CPM machine— moving only her right leg and not her left—had caused her lower spine injury to worsen.

Her cell phone rang. "What do you want, Richard?"

"Is that any way to speak to your favorite brother?"

"I'm hanging up now—"

"Wait, wait. Can I come over?"

Lex's alarm bells went off. "Why? You don't do sickrooms of any kind."

"Well, my friend and I—"

"A friend? Richard, I've kind of had *surgery*." She tried to stretch out and ease the pain in her back.

"You're okay, right? Not bleeding?"

"I've been puking for three days."

"Oh." He paused. "Can I still bring him over?"

Lex snapped her phone shut.

Venus punched the microwave touchpad. "He's been introducing you to a lot of guys the past few weeks."

"Yeah, I don't know why. Maybe Grandma got to him."

"But she doesn't have anything on him. Why would he do what she says?"

"Good point."

Lex was halfway through her tepid chicken noodle when the doorbell rang. "Mimi already?" She finished another spoonful.

Venus opened the door.

A very short Asian stranger stood in the doorway. His polite smile brightened when he caught sight of Venus. His eyes glazed over. "Hey, baby—"

"What do you want?" Venus's hand went to her hip.

"If I could rearrange the alphabet, I'd put U and I togeth—"

"Oh, come up with something original. Who are you?"

"Ben Shue."

Venus glanced over her shoulder at Lex, who shook her head and shrugged. Ben never took his eyes off of Venus.

"Sorry, we don't know you." Venus started to close the door.

"My mom told me to come here."

Venus just stared at him. Lex wished she could see her face.

Ben's gaze grew dazed again. "You have such beautiful eyes—No, no, don't close—!"

His voice came muffled through the door. "I'm supposed to help Lex Sakai with her surgery recovery."

Venus whipped it open. "What?"

"I live at an apartment building down the street. Lex, your grandma told my mom you needed someone to help you."

What? "No thanks." More like, *No way.* Lex took in his expensive clothes and the way he didn't even turn his eyes from Venus when he spoke to Lex.

Then another figure appeared in the doorway. "Is Lex here?"

"Hi, Aiden."

In contrast to Ben, Aiden's eyes barely skimmed over Venus before he peered inside and smiled at Lex. "How do you feel?"

"Come in, Aiden." Venus grabbed his arm and yanked him inside. "After all, you guys have been dating awhile."

Both Lex and Aiden stared at Venus, who gave him a meaningful glance with a quick motion at Ben, still standing in the doorway.

"Boyfriend?" Ben finally looked somewhere besides Venus's face. "Lex's grandma didn't say anything about a boyfriend." His eyes narrowed.

Lex put every ounce of desperation in her look to Aiden.

He turned to Ben. "Uh ... yeah. We're dating." He stepped into the apartment, maneuvering around boxes, and handed Lex the small bouquet of flowers he carried. Ben's dark scowl followed him.

Lex smiled and murmured through her teeth at him. "Give me a kiss."

He obliged with a hand on her shoulder and a peck on the lips. She had to concentrate not to flinch. It wasn't too bad, really. He smelled like soap, fir, and musk.

He immediately released her shoulder, but his voice sounded low and deep in her ear. "You really don't like being touched, do you?"

His words relaxed her. Maybe because he'd gotten it and she didn't have to explain it to him. "Just by men." She swallowed. "Nothing personal."

His look told her he understood and didn't need to know anything more.

Venus blocked Ben's view. "We're good here. You can leave now."

"Hey—"

Venus shut the door in his face again.

"What—"

Venus cut Lex's words off. She peeked out the window near the door. "So, Lex, good thing Aiden's here because he can remove all your ingrown toenails." Venus's voice boomed in the tiny room.

Aiden's face had gotten rather rigid, as if he were trying to decide how to answer that politely. Perhaps, *Is that so?* Or *How interesting*.

Venus jabbed her fingers at the closed door, eyes wide and meaningful, mouth moving silently in words Lex couldn't exactly decipher, but that she could understand. *Ah.* Lex picked her jaw up off her lap. "Yes, thanks, Aiden. And I'll need you to pop these blood blisters."

His expressionless mask cracked as he shot her a bug-eyed look.

Venus rummaged through one of Lex's boxes and pulled out what looked like a miniature tennis racket—oh, perfect. Dad would be so proud of the way they were finally using the electric bug zapper he'd gotten for her.

Venus pressed the battery button to charge up the metal strings lacing the head. "And Aiden can help you lance that bleeding mole on your butt." She stepped into position behind the closed door. "But I think that maybe that third hand growing out of your head needs professional surgery."

She cranked the doorknob and whipped open the flimsy door. The charged bug zapper racket came sailing down on Ben's head, where he crouched on her doorstep. *Crack! Fizz! Pop!* The scent of burning hair reached Lex's nose.

"Aaaiiieee!" Ben zipped away, hands grabbing his head.

Venus closed the door with a click and a triumphant wave of her racket.

Lex applauded her. "You are so evil."

Venus's smile reminded Lex of Catwoman. "I know."

"Good thing you didn't really hurt him."

Venus lifted a delicate eyebrow. "You don't know much about men and their hair if you think that."

"Huh?"

"Honey, he probably goes to Lana's or Vertigo every three weeks for a sculpted head like that. I just caused him abject pain."

The doorbell rang. Venus charged the zapper and opened it.

"Hi guys." Mimi sashayed into the room, then froze as she saw Aiden. Her slow smile would have put Jezebel to shame. "Well, helloooo there."

Lex had to stop herself from growling. Then she had to ask herself why she felt the need to bristle in the first place. Maybe she was still upset from when Aiden touched her. Shouldn't she not care that Mimi's hands were all over Aiden as they chatted?

"So, Aiden, where's your physical therapy clinic?"

"It's a combination clinic and fitness gym ..."

Lex stared at her bowl of soup, cold now. Her stomach burped. She set the bowl down before the sight of it did more weird things to her digestive system.

Venus cleared her throat sharply. "Mimi."

Mimi snapped out of vamp mode mid sentence. "Oh. Right. I brought all my stuff." Then she glanced at Lex's leg, exposed only as far as her warm-up pants would go. "Um ... we'll need to take your pants off."

"My cue to go." Aiden turned rather effortlessly from Mimi to Lex. "I just wanted to make sure you were okay."

"Thanks. And thanks for that ... thing with Ben."

"No problem." Aiden let himself out.

Mimi loosed a long, low breath. "What a hottie. He's cuter than Orlando Bloom."

"What is it with you stealing every man in my vicinity?"

Mimi blinked at Lex. "You mean Kin-Mun?"

"George. Crustaceans. You were even there with a date of your own."

"Ooooh." Mimi stifled a laugh. "Actually, I'm sorry about that, but I had to meet George so he'd ask me out. I had him drive me to Shoreline, and then I stole his car and stranded him there. Revenge for when he did that to one of my girlfriends."

Lex looked at Venus and saw her mouth open as well. "You're kidding."

"So, you see? It was for a good cause. You weren't enjoying your time with him anyway. I could tell even from across the restaurant."

Lex cleared her throat. Couldn't argue with that.

Mimi dropped her bag near Lex's bed. "Take off your pants and the bandages. Let's see."

Lex obliged.

Mimi seemed genuinely distressed as she saw the blisters. "Ouch. Okay, first of all, pump your foot up and down. Yeah, like that. You need to get your lymphatic system going to drain the swelling and the fluid."

She started pulling various jars from her bag. "These will help with the swelling and the blistering. There might be some scarring, but hopefully these will take care of most of it." She plopped down on Lex's bed.

Her serious eyes, so different from any other time Lex had seen her, made her start to tear. "Why are you doing this?"

Mimi glanced at the leg, then back up to Lex. She shrugged. "You've always been aware of what you were good at — fitness and volleyball. When Venus called . . ." She twisted the bottle in her hand. "This is what I'm good at. Plus . . ." Mimi pinned Lex with a more normal Mimi-like gaze. "Now you owe me."

Lex had a hard time taking it all in — her view of her younger cousin seemed too set to be shaken, but she'd just had a minor quake. Still, the fact that Mimi had come — despite the Siren-act with Aiden — revealed something honest in her words.

"Thanks, Mimi."

"Let's get started."

"I'm going to call Aiden." Venus walked into the apartment and dumped the bags of groceries on the floor.

Lex looked up from Venus's *Cosmo.* "Why?"

"I saw Ben lurking around outside. I think he's still suspicious about Aiden being your boyfriend."

"Gee, I wonder why, considering he's *not* my boyfriend."

"Well, unless you want Ben around, we have to convince him otherwise."

"Just don't answer the doorbell."

"I read guys pretty well, especially when they're in a predatory mode like that. I don't trust him." Venus punched in a number.

"Hey, how'd you get Aiden's number?"

"Aiden? It's Venus. Can you come over? That guy Ben is hanging around ... Thanks." She snapped the phone shut. "He gave it to me."

Lex frowned. "He didn't give it to *me.*"

Venus stared at Lex a long moment. Lex squirmed a bit under her strange, neutral gaze. Finally, Venus turned away to unpack the groceries. "He said to call if you needed anything."

"Oh. That was nice of him." Lex scratched her ear. "Do you think he still feels bad about tearing my ACL?"

Venus didn't bother to answer, just stuck the fruit into the refrigerator.

Lex checked her email. She only had dial-up, which took ten times longer than the cable modem at her old home. She had several responses to a message she'd sent to friends about physical therapy recommendations.

"Why does that name sound familiar?"

"Hmm?" Venus didn't even look up from her new *Entertainment Weekly* magazine.

"My insurance would only pay if I used one of two different physical therapy places, and all my friends say to go to Golden Creek Fitness and Physical Therapy." Lex tried to bring up the website, but her dial-up dragged along. "I've heard that name before, but I can't remember where."

"I know where."

"You do?"

Venus nodded and flipped a page.

"Well? You're not going to tell me?"

"No."

"Why not?"

"It's more fun watching you rack your brains."

The doorbell rang. Venus jumped up, grabbed the electric fly-swatter racket, and then opened the door. "Oh, hi, Aiden. Thanks for coming."

"No problem. Hi, Lex."

"Hi."

Aiden squeezed in between a few boxes so he could sit on the one filled with books. "I saw Ben on the way in, by the way."

"Oh good." Venus picked up her magazine and perched back on Lex's bed. "Can you just hang out for a while?"

"Sure."

Lex stared at her computer screen. Still loading. "Wait a minute ... Aiden, you're a physical therapist?"

"Yeah."

A dreading suspicion crept over her. "Where do you work?"

"Golden Creek."

Lex's shoulders sagged. "You're kidding."

His face remained neutral, but somehow sharpened to all hard edges. "Hey, it's a great facility."

"No, I know that—"

"And it's nearby ... Oh, I get it. That's where your insurance wants to send you."

"Yeah, pretty much." Somehow, having Aiden as her PT kind of weirded her out.

"I didn't tear your ACL on purpose, you know."

"No, I know that—"

"It's not like I'm going to tear the other one once I've got you on the table."

"I . . . I guess."

She'd never seen frustration on his face before, but he looked like he wanted to strangle her. "You're acting like you don't want to get better and play volleyball again."

"No, it's not that at all."

"So what's the problem? I've treated dozens of volleyball injuries, most of them ACL. All the ACL surgeries go to me."

"All of them?"

"I'm good at what I do, Lex." A dangerous glint appeared in his eye, making her backtrack with haste.

"I didn't mean to imply you weren't. I'm sorry."

"I'm good at helping players get back into shape. And now that I'm playing, I understand the injuries better too."

Didn't she want someone like that, who knew her sport, knew her injury? Why the hesitation? She knew he wasn't to blame for the injury, but a part of her didn't want to spend more time with him—and she wasn't sure why—while another part liked spending time with him too much.

What was her problem? She was such a basket case.

"Why don't I drive you to PT at Golden Creek?"

"Thanks." Venus answered before Lex could reply. "That'd be great."

Lex frowned at her. "Excuse me, I don't see the surgical holes in your knee."

"Excuse me, I don't see you needing to go to work right now."

"Oh." A flush rose from her neckline. "I'm sorry, Venus. You're right."

Venus turned to Aiden. "Are you sure it won't be a problem for you?"

"Not at all." He dug out his PDA. "Lex, I'll arrange for you to have my first morning session—actually, I'll give you my first two sessions—and then I'll take you home right afterward."

"Your boss isn't going to be mad?"

"He's my friend—we went to PT school together. It won't be a problem."

Aiden seemed confident, so Lex didn't see a reason to doubt him. "Thanks."

"Next week will be two weeks since your surgery, right?"

"Yeah, about."

"I'll schedule you. Give me your doctor's PT prescription."

Lex handed it over, trying to ignore the twinge in her gut. "I appreciate it." She really did. Why was she so afraid to have him as her therapist?

To spend more time with him. To get close to him.

That's ridiculous. She was never frightened. She faced things head-on.

He didn't scare her a bit.

TWENTY-SIX

No, he didn't scare her. Because in a few minutes, she was going to kill him.

"Aiden! That really hurts!" Sitting up, Lex pushed against the PT table, trying to escape his fingers massaging—no, *torturing* the outside of her thigh.

His calm voice made her want to scream. "The IT band runs from your hip down your thigh to your knee joint. When it gets tight, injuries happen." He kept kneading, but it felt more like slow kicks into her leg with combat boots.

Lex grabbed the edge of the table. "Haven't I had enough pain? Surgery, blisters, no pain meds? Remember? Yow!"

With another patient on the next table, the other therapist gave a sympathetic yet amused look. Her patient had turned white in response to Lex's screaming.

Lex didn't care. She would start cussing in a minute.

Finally he stopped. "I think that's enough for today."

"Ya think?"

"Keep it up at home. It'll get easier."

"Why do I not believe you?" Lex rubbed the area, but it felt hot and sensitive. And she had thought getting used to Aiden touching her would be the hardest part of physical therapy.

"Okay, time for some exercises in the gym."

Lex got down from the table. "Now exercises, I can do."

Aiden led the way out of the patient area into the public gym area. "Expect a bit of muscle atrophy."

"In the four weeks since I tore it? Come on. I was in the best shape of my life. That's got to count for something."

Five minutes later, she heaved like she'd run a marathon. With lead feet.

"Come on." Aiden stood in front of her. "Lift your leg higher." He had opted to guide her exercises himself rather than handing her off to an aide. Lex kind of wished for an aide. They seemed nicer.

She strained against the cord, attached to her ankle on one end and a pulley on the other, causing resistance to her forward straight-leg raise. Her quads burned. The outside of her hip burned. Her *good* leg burned.

"One more." Aiden watched her. "Higher. Good."

She dropped her leg a little too fast. The cord zipped back into place.

"Now to the side."

"The side?"

She finished her other exercises, heart slamming against her chest, lungs aching. She leaned against the abductor weight machine, which had been her last exercise.

Hubba, hubba. A hunk walked into the gym area—Jude Law in the flesh. Gym member, it looked like.

Aiden bent down to look closer at her knee. He seemed happy with it. "Okay, let's ice you down."

"Hang on, let me stretch a little." She wanted a little more time with the eye candy. The hunka-burnin-love paused near the free weights.

She spread her legs a little and reached for her toes.

Rrrrip.

She gasped so hard that she lost her balance and nearly tipped forward. Aiden nabbed her by the waist and kept her from toppling. She didn't even react to his touch—her mortification had kicked a hole in her gut.

Her warm-up pants had split right across her rear end.

She straightened—with Aiden's help—and reached around to finger the edges of the tear. Her face felt like she'd baked at 350 degrees for an hour.

Aiden didn't laugh—didn't even have a glimmer of amusement in his calm face. "It's just the warm-ups. Your shorts underneath are still fine."

"That's not the point." Her voice was doing that screeching thing again. "I've gained weight!"

Aiden took on that ultra-careful expression that men adopted when around women talking about their figures. "You don't look it."

"Oh, stop patronizing me. It means I'm out of shape. I've never been out of shape. I wasn't even a chubby baby."

"How do you know that?"

"Are you telling me I was a fat baby?"

Aiden's eyes widened. "No, no, not at all. Carry on."

"First, my body let me down when I tore my ACL. Now, my metabolism. My metabolism has never let me down like this." She swiped at the tears gathering in her eyes. "And I'm so weepy lately. I never cry. What's wrong with me?"

"Well, surgery will do that to you."

"Not to me. It just doesn't happen to me." She sniffled.

"Here. Step out of your warm-up pants."

She shoved them down over her shorts and held on to the leg press machine while Aiden helped pull her shoes free.

"Now, let's ice you down."

Lex grabbed her crutches and hobbled back toward the patient therapy area. She didn't even glance at the cutie, who probably hadn't even noticed her. Good thing.

She would be prepared for therapy on Wednesday. She'd start eating better. Aiden had given her exercises she could do at home. She'd do them five times a day.

And most of all, she'd massage that stupid IT band until it was looser than a granny's girdle.

Lex went into PT on Wednesday ready for Aiden and his IT band torture. She'd been faithfully massaging her leg.

But he did a change-up.

While she lay on her back, he lifted her ankle onto his shoulder and pressed down on her knee to get her leg to straighten back to 180 degrees.

"Ow! Ow! Ow!"

Lex's upper body lifted off the table at the pain of ripping, tearing across her kneecap.

"Scaring the other patients again, I see." Aiden eased up on the pressure for a second, then pressed down again.

"Shut up! Shut up shut up shut up!" Lex tried to focus on pleasant things. Like running a samurai sword through Aiden's bowels.

He finally let her leg down. Lex dribbled off the table onto the floor.

Aiden stared down at her. "Come on, get up. You still have your gym exercises to do."

She sat up and grabbed her crutch, but before she could swing it at Aiden's exposed kneecap, the other therapist walked in front of her.

Saved. Lucky dog.

She hoisted herself to her feet. Aiden pointed to her crutches. "Try walking without them."

"What?"

"It's only a few feet into the gym area. I'll grab you if you start to fall, but I don't think you will."

"You're not my doctor."

"No." He put his fists on his hips and struck a Superman pose. "I'm your therapist."

Oh, brother. She left her crutches and took an experimental step.

Hey, that wasn't too bad. She didn't feel as unstable as she thought she would. She headed toward the open doorway where Aiden waited for her.

He studied her feet. "Strike down with your heel first—"

Just before reaching him, her foot came down awkwardly on the ball of her foot, and she pitched forward.

Bam! Her right eye smacked into the doorframe.

Aiden grabbed her waist to keep her from going the rest of the way toward the floor.

And the hottie from Monday had just walked in the door. She was so brilliant, she amazed herself.

Stars flashed in front of her, then the throbbing started. Her cheekbone would come flying out of her skull any second now.

"You okay?" Pseudo-Jude Law winced a little as he studied her eye.

"Peachy." Lex tried to assimilate the fact that he had two heads.

Aiden shoved her hand away to study her eye. "It'll be fine. We'll ice it."

"Oh good." She started to turn around, back into the patient area.

"After your exercises. Where are you going?"

Okay, she was ready this time. Lex marched—well, hobbled into PT on Friday. She'd been massaging her IT band. She'd been working on her leg extension with stretches.

However, Aiden had a sadistic streak.

After her strengthening exercises on the table, Aiden peered at her surgery scars, the incisions made by the doctor. "They're healing nicely."

"Yeah, now that the blisters are gone."

He touched one of them. "It's got a lot of scar tissue under the surface."

Uh, oh.

Aiden got out a plastic jar of something white and slimy. He took a little onto his fingers, then started working it into her portal scars.

"Yiyiyiyiyi!" Lex slapped her hands against the table with each scream. "I don't care about my scars! Leave off!"

"They'll interfere with your extension." Aiden gave her a *You're such a baby* look.

Tears started to well. "See? You're making me cry."

"You're hormonal from the surgery's shock to your body."

"Do you have an answer for everything?"

"I have an answer for every complaint of yours."

Lex lay back and whimpered.

"Pansy."

"Am not."

"There's a woman named Mary—she's probably about my mom's age. She had hip replacement surgery, and she didn't complain even half as much as you do."

"You were probably nicer to her."

"I was even meaner."

"Not possible."

"And she still likes me. In fact, she got a gym membership and comes in faithfully three days a week to keep up with her rehab exercises."

"Must be your winning personality." Lex winced as he finished.

"Time to do your exercises."

He took her through her exercises in the gym area, then iced her down back in the patient area. "See? Wasn't that bad."

Lex glared at him.

"You're getting stronger, did you know that? I upped your weight today on the pulleys."

She paused as she strapped on her brace. "Really?"

"You couldn't tell?"

"No."

"See?"

Lex fastened the Velcro straps. Wow. Progress. How about that? She had to admit, Aiden pushed her the way she pushed her junior high girls. She shouldn't be complaining so much. In a weird, illogical way, she respected him for not giving in to her.

"Give me a sec." Aiden had a clipboard in hand. He waved her out to the front. "I'll drive you home after I finish this."

Lex stood by the receptionist's counter. The tiny Filipino lady, who looked like she could spit nails, nodded at her. "How's it coming along?"

"I'm getting better."

"Good." The receptionist went back to her computer.

The front door opened, and the Jude Law hottie strolled in. Perfect. Here was her chance. Lex smiled at him. *Be charming, not scary.*

He smiled back. Good sign.

She stepped forward. "Hi, I'm Leeeee—!"

Her leg, locked straight in the metal brace, didn't plant far enough to the side. She had no lateral balance. She started tipping.

"Aaack!" Lex grabbed at the receptionist's counter, but her wild arm movement sent her toppling backward instead.

"Ooomph!" She sat down hard. Pain jolted up from her tailbone.

She stared up at the cutie. At least he wasn't laughing. Heat radiated from her shoulders to the top of her head. Yup, she could feel the embarrassment prickling at her crown. She scratched at it.

"You okay? Are you hurt?" He bent down to help her up.

"Oh, Lex!" The receptionist's head appeared over the edge of the counter.

An Asian woman—maybe her aunts' age—entered the gym at that moment and saw the hunk helping Lex to her feet. "Oh, goodness. Are you all right?"

"Lex!" Aiden rushed from the patient area.

Lex sighed. Why bother trying to be cool anymore? "I have completely lost any dignity I might have had." She got to her feet. "Thanks."

"You okay?" the hunk asked her.

"I'm fine, the knee is fine, everything's fine." Although her tailbone might never be the same again. Yowsers, that hurt. She stopped herself before she rubbed it in public.

"Glad you're okay." Jude Law flashed a megawatt grin. "I'm Ike."

"I'm Lex. Nice to meet you. Thanks for helping me."

"No problem. See you around." The dreamboat headed back into the gym area.

The Asian woman who'd entered touched her elbow. "Are you sure you're all right? Looks like you've had surgery and all."

"I'm fine."

"You're Lex? Well, I'm Mary—"

"Oh! You're Mary. It's nice to finally meet you."

The woman's eyes crinkled with joy. "Has he been talking about me?"

"Oh, all the time." A dull ache started in her hip, and Lex flexed her leg.

Mary looked down at her knee. "I'm glad you're okay. Don't worry, these things take time."

Time. After so much of her life raced along, she hadn't really considered that her recovery would pace itself slower.

"Hey, Lex, Mary, sorry to rush you two, but I have to take Lex home." Aiden flashed Mary a familiar smile.

"Oh certainly, take her home. It was nice to meet you, Lex." Mary headed back for her workout.

Lex staggered out with her braced leg. "She's really nice."

"Isn't she? She just started dating again."

"That's great."

"She's been widowed a long time." Aiden held the elevator door for her. "I just hope her new boyfriend is treating her well."

TWENTY-SEVEN

"Come on! Faster! Keep up the pace." Lex clapped her hands at the junior high girls running blocking drills.

She had stood up rather than sit in the chair Vince had gotten for her, but it made her lower back ache. The CPM machine had screwed it up even more than before. She arched her back while she watched the girls sprint, block, sprint, block, but the ball of knotted muscle only seemed to twist itself tighter.

"Okay, that's it! Wrap it up!"

"Already?" Her assistant coach leaned in a little too close to murmur to her. She stepped away.

"I'm ... in too much pain." Lex couldn't look at him as she admitted it. She dug her fingers into the rough plastic of the chair and damped down a wave of frustration. She had nothing to throw, nothing to hit, nothing to break. She never expected the surgery to impact her ability to coach.

"Lex?"

"Yes?" Lex turned to two of her girls, sisters only thirteen months apart.

"We can't make it to playoffs this summer." The older girl sniffled. "We would if we could."

"Why? What's wrong?"

"Our grandpa's sick, and Mom doesn't want us away from home." The younger sister bit her lip.

Oh, man. What a summer these girls will have. "That's okay. You guys should be with your grandpa. That's the right thing to do."

After they'd gone to take off their gear, Lex sank into the hated chair. If girls kept dropping out of playoffs, she wouldn't have a team. She wouldn't even need Grandma to sponsor them for the summer. She wouldn't need to find a boyfriend. Lex didn't feel very loverlike.

She leaned over, trying to stretch her back. She was falling apart. Her team was falling apart.

I'm failing them already.

No, she couldn't think that way. She had to shake this defeatist attitude. It would turn into a self-fulfilling prophecy. She still had six weeks before the wedding.

She'd stretch her back more. She'd go to PT and work to strengthen her knee. She'd make her girls' team even stronger so they didn't need the lost players for playoffs. She could do it.

She could *do* it.

Oh, boy. She needed another ibuprofen.

Lex's stomach roiled as she waited by the curb in front of her apartment building for Aiden to arrive. She'd taken her ibuprofen on an empty stomach. Stupidity at its finest. Now she couldn't even contemplate food. Even worse, it had only blunted the edge off her back pain.

Aiden's car pulled up and she got in. As he drove off, he frowned at her. "What's wrong? Where does it hurt?"

How'd he know that? "My back."

"You look kind of sick too."

"I took ibuprofen on an empty stomach."

"Left your brains in bed this morning, I see."

"Oh, shut up."

"Here, have some bread." He reached for the backseat and threw a new loaf into her lap. "I went shopping this morning."

Lex downed a couple slices, and the desire to hang her head out the open window started to ease.

"So, your back …" Aiden pulled into the PT parking lot. "New injury?"

"Old. Lower back." Lex climbed out of the car awkwardly. The combination of her brace and her back problems made her as graceful as a waddling duck.

"What's it from?"

"Bad chair at my old workplace."

Aiden winced as he punched the elevator button. "The ibuprofen isn't helping?"

Lex entered the elevator and leaned against the handrail. "Not really."

He grew very still. He studied her, eyes searching … for what? Finally he seemed to come to a decision. "I can help you, if you want."

"How? Painkillers in an IV drip?"

The elevator doors creaked open. "I could give you a massage."

Lex halted mid-step. Her muscles clenched, making the pain throb in her lower back. She stared at Aiden as he waited for her to exit. The elevator doors started to slide shut again, and he thrust a hand to trigger them open.

She walked out. "I don't know, Aiden."

"Look, I don't need to know why you don't like it when men touch you, but you've gotten used to me handling your leg."

They entered the gym doors, and Lex signed in at the receptionist's counter. As she signed the credit card slip to pay for her session, she tried to make her back muscles relax. Her skin had become hypersensitive, feeling the rasp of her T-shirt.

"Oh, Aiden, your friend Spenser called." The receptionist handed him a message slip. "He said he'd be here in an hour."

"Thanks." He frowned at the piece of paper.

Lex tried to peek. "Problems?"

He crumpled the message. "No. Well, what do you think?"

She looked into his eyes, and the calm pooling there made the fluttering in her chest ease. This was Aiden. Her therapist. She had to fight this phobia.

"Okay."

Lex expected something to explode, or maybe some Hallelujah chorus to erupt. No, none of that. Just Aiden's slow smile, reassuring and gentle.

He set her up at a table a little apart from where the other therapist worked a shoulder surgery patient. He had her lie on her stomach.

As Lex eased her body down, her shoulder cramped. Then a little pit fire crackled on her lower back. It slowly dulled, but she couldn't seem to make the rest of her muscles unclench.

"I'll massage you through your T-shirt." Aiden's voice floated over her. He seemed closer to her than he'd ever been, even when stretching her leg. Maybe that's why she now caught a whiff of soap and fir and musk—just a hint. It soothed her. Her shoulder blades relaxed a tiny bit.

This was Aiden. She trusted him.

He started on her arm—a safe place. She couldn't stop herself from flinching. He continued his gentle kneading motion up her shoulder.

A brief flash of memory. Her date's breath against her neck, her apartment carpet burning her elbows and hands as she tried to scramble away. His hand on her arm, pinning her down, pressing her face into the carpet where she breathed in the wine she'd spilled, mold, rancid cooking oil.

She jolted. Aiden paused. "Do you want me to stop?"

"N-no." She had to fight this.

He continued. "Long, deep breaths."

Lex complied. Fir and that thread of musk. She imagined it cleansing her as it filled her lungs.

She focused on his hands, kneading slowly. His patience amazed her, but then again, she always moved at breakneck speed.

He massaged up her arms, and then she realized both his hands touched her shoulders and she didn't flinch, she didn't mind, she didn't fear. He rubbed circles in her neck. Oh, that felt nice. The tension at the base of her skull dissolved away. She never noticed the ache behind her eyes until it eased. He hadn't even touched her back, but the knotted ball at the base of her spine loosened a little.

His fingers pressed, circled, pushed. She barely noticed when he moved down toward her trouble spot. Her back unkinked, the burning cooled. Cool like fir, relaxing like a thread of musk.

"Okay, you're done."

The ache hadn't completely gone away—she still felt tender in that area—but she moved more fluidly than she had in weeks. Her spine didn't feel like a creaky mass of bones rubbing together.

She sat up. "Thanks, Aiden." A world of meaning in those words.

Lex knew he heard everything she didn't say, because his eyes locked with hers for a moment. She felt this strange stretching— almost a physical sensation—like Play-Doh being rolled together. She blinked, and it disappeared.

Besides, she hated Play-Doh.

She started to climb down from the table.

"What are you doing?"

"What do you mean?"

"You're not off the hook. Now that you're feeling better, we've still got your exercises to do."

Aiden knew he was being irrational, but he hurried Lex through her gym exercises like a drill sergeant. She had to be gone by the time Spenser arrived.

He glanced at the clock. Thirty minutes. If he pushed her a little harder, she'd be done with her ice and stim a few minutes before he came. Hopefully he'd be late, as usual.

She couldn't meet Spenser. She belonged to him.

There he was, being irrational.

He'd waffled about giving her the massage. He'd given dozens of massages, so the procedure itself didn't make him uncomfortable, but he knew it would be different with her. He knew that he'd be feeling like this — stronger than King Kong, victorious like an Ultimate Fighting Champion — if she overcame her fear with him.

Aiden didn't often touch people casually like gregarious Spenser did, but he stared at the nape of her neck as she sat in the machine, wanting to smooth the taut skin. To be comforting, encouraging . . . proprietary.

He never bonded with any of his patients — he kept his professional distance. But he had liked being with Lex even before he tore her ACL. He didn't know why. He always seemed to catch her at her worst. She created chaos like a tornado through his controlled, ordered world.

"Five more." His voice sharpened as he drove her on this last rep, but she smiled at him. She complained and whined, but he heard the note of teasing in her tone, the glimmer of mischief in her eyes. She appreciated how he pushed her. She had never mentioned it, but he knew the raging determination in her that rushed her on, focused on her healing and rehab. He could see that rage in her even now, as she grunted and strained to finish the set on the machine.

Why this connection with her? He'd been physically attracted to Trish, but he'd never been tempted by her, and he had rejected her advances without regret. Lex and Trish had too many similarities — face, family, religion. The last one had set his back up every time Trish mentioned it, especially because her actions contradicted the morals she claimed to follow.

Lex switched to the leg press and paused before starting. "Do you remember the first time we met?"

"At the —" No, she never saw him at the coffee shop — "grass tournament?"

"Yeah. You asked me about church. What did you mean by that?"

Had she read his mind, bringing up the subject he wanted to avoid? "Just curious."

She grunted as she performed a set. "I've been thinking lately."

"Don't hurt yourself."

She glared at him, but his bland expression seemed to amuse her. Then her mood shifted, and her eyes skittered away. "Trish ... came on to you."

He kept his face impassive, but a burst of tension rippled over his skin at the sound of her name. "Who told you?"

"Richard."

"Oh. Let's go, another set." He tapped the machine. He had to get her out of here.

She sweated and groaned through another fifteen reps. The weights clinked as she finished. "Trish and I became Christians in college."

He didn't want to hear this. "Really?"

"But the past few years, she's been ... wild. She stopped going to church regularly. With this current boyfriend, she stopped going to church completely."

This affects me, how? "And?"

"The way you talked about church ... after what she said about dating non-Christians ..." Lex sighed.

"Last set." Aiden leaned against the foot of the machine.

Lex strained through the set, breathing hard as she finished.

"Ice and stim." Aiden headed to the patient area, Lex trailing behind. Maybe he could distract her and she wouldn't—

"You're not Christian?"

His lips tightened, but he didn't face her, so she couldn't see. "I'm not."

She didn't reply, but he knew the topic wasn't over. She followed him to the patient area and got up on a table. He started attaching the electrodes around her knee.

Lex's eyes flitted to his face and away, as if she couldn't quite meet his eyes but she wanted to. "Because of ... Did Trish? ... Why? ..."

Aiden sighed. "Do you really want to get into a discussion?"

"I just want to know."

"Why?"

"I don't know."

Her candor never stopped surprising him. He rubbed his forehead. "It's partly because of Trish, but mostly because of another girl I dated a long time ago who said she was Christian. And before you say not all Christians are like that—" He stopped her as she started to interrupt—"I've met a lot of hypocritical Christians."

But then his friend Spenser's face flickered before his eyes. Spenser, who never nagged or questioned or argued about religion. Aiden thought he was a little too flirty, but Spenser was always there for him as a friend.

He finished attaching the adhesive pads to her knee.

"Am I ...?" Lex asked.

She looked at him now. He realized he'd never thought about it with her. "No. I know a few sincerely loving Christians. But I also know plenty of sincerely loving atheists."

Lex nodded and looked down, but she didn't say anything.

He needed to hurry. Aiden got her ice bag, wrapped her knee, and started her stim.

He should have just walked away, but he didn't want to leave her like that. "Look, I'm not one of those people who loves to argue and try to debunk or fluster Christians. But I won't lie to you or anyone else who asks about what I believe or don't believe."

She didn't seem terribly upset—he had expected more defensiveness. What had he expected from her? Derision? He knew her better than to think she'd react that way.

Instead, she shrugged. "That's you. That's fine."

Somehow, her disappointment sliced like a razor blade.

He kept watch on the clock. She finished her ice with three minutes to spare.

"I'll wait for you out there." Lex headed to the waiting area.

The receptionist entered the patient area as he cleaned up, and he turned to her. "Could you please tell Spenser I'll be back in—"

"Hi, there." From the waiting area, the familiar purring voice carried back to him.

Oh, no.

"I'm Spenser."

"Nice to meet you. Are you always this friendly?"

Her mildly sarcastic reply made Aiden pause as he turned the corner. Spenser hovered next to Lex, who leaned casually against the receptionist's counter.

"Spenser, this is my patient, Lex."

"Pleasure." Spenser used his infamous double-hand clasp. He didn't seem to notice when Lex's shoulders snapped tight and her smile hardened. She snatched her hand away.

Aiden couldn't resist. Maybe he just wanted to test her, to affirm ... what? He didn't think. He came up behind her, and making sure Spenser couldn't see it, he placed a gentle touch at the small of her back.

She didn't react.

Something bloomed in his chest. It felt like when he made a free throw that swished through the net.

Spenser gave a charming smile. "Aiden isn't pushing you too hard, is he? I'll school him for you."

She regarded him with half-closed eyes and a cool expression. "He pushes me hard enough."

"How dare he push a sweet thing like you? You put Hershey's out of business."

She burst into laughter. "Oh, come on. You can do better than that."

Aiden had to admit Spenser took it in stride with a warm, more genuine smile than before. However, Aiden wasn't going to let her stay and taste more of his magnetism, much less discover that he had recently broken up with his girlfriend and was Christian. Although to Aiden right now, he was more like the snake in Eden.

Aiden moved away from her, even though he wanted to stick to her like PB and J, but his physical distance would fool Spenser into believing his professional distance from her. "Sorry, Spenser, but I'm Lex's ride home. I'll be back in fifteen." He headed out the door.

He paused outside so Lex could catch up to him, still staggering in her straight-legged brace. "He works at the same pharmaceutical company as Trish."

Aiden glanced sidelong at her. "He does?"

"I didn't actually meet him, but you went out to lunch with him that day I went to eat with Trish."

Now he remembered. "He's a good friend."

"You guys are like oil and vinegar."

"Who's the oil, and who's the vinegar?"

She giggled. *Giggled.* She'd rarely done that with him. "Oh, you're definitely the vinegar."

"So, he's the oil?"

"Actually it fits him."

"What do you mean?"

"Don't get me wrong, he was nice. But he's also slick. Like my brother Richard."

Aiden thought he hid his surprise, but she frowned as they waited for the elevator. "What?"

He shrugged. "Most women use words like 'charming,' 'sweet,' 'cute.'"

Lex guffawed. "Oh, please. I grew up with guys like him. Richard's the worst out of all my male cousins." They entered the elevator. "They're just boys with nice smiles. All my life, I've heard what they really think after the girls have gone home."

Her mobile, expressive face smiled at him. Such a contrast to the slightly cynical mask she had with Spenser. She even looked at him differently than she looked at other guys.

Maybe *she* was different.

TWENTY-EIGHT

"Aw, come on, Venus. Please?" Lex tried to keep her cell phone on her shoulder as she struggled to strap her leg more firmly into her brace.

"No, I'm too busy at work. I already called Trish to come pick you up."

"Trish? Since when is she my favorite person?" Lex stood and maneuvered past her boxes toward the bathroom.

"Jenn is out of town this weekend—rather conveniently, if you ask me. So it's either Trish or Mariko."

Ew. "Okay. When is she coming?"

"I caught her as she left home, so she should be there soon." A murmuring in the background claimed Venus's attention. "No, write an action item . . . No, not—Lex, I've gotta go." *Click.*

The doorbell rang.

Trish had lost weight. Dark bags sagged under her bleary eyes, and her mouth drooped in a petulant frown. "Let's go."

Once in the car, Trish broke the silence first. "I don't want to talk about it, okay? We both have to survive Uncle's birthday party, so let's just ignore it for now."

"Fine." Lex's teeth clicked together, but she uncrossed her arms. "So . . . uh . . . How's PT?"

That's a loaded question. A few weeks ago, she would have told Trish all about getting the massage, conquering her fear, the triumphant feeling afterward, like . . . an Ultimate Fighting Champion. "It's going well." She couldn't resist adding a little dig. "You know Aiden's my therapist?"

Trish's eyes ballooned. "Aiden's your PT? How is he?"

"He's really good. All my volleyball friends recommended him."

Trish sniffed. "Has he bitten your head off about your Christianity yet?"

"Is that what he did with you?"

"He kept going on about it. Finally I told him I couldn't work with him anymore because he wasn't Christian. I didn't like him harping on me."

Harping didn't sound like Aiden. And her current attitude about Trish didn't put Lex in a mood to believe her cousin's version of Aiden.

She kind of liked him, even though he didn't really fit the List. But he fit one thing she hadn't thought to add: *Someone who doesn't make me freak out when he touches me.*

She wondered if it would go anywhere with him. If not, she wondered if he might be willing to pose as a boyfriend in front of Grandma. Except that would be kind of, well, *lying.*

They arrived at their uncle's house, which already rang with childish screaming and collective male groaning—the Giants' game? Probably.

Eat and leave. Here we go again.

Trish had to park a few blocks away because the earlier arrivals had taken up all the curb space. She grunted in frustration. "I hate walking. Especially in these shoes."

She started off at a fast clip, then turned to give Lex an impatient look. "Any time this year."

Lex stumbled after her. The doctor had cleared her off her crutches, but she wished she'd brought them so she could get in a good *thwack* to the upside of Trish's head.

As soon as she walked in the door, an uncle's beer-soaked breath reached her a millisecond before he grabbed at her. "Hey, Lexie, Trish."

Lex snapped stiffer than an ironing board and shoved him away. Their harmless uncle became overly affectionate when supplied with Miller Genuine Draft.

"Where's the food?" Trish headed down the narrow hallway toward the kitchen. Another cheer came from the living room— hmm, maybe they were watching the A's game instead.

"I got you! I got you!"

Lex had only a half-second warning before two of her cousins' children barreled around the corner of the hallway. They swished past Trish's skirts and rammed straight into Lex's brace.

Bonk! The little girl ricocheted off the metal frame and bounced on the wooden floor. The impact sent a sharp jolt through Lex's knee joint.

"Ow!"

"Waaaaa!"

The child was louder.

The brat—er, kid's mother hustled into the hallway. "Lex, what did you do?"

"What did I do?"

"You're the one with bulletproof armor." Her cousin picked up her battering-ram daughter. "Poor baby. Did the bad Robo-Lex hurt you?"

"Waaaaa!"

The little boy who had been chasing the girl eyed Lex's steel-encased leg with a speculative grin.

Lex made a threatening move toward him.

He backed off.

Her cousin gasped. "Big bully."

Lex rolled her eyes and stilted off after Trish's disappearing skirt.

She found the food, scrambled around on the kitchen table. The kids had already mangled the fruit plate, but the *sashimi*—fresh raw tuna—fanned out in cool pink glory next to *makizushi* sushi rolls. Marinated *mochiko* chicken still steamed, crispy fresh from the deep fryer, and Grandma's homemade pickled vegetables—*takuwan* and *tsukemono*—lay in small dishes next to it.

"Oooh, one of the aunties made shrimp *tempura*." Trish piled hand-battered, deep-fried shrimp on a paper plate.

Lex grabbed a plate—this was the only reason to attend these things. Even Grandma muted her nagging when eating good Japanese food.

"Hey, Lex." Richard's jovial tone stiffened Lex's shoulders and set her jaw.

Yup, she was right to be wary—he dragged a short, thin Asian guy behind him, whose gaze had leeched onto the food.

"Lex, meet my, uh ... friend."

Food Leech didn't respond. Richard nudged him with an elbow.

"Yeah, yeah." Food Leech didn't even glance up at her. "Can we start eating?"

To add to the Ephesians List: *Common courtesy would be nice.*

Lex stepped out of the way as Food Leech bulldozed through the musubi—both plain rice balls and the ones with fried Spam— the shoyu-braised hotdogs, the *inarizushi* looking like golden dumplings in their deep-fried bean curd pouches. Okay, Lex would like her future boyfriend to appreciate food, but not at the expense of proper manners.

"Richard, where do you get these guys?" Lex didn't bother to drop her voice. Not that Food Leech even noticed.

Richard sputtered. "These are my friends—"

"Yeah, right. These are your friends like your kitchen is the most-used room in your apartment."

"Hey, I cook sometimes."

"Once every third leap year. Why the sudden parade of *Dating Game* rejects?"

Richard's "innocent" face never failed to incite suspicion. He shrugged. "I don't know what you mean."

"Cut the act. What does Grandma have on you?"

Richard stuck his nose in the air and smoothed his mousse-laden hair. "Unlike you, I have an excellent relationship with our grandparent."

Lex snorted.

"Very ladylike."

"Lex, come meet Mrs. Inawara's nephew." Grandma entered the kitchen with a tall, pale Japanese boy in tow.

Trish nipped out of the kitchen faster than a dog with a steak. Food Leech must have sensed imminent conflict, because he tailed her out of the danger zone.

"Lex, this is Derek, my friend's nephew." Grandma hooked his arm and thrust him forward, a sweet, butter-wouldn't-melt-in-her-mouth smile on her face.

Lex gritted her teeth. She didn't like his aunt very much, but no harm in meeting him. He might actually be nice —

As he approached, the smell assailed her. She gagged. Even Richard cleared his throat and stepped back. Grandma must be losing her sense of smell. The guy *reeked*.

"Fphaaugh! When was the last time you took a bath?" Lex held out an arm to keep El Stinko away.

"What are you talking about?" He took a whiff of his armpit.

Another odiferous wave crashed over her with his sudden movement. "Ugh. I'm going to lose my breakfast. Grandma, at least make sure they have good hygiene."

An affronted gasp sounded from the doorway to the kitchen. Grandma's friend — and El Stinko's aunt — stood there, white and quivering. Lex wasn't exactly upset, considering Aunty El Stinko always had something nasty to say about Lex's unfeminine interest in sports.

"Come, Derek. We're going home." Aunty El Stinko pivoted and marched away.

El Stinko spun around and followed her, but his action sent a BO-saturated breeze at Lex. She grabbed her stomach. Richard coughed.

"What is wrong with you?" Grandma's hiss carried louder than a shout.

"Uh ..." Richard glanced from Grandma's sparking glare to its victim, Lex. He took a giant step back and escaped the room. Coward.

"Grandma, will you stop siccing your friends' sons at me? How many of them do you have, anyway?"

"What's wrong with them? You don't think far enough ahead, that's your problem."

"They're only after me because you told them I could get them college game tickets. How is that thinking ahead?"

"That means they like sports, just like you. If you'd go out with them, you'd get to know them better."

"I have yet to meet one who doesn't set off my dweeb-meter."

"You're not open-minded enough." Grandma's cheeks started to flush under her makeup.

"How open-minded do I have to be?" Lex stabbed a finger at the empty doorway and the now-departed El Stinko.

"You're so picky." Grandma jerked her own finger at Lex's chest. "He has to be American, he has to be Christian—"

"No, we're not going into this again. His faith is important to me."

"Why does he need to be Christian? Does it matter as long as he can provide for you and your children?"

Grandma had already jumped to progeny. "Yes, it does matter. It's a deeply personal issue."

Grandma started talking with her hands. "All the Christian boys are so boring. You'd never date any of them."

What could Lex say to that? She had yet to meet a Christian boy who made her pulse rocket out of her wrist. But she wasn't about to let Grandma know that. "I'm not budging on this. He has to be Christian."

"You're being unreasonable." Lex could almost see the steam rising from Grandma's permed and colored head.

"*I'm* being unreasonable?" Lex flung her arms out.

She pursed her lips, and her eyes sparked black fire. "Grandma's trying to help you."

Great, Grandma was so upset, she was speaking in third person.

"My love life should be my business."

"Fine." Grandma turned smartly and marched to the doorway. "Good luck finding your exciting Christian boy." She paused at the threshold with a dark Dracula expression aimed at Lex. "Grandma still means what she said. If you don't have your *Christian* boyfriend by Mariko's wedding, Grandma's cutting funding to your girls' team the very next day."

"They're only girls—"

"And don't try to fool Grandma. She'll know if he's a boyfriend or not." She exited. The only thing missing was a melodramatic swirl of some dark cape.

Lex sagged against the kitchen counter. She crossed her arms tight to still the trembling of her hands. Why'd she let Grandma get to her? Now she couldn't even ask Aiden—very vocally non-Christian Aiden—to pose as her boyfriend.

She supposed she shouldn't have been thinking of him, anyway. If she started liking him, it would make things complicated. She knew their difference in faith—her belief and his lack of—would make any deeper relationship rocky at best. She had let his soap-fir-musk scent and magic hands cloud her judgment.

Back to the drawing board.

TWENTY-NINE

Was it really a good idea?
No, how could it be?

But maybe it would work out. She was different. What was the harm in asking?

Aiden needed to hurry up if he intended to ask her on a date. Lex only had the leg press left. He'd taken too long waffling. She sat in the machine but stared out the big picture window without seeing. Here was his chance. "So, Lex—"

"Where do you meet girls?" She didn't turn to look at him.

He blinked. "What?"

"You know. Where do you pick up chicks?"

He gave her a blank stare.

She glanced at him with raised eyebrows. "Going cruising? Scoping out? I'm running out of phrases here."

"I'm trying to decide if I want to laugh at you or increase the weight for your sets."

"No, don't up my weight. I really want to know."

"Why?"

"Well . . ." She had a hard time meeting his eyes.

Aiden suspected she was searching for a lie to tell him. He reached for the weight key.

"No!" She put her hand out to stop him. "I need to meet guys."

"Your grandma's supplying those pretty well, don't you think?"

"No, I mean nice guys. Ones who don't need Berkeley tickets."

"That's all?"

"And Christian."

He surprised himself by rolling his eyes rather than keeping his habitual calm, expressionless face. "That again?"

"It's important. Do you know how many divorces are the result of mismatched religions?"

"No, do you?"

"No, but I'll bet it's a lot."

Aiden folded his arms and stared down at her. "You're not working hard enough." He snatched out the weight pin and moved it down a slot.

"Hey!"

"You should be sweating too much to ask dumb questions."

"It's because of my grandma. She's going to pull funding from my junior high girls' volleyball team if I don't find a nice Christian boy to date. And marry."

"That's the dumbest story I've ever heard."

"It's true. Grandma's nuts. You'd think she doesn't already have tons of grandchildren and great-grandchildren. She's such a control freak."

"Pot, meet kettle," he murmured.

"What?"

"Nothing."

"You don't understand. I'm desperate. And he's got to be someone I can trust, because ... well, you know. The touching thing." Red stained her cheeks, but not from the workout.

And suddenly he realized how difficult this must be for her. A Christian boy would be safe—no French kisses or heavy petting in the backseat of the car.

But a part of him wanted to shake her. She was already comfortable with *him*. Why some boring, hypocritical Christian guy?

"Hi, Lex, Aiden." Mary walked past them on her way to the women's locker room.

A stunning smile appeared on Lex's face. "Hi, Mary. How's your shoulder feeling today? Any better from last week?"

"Oh, yes. I iced it a lot this weekend, just like a certain handsome physical therapist told me to do." Mary winked and nudged Aiden, then disappeared into the locker room.

Lex finished a set and sat there panting. "Maybe I should go church-hopping. Are there any Christians-only non-alcoholic bars?"

Aiden snorted. "Why don't you just camp outside a seminary? Hold up a sign, 'Will work for date.' Or better yet, 'I'm unsaved. Take me on a date.'"

Her glare could have burned the hair off his body. "Ha. Ha."

She finished her last set, and they headed back to the patient area for her ice and stim. "You're lucky. The doctor gave me the okay to drive as of tomorrow."

"Tomorrow?" He let her walk ahead of him down the ramp.

"He said three weeks. Tomorrow is three weeks."

"I better stay off the road."

"Oh, you're just so clever. I could always smear something nasty on your car seat today when you take me — " She came to a grinding halt. Aiden knocked into her from behind. She tipped forward, so he grabbed her waist to keep her from falling.

She didn't even notice. Ike, a regular at the gym, had captured her attention. He wore a bloody pierced-hand Christian T-shirt with "Consider this an engraved invitation" scrawled across it.

If anything, Lex wasn't shy. "Hi, Ike. Nice shirt."

"Thanks." Ike flashed his girl-magnet grin at her. Aiden's hand, still on Lex's waist, tightened.

She stepped away from him. "So ... you're a Christian?"

Oh, no way. Aiden crossed his arms.

"Yeah, I go to Valley Bible Church in Sunnyvale." Ike stepped forward to exert his charm.

"Oh, perfect."

"Huh?"

"I mean, that's great. I go to Santa Clara Asian Church in Campbell."

"I didn't know you were Christian." Ike shifted from "mildly interested" to "intently intrigued."

"Yeah. I've been wanting to visit Valley Bible Church for a long time."

Did she actually flutter her eyelashes at him? *Give me a break.*

Ike responded favorably to the fluttering. "Why don't you visit this weekend? You can sit with me and the rest of the Singles Group."

"Oh, that would be terrific." Lex sounded like it would be more fun than beach volleyball.

As they discussed time and directions, Aiden tightened his jaw. Lex knew guys. Was she really falling for his act? Aiden had heard Ike and his friends in the gym locker room after their workouts. He knew who they really were, what they thought about women.

She's a grown woman. She can take care of herself.

But then again, Lex was desperate. What wouldn't she do if she needed to accomplish something?

"Thanks." Lex gave him a dazzling smile.

"See you Sunday." Ike headed up to the weight machine area.

"Valley Bible Church?" Aiden couldn't keep a hint of derision from his tone.

"Don't knock it." Lex's look snapped from charming to chilly. She continued down the ramp.

Aiden's friend Spenser went to Valley Bible Church. He'd ask him to keep an eye on Lex this weekend.

"Why not?" Aiden strained through another set of bicep curls.

"I'm not your servant. Come to church yourself." Spenser got on the bench for barbell triceps press exercises.

"But you're already going to be there. All I'm asking is for you to look out for her, not be her bodyguard." Aiden set down his free weights.

"So, why can't you come?"

"She's going to see me there, and then what?"

"Naw, it's a big church."

"With my luck, she'll see me as soon as she walks in. She knows how I feel about all this church stuff. She'll think I'm stalking her."

"Which you are."

"No, I'm asking you to stalk her. Big difference." He flashed a grin.

Spenser glared. "I'm not stalking her, even for you."

"You're going to be at church anyway."

"Why can't you pretend?" Spenser dropped his barbell and turned to face him.

"She won't believe me."

"She'll believe me." Spenser's voice had that strange tone to it.

"What do you mean?" Aiden wasn't going to like this.

"I'll go up to her and tell her what you asked me to do."

Visions of lots of blood and guts flashed in front of him. Lex wouldn't stop there either. "You wouldn't."

"I would. I'm being truthful."

Aiden wanted to slug the smug smile off his face. "Forget it."

"Nope. Too late."

"Why does it even matter? This is stupid. I'm not going."

"It's only for one Sunday."

"She's a grown woman. I don't need to protect her. Besides, Ike isn't going to do anything. Just deceive her a little about how morally upright he is."

"And women just love being lied to. Just like she'll love when I tell her the little white truth about what you asked me to do for you."

"Okay, okay, I'll go."

Ike met her at the front of the church, just as he said he would. Another thing for her to add to her Ephesians List: *Someone who keeps his appointments.*

"Hey, Lex." Ike beamed at her.

She gave a weak smile in return. "Hi." She blamed her testy mood on the slight headache buzzing at her forehead.

"Let's go inside."

The large church overwhelmed her a little, but she soon realized she was only another face in the massive crowd. Ike led her to a middle section already half-filled with young adults. They sat down.

"I'll introduce you after the service when we all go out to lunch."

She glanced around at the guys. Most okay-looking, although a few were kind of strange, like that pale kid with the shock of red hair, and the bug-eyed goldfish-looking guy.

Then she noticed a few hostile stares from the women. Well, she sat next to a very cute bachelor. Although Ike's arm across the back of her seat annoyed her. He didn't touch her — just let his arm hang out there, over the seat edge.

The service started with a Bible reading. At that point, Lex realized they sat right under the speakers, and the buzz and vibration bumped her headache up the Richter scale. The words pounding out over her also made her realize she hadn't read her Bible in a while. Well, she'd start up again as soon as she got rid of the pain pulsing behind her eyes. She searched through her purse. No ibuprofen.

The worship music, although loud, drew her in. She knew most of the modern songs. For those few minutes, she checked her baggage at the door and rediscovered the joy of just being with Him. He didn't speak to her, but she felt happy singing to Him. She almost forgot her headache.

The sermon spoke to her about her tepid prayer life. Yeah, she really should pray more. Listen to God more.

During the announcements, she massaged her temples, and her attention wandered. There were mostly Caucasians in this church. No — one Asian couple sat near the front.

Since when had she become so ethnocentric that she couldn't feel comfortable not surrounded by her yella-fellas? It couldn't be because of the attack, could it?

He was so much larger than her Asian guy friends or her cousins. His pale wrist, smashing her clenched fist against the carpet, lay inches from her face. She couldn't stop staring at it as he fumbled with his belt . . .

A touch across her shoulders.

"Aaaah!" Lex jumped in her seat.

Ike jerked away from her, snatching back his arm. The worship leader paused in telling about the church picnic next week.

Everyone stared at her.

Oh, God, just open the ground and swallow me now.

The worship leader smiled kindly at her. Lex gave a weak smile back. He continued reading the announcements.

The speaker boomed, and her head boomed with him in boluses of sizzling pain. When would he just stop talking?

"Thanks for joining us for service today. God bless."

Finally.

Ike ushered her toward the social hall in the back of the sanctuary, where the Singles Group apparently gathered. Young people started filtering into the small, empty space. And several of them were definitely young. How old were these kids, anyway? Lex suddenly felt every one of her thirty years.

Ike introduced her around. The good thing was that no one knew about her job.

"This is Robert."

A bored-looking yuppie-type gave her a limp hand to shake. His massive gold pinky ring cut into her finger. "I'm in finance. What do you do?"

"I work for a website company."

Robert rolled his eyes behind designer-frame glasses. "The dot-coms are bombing."

"I like my job."

"Good, because you won't have it in another year."

To add to the List: *Someone who isn't snide, nasty, and snobbish at first impression.* His peevishness made her head throb.

Clark looked like a goldfish—he had buggy eyes, a pale yellow shirt straining its buttons over his round stomach, and a five-second memory.

"So what do you do, Clark?"

"I sell products door to door. I like it."

"What do you sell?"

"I sell products door to door. I like it."

"What kind of products?"

"Door to door. I like it."

To add to the List: *Able to hold a normal conversation.*

"Hi, I'm Jaspar." The tall, thin boy with thick red hair sprouting toward the ceiling had pale, almost translucent skin. He wouldn't meet her eyes, just stared at the floor.

"What do you do, Jaspar?"

"I sell products door to door." He aimed his mumble at her shoes.

To add to the List: *No door-to-door products salesmen.*

"That's interesting."

He sighed, as if his soul were falling into abject despair. "I suppose." He was having a lovely conversation with her sandals.

To add to the List: *Someone who will speak to my face and not my footwear.*

"So do you have any hobbies?"

"Yeah." His eyes rose to her shoulders. "I like going to movies."

"What movies?"

His bright green gaze popped up and locked with hers. In a flash, his demeanor had gone from sad to spiffy. "*Star Wars* changed my life."

"Uh ... the movies?"

"I used to be really into *Star Wars*. Their light sabers are really cool." He erupted into a few wild moves, swinging an imaginary sword—no, light saber. Then abruptly, he deflated back to his original, shoe-speaking self. "Now I'm into Jesus." He ended with a depressed sigh.

Real Jesus freak, aren't you? Her headache stomped with a vengeance.

The girls she met all showed their teeth when they smiled. Lex got the impression of bristling dogs guarding a bone — Ike, possibly? Were there any normal people in the bunch?

Lindsay twined her bangled wrist in Ike's arm as Lex approached. *That's real subtle there, sister.* "Where are we going for lunch?"

"Let me go ask some people." Ike left her to the mercy of Lindsay. The pretty woman stared at her like a piece of gum on her stilettos.

May as well clear the air. "So, are you or any of the other girls dating Ike?"

Lindsay's eyes reminded Lex of a cobra she'd seen once on TV. "He just broke up with a girl. He's still getting over her. He and I are *good friends.*"

Translation: *Keep your grimy hands off my man, I have first dibs.*

This had to be the worst Sunday service she'd ever had.

THIRTY

Aiden couldn't be more bored. The Scripture reading took forever. Did they have to read the entire chapter from Psalms?

The worship music wasn't much better. Repetitive, slow. He should have sat with Spenser in the front row rather than hiding here in the back.

Then he saw Lex. She had a quietness he'd never seen on her face. Peace, relief.

He became uncomfortably aware that while he mocked the music, it seemed to help unburden her. When was the last time he'd unburdened himself? He never unloaded, not to anyone. He never felt any kind of release or relief.

He was thirsty.

Aiden left the sanctuary—most people didn't even notice him leaving. The water fountain stood next to the men's restroom.

He took a drink. Took another one. He wasn't going back in there just yet. He wasn't. He took another drink. His stomach protested the excess water, but he slurped it up anyway.

The music stopped and the pastor started his sermon. Aiden dragged himself back into the sanctuary.

Boring, boring, boring.

He made a mistake when service got out. He should have left first. Instead, he ducked down in his seat as Lex and her escort shuffled down the aisle to the back of the sanctuary. When he got up after them, he realized they'd gathered at the entrance to the Social Hall—

which looked right out into the lobby. Lex would see him if he tried to waltz out of church.

He hung back, wondering if the sanctuary had another exit.

Suddenly, Lex appeared in the lobby area with another girl. Aiden ducked down to pretend to tie his shoe. Which had no laces.

"Hi, Ike—oh!" A sultry voice sounded above his head. "I'm so sorry. I mistook you for Ike."

Aiden straightened, and a twenty-first-century Lolita invaded his personal space with a flirty tilt to her blonde head. Lex had disappeared. "I'm Salome."

"Aiden."

"Nice to meet you." *Flutter, flutter* went her eyelashes.

"Er ... nice to meet you too."

"So ... are you here alone?"

"Uh ... yeah." Why did he feel like a gazelle stalked by a hungry lioness?

"Why, how nice. Let me introduce you to our Singles Group."

"No! Uh ... thanks."

"Oh, we're a nice bunch. There's a new girl today too." Her slightly brittle smile indicated she wasn't as thrilled about that as her words implied.

"Sorry, I'm committed to lunch with someone."

"Oh, who?" She glanced around.

Oh, great. "Um ..." He pointed toward the right. "There."

She looked.

He ducked left.

He darted down the first hallway he found, dotted with closed doors. He opened one and slipped inside.

Darkness surrounded him. He listened at the closed door. He heard light footsteps that approached, then receded.

"Let me guess. Salome?" The gentle male voice shot a bolt of adrenaline into Aiden's heart. He spun around.

The pastor sat at his desk in the darkened office, surrounded by books.

"I'm sorry, the door was open, and it was dark—"

He smiled and waved a careless hand. "I was just sitting here. You have the look of the hunted, and only Salome causes that in young men." He gestured toward the wall. "Turn on the light."

Aiden did. The office brightened. Books surrounded him, some old, some new, all crammed onto the shelves. But on the wall across from the desk, where the pastor would look up and immediately see it, was a painting.

It stretched from ceiling to floor. A crucified Christ—bloody, gruesome, painful. His agony etched on his face, evident in the curl of his body. He lay pinned to the Roman cross, naked, legs pulled up sharply. It was worse than the *Passion* movie.

"That's a true crucifixion." The pastor shifted in his chair, causing the leather to creak. "Not the sanitized version from movies."

Aiden couldn't look away. A trembling took over his hands, his legs, his chest. The picture made him ache. It made him want to crash to his knees, howling and weeping. It shocked and stripped him, all at once.

Aiden didn't know how long he stood there staring.

The pastor never spoke. Finally he got up from behind his desk and moved around the cramped space to reach the door. "Feel free to stay." He exited his office, closing the door behind him.

Aiden couldn't have moved if he'd wanted to.

THIRTY-ONE

Lex was drowning in bills.

Medical bills, to be exact. She'd been paid a little during her medical leave, but the sheer size of her MRI bill made her want to cry. She'd go back to work in about a week—and hopefully be able to pay this when she got her paycheck. She was thankful for her insurance; otherwise, her bills would be much larger.

Her cell phone rang. "Hello?"

"It's Chester."

"Hey, coz, what's up?"

"I know you're on medical leave, so I thought I should tell you—they announced sitewide paycuts today here at SPZ."

"*What?*"

"They're trying to make up for a bad quarter with a 10 percent paycut for everybody rather than laying anybody off."

Well, she supposed she should be glad they hadn't let her go. But 10 percent? "Chester, I've got surgery bills."

"Don't whine to me. I've got a mortgage."

Lex sighed. "Thanks for letting me know."

"No prob." He hung up.

Her phone rang again immediately. "Hello?"

"Hi Lex, it's Ike. I was free tonight and wondered if I could come over with ice cream."

Whoa. Talk about coming on strong and fast. Still, despite his touchy-feely tendencies, he was charming, nice to look at, and a good conversationalist. "Sure." She gave him directions.

He arrived with four different pints of Ben and Jerry's. "Didn't know what you liked, so I bought a bunch."

"Aw, that's so great of you. Usually my brother and my dad get whatever they want without asking me." She closed the door behind him.

Ike turned mid-stride on his way to her kitchenette. He looked deep into her eyes. "Yeah, well, I'm not your brother."

Dark blue eyes. Rugged face. *What's not to like?*

She snatched the Chunky Monkey, he picked up Cookie Dough. The rest they crammed into her teeny freezer.

They ate leaning against the counter and talking.

He liked weekend warrior-type sports—the occasional pickup basketball game, football with friends, softball with the church. He kept in shape primarily through the gym. "I just felt like we never got to talk on Sunday, and I wanted to get to know you better."

Lindsay's feline face hovered in her mind's eye, but Lex gave a mental snarl and it dissipated.

Ike loved classical music and jazz, but he didn't play it when with friends unless they liked it too. He didn't have a favorite restaurant—he was happy with whatever someone else preferred. He liked going for long drives. "And I like hanging out with friends."

Lex licked her spoon. "Thanks, Ike. This ice cream hits the spot." Better than worrying over her bills. What a great time getting to know him. He was so easygoing, so down-to-earth.

Ike reached around her to throw his spoon in the sink, and came face-to-face with her.

He was incredibly *male*. His blue eyes seemed very close. He wore a spicy cologne—not too strong, but hecka sexy. His gaze fell to her lips.

She'd read a lot of romance novels, so she knew her pulse should start racing right about now, and her breathing should come in little gasps. She felt tense—did that count?

He was going to kiss her, and she was ready for him. Her first kiss ever. Well, second kiss if she counted that peck Aiden gave her to deceive Ben—

Don't think about Aiden. Ike is about to kiss you.

He took his sweet time. He stared at her mouth for so long, she wondered if she should move in and plant one on him. But even though she moved through most of her life aggressively, something about this made her feel shy and scared.

No, you're not scared. You're anticipating. It's different.

"You have ice cream on your lip." Ike's low, husky voice sent a chill—no, a thrill, that was a *thrill* she felt—down her spine. His finger came up and touched the corner of her mouth.

Her jaw flinched and banged against his knuckle.

"Sorry."

He chuckled low in his chest. She guessed her nervousness encouraged him.

His head came down.

At the touch of his mouth, her heart slammed painfully against her chest. Ants crawled all over her skin, biting her collarbone, her neck. She hunched her shoulders, gasped against his mouth, twisted away.

He'd barely touched her and she freaked. She couldn't imagine what he thought of her. The kindness in his eyes made her want to cry.

"I'm sorry, Lex, I jumped the gun."

"No, I'm sorry." She didn't deserve his understanding. "You're—" She checked herself. What had Richard told her once? She shouldn't tell a guy he's nice because he wouldn't want the "nice guy" syndrome. "I'd like to get to know you better."

"I would too." He dipped in and brushed a soft kiss against her cheek. She moved her head at the same time so he wouldn't notice her automatic flinch. She had to stop doing that or she'd chase every guy away.

"I'll see you at the gym."

"Yeah."

"No, don't move. I'll let myself out." And he did.

She stared at the closed door. She was so stupid! What was wrong with her? It had been perfect! Perfect! Why couldn't she just kiss a guy?

I'd like to kiss Aiden—

Stop it, stop it, stop it! She flung her spoon in the sink.

She'd like to kiss Aiden ...

"Hi, Dad—whoa! Spiffy!" Lex stared at her father, standing at the open door to Uncle Howard's apartment. "Going out to dinner?"

Dad flushed. "No, no. I'm doing laundry."

"Oh. Well, can I come in?"

"Uh ... sure." He stepped aside so she could walk in, carrying paper shopping bags.

He shifted his weight from one leg to the other. "Uncle Howard's out bowling tonight."

"Yeah, I know." She dropped the bags to the floor and bent to rub her knee. Man, it ached.

"You doing okay?"

"I got my brace off a couple weeks ago, but stairs are still killing me. Especially when I'm carrying something." She opened one of the bags. "I found some of Mom's stuff in my boxes. I wanted to know—"

The doorbell rang. Lex moved to the door.

"No, wait, Lexie—"

"Mary?" In a pretty pink dress, Mary stood on the doorstep. It was weird not to see her in gym clothes. "What are you doing here?" At Dad's place. With Dad home, but not Uncle Howard.

Then it dawned on Lex.

Mary realized it at the same time. Her gaze shifted to the living room behind Lex. "You didn't tell her?" Her irate voice shot over Lex's shoulder like a bullet.

"Mary ..." Her father's voice sounded softer than Lex had heard it in a long time. But also more frightened than she'd heard it in a long time.

"*Baka!* I can't believe you didn't tell her." Mary pushed her way into the apartment and stood toe to toe with Dad.

The late evening sun glinted into the living room, illuminating her father looking a little shriveled next to Mary's strong, highly annoyed frame.

A smile tugged at Lex's mouth.

Her dad cleared his throat. "Mary—"

"Martin, you give her no respect. She's your daughter. You know better than that."

An unexpected tightness clenched behind Lex's eyes. How strange. She sounded too much like Mom, but in a voice so different.

"Now, M—"

"The girls are always the last to know! Like she's an afterthought."

Wait a minute. "Dad!" Lex stabbed a finger at him. "You told Richard and you didn't tell me?"

"Well—"

"Dad, I can't believe you!"

Mary waved a finger in his face. "She's the one who took care of you for years, but you bothered to tell her brother and not her? Shame on you."

"I was going to—"

"I came over last week and you never said a word about dating anybody!" Lex's voice roared in the little room.

"Lexie, I was going to tell you. Mary, this is Lex—"

"We've met!" they both snapped at the same time.

Suddenly, Lex wanted both to laugh and cry.

Mary turned and approached Lex. "I'm sorry. When we met at the gym, I thought you already knew."

Lex thought back to their first conversation. "No, Aiden had been talking about how faithful you were in coming to the gym every week, so I thought you were talking about him."

"Aiden? Oh, he's such a sweetheart. Unlike some men I know." Her voice hardened. "Did you and your dad want some time—?"

"No, go out to dinner." Lex opened the door. "I need to be alone."

"Lex ..." Her dad's eyes peered at her with worry. Concern. Sorrow. Regret.

"I'm fine. Really. I just need some time. I'll talk to you about it later." She shut the door behind them.

"No, you're going too fast." Aiden snagged another exercise ball and joined her on the mat. He lay on his back and placed his feet on top of the ball. "Copy me."

He lifted his body up off the floor in a bridging exercise, keeping his shoulders to the ground. She followed him. He lowered excruciatingly slowly. Her hamstrings burned.

"Good." He set the pace for her entire first set of fifteen. She gulped for air when they finished, but he hadn't even broken a sweat.

Too soon, he got into position again. "Ready?"

She got into position and nodded.

"One."

"Hey." Lex noticed Aiden had lifted one foot from the ball and extended it out, performing the exercise single-legged. He'd also moved the ball out farther.

"If I have to set your pace for you, I may as well get a little workout in."

She ignored the jibe. "I want to try that." She extended her good leg and tried a rep. Lex couldn't even get her butt off the ground.

"Oomph! My bad leg isn't strong enough." She switched legs.

Oh, man! Lex barely got three inches of air before her back struck the mat again. She rubbed her aching hamstring.

Aiden did another rep single-legged. "It's more advanced."

Advanced? It was Superman-level.

"Come on, both feet on the ball. Keep up with me."

She kept up with him—sort of. She had a tendency to drop back down faster than he did. He glared sideways at her. "Slower. Don't cheat."

Any second now, her hamstrings were going to twang out of her thighs like snapped guitar strings.

Lex liked just watching him—effortless, strong. Like when he'd pushed her on that run. A pleasant tingling spiraled in her stomach. She was such a sucker for an athlete. She forgot that Aiden excelled in sports other than volleyball—she kept seeing him like that first night at Nikkei, awkward and wild on the court.

He's cute.

But he's not a believer.

She struggled to finish the set. As she lay panting, she watched him do a few extra reps.

Look, but don't touch. And don't let him know you're feeling this way.

It was all her back's fault.

Lex had been feeling achy, so she yelled at the girls more than usual. After the girls had left, Vince pulled her aside before she walked out of the gym with her bag. "You were hard on them again today."

She knew it but didn't want to admit it. She shook off his hand. When would he get the hint and stop touching her? "Playoffs are only a few weeks away."

"No, this is different. This isn't playoffs. This is something to do with you."

"What are you, my shrink?"

"I'm your assistant coach, and you're not coaching them well."

"What do you mean?"

"What are your real motivations for pushing them? Is this about them? Or about you?"

"I have no clue what you're getting at."

"Look, I know that your mom used to coach these girls' mothers. I know why you formed this club team."

"You only think you know." Coming from Vince's mouth, it seemed like such a sad, pathetic thing for her to do—something in honor of her mother.

"Getting the girls to win isn't going to bring your mother back."

"What? That's ridiculous."

"It seems like that's what you're trying to do."

Lex rolled her eyes. "You are way off the mark, Vince. I've been having back problems, and it's making me crabby. Should I admit that I'm PMSing too?"

"Now you're making excuses to validate your denial."

With a gust of frustration, Lex marched toward her car. "Good-night, Vince."

She had driven almost half a mile away when she realized she'd left her purse under the bleacher seat. She turned the car around, ignoring that alarming sputtering from the engine.

Vince's accusations horrified her. Bring her mother back? Now that was just morbid.

Except ... did a part of her sort of think that way? Did a part of her want to be here for these girls because her mother had been forced to abandon her old volleyball team, to abandon Lex years ago?

Mom had cancer. It wasn't her fault.

But Lex had still felt abandoned. And she drove these girls and sacrificed for them because she didn't want to abandon them either.

Oh, come on. This was stupid. Lex would not fall into some psychoanalysis pit. She was too complicated to compartmentalize like this.

She pulled into the parking lot. Another car had pulled next to Vince's. It looked like Jennifer's truck. No, it couldn't be. Jennifer didn't even know Vince. Lex got out and headed toward the gym.

Vince had company. She heard the voices as she approached the open gym doorway.

"Mrs. Sakai got you that coaching position at Olympic Boys' School."

Mrs. Sakai—Grandma? Coaching position? And that voice sounded a lot like Jennifer. Lex slowed her steps.

"Good. Tell her thanks."

"The job starts in a couple weeks. You'll honor your agreement with her and quit this job by then, right?"

What? Vince couldn't quit. Lex needed him for playoffs. A volcano erupted in the pit of her stomach, with rolling, pitching, acidic heaving. She wanted to spew lava at somebody. Or two.

"This isn't a real job, just volunteer. But yeah, I'll quit."

Traitor. Betrayer.

"Olympic Boys' School will contact you this week about starting." Jennifer's voice moved closer to the doorway.

Burning, Lex stepped into the gym.

She stood nose to nose with her cousin. Jenn gasped and jumped back. Vince paled, but straightened.

Lex didn't know what she looked like, but she certainly felt as lethal as Medusa. She pointed a venomous gaze at Vince. "Our conversation tonight wasn't about me. It was you justifying leaving the girls, you slime."

"You're not going to have funding for playoffs anyway." Vince picked up his bag and pushed his way out the door.

Lex skewered Jennifer with a jagged-edged stare. "Since when did you become Grandma's messenger girl?"

Jennifer's lip trembled. Her face screwed up tightly.

"No, no, no. Tears aren't going to get you out of this one, Jenn."

"You have no idea what I've been through!"

Lex started. Jenn yelling was like Grandma being quiet.

Jenn started sobbing in earnest. "Grandma's over at our house all the time, asking about you. I stopped calling you so I wouldn't have anything to tell her."

"Grandma nagging is different from this. You betrayed me."

"You still don't get it." Jenn snuffled loudly. "You're strong. I'm not. It wasn't just Grandma—it was Mom and Dad and my sisters. Grandma complains to them about you, so they complain to me."

"This was their idea?"

"No, it was Grandma's."

"Figures."

"They bullied me into doing this."

"You could have said no." But even as she accused her, Lex knew Jennifer never told her overbearing family no.

"No, I couldn't." Jenn started heaving with sobs. "I don't control anything in my life anymore."

"Jenn, I'm stranded and you betrayed me. You should have come to me instead of going to my assistant coach behind my back, arranging for Grandma to buy him off."

Jenn shook her head and kept crying.

Her tears only fed Lex's fire. "What could your family have done to you? You know who's going to suffer? These junior high girls." Lex turned away. "They don't deserve any of this. I'm doing my best."

"Grandma heard you were trying to find another sponsor."

"I'm trying to save them."

"Grandma wants you to have a boyfriend."

"Grandma wants more great-grandchildren. Her immortality. A boyfriend is a means to an end." Lex pressed her fingers to her temples. "I'm really trying, Jenn. I have one more month before the wedding, but you've just made things more difficult for me. You've made things harder for those girls."

Jennifer sniffed.

"Just leave." Lex went to grab her purse from the bleachers. When she turned around, Jennifer had gone.

THIRTY-TWO

A iden took a deep breath, then knocked on the door.
"Come in."

He felt like an interloper as he entered. "Pastor, we met—"

"I remember." The pastor waved Aiden inside.

No cheesy smiles, nothing even remotely resembling a salesman selling something. The pastor gestured to the chair in front of his desk.

"I'm Aiden." No last name. "I came to see the mural again."

"Go ahead."

It kicked Aiden in the gut, just like before, actual physical pain. He never expected it from a mere picture. "Who painted it?"

"Another church commissioned an artist to paint it for their sanctuary, but the result was ... a little too shocking. So I bought it."

"Why?"

"You know why." The pastor's matter-of-fact voice remained neutral. "You're the one who came back to look at it."

Aiden couldn't stop. He shuffled his feet. "I—"

"You don't have to say anything if you don't want to. I don't mind if you want to just look at it again."

Sincerity in this man's eyes. Aiden suddenly realized how different that was. He always felt closed. Controlled. "What do you feel when you look at it? Do you get used to it?"

The man's eyes saddened as he looked at the picture. "I don't get used to it. I pray I never do."

293

Aiden didn't say anything. He reached out a hand to trace a nail biting into his flesh.

"Christ's pain should always be my pain. I should never forget. I never want to. I want to keep reaching out to other people in pain." He sighed. "It doesn't always work that way. I fail more than I succeed."

"Why try?"

"Because I can't afford not to. Look at Him." He stretched out his hands as if beseeching the picture. "He wouldn't give up."

Aiden shook his head. "He doesn't make sense to me."

The pastor shrugged. "He does when you believe. That's all I can tell you."

"That makes even less sense."

He sat back down in his chair. "Take a couple days and think about it. Come back and tell me what you think."

"You'll just argue with me."

"I won't." And he hadn't, not the entire time Aiden had stood in his tiny office.

"Maybe." Aiden twisted the doorknob.

"You don't have to leave if you don't want to. I'll even leave the office if that'll make you more comfortable." He wasn't eager or pushy. He was matter-of-fact. He met Aiden with clear eyes.

Aiden had never been as transparent as that. He almost wished he could be. "No, I've seen enough. Thanks." He shut the door behind him and headed out to the church lobby. Maybe he'd come back.

"Lindsay, sweetie."

Ike's voice stopped Aiden before he erupted into the front lobby. He peeked around the corner.

Ike held Lindsay in a loose embrace. His murmured words didn't carry to Aiden, but they clearly pleased Lindsay.

Aiden had seen Ike flirting with Lex the other day at PT.

He wasn't surprised. He had overheard Ike enough at the gym, in the men's locker room. He knew Ike flitted from girl to girl. He loved whatever girl he happened to be with, no matter how much he flew back and forth.

Lindsay today. Lex tomorrow? Not cool.

Except Lex wasn't Aiden's to protect. If she made a bad choice in men, what was it to him?

Ike took Lindsay's hand and led her out the side door.

Bile left a bitter taste in Aiden's mouth. He forced his jaw to relax and stop clenching his teeth together.

Lex didn't deserve to be played.

You don't feel this protective of Lindsay.

Lex wasn't his, but she was a friend.

She would never want you to interfere with her life.

She'd never find out.

The Goodwill guys had put it in her car for her—even if it did stick out the back a little—but who would bring it into her apartment?

Lex frowned and stared at her new/used exercise bike. It wasn't nearly as nice as the ones at PT, but it would do the job. If she could cycle a couple times a day, the swelling would stay down in her knee.

Assuming she could get it into her apartment. And assuming she could find someplace to put it. Well, the CPM machine had been returned long ago, so she really should rearrange the boxes.

Maybe somebody would come by. Or maybe she could call someone. She'd leave the bike in the car until then.

Lex walked slowly over the cracked walkway to her apartment. She still didn't feel very stable without her brace. The doctor assured her she'd get stronger once she got used to not having it on.

What was that on her door? Lex pulled the yellow sheet of paper from her peeling paint.

The apartment building was being sold. Lex had four weeks to move out.

A hammer sent blows to her breastbone and her stomach at the same time. She gripped the doorframe to keep from falling.

This couldn't be happening.

She needed ice cream.

Lex jammed her key in the lock.

"Rex?"

She turned. "Oh, hi Mrs. Chang."

Her cheerful round face had turned into a weepy moon. She held her own notice.

"Oh, Mrs. Chang. Do you understand what that says?" Lex pointed at the paper.

Mrs. Chang nodded. "I call nephew, he read."

"What are you going to do?"

She shook her head while another fat tear dropped from her downcast eyes. She gave a rather loud, wet sniff, then a hacking sound from the back of her throat.

Okay, that was just gross.

"I live wit' nephew. He help."

Lex awkwardly patted Mrs. Chang's round shoulder. She nodded, then waddled away.

What would happen to her? Would her nephew find her another place or take her in? It sounded like he knew his duty—he'd take care of his aging relative in some way. Lex had never been so relieved at the old cultural obligations. She'd stop hacking at them after this.

She needed ice cream.

She pushed into her studio. The unnatural silence confused her. What was missing?

The hum of the refrigerator.

Lex dashed to the kitchenette and saw the drips of water from the tiny freezer, all the way down the front.

She wanted to cry. No ice cream.

She had just finished cleaning out her spoiled food and slurping down some melted ice cream when her cell phone rang. "Hello?"

"Hi, it's Aiden. I'm in your area—I'm meeting some friends for dinner. Want to join us?"

Not a date, then. Lex wasn't disappointed, not really. "Your timing is perfect. My fridge is broken."

"Hooray for old appliances."

"Gee, thanks."

"I'll pick you up in ten minutes."

He arrived in eight minutes, actually. She opened the door before he rang the bell. "Where are we going?"

"Chinese?"

"Excellent."

Aiden kept tapping the steering wheel as he drove. Even Lex, as unobservant as she tended to be, noticed his uncharacteristic nervousness. "Are you okay?"

"I'm just hungry."

"Not that I'm complaining, but what made you call me for dinner with you and your friends?"

Aiden's face seemed smoother than glass. It seemed almost as if he were hiding something. No, that was ridiculous. "You did say you wanted to meet more guys, right?"

"Oh." She had said that. "Right."

"One guy is Christian, I think. At least, he says he is."

His cynicism pricked her. "There are sincere Christians, you know."

He grew quiet. "Yes, I know." His voice thrummed low and thoughtful.

They pulled into the parking lot. "Is that them?" Lex saw two figures half-hidden in the dark.

Something made her pause before opening her door.

It couldn't be Aiden's friends—it was a couple. The man kissed the woman in the dark, a romantic picture. The woman's light-colored hair shimmered almost silver.

That looked like Ike. And Lindsay.

The man lifted his head.

"Ike?" She didn't recognize the croaking voice. Was that her? She swallowed. A wadded up ball of tape stuck in her throat.

The man smiled. It was Ike.

Aiden hadn't gotten out either. He stared hard at the couple.

Lex swallowed. "Can we not—?"

"Sure." He started up the engine again, no questions.

"Please just take me home." She wasn't hungry anymore.

They drove out of the parking lot. As they passed Ike and Lindsay, Lex felt only a twinge like a snapped rubber band in her chest.

Well, at least she wouldn't have to kiss him now.

She glanced at Aiden. She'd like to kiss him—

Look, but don't touch.

Rats.

THIRTY-THREE

A iden thought sitting in the front pew with Spenser would make him a target for the full force of the pastor's sermon, but the man barely glanced at him.

The message aimed at hearts more than minds. It contrasted with the talks Aiden had with him the past couple weeks, where Aiden asked and the pastor responded with logic.

"God gives us freedom." He studied his notes and sipped some water before continuing. "But freedom isn't the same for everybody. Freedom could be from physical prisons or mental prisons. Freedom from inadequacy and hiding."

Aiden wondered if that was a message to him. They'd talked about his tendency to hide behind his impassive mask, to always seem calm and in control.

From the pulpit, he swept a pointing finger at the congregation. "God wants to free you. He cares about each of you, individually."

Aiden had a hard time believing that. The pastor had told him to set out a fleece, but Aiden wasn't sure how.

One thing the pastor had said still resonated in his mind. *Aiden, you don't need to have all the answers before you step out in faith.*

Listening to him now, Aiden struggled with the fact that he didn't have enough to go by, and that *that's* what faith was.

Okay. He sat back. He wasn't sure how to open a channel to God, but he assumed He'd hear him. *Okay. Prove Yourself to me. I'm not promising to believe, but I'll listen, for a change.*

That's it.

No thundering revelation. No fireworks, no surge of emotion.

Well? He didn't feel any different. Was he supposed to?

The pastor suddenly glanced at Aiden, paused in his sermon. Then he picked up his sentence and continued.

That seemed odd.

Spenser turned in his seat, gave him a long look. He turned back around.

Hmmm.

Then Spenser leaned sideways. "Let's go fishing after service."

"Okay."

"I've been talking to your pastor." Aiden cast his line into Calero Reservoir. The hot day didn't say much for their chances of catching anything.

"He's a nice guy." Spenser cast out his line and moved a step farther away.

"I like the picture on his wall."

"Me too."

Aiden's lure stuck on something. "Aw, man." He tugged, but no dice.

"Stuck?"

"Yeah."

Aiden cut his line. It had been a cheap lure anyway. He selected another one and started stringing it. "I'm starting to understand this Christianity stuff." He didn't look up at Spenser.

"Great." Spenser didn't say anything more, just kept jibbing his lure. Aiden looked at him.

Spenser smiled. It wasn't brilliant, or startled, or even different from normal. But something about it ... Aiden somehow felt that now he knew Spenser better than he ever had before.

He cast his lure. Yeah, maybe this was right.

"So this snooty guy comes up and says, 'Welcome to Green Pastures Church. Are you a visitor today?' And I was like, 'Well, duh.' And then he asked me if I was a Christian, if I went to Bible study, blah, blah, blah. And then he started harping about how I needed to learn Greek. Greek!" Lex shoved at the leg press so hard, her foot caught air.

She could tell Aiden tried hard not to be amused. "Greek is a worthy study."

"Oh, don't start. So then I told him—"

"Hey, Aiden, where were you, man?" Ike walked up to Lex's leg press. "Hi there, Lex."

She stifled the urge to knock him to the mat, the two-timing flirt. "Hi, Ike."

"So, Aiden, me and Lindsay waited twenty minutes for you, and then we just went inside to order."

Aiden had gone still—so subtle, Lex almost didn't notice it. He shrugged. "Sorry. I tried calling you, but my cell phone died."

"No prob, no prob. Next time. That Chinese restaurant was great."

Lex almost didn't pick up on Ike's words except that Aiden's mask had subtly shifted at "Chinese restaurant."

"When were you guys supposed to meet?" She paused at the top of her rep.

Aiden cleared his throat. "This past week."

He was never vague. Lex's eyes narrowed.

"I think it was Wednesday, right?" Ike patted his stomach. "That restaurant on Bascom."

"You set me up!" Lex swung off the machine. The weights crashed down.

"Whoa, whoa!" Ike backed off. Lex ignored him, advancing on Aiden. His face had become fluid, flowing from shock to calculating, from guilt to regret.

"You wanted me to see Ike with Lindsay."

"You saw us? What?" Ike paled to paste. "Oh, man."

"You—" She whirled and advanced a step at Ike, who backed into the freeweights shelves—"are a dork. You never had a chance. And you—" She turned to stalk Aiden—"are just as bad as Grandma."

She stood there, nursing a strong urge to knock *him* to the mat instead of Ike. She had never thought Aiden would trick her. Aiden was the one person she had thought she could trust to be honest. Wasn't that one of her original points on her Ephesians list? Honest? Not manipulative?

"It's true, I did know Ike and Lindsay would be there, and I took you to see them. But I didn't make them start macking."

"You saw that?" Ike plopped onto a gym bench. "Oh, man."

"You had to have known what he'd do with a pretty female in a dark parking lot."

Aiden's mask dropped and shattered. "Do you really want to date someone like that?" He flung his arm at Ike.

Lex had never seen Aiden upset like this—even on the volleyball court, she'd never seen him so mad—but anger fired through her veins too. "It's not your business. You took that choice away from me."

"You don't like not being in control of everything."

"Look who's talking."

"Guys." Ike stepped between them and extended an arm to each. "Now, you're just getting snipey. Let's try to keep communication open—"

"Shut up!" "Stuff it."

"Okay." Hands up, he backed away. "I can see I'm not wanted."

"I don't like being manipulated." Lex wanted to grab something and brain Aiden, but the weights were a little too lethal.

"You'd rather be manipulated by the player over there? I was trying to protect you."

"I—" Lex ground her teeth. That was actually kind of nice, but she wasn't in a mood to appreciate it. "You just keep out of my life." She marched down the ramp and turned left to the waiting area.

She ruined her exit by coming back to get her purse from the women's locker room. She gave Aiden a heated glare when she passed him the second time.

With nose pointed straight up in the air, Lex stormed out.

THIRTY-FOUR

Hey, Lex, meet my friend—"

"Not now, Rich." Lex stomped through Grandma's front door, past Richard, who held it open, and past his skinny male "friend."

"Hey, hey." Richard snagged her arm before she got too far.

"I need to say hello to Grandma."

"She's talking with Jenn's mom. She can wait. This is—"

"Hi." Lex stuck out her hand. Mr. Skinny shook it with his own slimy one. "I'm Lex, and I'm not interested, no matter what Richard told you." She turned toward the kitchen.

"Lex." Richard caught up with her, thankfully leaving Mr. Skinny in the living room. "Come on, you have to be nice to me today. It's Boys' Day."

"No, it's May fifth. Technically it's Children's Day, not Boys' Day, which means I don't have to be nice to you ever. What's up with all the guys?"

"What guys?" Richard suddenly found the linoleum fascinating.

"You've turned into a one-man male escort service."

"What?" Apparently the jab at his masculinity pricked him. "I have not. I'm *sociable*. Something you need to learn to be."

"And you're trying to teach me by introducing me to the latest Loser from the Street? You hardly know these guys."

"How do you know? We could be best buds."

"I've seen all your friends. They're all like you. You wouldn't be seen dead with Mr. Skinny in the living room, or that Food Leech at Uncle's birthday party, or—"

"I'm trying to find sensitive men who would appeal to your feminine sensitivities." Richard raised a hand to cover his heart. "I have only your interests in mind."

Lex laughed in his face, the first non-depressed feeling she'd had since her fight with Aiden that morning. "Try another one."

Richard tried to think fast, but instead gaped like a goldfish.

"While you're coming up with something, I'm going to say hi to Grandma before she disowns me."

She heard Grandma before she entered the TV room at the back of Jenn's parents' house. "Oh, Trish, your boyfriend is so nice. He has such a wonderful accent when he speaks Japanese to me."

Lex entered the room, already milling with cousins, aunts, and uncles. Grandma perched on an overstuffed wing chair in the corner, Trish sitting beside her on the couch. Jenn sat rather dejected on her other side, while Venus leaned against the couch arm, looking bored.

The sight of Jenn and Grandma unleashed the dam of anger and betrayal. The sound of praise for Trish's boyfriend—who'd been influencing her to stay away from church—made Lex's body go rigid.

Why couldn't Lex find a nice guy? Why'd Grandma throw all those losers at her? Why couldn't Grandma leave her alone? Why'd she turn Jennifer against her? Why was she so nice to them and so horrible to Lex?

"Hi, Grandma." Lex stood a few feet away and spoke through clenched teeth.

Grandma gave her a cool smile. "How's your girls' volleyball team?" She said *volleyball* as if it were *Ebola*.

Then it clicked in Lex's head, like the difference on the radio between the 670 AM and 680 AM KNBR station ("*The* sports leader"). Grandma didn't want Lex playing volleyball with those girls *at all*.

"What do you have against those girls?" Lex took a menacing step forward. Her outburst caused the noise level in the room to drop.

Grandma's nose went straight up in the air. "I don't know what you're talking about."

"What is so wrong about me coaching that team?"

"You're always coaching that team. Every time I call you, you're out coaching them or playing with your friends."

"So, you shut down my team?"

"Not at all." Grandma had a good facade of reason and sweetness. "I said I'd keep up funding if you found a boyfriend."

"I don't want a boyfriend."

"Now, that's just silly—"

"And I'm tired of being controlled and manipulated." Lex had started breathing hard. "First you, then Aiden. This is *my* life! What I do with my time is my business."

"You play volleyball too much. It's unfeminine. *You're* unfeminine."

The words had stung when Lex's girly cousins taunted her as a child. They hit her like a slap to the face now, coming from her coiffed and perfumed grandmother. "I'm fine the way I am. There's nothing wrong with me!"

"Lex!" Jennifer's mother stepped up to bat. "You don't talk to Grandma that way."

"She shouldn't treat me this way!"

Grandma's eyes blazed, causing the flush in her cheeks. "Grandma's treating you the way you should have been treated years ago. Your father spoiled you. You turned out wild and uncouth just like your mother."

Jennifer, Venus, and Trish all sucked in gasps.

A red film fell over Lex's eyes. "You shut up! Don't you talk about Mom that way!" She lunged.

She actually *lunged*.

Grandma flinched back in her chair. Jennifer jumped in surprise and fell off her seat. Trish and Venus leaped into Lex's way, holding her body back while her grasping arms still reached for Grandma's pearled neck to wring.

"Lex!" "Lex, calm down!"

Her cousins' alarmed voices brought her back from the wildness that shook through her limbs. She had actually yelled at Grandma.

She had told her to shut up, even. She looked at her hands. She had acted on her fantasies and tried to strangle Grandma. No, that hadn't been her, had it? She had ...

She sagged against Venus, who grabbed Lex's arm to keep her from falling. "It just isn't fair! There's nothing wrong with me! My mother was beautiful and feminine!"

Lex grabbed her head. "I was trying really hard, but they were all dweebs! My List is so long! I'm going to grow old and die without anyone because I can't kiss a guy! And the one I want to kiss took me to see Ike kiss Lindsay, and he's such a slime! And if I can't find someone else in three weeks, Grandma is going to let innocent girls suffer!"

She covered her face with her hands and sobbed. "And my body is falling apart! I've probably lost six inches from my vertical jump! Everybody thinks I'm a big, dumb jock, and no one could ever be attracted to me! And they're right! I'm only good for college sports tickets!"

One of her cousins zipped in front of her, his ears perked up. "Tickets?"

Lex stared dumbly at him, but Venus lanced him with a look that should have stopped his heart. "Don't. Even. Think it." She shoved him away.

Lex erupted in another chorus of caterwauling.

Venus grabbed her chin and rammed her mouth shut, stopping her mid-cry. Lex barely missed biting her tongue.

"Come on, I'm taking you home." Venus pulled at Lex's arm to haul her toward the open doorway.

"But you didn't drive." Jenn handed her Lex's purse and her own.

"I'll drive Lex's car. Where are her keys?"

They exited the eerily silent living room. Lex didn't even glance at Grandma. A remote part of her realized she'd be in the doghouse for life, but she really didn't care.

Venus settled her into her junk-mobile. After a few false starts, the engine caught and they rumbled away from Jennifer's parents' house.

Lex stared at her cracking dashboard. The tears still stained her face, although she'd stopped crying. She didn't feel anything anymore.

Then a bomb exploded under the hood.

Well, maybe not a bomb, but something exploded. The *boom!* jolted through the car, but no fireball engulfed them. Smoke poured out from under the hood like gray floodwaters. Venus pulled over.

Lex and Venus escaped from the car—after all, she'd seen enough cars explode in movies not to take any chances. They couldn't get close enough to the hissing hood to lift it up.

Lex coughed. "Think it's bad?"

Venus just looked at her.

"You don't understand. I ... can't afford to pay for it." She'd lost all shame—why not advertise her penniless state? "God's got it in for me."

"God does not have it—"

"Yes, He does. Grandma's probably going to charge me with assault and send me to prison. Without my club team, my junior high girls will descend into drugs and prostitution. I'll become fat and get high cholesterol and diabetes, and I'll have a heart attack and die."

Venus crossed her arms. "Are you done now?"

"No, I'm not. God's being mean. Was I so bad a Christian that He had to punish me like this? Why is He punishing my volleyball girls? He's not the God I thought He was."

"Why are all Grandma's actions God's fault?"

"It's not just Grandma's actions. Why can't I just find a nice guy? How hard is this supposed to be?"

"Lex, singles in the entire Bay Area are asking the same question."

"But I used to succeed in everything whenever I gave my best. Why not in finding Mr. Right too? Or at the very least, a sponsor?"

"Let me get this straight. You're complaining because you, like practically every woman in the United States of America, can't find either Mr. Right or Mr. Rich? What planet are you living on?"

"But I've been trying so hard—"

"I'm not a super spiritual person, but even I know that sometimes you just have to stop trying."

"That's stupid. If you stop trying, then nothing happens."

"No, it's like . . ." Venus thought a moment, then snapped her fingers. "It's like Indiana Jones and that cliff, remember? You tell Him, 'God, I just trust You to help me do whatever You want me to do. If You want me to fall, then I'll fall. If You want me to succeed and find the grail and start that massive earthquake, then I'll succeed.'"

"He didn't start the earthquake, that blonde chick did."

"Whatever. It's that whole 'walking off a cliff' thing."

"So . . . walk off the cliff, just like that?"

"Sure. If you could see the bridge, it wouldn't be faith, right?"

Lex didn't realize she'd been leaning against the car until the heat began toasting her buns. She scooted away. "Venus, I don't know if I can do that."

"Well, if it were easy, everybody would be obeying God."

"But I mean . . . not moving forward, not giving my all, not doing anything? Just waiting for . . . whatever?"

"Maybe that's what God's asking you to do."

"That just seems wrong."

"Did you even pray when Grandma started getting all Big Brother on you?"

"Uh . . . sort of." More like *no*. "I just . . . acted on it."

"You didn't wait for an answer from God about what He wanted you to do?"

"I never wait."

Venus rolled her eyes. "That's your problem." She coughed. "Hey, the smoke's cleared." She reached to lift the hood, making sure it wasn't too hot to the touch.

Wait on God? Lex didn't want to wait. She didn't want to *ask*. She didn't want to hear God say no when she really wanted something. She'd never be able to accept that.

She needed time to wrestle with it.

Venus didn't look too hopeful as she stared at the blackened engine. "It had a good life. It went out with a bang."

"Literally."

"Look, Lex." Venus's cynicism melted away into a serious, loving expression. "I know you hate charity, but I can pay for a used car for you."

"No." Lex stuck out her chin.

Venus gave a sigh that sounded more like a frustrated howl. "You just admitted you don't have the money."

She did, didn't she? Tears stung her eyes as she stared at the mess under her car hood. Must be the smoke fumes. What had happened to her? She always could take care of things herself. But now, she was gimpy, weepy, and dirt poor.

Venus coughed. "I'll even charge you interest."

Lex perked up. "Really? You'd charge interest just for me?"

Venus closed her eyes a moment. "You're such a weirdo. Yes, I'll charge interest since it's obvious you're not sane enough to accept the cash."

"Can you help me find housing too?"

"I'll ask. Actually, the person you should talk to is Richard. He has more contacts than I do."

"Rich, it's Lex." She adjusted the cell phone as she tried to cram another pair of shorts into the cardboard box.

"Yes, sister dear?"

"My apartment building is being sold. I need housing fast."

"Oh. Well, there's George."

"George, as in, the dweeb you set me up with a few months ago who shafted me with the dinner bill?"

"He's a good real-estate agent."

"He's also a big, fat no."

"Okay. There's a guy I know, although not very well. He mentioned his sister needed a roommate for her town house."

"Who?"

"You've met him. Oliver. He was at Hot Pot Town when you ... uh ..."

"Yes, the night is pretty clear in my memory."

"He actually called me afterward to see how you were doing, since he was there when you ... you know."

"Can you manage not to bring it up every ten seconds?"

"I'll have to find Oliver's number. When do you need it?"

"I've got to move out soon, Richard."

"Well, I do have one other lead."

"What?"

"You won't like it."

"Why?"

"The family from Grandma's rental house is moving out this month."

When pigs fly. "Get me Oliver's number."

THIRTY-FIVE

Lex stared up at the endless line of stairs. "Your sister's on the fourth floor?"

"Yeah."

"And there's no elevator?"

"No elevator."

"Oliver." Lex turned to him. "My knee's getting better, but I still can't go up stairs without a lot of pain."

He winced, flashing bright white teeth against his darkened skin. "It won't be well enough by the time you move out?"

"I don't know. I'm working hard on my physical therapy." *Liar. You've canceled the last few sessions, you coward.*

"How's that going?" He led her back to his Mercedes convertible.

"Fine. I'm healing slowly, though."

"Yeah, that's always the way it is. In college, I tore my meniscus, and it took me six months before I could play beach volleyball again."

"You play beach volleyball?" Oliver did have a rather fine physique.

"Not anymore." He gave a rueful smile. "My knees couldn't take it, so I retired."

"That must be awful." Lex would have had to be in a wheelchair before she stopped playing. And even then, she might still play and run people over.

Oliver shrugged. "It's not as bad as I thought it would be. You play, right?"

"Coed on Mondays and Fridays, women's SCVA on Wednesdays. And I coach a junior high girls' team."

"Oh, really? That must be fun. How are they doing?"

"Uh ... they're doing well, but I might lose funding after May." In fact, she wouldn't be surprised if Grandma cut funding as of Wednesday night.

"Really?" Oliver paused as he opened the passenger side door for her. "How much?"

Lex's entire body turned into a buzzing beehive where she stood. She told him the amount they'd need until September. "It's a lot because we're traveling for playoffs this summer."

His Egyptian-shaped eyes narrowed in thought. "I might be able to swing that."

"Are you serious?"

"Well, no promises. I still need to think about it and do a few calculations, but I've been considering something like this for a while. No offense, but it would be good for my business."

"Oh, of course. I understand that."

"And my pastor always says to give back to the community the way Jesus did."

"What church do you go to?" Lex couldn't believe this. Oliver became more perfect with every word he said.

"Green Pastures Church."

"I go to Santa Clara Asian Church." *Read: We could be equally yoked, hot-stuff.*

"That's really great." Confidence made his gaze clear as he faced her. "Actually, I wondered if you'd like to go out to dinner with me tonight."

"Me? Tonight?" This handsome, swarthy guy actually wanted to spend more time with her?

"If you're free."

"Sure." She'd have to be dead not to want to spend more time in his luxurious car.

Oh, and his company was pleasant too.

"I had a great time, Lex." Oliver leaned against the doorframe to her apartment, easing closer to her.

"I did too." It was true. He reminded her of Aiden—calm, controlled. He didn't tease her like Aiden did, but then again, she'd only been with the guy for a few hours.

"I hope we can do this again." His voice had gone low and husky.

"I'd like that."

Oliver's exotic eyes dropped to her mouth. That must be some unspoken guy signal telling the girl, *I'm going in!*

She didn't mind, right? He'd been easy to talk to, nothing creepy about him. He had all his teeth, he didn't smell, he talked to her face and not her shoes.

He touched her cheek in a gesture right out of something like *You've Got Mail* or some other sappy chick flick. Lex flexed her jaw but didn't flinch. Hey, she did pretty good.

He came in slowly. Lex would have preferred he just get it over with.

No, she needed to rearrange her attitude. She had to beat this fear. It wouldn't impact her life anymore. She would kiss Oliver and she'd like it!

She also had to think of her girls. Oliver would be a great boyfriend who might sponsor her team.

His kiss started off very soft, sweet as honey. *That's not too bad, I'm doing okay.*

Then he started breathing heavier, kissing her harder. Moving in until she leaned against the door. Lex felt suffocated. She pulled away.

His eyes were cloudy, blacker than black. Then he blinked, and they grew rueful. "Sorry. You're so beautiful, and I had such a good time."

She supposed that was a compliment. "Thanks for a great dinner." He'd even paid for it. "I'll, um ... I'll call you." Yeah, now she sounded eager for his company.

Lex let herself into her apartment, squeezed in by all the half-unpacked boxes that would need to be re-packed soon.

Funny, that's what her life seemed like.

Lex flipped open her cell phone. "Hey Richard."

"So how'd it go?"

"How'd what go?" The refrigerator stopped humming for a few seconds. Lex smacked it hard, and it started up again.

"Your dinner with Oliver."

"How'd you know about that?"

"I asked him."

"*You* asked him? Since when are you so interested in my love life?"

"Uh ... just curious."

Lex planted her hand on her hip and stared at the fridge, imagining Richard's oh-so-innocent face. "You're never curious."

"Never mind. I'll talk to you later." *Click.*

Lex dialed.

"Hello?"

"It's Lex. I need a ride."

"Now?"

"Are you free?"

Venus sighed. "Yeah, I guess. I'll be there in thirty."

"Good, he's got someone over at his apartment." Lex tapped the glass toward a candy-apple-red Mitsubishi in one of her brother's two alotted parking spaces.

"Can you not leave fingerprints on my window?" Venus swung the car into a visitor's stall.

They got out and Lex took the stairs to Richard's apartment slowly, step by step. Now her good knee started aching from all the use going up and down stairs. *Just great.*

Venus rang the doorbell. "This better be worth pulling me out of a relatively light day at work."

"You're working on a Saturday?"

"Hello—it's a start-up. I work every Saturday."

"But today's a light day?"

"On light days, I can close the office door and sleep at my desk."

The door swung open to a tall Asian girl, skinny enough to be a model. "What you want?"

"Mei-Ling?" Lex couldn't believe it. "What are you doing here?" Months after Richard broke up with her, Psycho-Chick herself was there in the flesh.

"You brother ask me ovah." Heavily made-up eyes slanted over her shoulder toward the living room. "I more important now. You come back later."

Lex slammed her hand into the closing door. "I'm his sister. Try and stop me." She and Venus could take her, psychotic or not.

"If it's Lex, I'm not here." Richard's voice boomed loud enough for his neighbors to hear him.

Venus closed her eyes and shook her head. "Are you sure you guys are related?"

"See? He no want talk to you!" Mei-Ling's voice had risen to a falcon screech. Manicured talons fingered the plunging neckline of her straight-from-Hong-Kong fashion blouse. "You go!"

One of Richard's neighbors peeked her head out the door at Mei-Ling's raised voice.

Lex leaned in close. "If you don't let me in, I'm going to key your red convertible."

Mei-Ling gasped, her siren-red lips as wide as a rice bowl. "My baby!"

Venus pulled out her car keys and jingled them.

Mei-Ling flung open the door.

"Greetings, earthling." Lex stalked into Richard's living room and kicked his feet off the coffee table. "We do not come in peace."

"Wha—? Oh, great."

Lex turned to Venus. "See? He knows he's in trouble."

"I'm not in trouble." Richard sunk lower in the couch cushions.

"Then this should be an easy question for you. What's up with the man-parade? Were they really your friends?"

Mei-Ling's eyes popped open. "Reeechahd! Is there something you no telling me?"

"Lex, you idiot. *Yes*, they were my friends."

"So what was the name of the guy at the Children's Day dinner?"

Richard blinked exactly three times. "Uh ... Marshall?"

Well, Lex hadn't caught his name either. "How about Uncle's birthday party?"

This time, Richard blinked seven times. "Carl?"

"Bzzzzt. Some friend you are."

"I, uh, can't remember who I brought."

"So, why were you so interested in my date with Oliver?"

"I wasn't. Don't flatter yourself." Richard grabbed the remote control and turned the TV volume up.

Lex snatched it and turned the TV off. "Hey, Mei-Ling. Did I ever tell you about when Richard was six and I was five?"

"Hey, hey, hey!" Richard flapped his arms around as if he had a magic wand to stop up Mei-Ling's ears and sew shut Lex's mouth.

Ha! He wished.

Richard's glare at Lex fizzled in a splash of fear. "You wouldn't."

"Wanna bet?"

"Okay. I'll talk to you outside."

"No way! You'll just lock the door behind me."

Venus looked up from studying her nails. "In that case, you can shout it loud enough for the neighbors to hear you."

Richard paled under his golf tan.

Lex sat on the arm of the couch, her leg dangling. "Talk."

"Grandma offered to buy me a new car if I found you a boyfriend."

"*What?*" all three women screeched at once.

"Grandma bribed you?" Lex hopped off the couch. "Why am I not surprised?"

"Richard, your sense of self-preservation never ceases to amaze." Venus sneered at him.

"You Acura only three years old." Mei-Ling pinched her lips and crossed her arms. "And you no get back together with me?" As if it were a national crime to not drive her around in prime wheels.

Richard's eyes wandered sideways, but he didn't look any of them full in the face.

Lex moved to stand in front of him. "How well do you know Oliver?"

"Uh ... not well."

"So, you could have set me up with an ax-murderer? I love you too, bro."

"Hey, he wasn't as dweeby as the guy at Uncle's house." Richard pouted.

"Richard, you are such a bum." Venus moved to the door. "Let's go, Lex. Leave him to Mei-Ling's care."

Mei-Ling smiled and cracked her knuckles.

"Aw, come on, Lex. I only wanted to help." Richard's desperate eyes beseeched her while casting a wary glance at Mei-Ling's stormy face.

"Help me into a bad date? I'm really feelin' the love."

"You were kinda hinting you were looking for a guy. And Grandma wants you to date too. What was the harm in trying to set you up?" He gave a desperate smile.

Lex's glare burned the smile off his face. "You could have chosen *nice* guys, Richard."

"I did. Aiden? Oliver? You had a good time, right?"

Lex followed Venus out the door. Well, she did owe him one.

"Yes, Richard." She grabbed the door handle. "Despite you, I did like Oliver." She slammed the door shut.

THIRTY-SIX

If she ever got married, she was eloping.

Lex staggered into the Pagoda Bridge Restaurant behind Mariko's giggling bridesmaids. Four hours on her feet, standing next to Squawking Tiki—thank goodness Mariko stuck Lex on the end of the line—was as joyful an experience as getting her tooth drawn. Without Novocain.

At least the actual wedding will only take an hour. With the rehearsal finally behind her, she could find Oliver, sit down for the first time in four hours, and enjoy a very expensive rehearsal dinner meal paid for by Grandma.

One more week, and this torturous stint as bridesmaid would be done. If only the wedding were tomorrow instead of next week Saturday. Mariko had insisted on Pagoda Bridge for her rehearsal dinner, and it hadn't been available the Friday before the wedding.

Venus found her first. "You're not going to like this."

"What—Mariko sat me with Uncle Fitz and I have to feed him?"

"Worse. You're with Trish and Jenn, and I'm at a different table."

Lex closed her eyes as a headache exploded behind her eyeballs. "Maybe I'll grab Oliver and we'll leave early."

"Too late, he started eating. It gets worse."

"How can it possibly get worse?"

"Mimi's here—"

"Hey, I get along with Mimi now. Sort of."

"She brought Aiden as her date."

Ugh. It had gotten much, much worse. Suddenly Trish and Jenn didn't seem so bad. "Has Aiden met—"

Venus nodded. "Too late. They're at the same table."

That's just great. Lex couldn't even enjoy her food because she'd be trying to enjoy her time with one guy when she'd rather be with the other, whom she'd avoided for a week, who wasn't an option because he wasn't Christian, even though she'd dreamed about kissing him every night for the past five days.

Lex hated round tables. Her seat was squished between Oliver, digging into his eggrolls with gusto, and Aiden, chatting amiably with Mimi, the little tart.

Lex sat, smiling at Oliver and refusing to even glance at Aiden or Mimi. Luckily, Trish and Jenn—both dateless—also seemed to be avoiding her eyes.

"Hey, Lex." Oliver passed her an eggroll. "And try the pot stickers—they taste just like my grandma's."

Grandma then strolled past their table, the grande dame, overseeing her grande feast. First, she bestowed warm smiles on the uncle and aunty who filled out the eight-person table. Then she gave gracious smiles to Jenn and Trish, who returned with weak grimaces. Grandma gave a strained smile to Mimi, probably because of Mimi's fire-engine-red, skintight blouse, which plunged into her cleavage.

Grandma's brow wrinkled as she gave Aiden a polite nod. She skipped over Lex—no surprise there—and eyed Oliver with curiosity. Then she moved on.

Lex released the breath she hadn't realized she'd been holding. She wondered if Grandma would pull funding just to spite her, despite Oliver's presence. If they started dating seriously, he'd help her with funding if Grandma pulled out, right? And he wasn't exactly difficult to like.

On a separate table, the waiters laid out dessert—little squares of heavily iced cake. When Mimi hopped up to get a plate, Lex followed her.

"Hey. I didn't know you knew Aiden." Had Lex's voice come across as plaintive? Jealous? Snipey?

Apparently. Mimi gave Lex an arch glance before she scanned the cake slices. "Don't you remember? I met him when I came to your apartment right after the surgery."

Oh, when Lex was miserable and on her back? Her memory was a little fuzzy. Or maybe her mind tried to block out the memories of that time.

Mimi stuck her finger into the icing on a piece and licked it. "Yeah, he and I have been emailing." She picked up a different piece of cake. "Don't you think he's cute?" She flounced away.

Cute? What would be cute would be that cake plastered all over her snide little face. Cute.

Aiden wasn't cute. He was a lying, weaselly, sneaky, overbearing, rat fink cockroach. Whom she'd been dreaming about kissing.

"Lex." Trish crept up from behind her. She tucked a lank strand of hair behind her ear. As she scanned the pieces of cake, the restaurant's lighting made the bags under her eyes look larger than used Liptons. She blinked rapidly and cast nervous glances at Lex.

"Where's your boyfriend?" Lex didn't dull the edge of her tone.

"We broke up." The noise from the party almost drowned Trish's voice.

"That's too bad." She tried — she really did — to keep the sarcasm from her tone, but she failed miserably.

Trish went on the defensive. "You're all superior now because you have a man and I don't. Well, I'm fine being single, while you were desperate trying to find someone who didn't think you were too weird to hang out with."

Lex flared her nostrils. "I searched for a guy who would respect me rather than telling me when to go to church, when to spend time with my friends — "

Trish gave a sob and ran out of the reception room, flinging open the women's restroom door. At the table, Jenn saw her flee and gave Lex a reproachful look. She got up to follow Trish.

Lex had to get out of here. She turned in the opposite direction and saw the glass doors leading out to the Japanese garden in back of the restaurant.

The night air cooled her skin but not her temper. She marched down the path toward the bridge that spanned the *koi* pond, swatting at fern fronds in her way.

A chill emanated from the stone bridge. Lex shivered but climbed the arch to stand in the middle.

"Lex."

At first she thought it was Aiden. No, Oliver. "I saw you fight with that girl and then head out here. I thought you might like company."

Not really, but he'd been very sensitive to notice. Why couldn't Lex appreciate him more? Why couldn't she feel more for him?

Oliver came to stand close. His hand brushed her arm. "You're cold." He removed his sports jacket and set it over her shoulders.

Aw, how considerate. But then he wrapped his arm around her waist.

Lex took a deep breath to force her muscles to relax. This wasn't a smart idea. The darkness, the intimacy. She usually didn't put herself in situations like this.

But this was Oliver. Potential boyfriend and/or volleyball sponsor. She'd already let him kiss her. This was nothing, right?

She couldn't get herself to relax.

Oliver misinterpreted Lex's tension, pulling her closer and turning her to face him. His mouth came down on hers.

It wasn't too bad a kiss—a little harder than she'd like. His hands kneaded her sides—that, too, was a little harder than she'd like. They moved up, higher than she was comfortable with. She tried to push them down, but her hands skidded over his knuckles. He drew her closer than she wanted to be.

He deepened the kiss, his breath harsh against her skin. No, she didn't like this. Her skin crawled—too much touching. She didn't want to be touched anymore. This was too difficult for her. She wasn't ready. She broke the kiss. "No, Oliver."

He smashed his mouth against her again. She twisted her head and pushed him away. "No."

"Oh, baby." He rammed her against the stone railing and wrapped his body around her.

He had trapped her. He touched her all over. She struggled, but it seemed to enflame him more. He grabbed her wrists and pinned them to the railing.

"No, Oliver!"

"You can't just lead me on." He pressed closer, suffocating her.

Oh, God. God, help me. She cringed inside herself, transported back eight years, but only for a moment. Only for a moment.

She reacted automatically. She slammed her heel down hard on his instep. When he took a step back and bent over, she kicked her knee up and broke his nose. She shoved him away.

Lex staggered down the bridge and turned left toward the gate out of the garden, into the parking lot. She rammed into the gate, fumbled with the latch. She tugged it open and stumbled out.

She didn't expect the cracked cement steps. Her foot twisted. Her back twisted. Her knee twisted—her right knee.

Pop.

A burst of pain, like a water balloon exploding in her knee joint.

No.

Nonononono.

No, God.

No, please, no.

Please, no.

Lex grabbed her bent leg and clawed at her knee as if she could stop the swelling rushing into the joint, as if she could reach in and repair the ligament. As if she could undo what she'd done.

Oh, God. Oh, God.

Screaming. She was screaming without a sound. She couldn't see. Tears made the darkness into a melded blur. The pain faded, leaving a narrow ache under the skin.

Oh, God. Oh, God.

Lex, I'm right here.

Her chest collapsed. The aching rushed past her tight throat, flowed out of her nose, her eyes. Her mouth opened wide, the cries pouring out of her.

Oh, God, where did she go wrong? Why was this happening to her? She was so tired. She was so tired.

Rest.

And suddenly she felt arms around her, and she was held.

The roaring in her ears died to a whisper, like wisteria brushing against a window screen. Her heart pulsed, squeezed tight, and then released. Warmth spread from her chest, over her arms, into her belly.

She looked up through watery eyes. There was no one, but she still felt arms holding her. A hand settled on her head. She closed her eyes.

Hot tears fell onto her knee and dribbled down her leg. The gravel bit into her butt. Crickets screeched. A breeze wicked away tears and cooled her face.

She heard sandals crunching the gravel, getting closer.

"Lex."

She looked up. Mimi's face in front of her. No, not Mimi. Not Mimi. Where was Venus? Trish? Jenn?

"I'll get Venus." Gone, Mimi had gone. *No, come back. Don't leave me alone.*

Lex wasn't alone. The arms still held her.

"Lex!"

Mimi had brought her three cousins. Venus ran up to her, saw her hands around her knee. "Oh, no. Oh, God." A whisper, a prayer. She touched Lex's shoulder.

Lex flinched violently. Her skin had become painful, like a sunburn. *No, don't touch me.*

"Lex, what's wrong?" Venus's hand hovered over her.

Trish pulled Venus's hand away and turned to Mimi. "Get Aiden."

"Why Aiden?"

Trish held Lex's numb gaze. "He's her therapist. He's been touching her for weeks. It has to be Aiden."

Jenn knelt in front of Lex. She sat there, breathing her air, staying close. Trish whispered something to Venus.

Who cares if they know about the rape? Even thinking the word made her shiver. *It happened years ago. It doesn't matter anymore. Nothing matters.*

Their whispers reached her. "How do you know that's what happened now?"

Trish's answer was fierce. "Put two and two together. Oliver followed her out here but came back alone. Lex ran hard enough to hurt herself, and she doesn't want anyone to touch her now, even us. It's just like before."

Before. Lex couldn't remember before.

Jenn shifted in the gravel. It must be puncturing her bare legs. She leaned close. Then Lex realized she was praying.

Lex suddenly felt safe.

The crunch of more gravel. A deep voice—a male voice. "What happened?"

Trish whispering. "About eight years ago ..."

No reply.

Lex's muscles locked, rock hard. Her shoulders started quivering. She had a hard time breathing.

Then Jenn backed away. A shadow over her. She curled up.

"Lex, I'm going to carry you to my car." Aiden's voice. Gentle. Soothing. But she couldn't relax.

Then he bent in closer, and she smelled it. Soap, fir, and a thread of musk. She remembered that smell. She remembered the soft pressure of his hands, easing the pain away.

His hand touched her back. Another arm under her leg. The smell filled her lungs, wrapped around her. Her back muscles loosened.

"Arm around my neck, Lex." She complied and smelled a stronger whiff of fir and musk. Like a sedative, it worked into her body, into her muscles, untangling the tension.

He lifted her up, and pieces of gravel fell away from impressions molded into her skin. He bounced her a little, adjusted his grip, wrapped his arms more firmly around her. Then he walked through the forest of cars.

She closed her eyes and breathed.

Aiden took her to his car, followed by her cousins. He clicked in her seatbelt.

Venus, Trish, Mimi, and Jennifer gathered around the open passenger door.

"Aiden, take her to her dad's place."

Yes, Lex wanted Daddy.

"I'll find her dad and her brother." Mimi darted away.

"What about Grandma?" Trish frowned. "I don't want her asking questions."

"I'll take care of Grandma." Jennifer straightened. Lex noticed the stronger line in her back, and her eyes met Trish squarely rather than flickering around.

"What about . . ." Trish's mouth pulled into a tight line.

Venus's eyes glittered like a dragon's. "I'll tell Richard. He'll want to know."

"Let's go." Trish climbed into Aiden's backseat.

Trish directed him to Dad's apartment. Dad and Mary arrived a minute after they did. Aiden carried Lex into the living room and laid her on the couch.

Her father had aged, with lines crossing his mouth, his hands. He sat on the couch with Lex, not saying anything. Lex heard Mary murmuring, and then it was just her and Dad. He didn't touch her.

He hadn't touched her then, either.

After the first attack, she'd sat, face hard like a porcelain *Noh* mask, her body a mass of rubber bands stretched to screaming tautness. She had spoken in monosyllables, and she hadn't wanted anyone to touch her.

This time, it was different. It could have been worse. She bit her lip.

Dad shifted on the couch. Then he reached out and touched her finger.

She moved her hand forward and clasped his hand.

He squeezed tight. Her fingers grew numb, her bones felt as if they'd break, but she didn't protest. A tear fell down her cheek.

Then she was crying, sobbing, reaching arms around Daddy and burrowing into his shirt like she used to. His hands went around her, and she was held again.

I'm here.

Oh, God. She was so sorry.

THIRTY-SEVEN

Lex's foot caught against the side of a cardboard box, and her knee twinged. She hissed against the pain until it dissipated.

She should be looking for housing, not packing her stuff. But she had to keep moving, doing something, so she couldn't think about what happened.

The doorbell rang. She made her way through the boxes, sliding her feet in small steps.

Trish.

"Can I come in?"

Lex moved aside. "There's not much room."

Trish wove her way to the bed and sat down. Lex stood by the door a moment, then followed her to the bed.

Trish chewed the inside of her cheek, kept her head bent. "I'm sorry, Lex."

Sometime last night, in resting in Jesus's forgiveness of all her headstrong stupidity, her reasons for being mad at Trish seemed just plain dumb. "It's okay."

"No, it's not okay. You were right about Kazuo. I let him tell me what to do."

"He's gone now. It's over. Clean slate."

But Trish started sobbing. "It's not over. I slept with him."

Lex jumped. But really, she shouldn't be surprised. Hadn't she suspected it, even though she shoved it aside in denial?

"I got drunk one night. And it happened." Tears rolled off Trish's nose and dripped onto the sheets.

Lex heard her own breathing in the quiet, heard Trish's soft weeping. What was she supposed to say? To think?

"I'm so numb." Trish sniffled. "Shouldn't I feel something more than this?"

Lex understood numb. "I don't know." She stared at her hands.

After a few minutes, Trish rose. "I'll go."

"No, don't go." Lex reached for her.

"You need someone else with you."

"I need you."

"What could I ever do for you?" Trish's voice broke.

"I love you, Trish."

Trish's face crumpled. She dropped back down to the bed, stuffing her head in the covers. She heaved and wailed. Lex touched her head, her shoulder.

It took Trish a long time to calm down. She lay staring at the wall. "I never thought to ask God about Kazuo."

"I never thought to ask God about Oliver. I never thought to ask God about anything I did. I just did it. And things got worse and worse."

The doorbell rang. Trish bolted to her feet, then glanced at the bathroom.

Lex stood. "Go. I'll get the door."

She opened it to the sight of the top of a female head and a male chest. She looked down. Oh, Mimi. She looked up. Who was that?

Mimi pushed her way in. "You really need a larger place, Lex."

"I'll remember that when I win Publisher's Clearinghouse."

Mimi waved a hand, Vanna-like, at her escort. "Ta-daaaaa!"

Lex looked. Trish came out of the bathroom and looked.

"And?"

Mimi huffed. "Doesn't he look like Oliver?"

Lex shrank back at the name. Trish took a step toward Mimi. "Are you nuts? What are you doing?"

"Grandma saw Lex last night with Oliver. This is Trey, who looks just like him."

Trey smiled at Lex.

"You want me to take Trey to the wedding next week?"

"Bingo!" Mimi beamed. "Just be a little lovey-dovey with Trey, here, and Grandma won't cut funding. I mean, that's the only reason you were after Slimeball in the first place, right?"

Sort of. She'd wanted to conquer her fear, and Oliver had fit everything on her List. But right now, weren't her volleyball girls all that mattered?

Lex stared at Trey, and the panic whirled like a class-five hurricane in her stomach, clawed up her throat, and squeezed tight. Her hands shook and she grabbed at the wall next to her.

Mimi saw the gesture, and her smile faded.

Lex couldn't fail her girls. She couldn't. It would be so easy to just take Trey to the wedding. She could do it. She could hold his hand—

She bit her lip and tasted blood. She screwed her eyes shut. She breathed in through her nose. Exhaled.

"Lex."

She opened her eyes to look at Trish.

"You don't have to do it." Mimi shook her head.

"I can't. I'm sorry, Mimi. I appreciate—"

"That's okay. Trish told me. Don't force it. It's okay." She nodded and then hustled Trey out of the apartment. "It'll be okay." They left.

Now Lex had to tell the junior high girls.

She couldn't do it. She'd had all the practice, and she couldn't do it.

Lex sat in the parking lot outside the gym in her car—a rental Venus had gotten for her because Lex went back to work next week. She stared at the closed gym doors.

She'd failed them. Completely.

She couldn't pray. She had to pray. *God, please.* Wasn't there something He could do?

Silence. But it seemed a friendlier silence than from the months before.

Please do something. She'd wait for Him to do something. She'd wait for Him, even if He didn't do something.

Her phone chirped. "Hello?"

"It's Mimi."

"What's up?" Lex started up the car.

"I've found housing for you."

Lex slammed on the brakes. "Really?"

"Yeah ... with me."

She wished she could see Mimi's face, because her voice differed from normal. "In your apartment?"

"No, a few months ago, Mom and Dad got me a condo. My roommate just moved out, and ... Want to move in?"

"Where do you live?"

"South San Jose."

It would be a commute, but ... "How much?"

"Free."

"Free?"

"It's ... kind of a dump. A fixer-upper. If you don't mind."

"As long as it's got a roof and no rats."

"Oh, yeah, nothing like that. I was going to ask a fix-it guy to room instead, but I know you don't have anyplace and you'll be having surgery again soon."

"Yeah." Lex had hesitated asking Venus to help her again, taking her away from work.

"Well, I don't mind taking care of you. And I know you'd be willing to help with renovations once you're feeling better."

This whole conversation seemed kind of weird, but hadn't Lex just been praying? "You're doing this, why?"

Mimi cleared her throat. Hemmed and hawed a bit. "Well, you need help. I need a roommate. I know you're strong. You're the 'reliable' cousin, so Mom and Dad won't freak out if I live with you versus some guy they don't know. You're not going to steal my boyfriends. I dunno. Do I need any other reasons?"

"Yeah."

"How about you score me some sports tickets?"

"I guess I can do that." She could ask for a few favors from scouts, alumni association reps.

"So we got a deal?"

"When do I move in?"

THIRTY-EIGHT

Lex fingered the diamond earrings. She hated touching them. They were too delicate for her clumsy fingers. She was more comfortable with a volleyball.

Mom had put these on when she came home to die.

Lex had never worn them, partly for that reason. Mom's face had been tired. She'd given up. It had been a relief.

Lex never gave up. Mom shouldn't have either.

She knew it was irrational. Mom hadn't been able to hold back death. But the earrings reminded her of that moment Mom gave in, gave up.

Lex was giving up too. Giving it into God's hands.

No joyous peace, no incredible assurance that all would be well. Just calm hope, and a little numbness. Maybe it would work out okay, maybe it wouldn't. She'd wait and see.

She put on the earrings.

Her bridesmaid dress took a little while to struggle into. The floaty skirt in sickly lavender kept tangling around her clumsy knee, and she couldn't wear the dyed-to-order pumps unless she wanted to tear the other ACL too.

Lex chucked the shoes into a box and reached for her sneakers. The long skirt hid them. Sort of.

Now, crutches or no?

She glared at the crutches against the wall. They had come out when she was vulnerable and in pain.

But what was the point of being strong, or pretending to be? Lex purposely reached up to finger the earrings. She grabbed her purse and the crutches.

Besides, Mariko would go postal when she saw Lex hobbling down the aisle with them.

She went out to the curb. An SUV parked there, but she didn't see her dad's car. Lex was already late. Was he late too?

Wait, she knew that SUV.

Aiden walked around the back side and unlocked the trunk.

"What are you doing here?"

"I'm your ride." He took her crutches and slid them into the back.

"Where's Dad?"

"Already on his way to the church with Mary."

Lex couldn't read Aiden's bland face. "Why?"

"Why should he wait for you when you'd be late as usual?"

She glared.

He grinned.

Grinned.

"I guess I can handle a change in chauffeurs."

"Before we go, I have something I should have told you a couple weeks ago."

"If this is about Ike—"

"No, but it's about his church."

"His church? You hate church."

"I've been going to his church."

Lex swayed. Aiden leaped at her, but she thrust a hand in his face. "I'm fine. Repeat what you just said."

"I'm going to his church."

"Since when?"

"Since two weeks ago. I'm starting to understand Christ a little more."

Lex couldn't speak. She considered trying to say something, but it seemed the information needed time to seep into her consciousness.

Then she realized what she'd put herself through. How her problems could have been solved earlier. Well, maybe. Sort of. Assuming she'd gotten over the whole Ike thing sooner. She was supposed to be happy Aiden had let her make herself miserable over him? "Why didn't you tell me this?"

He backed up a step, probably because her tone hadn't exactly been "Welcome to the body of Christ."

"Why did it matter? You said faith was personal."

"Personal? Personal? I've been chanting to myself, 'Look, don't touch. Look, don't touch.' And you were—you had—Aargh!"

Aiden looked like he was reconsidering letting a madwoman like her into his vehicle. "Um ... what do you mean, 'look, don't touch'?"

Lex headed for the back of the SUV. "Where are my crutches?"

"Why?"

"Because I'm going to brain you with one of them."

"Let's try it."

"No, she'll know."

But Aiden headed straight for Grandma, holding court at the far end of the reception hall. "May as well try. Besides, your dad's there too. He'll help."

"Aiden!" Lex hissed and hobbled after him with the crutches.

He looked over his shoulder at her. "Come on."

Lex caught Trish's eye across the room and made a *Get-your-butt-over-here-now!* face. Trish got Venus and Jenn's attention and moved to rendezvous with Aiden and Grandma.

Aiden's smile transformed him into someone she didn't know. Since when had he become so charming? "Hi, Grandma."

"Who are you?" Narrowed kohl-lined eyes, pursed fucschia lips.

"I'm Aiden. I was at the rehearsal dinner last week. I'm Lex's boyfriend."

Grandma's gaze hissed and smoked like mochi rice dumplings burning on a hibachi grill. "No, you weren't. She brought that other boy."

"No, Grandma." Trish brandished her digital camera. "See?" She shoved the tiny screen into Grandma's face.

Lex peered over Grandma's shoulder at a candid shot of their table—Mimi, Aiden, Lex, Oliver, Trish.

"See? She's with that dark-skinned boy."

"No, Grandma, Oliver was my date." Trish pressed a button to forward frames. "See?"

A candid shot of Trish standing next to Oliver, waiting in the restaurant foyer. It must have been taken before the bridal party showed up.

Grandma blinked. Then she darted from Trish, to Lex, to Aiden. "How do I know you're a boyfriend and not just one of her volleyball friends?"

"Mom, don't you remember?" Lex's dad spoke up. "I told you about Lex's physical therapist a few weeks ago."

"This is him?"

"Yeah."

Grandma's face could only be called pouting. Lex could almost see her brain working to find a loophole.

Lex wasn't going to let her wiggle out of this. "Grandma, you have to honor our agreement."

"No, I don't. You can't prove he's your boyfriend."

Lex crossed her arms. "Then the other cousins won't even bother trying to find boyfriends."

"What do you mean?" Grandma's hands tightened on the arms of her chair.

"They'll know you'll reneg if you don't like who they date. So what's the use?"

Venus, Jenn, and Trish all crossed their arms and stared Grandma down.

Grandma's frown deepened, but she threw her hands in the air. "Fine, fine."

Lex could breathe again. "Thanks, Grandma."

"But Grandma's watching you." Her eagle eyes sliced into Lex's. "And she's cutting funding if you suddenly break up with him." She flicked a hand in Aiden's direction, like waving away a bug.

Aiden lightly circled Lex's waist, touching her filmy dress instead of pressing against her. "So cynical, Grandma." He led her away. Her hands, gripping her crutches, started to shake as they walked.

"Here, sit down." Aiden pulled out a chair from one of the reception tables. Most of the guests gathered around the dance floor, where Mariko waited near the cake table for the cutting.

Aiden sat next to her and didn't speak. The house lights dimmed, and the DJ started the couple's first dance.

He'd done it. *God* had done it. Lex followed Mariko's white gown around the floor. God led, she'd only needed to follow.

"Everyone is welcome to join the happy couple." The DJ's smooth voice flowed over the darkened hall.

"Let's dance." Aiden stood up and moved in front of her.

"Dance?"

"Let's move back and forth or side to side gently and rhythmically."

She laughed. "Dork." But Lex reached for her crutches, leaning against the table.

"Leave them. I'll hold you up."

Dancing. Slowly. Being held. "Um ... okay." She stood up.

Aiden didn't touch her immediately. He came close and looked down at her with eyes glittering like star sapphires. She reached out a hand to touch his shoulder.

His hand cupped the small of her back, softer than the silk of her dress. His fir-musk scent surrounded her. She didn't even have to think—her back, shoulders, and neck loosened.

It felt odd and yet comfortable being embraced. Aiden wasn't touching her as much as when he massaged her, but he seemed closer. She liked feeling surrounded by him.

She limped forward a step. His hands tightened, steadying her.

Lex moved her face in close, breathed deep. A cedar-closet scent lingered on his suit jacket. He bent his head, and then his cheek touched hers.

Slightly prickly from a not-so-close shave, but smoother than she expected. His skin felt oilier than hers. How weird. Warm. And oh, his soap-fir-musk filling her pores.

They swayed like that, barely moving, for minutes, hours, days. She leaned back into the strength of his hands at her waist. He cradled her closer to him.

A whisper of breath at her cheek. Skin sliding against skin. Soft lips on the corner of her mouth.

Her heart fluttered.

She turned her head into his kiss.

GLOSSARY OF ASIAN WORDS (CAMY STYLE)

Ahi — (ah-hee) tuna (Japanese), pink-red in color when it's raw, yummy and delish. A favorite type of roll in sushi bars.

"Aaaaiiiiieeeee!" — (eye-Eeeeee) a modified form of aiyah (below) with added emotional emphasis, such as when you spot a mouse in your sock drawer.

Aiyaaaah — in actuality, aiyah (eye-yuh) but with the "uh" sound at the end drawn out, usually in dismay. Loosely translated from the Chinese, "Aw, man!"

Baka — (bah-kuh) "stupid" (Japanese). Very useful slang word, especially around annoying siblings or best friends.

Char siu and char siu baos — (Chah-shoo) Char siu is reddish-colored marinated barbequed pork. Baos (bow as in b + ow!, the expletive when someone hits their thumb with a hammer) are steamed bread-like Chinese dumplings that look like little white round pillows, ranging in size, with char siu hidden inside. Very delish.

Chou dofu — (chew doh-foo) Chinese fermented tofu, also called stinky tofu. Smells like a sewer. Not something to eat on an airplane.

Domo arigato — (doh-moh ah-ree-gah-toe) "thank you" (Japanese), made famous in the song "Domo Arigato Mister Roboto" by Styx and often heard in TV commercials with strange people dancing to it.

Geisha — (gay-shah) a professional female Japanese artist and entertainer. NOT a prostitute. Geishas are like ballet dancers or composers or any other professional in the arts and entertainment business.

Goma seeds — (go-mah) black sesame seeds often used in Japanese cooking.

"Hajimemashte. Boku wa Akaoki Toya. Anata no obaasan — " — "Hello, nice to meet you. My name is Toya (first name) Akaoki. Your grandmother — " (Japanese)

"Ichi, ni, san, shi, go! Hitotsu, futatsu, mitsu, yotsu!" — "One, two, three, four, five (counting numbers)! One, two, three, four (counting objects)!" (Japanese)

Inarizushi — (ee-nah-ree-zoo-shee) a type of sushi in which vinegar- and sugar-flavored rice is stuffed into pouches made from fried bean curd. They can look a little bit like mini-footballs.

Koi pond — (coy) Koi is Japanese for the fancy carp fish colored white, gold, red, orange, black, or a combination of all colors. They don't do much besides look pretty and require a ton of work to maintain.

Makizushi — (mah-key-zoo-shee) a type of sushi that's made by rolling pickled vegetables, shrimp powder, sometimes canned tuna, and various other Japanese things I can't pronounce in vinegar- and sugar-flavored rice, with seaweed around the log. The log is then cut into bite-sized rounds. Makizushi can be very fancy if made in a restaurant, but this is the country-style makizushi I'm used to.

Maneki — (muh-neck-ee) a Japanese "welcoming cat," typically a small statue at the entrances of stores to welcome customers inside.

Mochiko chicken — (moh-chee-koh) marinated and deep-fried chicken. The marinade usually involves mochiko flour, or flour made from sweet rice, which is different from regular rice. My mom's recipe is fabulous.

Monku-monku-monku — (moan-coup) "complain, complain, complain" (Japanese American slang), often accompanied with a raised hand opening and closing like the other person's unabated mouth.

"Moshi-moshiiii! Otearai e itte mo iidesuka?" — "Hello (answering the telephone)! Where is the restroom?" (Japanese)

Musubi—(moo-sue-bee) a simple triangular "ball" made of white rice with a strip of seaweed wrapped around it. Often eaten by Japanese Americans with fried chicken, which isn't traditional Japanese but very tasty anyway.

"Ni hao ma?"—"How are you?" (Mandarin Chinese)

Noh—(no) ancient Japanese musical drama, often recognized for the ghost-white painted masks used. There are also some red demon masks scary enough to give you nightmares.

"Okaasan—"—"My mother—" (Japanese)

"Otearai"—"bathroom" or "restroom" (Japanese)

Sashimi—(sah-shee-mee) a general Japanese term for sliced fish eaten raw, but often referring to tuna, since that's the easiest variety of raw fresh fish available at the supermarkets. There are different grades of tuna sashimi, and that stuff can get pretty expensive. Sashimi is usually eaten on special occasions and at parties.

Shrimp tempura—(ten-poo-rah) shrimp dipped in an egg batter and deep fried. Some tempura batters are similar to British beer batter for fish. Shrimp and deep fried—what's not to like?

Sukiyaki—(sue-key-yah-key) another name for the original Japanese song *Ue o muite arukô* by Kyu Sakamoto, rereleased in English by A Taste of Honey. Also, sukiyaki is a yummy Japanese winter dish of meat, vegetables, and noodles simmered in rice wine, soy sauce, and sugar. My grandma makes a mean chicken hekka, which is like sukiyaki except with broth added.

Takuwan and tsukemono—pickled vegetables. Tsukemono (sue-kay-moh-no) is the general term for pickled vegetables, while takuwan (tah-coup-won) is specifically pickled radish. However, for our family, tsukemono usually meant Grandma's pickled cabbage and cucumbers.

Ume—(oo-may) a Japanese pickled plum. It is an unnatural red-pink color and can sometimes be sour enough to make you pucker for an hour after eating it.

Yakudoshi—(yah-coup-doh-shee) Japanese birthday milestones, with different ages for men and women. They are considered "calamity years" which Japanese celebrate with huge parties in order to ward off the bad spirits or bad luck. For contemporary Japanese Americans, it just means we're getting old.

Yakuza—(yah-coup-zah) Japanese mafia. Not a good group of guys to anger.

Three ways to keep up on your favorite Zondervan books and authors

Sign up for our *Fiction E-Newsletter*. Every month you'll receive sample excerpts from our books, sneak peeks at upcoming books, and chances to win free books autographed by the author.

You can also sign up for our *Breakfast Club*. Every morning in your email, you'll receive a five-minute snippet from a fiction or nonfiction book. A new book will be featured each week, and by the end of the week you will have sampled two to three chapters of the book.

Zondervan *Author Tracker* is the best way to be notified whenever your favorite Zondervan authors write new books, go on tour, or want to tell you about what's happening in their lives.

Visit *www.zondervan.com* and sign up today!